The Mermuring Maiden

The Mermuring Maiden

A NOVEL

MICHELE LAMAR RICHARDS

KarmiChange Books
Sedona, Arizona

Jacket Design by Andy Mays

Cover and interior concept created by Michele Lamar Richards
www.michelelamar.com

Interior Design by HeatherUpChurch
www.expertsubjects.com

Author Photo ~ Mark Sachet

ISBN: 978-1-7328079-1-4 (paperback)
ISBN: 978-1-7328079-0-7 (hardback)
eISBN: 9780999361351 (ebook)
Library of Congress Number – 2018943954

Printed in the United States of America

Published by KarmiChange Books
Sedona, Arizona

ACKNOWLEDGMENTS

I would like to thank those that held the space for me to finish this book; Adrienne Harris and Yvan Rochon for giving me a place to be while writing it, Tish Merritt-Arana for her loving encouragement and the Porters, Lees and Richards' families for allowing me to use their essence. With all my heart I thank my Diné brother, Johnny. "Ya'at'eeh shi'kis." I miss you, my relation! Thank you, Cuz, a.k.a. Pastor Sharper for praying me through it all and of course my Earth Mother who grounded me in her nature so I would finish it.

If I've stolen something sacred from anyone's beliefs and used it to create this book, please allow me. I simply took from my life experiences thus far and created a fictional community based on several indigenous cultures. Then I added water and an elemental love story began to flower, because at the root of everything the origin has always been love.

I dedicate this story to Africa, especially her children, which genetically speaking are all the children on Earth. The children incarnating today are born aware and desiring of a way of living that entails more than simply surviving. I would like to write their stories, for I am that child.

If I split myself in two,
is there more of me or less
or am I just broken?
I believe I am.

BOOK I

TRANSMUTING INNOCENCE

CHAPTER 1

You can outdistance that which is running after you, but not what is running inside you. Rwandan proverb

The prince got off the plane and quickly grabbed his bag before catching himself and carefully replacing it back where it was on the tarmac.

"Look at you, my friend," boomed Elouba as he approached. "You must be hot," he laughed. "I should talk. Here I am dressed like a tourist. Do you like it?" chortled the large-bellied man dressed in a tie-dyed dashiki. Then he grabbed the prince's luggage and began pushing his way through the crowd towards the parking lot.

The prince was indeed uncomfortable. His three-piece woolen suit didn't fit in under the hot African sun. He was sweating profusely. But he needed the excuse. He couldn't let his family know how nervous he was about returning. It all happened so fast. He was there one moment and now here the next. It was like watching his life through time-lapsed photography as it passed from one season into another like it did up north. He would miss that.

"This way," Elouba said. "They are all waiting. I hope you're hungry because they've been cooking for a long time," he roared.

The prince was looking forward to eating again. He'd had his share of grease and grass for meals. He never got used to salads and the English's love of cow's milk still sent his stomach churning. The colonials didn't even suckle their own children. They did nothing for themselves. No wonder they were always looking for home elsewhere.

The prince stopped and wiped his brow before getting into Elouba's truck. It was a wise choice to send him. It was his father's choice. He probably chose Elouba because he'd left Librebe years ago too. He'd moved to the city and had made a fine life for himself driving supplies and people around here and there. He knew what it was like to have a multi-viewed perspective on life. His father chose someone sensitive enough to allow him time to take everything in, but compassionate enough not to make fun of him. His father was right. Elouba never teased him for swatting flies or covering his nose when he smelled rancid meat in the market place or for pitying his tribesmen's woes. He knew he'd adapt soon enough and life would go on as if he'd never left three years and two months ago.

The three-hour drive went by quickly. His memories alone covered more distance than the ride from the airport to the road leading to his village. He remembered everything down to the rocks he'd stubbed his toe on when making his escape. He was at the ledge under the huge fig tree when he decided to leave. He was upset because his father had critiqued him in front of his aunt.

His father, their king was disappointed because his son wouldn't fight during his manhood ceremony. The prince couldn't understand the point of it. If they were learning to use the stick to govern instead of using it as an instrument of war, then why fight in the first place. It was a medieval concept to him, to war with those he was to govern later. But his father was a competitive man who wanted to see if his son was as strong as he was at that age. The thought of his being judged based on his father's experiences made him ill. He decided to lie down and wait for the gods to test him. They ruled over everything, even his father.

The prince drew a protective circle in the dirt around his body. He stopped listening to anything. He let his awareness go deep into the earth. He went so far inside himself, he could see the eagle's eyes when it looked at him from above and he could feel the mole burrowing underneath where he sat. He communicated with his animal brothers because they felt close to him. They felt closer to him than his father.

His manhood ceremony was an amazing oxymoron. He finished

the quickest in the history of the ceremony, and it was the most fulfilling experience he'd ever had. However, the people wondered if he'd had enough time to become a man, so they never stopped watching him to see if he'd indeed changed.

Thus, he found solace in his studies. He looked forward to his time with the foreign tutor. It was the Belgium man that convinced him to take his tests in the city. The burly red-haired man that incessantly drank and was quite flatulent (his nanny would scream 'you're toot-toot is here' and she didn't mean tutor) wanted him to succeed. He made it possible for him to get his associate degree then his bachelor's and he inspired him to get his master's. One day when his tutor came to work drunk he insisted he "be the best". He told him he had to make up for his king who had cut off the hands of the people. This gassy man validated him more than any other person he'd met. That's why the prince left and went to live in a land full of strangers because he felt strange, even to himself.

The prince was so busy confronting his past that he hadn't realized the truck had stopped at the path leading up to his village until Elouba opened the door wearing his rucksack. The bear-like man gave him a hug then jumped into his truck and warmly waved goodbye. As he returned his countryman's greeting, he inhaled a large mouthful of dust from the wake of the truck. Before he'd thought it through, he grabbed his bottle of water and drank half of it in one gulp. He had a two-hour walk uphill ahead of him. He needed to conserve his water. He couldn't twist a spigot and refill his bottle at will anymore. He was back in Africa.

The prince slowly stopped walking. He knew this was all the time he'd have to be alone, after that everything would be done with the community. He leaned against his rucksack and looked at the diploma the school had given him. He was the first from his country to receive such an honor, but no one at home would be impressed. Only a handful even knew what having a master's meant. To them having a master was not a good thing. When they offered him a full scholarship to get his doctorate he felt pride until reality checked in. What good would a doctorate in environmental engineering do for his village? His people had survived on renewable energy ever since time began. They were still using the first well ever built there and it was built three days before Vitruvius built his.

He knew he was exaggerating. He was just proud of the way his people replaced more than they consumed. Librebe was very resourceful. He himself had climbed down and sealed the old well so they didn't have to sift the soil out of the sweet water. He did the same when building their new well too. The Hogons of his village could smell out water better than any hydro-geological survey. The villagers assumed he went north to bring their foreign ways south, but it was the other way around. He wanted to take the primitive, original ways up north. Although in the end, all that was gained in his three years there were some better tools for his work kit, synthesized vitamins and medicines to use when fresh herbs were not available, and a fancy piece of paper that said he was the master of all he knew.

The prince sat down and examined the presents he'd gotten for the family. For the children he bought hard candies, a set of marbles, a game of *Pictionary*, and some colored pencils and notepads from the Chinese store. He decided on beaded barrettes and silicone potholders for the women, and fishing line, wet wipes and matches for the men. (The wipes and matches he saved from his visits to the fish shops and pubs in his area.) For those that could read he bought all the books he could find in print by African authors and a couple of gossip magazines for laughs. He got his auntie a linen jacket, and for the Herb-Woman a colorful tote made of oilcloth. For his nanny he found a vintage silk umbrella to protect her from the sun, and he gave her all the little raw sugar packets he had saved from the expensive coffee chain near school. He gentle repacked the 198 packets of sugar and the umbrella in the cotton bag they'd given him at university to promote recycling. He purchased a silver flint-stone lighter kit for the Fire-Tender, and a small tin of biscuits and black tea for the Man-of-Medicine. He had no idea what to get his father, the King-Guardian of his village. Whatever he gave him wouldn't be enough or would be more than he should have spent. So, he decided to give him his diploma and a good Cuban cigar in a small box with a picture of a beautiful brown woman dancing. His father loved women. Satisfied he hadn't forgotten anyone, the prince slung his rucksack over his shoulders and began making his way up the hill, home to Librebe.

He could see every wooden step hidden in the rocky soil and dry vegetation. They'd been placed there ages ago to deter intruders (slave traders mainly) and those that came to steal the yellow metal holding Mother Amma's mountains together. Gold fever had destroyed every culture he knew or had studied. His brothers in the northeast had taken to building triangular mountains to preserve their stashes of gold. An elder once told him it was because they had become slaves of the gold themselves. They'd given over their free will to those beings that came seasonally from the stars. The elder forgave them, because it had all been done in exchange for healing information and techniques that allowed them to grow yams and other plants in Africa's harsh climate. That's why the prince wanted to learn everything he could for himself. He didn't want to be an alien's slave or become mesmerized by a color.

In the end, those star beings asked for more than gold. They asked to be worshipped and revered. They wanted his northern brothers to bow down to them and build them temples that touched the sky. But their pointed temples were not Amma's mountains and his people knew this. His ancestors knew all of creator's beings were to be revered. Librebeings knew all life was a part of their family. They believed all life mattered. So, they climbed the hill and made their home in the mountain where they could live in alignment with life. From there, they watched their brothers die like ants as they built the stone triangles that stored the stolen gold.

The prince was on the sixth step. He looked up the hill and saw the seventh at the foot of the sacred tree. It was placed there so strangers would confuse it for a root that had simply broken through the ground. Only a Librebeing would know it pointed to the eighth and final step before entering their village. Even their friends and fellow traders were unaware of this. They would begin singing and ringing bells or beating their drums to alert the village of their presence. Then someone from the community would come to welcome them home. But the prince did not take that final step. He went beyond the roots of the sacred tree toward the cave that held the spring that filled their wells. It tasted cool and sweet, and it refreshed his memory of all he'd left behind. He was finally home. He was back home in Librebe.

It was the women of the village that rushed to see the prince first. They were screaming and crying and wailing and ululating and throwing herbs and flowers at him from all directions. Next the men of the community came and blew smoke on him and whistled and then teased and pushed him. Afterward they bowed and made promises to take him fishing. The children rushed past the men and knocked the prince flat on the ground. They were honest in their joy and were honestly waiting for the treats that were sure to be found in his bag. The prince was so grateful for the children shielding him from the questioning eyes of the adults that he began distributing the candies immediately. This vexed the women so much that they sucked the air through their teeth. They were not pleased. They'd been cooking for over a week and the only taste they wanted in anyone's mouth was the meal they'd prepared. The children, feeling the vacuum from their mothers' teeth-sucking scolding, immediately pocketed the sweets and ran off to play marbles.

After the children parted the prince's aunt, the queen, came to his rescue. She rushed over and covered his face in so many kisses she was sure she'd made him invisible to the others. Then she grabbed his hand and proudly walked him out of the square and up the stairs that led to his father's lodging.

The king was waiting for him in a chair by his altar. This was not a good sign. It meant all that had past, was now over. His father was going to assign him quests and goals to achieve immediately. The ancestors would want it that way, or that was the way his father would rationalize it.

"My son, you are home! You have grown. Mostly around your waist, I see," said the King before laughing. "Too much mother cow's milk," he said with a conspirator's smile.

The prince knew his father had studied for this visit. He had read up on all the customs of the northerners, so he could speak with great knowledge when the prince began talking. That was if he was permitted to recount his experiences before his father covered every subject on being there. The prince was already looking for a way out. By this time, he would have gone fishing or had some chore to do as an excuse. He would've run for the hills or hid in his room, but he had no idea where his room was anymore.

"He looks tired," the Queen said.

His father's sister had been coming to his rescue since he was born. She would always align her heart with his so when it started to close she could rush in and fling its chamber's door wide open. That was how he got out.

"Thank you, Auntie, but I could not sleep even if I tried. I'm a little too excited from seeing you all. It's been a long time," the Prince said.

The queen could hear the maturity in the prince's voice. He'd grown up. She could feel it. She'd no idea what happened to him overseas, but something had. She also had no idea how much she'd missed him until that moment. No matter whose womb he'd come out of, he would always be her son. "You've grown," was all the Queen could say.

The prince adored his aunt. She was nothing like her brother. His father would never admit or reveal any thought he had on any matter. One day he asked his aunt what happened to them as children that his father was so cold now, and she told him nothing happened. She said he'd just became king and human frailty had no place when people's lives were at stake. Although, she did mention how in his youth he'd been a sensitive compassionate boy that never stopped begging for sweets.

The king's sugary habit turned to women, as he got older. He'd been married four times; two before he fathered a male child with his third wife. His father had always been a cautious man. He'd never have even thought of having children unless he knew they'd have more than they needed, not less. His father was different. He was quite liberal in his thoughts but primitive in actions, and no one ever knew which direction that would take.

"Are you thirsty? There are no water fountains on the road here, so I imagine you would like some water. My Queen, water and a nice pot of bush tea for our son, please. If I may impose on you?" he asked. His father always made sure when telling his older sister to perform a chore to ask her politely.

The queen left the room but before closing the door she turned and looked at her nephew and gestured that she was only an eye roll away. It'd been their signal since he was a boy. His auntie would roll her eyes to let him know she had his back, and no one could bother him. The only time he tested their sign language was when his father demanded he marry a young woman from the Fermemi village because he found her attractive. His aunt rolled her eyes, then folded her arms. So, the prince stood up and told his father he did not want to marry the woman with the large bosom. He was fourteen at the time. His aunt laughed so loudly the king left the room and didn't return until the next morning. But when he did return, he demanded that his son marry the woman. His aunt went outside and got a pregnant ewe and she told her brother that she would rather see the prince mated with a sheep than coupled with a cow. Afterward she took the prince's hand and walked him out of the room leaving the bleating ovine there. That was the last time his father asked him to marry anyone.

"They are planning a ceremony for you. Your nanny is waiting outside to take you to your new lodgings," he said. Then the king stood up and walked the prince to the door and clapped him on the back. "I'm happy to have you home, my son," he said before closing the matter on his being gone altogether.

CHAPTER THREE

There it was floating directly above her head. The generator's light had exposed it. The aquamarine cluster, which supplied the entire village with energy, bathed everything in its blue hue. However, being they were in water, its tint made it difficult to see. Nevertheless, the mermaid loved the delicate high-pitched hum it made, especially when the sun touched it like it did in spring. It was November, Sedina's favorite month because the sun finally made its way down to the depths of the sea and everything came alive again.

The mermaid watched her amethyst earring circling in the warm current. She found it quite amusing. It appeared to be dancing and flirting with her. 'Can't catch me', it seemed to say before it married the sunlight and disappeared from view. "Hey, come back here," she said as she darted off. As she swam toward it, her body blocked the light and the jewel reappeared, so she quickly grabbed it. "Now I have you," she told herself. When she lifted her arm to replace her earring, her body floated upward, and she overheard her parents talking in the cavern above.

"No, now," said the firm voice. "And that is final. We must go now," her father calmly said.

Sedina could hear her mother pleading with him to reconsider, but her parents must have moved further into their cave, because she couldn't hear them anymore. The young mermaid quietly floated toward the opening between their dens. She coiled her tail around a piece of gypsum sticking out from the cave's ceiling and stretched her body as far as it would go. After balancing herself on the ledge, she inched her head closer. She was clasping her earring so tightly it left a deep mark imbedded in her palm. "Relax," she reminded herself. As she started to ease her muscles her tail unfurled, and she began to slip. Yet, the reflexes of a mermaid are quick. They engage instantly.

Sedina simultaneously readjusted her tail and arranged her rose-lilac hair in a bun. She didn't want to be caught eavesdropping, especially by a strand of hair. She was the only mermaid created with rose-lilac locks, so everyone would know it was her listening. Her mother believed her hair's unusual color was because she adored kunzite. Kunzite was a very sensitive crystal that was unable to hold a negative impulse, nor would it wish to. When she was in her mother's womb she would swim and make gurgling sounds whenever she wore the stone. The unborn mermaid would giggle so much the lilac crystal would glow pink. Her mother often teased her about her it. She said her hair had grown long and turned pink because the kunzite-stone-elder got embarrassed at all the attention she gave it. Secretly her mother loved the connection she 'd made with the mineral. Stone elders were hard to hear, and their silent ways made talking to them almost impossible.

The Mer-ones were suspicious of their queen's unborn merchild. The baby's attraction to the kunzite crystal while still in the womb, scared them. It took them a long time before they stopped fearing her birth. There were rumors she'd be an enchantress or worse, a mad-merwoman. When the fetal Sedina heard her kinsmer's thoughts, she became as still as a sea turtle. This scared them even more. Now they were certain she'd cursed them. Nevertheless, Sedina was beautifully born. In fact, she was so attractive those same merfolks stopped in awe or swam into rocks when she passed by them. However, she pretended she didn't notice. She truly wanted their love, so she never giggled at the expense of anyone, or thing, ever again.

"But the omen, my love, what of the omen?" her mother asked. Her father did not respond and when her father said nothing, it meant everything he previously said would remain the same.

"What omen?" pondered Sedina. She hadn't heard of anyone having a premonition recently, especially regarding the Sacred Ceremony. Her friend, Oola had a vision about meeting a sea-god that would take her away to dimensions beyond, but she was always predicting that, or was wishing it'd come true. Sedina seldom thought about mer-unions, or babies, or co-living situations. She thought about the stars. She could bask on a rock and watch the constellations revolve around her for years.

"Again, my dear," her mother sighed. "Again, you are sea-dreaming your time away."

Sedina's mother startled her. The mermaid slipped and fell backward off the sapphire ledge onto her seaweed bed. Her hair got tangled in the algae and cast a sulfur-colored glow around her face. She looked absolutely unhealthy. Worse, she looked like a hatching turtle. She was a slimy green, and her face was all squished up. Her appearance made her mother laugh so hard that her strands of quartz tinkled as well.

"What omen, merma?" Sedina cautiously asked. "What is this omen that's circling around?"

Her mother stopped laughing. "It's just a silly rumor, my love. It's nothing to be concerned about," she replied.

Sedina quietly mused over her mother's words. No rumor was silly. Words often spread like a tsunami and washed away all common sense, so she continued questioning her. "Tell me, merma. I'm fully-grown now. I've passed my rites," she added. "How can a lineage disappear? How can what has already been created, no longer exist?"

Needless to say, her mother would not discuss the matter any further. In fact, she completely changed the subject. "Oh, dear one," she said. "This is no matter for a beautiful young mermaid, especially one that has come of age to perform her Life's Union. Have you thought about who you will choose?"

Sedina wasn't expecting this question. In fact, she'd been avoiding it for some time now. "I haven't had a chance to meditate on it yet, Ma-mere," she replied.

The young mermaid tried to deflect answering her mother's question by using her pet name for her. 'Ma-mere' was a double, or triple entendre given where her mother came from. It was the French word for sea–mer and for mother–mere.

Her mother was silent for a good long moment. It was more her father's way to show disapproval by not speaking. Normally her mother would try a more loving approach to accomplish her goal. She would complement her only merchild and remind her of her responsibility to her mercestors. She would recite story after story about the joys of creating life and how the life-creating miracle had indeed changed her. She would continue explaining how giving birth had expanded her awareness of life. And she would finish with, how she—her only child, had become her favorite gift in life, but her mother did none of these things.

"Are you hungry?" Her mother asked.

Sedina knew her mother had been listening in on her thoughts, so she tried to clear her mind before answering. "Yes, some fresh sea grass would do nicely," she responded.

"Wonderful. Let's go have a meal with the others. Then you can tell me what you saw in the stars last night," her mother adoringly said. Before leaving the Mer-queen gently released her daughter's hair from the tight bun. "There," she said before gracefully swimming out into the waterway.

Sedina combed her hair with her fingers as she quietly followed her mother out of the cavern. No matter how much or how often she'd worried or frustrated her mother, she was always patient with her. Her heart swelled with admiration as she swam beside her mother into the Great Hall of the Merfolk.

CHAPTER FOUR

It was complete pandemonium in the Great Hall. The community was collectively preparing for the annual ceremony honoring their ancestors. Everyone was getting ready for the long voyage to the Sacred Waters of Creation. Every table was filled with some gadget, or bag, or basket, or shell—something. Normally it was a happy time, but the strange premonition had left everyone anxious.

"Strange times. Strange times," muttered an elder merman as he tightly wrapped his seaweed into tiny shrimp crusted balls. Another elder was designing a new portable crystal activator that could create heat as well as light in case they needed to descend further into the sea's floor.

When Sedina and her mother entered, everyone immediately stopped their tasks and all hands gently floated beside their conch shells of food. Sedina didn't know who began the Life Song, but they were all humming it now and in unison. It sounded so peaceful. The aquamarine geode must have agreed because it was shimmering. It always emitted a delicate, turquoise colored light every time it was pleased with the flow of energy, and now its light was radiantly blue. It was so stunning it made Sedina's heart vibrate.

Their Mer-family continued oohing the Life Song in honor of their queen. They adored her. Their queen was of pure lineage. Her natal star fell with her into the sea the night she was born. Heralded by the comet's tail when it hit the Mer ley-lines off the French side of the Pyrenees, the Mer-queen became known for her entrance on earth and also for her intelligence and capability to remain connected to all. That is why Sedina's father traveled by ocean to the sea and then through rivers to find her. Her mother gave him balance and her beauty opened his heart. Thus, the Mer-ones worshipped her father even more because of his choice for his Life's Union. How could Sedina live up to that?

Her mother's egg sack never went empty. She was always filled with her father's love. But when her anatomy did not adjust to the strange earthly waters, all her babies died. All but one, the one her parents placed in a recess of the core crystal. Thus, Sedina was born. The warmth of the crystal generator incubated her. No wonder she loved the stars so much. She was born of light as much as water.

"Hooloo, my love, are you in there?" Sedina's mother was still holding the seaweed ball she had gently rolled in ground abalone shell for her daughter.

The young mermaid had no idea why her mother's displays of affection embarrassed her, but they did. She already felt separated from the others by her strange birth from her alien stellar merma and being of her father's regal Mer-lineage didn't help her feel connected either. However, the community would not continue eating until she took her first bite. It was tradition. It was humiliating, plus it made her feel like a baby. Still it was the way it was, so she let her mother feed her in front of the entire village without one complaint, or downcast eye, or low humming sound.

Her mother sensed the arrival of the wise Mrage first. She rose up vertically to greet him. She had felt his rhythmical swaying in a wave of blooomp-blump, blooomp-blump and she smelled his familiar scent of sea-roots mixed with whale blubber. It was intoxicating. The rest of the community rose as well. They were following their queen.

Sedina lagged a few milliseconds later so she could hide behind the efforts of the others. She'd been doing this since she was a wee tadpole. She would exit or enter on the downbeat so those moving upwards would gather the attention and she could remain unnoticed. For the most part it worked until the wise merman smiled and began to take notice of her first. Manulir (the Mer peoples' wise counselor and seer—their Mrage) knew exactly what she had been doing and found a way to halt her game of becoming invisible before it made her un-visible to herself. She knew this because he so much as told her so.

"Good day, my ladies. My dear, Queen you look beyond radiant today. You look light filled," boomed the wise merman. His words always exited his being as if he was releasing them out of a blowhole instead of silently thinking them with his mind.

"Blessed day to you as well, cherished Manulir," her mother replied. "What a delightful surprise to see you here."

"And you, young beauty, are you surprised to see me too?" bubbled Manulir.

Sedina slid from behind her mother and humbly smiled at him. He always managed to catch her only to release her immediately after.

"Well, lady Waheen, I had tea with the king, but you were not there, so I came here," he remarked.

Sedina's mother's spirit gently drifted away leaving a frozen smile upon her face and not a thought in her head. She'd never seen her mother do this before. Her mother hadn't disassociated (she had a stronger character than that) she'd left her fleshy existence and went outward to get a better view of what was taking place. So, the young mermaid took the opportunity of her mother's absence to ask the Mrage about the cryptic omen floating around the community.

"Sir, why is everyone so anxious? Is there a predator in our waters?" she quietly asked.

Manulir got very silent and his silence stole all the ambient sound out of the hall. He held his hands gracefully across his heart and lifted his fin and gently stroked Sedina's shoulder and in the loudest sound she'd ever heard in her life, he spoke. "Dearest Merfolks of the legions of light. I have come to tell you a story," he said and aloud for all to hear. Then Manulir rose to vertical and took a place in the west.

The stunned school formed a circle that connected on both sides of the sage. No one had ever heard the sound of his voice before. He usually only spoke through thoughts or sonar waves you could feel more than hear. Now everyone understood why he only communicated in silence.

His voice was too enormous to be heard. Sedina had to grab on with both arms and her tail so she wouldn't be knocked clear out of the Great Hall, and as she scanned the room she could see everyone there was holding onto something. They'd even put stones in their baskets and then set them on their laps to hold themselves in place.

Manulir was a huge man and an even larger fish. His Hu-man side came from the northern waters of the Celtic tribes. He was freckled and had red, coarse, wiry hair. He had massive arms and a scent that made you want to mate immediately. His fish family was more of the mammal variety like a dolphin or whale. He was sleek but strong and his grey dorsal fin stuck up in the air no matter how calm or warm the water had become.

The wise Manulir knew he had frightened his Mer-family as much as he'd impressed them. This had always been the way. No matter how gentle or graceful he tried to be in expressing himself, the listener would shudder, or bow, or curl into a ball, everyone except Waheen. The queen would disappear then reappear when it was her time to make a statement. The only time he'd ever left his Mer integrity and resorted to Hu-man tactics, was to impress this mermaid. He would never do that again. Manulir slowly descended and floated prone, closing the gap in the circle of Merfolk.

"Once upon a time many lifetimes ago in the hot deserts of the Americas, there was water," toned the wise merman. "There was a sea, an enormous ocean that fed all forms of life, and in the deepest part of this ocean, there was a city," he softly thought. When Manulir returned to his silent way of speaking the school of merfolk relaxed into a comfortable ball.

"The city was built on the side of an immense mountain that extended from the bottom of the seafloor and exited into the sky. It was carved by master carpenters and encrusted with gemstones that were set in gold by the universe's finest artisans. They even cleared the undersea growth from around the aquapolis, so the sun would shine directly down upon it. And the city glowed as if it was made of light. It was a most amazing place and all the beings in the sea were very proud of it, so they called it Grand City."

"But a time came when the sun burned too bright and dried up all the water and the city began to crumble. Many perished and those that survived were forced to leave. They had to find water. So, they traveled the rivers flowing deep within the earth's belly until they came upon another body of water. These waters were pure and were teeming with life. There they built a new city and they called their new home Mer. And the Mer-ones still live here to this day."

Waheen was baffled. She didn't understand why the wisest merman in their midst, or any ocean for that matter would speak aloud a story their kind knew by heart.

"And tomorrow morning, we children of Mer will begin our annual pilgrimage to the rock remains of Grand City. We will return to the home of our mercestors, those kinsmer who have passed on and those yet to be born. It will be a long and difficult journey. Nevertheless, no matter how long or how difficult it may be, we will look forward to this time. Shan't we?" he asked looking directly at Sedina.

The queen fell watched the wise merman smooth out the kinks in her daughter's hair. And with every stroke of his hand across her head, Sedina's aura changed color from violet to silver, then magenta to gold.

CHAPTER 5

Leboya had been the prince's nanny since his mother died in childbirth. She was the one he suckled when he cried. She was the only mother's milk he knew. She was his true mother. When he exited his father's chambers she turned around in circles like a puppy and yipped. "Look at you! How big you've become, and you have hair everywhere," she said. She was so delighted to see him. "I am glad you are home safely. Now I have someone to cook for again. I made all your favorites," she said.

She was happy her prince had returned. She hadn't realized until that moment how big of a hole he'd left in the community, but he was home now. She tried to walk slowly enough for the prince to take in his surroundings, but fast enough so his peers would not accost him. It was not the time to catch up on old friendships, not yet. It was hard for her to continue walking when all she wished to do was stop and stare at him. She wanted to take in all the changes the years had drawn into the folds of his face. He was paler now. He had lost his rubbed mahogany texture and was more like the cotton tree. He lacked sun, but he didn't appear unhealthy. His hair had grown out and was springing all over his head. He looked like a musician in a beer ad. His body was firm and riddled with muscles, but it had a strange odor. He smelled more floral than musk. He smelled like the missionaries. His voice was lower, and his eyes were brighter. That was good. His step was cautious, but it was still his cadence. He was always a quiet walker; so quiet he could sneak up on you like the great cats when stalking their prey. He seemed old for such a young man, yet a purity still remained in his face. With all the wisdom he'd gained, he had not loss his innocence, but she could tell he was sad.

Leboya looked down at the earth and continued walking toward their new lodgings. She didn't want to see anymore—not right now. "Here we are," she said, and with a childlike hop the old woman ran up the stairs and opened the door. "You are home now, my Prince," she said with great sincerity.

The prince solemnly smiled and followed her into the house. They had given him larger lodgings, but everything looked the same. Even after relocating not one thing had changed. His room was exactly as he'd left it three years and two months ago.

"I did not let a soul touch your things, my Prince. I knew you were coming home," she screamed from the kitchen.

The prince had no idea people believed he wouldn't return. He was their prince. What did they think, that he would marry a pale foreigner and take up golf, or start dating big-bottomed video vixens and hang out in nightclubs all day? Did they not know him at all? He loved his home. It was who he was. Everything he did was for his people. The prince sighed. He knew that wasn't true. He loved his village—that was true, but he didn't want to be a prince. He worshiped his time alone. Having people smile and wave and tell him their problems every time they saw him was annoying. The only person that ever asked how he was and listened for his response was the Fire-Tender's daughter.

"Here you are. I should have known you'd be at your desk," his nanny said. "Here's some good bush tea." Leboya poured the prince a cup of tea and waited for him to take a sip.

The prince stopped unpacking. He set his backpack on the floor and took a small sip of tea. "Aah," he said. And then he smiled in approval at the grinning woman.

"You see. You can't get that at the white people's palace," Nanny said.

The prince knew she meant no harm by the comment. His nanny believed the pale capitalists had created all the bad in the world, even though she had never seen a white person in her life. She'd never seen a yellow, red or purple person either. On those rare occasions when his tutor or some missionary came to the village, she escaped into her kitchen and stayed there until they left. Nanny Leboya never left Librebe. It was her choice. She'd never seen an elephant or giraffe, or drunken Indian chai, or been to a bazaar. She barely read. She could only make out the words applicable to her lifestyle. She knew honey, bleach, dish, meat, and soap—maybe perfume, but any written words of tenderness would have been lost to her. However, no one knew she was barely literate because she could read everyone like a book. In Leboya's mind every person deserved a happy ending, so she told you what was holding you back from being happy, and then she made the happiness happen. It was her way of creating justice in the world.

"Here," she said as she put a clean linen sheet on his bed. "We can catch up in a couple of days. Sleep now." And before the prince could protest or thank her, she closed his door and left.

The prince took off his suit and examined his body. He was still himself, but he could see the changes the last few years had made. His skin was soft and moist like a baby's. He hadn't noticed the effects of being enveloped in fog until now. He wiped his eyes. They were sore from trying to shield themselves from the African sun. He stopped wearing sunglasses earlier in the year to prepare them, but he still squinted when he got off the plane.

The prince placed both hands on his chest and repeatedly pushed while exhaling through his nose with great force. Afterward, he walked over to the small armoire his father's fourth wife had given him and stared in the mirror. He couldn't see himself in entirety. He had to stoop down. So, he took two steps backwards until he could catch his image in full view. He was taller now. His body had grown from all the cooked meats and grain he'd consumed overseas. He placed both hands over his heart and felt it beating for a good—long—moment. He decided to give all the small colonial furniture his stepmother had given him to his nanny. He'd outgrown it all. He hung his suit jacket on the mirror's sconce before going over to his bed and collapsing onto the mattress. He'd keep his bed. It still fit him, and it was comfortable. It sunk in all the right places and supported him too.

He was finally alone, more alone than he'd ever felt in his life and he'd had plenty of experience at being alone. He spent the majority of his time alone. He was always fishing, studying or hunting in the woods. He lay on his back and placed both hands behind his head and watched the night sky drop down from above. Venus was rising, and Sirius would soon follow.

The prince rolled over onto his side and immediately sat straight up. He had an epiphany. All that time he'd been telling himself to go out and see the world, so he could have exotic memories before taking up his position in the community had been a rationalization. He'd run away, and now he knew why he'd taken such drastic steps. He felt like all of Africa was closing in on him.

The prince was having trouble breathing. He'd been home for less than two hours and he was already scrutinizing himself. If he thought the people were watching him after his manhood ceremony, they were surely going to keep vigilance now. They were going to watch to see if he'd become westernized like the musicians that recorded their music in English instead of their native tongues. The people needed to know he was still one of them. Yes, he nodded to himself and his imaginary jury. Of course, he was an African. He simply left to get more knowledge to mix with his own. There was no other agenda. He knew who he was. Of course, he did. He was the Prince of Librebe!

This was not good. All this thinking was not good, and the prince knew it. He didn't want the revelations Mother Amma was telepathically sending him right now. His entire life had been one long vision quest and it was exhausting.

"Breathe," he told himself. The prince took a deep breath and slowly exhaled. This was not good. He had to find a way to get the hell out of Librebe, and soon.

CHAPTER SIX

The Merfolk jubilantly left their home within the earth and headed toward the surface of the ancient seabed. Manulir led the way. The entire school respectfully followed their Mrage's silent trail of bubbles. Even their Sea-mother, Waheen, and their Mer-king, Nehtoon, deferred to the wise merman's guidance, yet the cold waters of the north seeped in, forcing them to change directions. Now they had to go around the back of the mountain's base toward its entrance making the long journey even longer. So, they clustered together in a tight group for protection and zigzagged on their way.

It was proving to be a most difficult trek. The sun's light wasn't reaching the currents they wished to travel, plus the rapid streams were strong like storm winds. The water was so icy nothing grew there. Without plants or sunlight there'd be no plankton, thus no small fish for them to eat either. Everything they carried was all they had to survive.

The younger more fit of the Mer village swam on the outside edges of the school providing a shield for the elders. It was here at the very end where Sedina had placed herself. She cut through the icy waters with determined dignity. Her lean form suspended in the water, reflected the emerald and beryline blues of the freezing sea and it made her eyes glow like sapphires.

Her parents flanked Manulir. They were sheltered from the elements by the Grand Protectors—the sacred swordsmen for the royal lineage. These amazing mermen had foregone their Hu heritage and shape-shifted into the full form of the sleek predator of the sailfish. Their long dorsal was more impressive than any Hu Norseman's sword and even stronger than King Arthur's mythical blade. They could take their tooth and rapidly impale their prey faster than the eye could see, and before a drop of blood could leave a trace. Their dorsal bone had been dipped in the strongest alloy on earth, although the substance used was from a meteorite, which had fallen into the sea from some unknown planet. These Mer swordsmen were indestructible. When they had lived their full life cycle they would journey to the earth's core and all that would remain was their meteor-coated tooth. To find one was an honor given to no one.

Sedina could feel her mother's hesitation at being led by warriors and she had to admit she agreed with her on this point. It did give off the wrong message and almost invited doom more than prevented it. However, she understood her father's point of view as well. The prophecy had left everyone on edge, thus the Grand Protectors made the school feel safe. They inspired discipline so everyone worked together efficiently. Manulir added the Mersongsters. Those gentle mermen with a balanced feminine and masculine countenance glided beside the warriors and gently oohed praises on the school. All in all, it was quite comical. That was why Sedina chose the rear, to avoid all the pageantry of the front. Now she could look up at the stars and bathe in their light the entire way.

On the ninth day of their journey they finally approached the jagged stones surrounding the Sacred Mountain. Manulir signaled for them to stop and begin preparing for the ceremony, but Sedina did not hear him. Not because she was in the rear; it was because she was too busy looking elsewhere. There to the left of the school, emanating from within a cave was a tiny speck of light. Sedina motioned to Oola to look, but her friend misread her gesture and realigned her focus on Manulir all the more. Yet deep within the belly of the Sacred Mountain the light flickered again.

Mer-ones believed the icy waters surrounding the mountain was where the Spirits created all life, and these caves were the entrances to the Unknown Waters of Creation. They were the openings to the womb of life itself. That was why it was strictly forbidden to go inside one; because once you did you were never heard from again.

Nevertheless, the old stories did not frighten the young mermaid. She tried to contain her curiosity and pray with the others, but the light kept blinking on and off like a vampire squid. She was mesmerized. Maybe someone was trying to communicate with them. She became so fascinated by the light on the other side. She began counting the moments it stayed on and the moments it stayed off, but the flicker was too irregular to establish a pattern. Plus, she began to anticipate each blink, which made her blink and lose count. Whatever it was, it was hard to decipher. It could have been anything; a sparkle off a white-capped wave, or simply the light reflecting off the water, or maybe it was a piece of Hu garbage or possibly a decaying sardine. It truly could have been anything. Thus, the blinking went on and on.

The mermaid tried to focus on something else. She tried dismissing every thought she had of it, but she could not look away. She didn't hear a word Manulir toned because she was too busy counting the blinks, or the time in between blinking. She knew she was missing the ceremony, but what she didn't know was she was slowly floating out into open water. Then as if magnetically pulled, Sedina drifted into the cave and in the blink of an eye, she was gone.

CHAPTER 7

The prince couldn't eat anymore. He'd had his fill of food and people's questions about living outside of the village. How does one describe something the other hasn't seen? No matter how many details he gave them, they would blankly look at him and then tell him how happy they were that he was home now and away from all the strange things he'd gone through. The worst part of returning home was all the attention the single women of the village gave him. It seemed his only reason for being alive was to marry one of them and produce children. Then the people would have had an excuse to organize more ceremonies. No one cared about what was happening in the world. No one acknowledged the wars going on around them or the famines and diseases claiming their brethren. They danced. The only time they allowed anyone from the outside in was when someone from home accompanied them, and since those from home never ventured far, the only people to visit were from the village below, or the occasional missionary that came and bored them to tears with images of torture and suffering.

The children were the only ones that asked him questions, but unfortunately, he couldn't answer any of them. He didn't know who made candy and he had never been to Disneyland. He had never kissed Beyoncé, nor had he seen LeBron play ball. He had no idea how to make a rap song, (he'd never seen anyone shoot another person) nor did he know any millionaires. He never wrestled the Rock, nor been to a rodeo or shaken hands with the Black American president. He didn't get AIDS or the avian flu. He never drove a mechanical jaguar, nor did he use a bicycle to travel.

He didn't have cable television or live in a palace and the suit he wore was the only suit he owned. In fact, the only question he could answer was the queen never walked around the streets waving to the people, but by then the children figured he didn't know much so they went back to their day like they normally did.

The prince went fishing. He escaped his auntie's kisses and his nanny's never-ending pots of bush tea. He ran away from the women wearing their best jewelry and avoided the men wanting to give him their favorite amulets. He even fled from his father's hopes and aspirations by sneaking out the back door, up the path to the ledge that led to the hidden pond.

Finally, he was at peace. He'd forgotten how beautiful Africa was. The small pool that seeped in from the aquifers underneath the ocean floor created a beautiful blue. The water was so still it looked like liquid rock, or so it appeared at that time of day. No one but his people knew the pond existed, and no one understood how it came into existence. Nothing disturbed its serenity. It was a well of fresh water that bubbled up in the mountain. Its whirlpool could suck in the largest fish from the bottom of the sea. He could reel in a nice catch without going beyond the comfort of the flat rock he sat on.

He never understood why no one else fished there. Every time he came to the spot the only other living entity there other than him, was an eagle that occasionally swooped in to make fun of his fishing. One day the bird dove down, caught a fish and then circled above him gloating. Afterwards, it went up to the top of the sacred tree and had his lunch. The prince couldn't tell if it was a male or female, but its good-natured teasing made him believe he was male. Once when the prince was searching for his mother's ring, the eagle was there. It watched him cast and recast his fishing line over and over again. The eagle felt so sorry for him it circled overhead, signaling him where to cast his line. The prince never found his dead mother's ring, but he caught a lot of fish that day.

He never really expected to find her ring. He was a boy when he lost it. He was only seven-years-old and terribly angry with his father. His father had married his fourth wife and she was mean. She didn't want anyone around that reminded her of his other wives, so she banned his children from sleeping in the same house with them. The prince's half-sisters quickly married and left the village, but he was too young to escape. She had them build a beautiful house like in a storybook for the prince. It had hidden rooms and a garden with swings, but he lived there alone with his nanny. His stepmother was a true witch, or that's what his nanny called her before the witch died. He never understood why his father allowed her to do this, but he did. So, one day when the prince was imitating the witch and his father, he stood on the rock and flung his pointed finger out into the bay demanding the tide to recede. It was then his mother's ring flew off his hand and sunk into the water below.

That ring was his favorite present from his mother. She was wearing it the day she died. He was sure the first thing he saw when he came into this world was his mother's shiny ring. He wanted to jump into the bay after it, but he knew he'd never survive. The pool was as savage as any wild beast. One minute it was kind (you could walk beside it or even tread its water) but the next step you could find yourself in a hole so deep you'd wind up at the other side of the ocean, or that was what they told seven-year-old boys back then.

The pool resembled a woman's body. The sacred tree's roots met along the edge of the water, and it looked like a woman's legs around a basin. The prince began to understand why he always came to this spot. The pool became his mother. He mourned all the sadness he'd experienced in life alongside this pool. Everyone knew when he ran away he always came to this spot. It all made sense now. That's why no one came here. The people went to the well even though it was further away. It wasn't because the prince dug the well himself. They went there because he was always here. The people gave him this spot.

The prince became silent for a good long moment. Why was he seeing some of the most important aspects of his life fifteen years later? How could he govern a nation when he was just seeing what was out of order in himself? He had to let go. He simply didn't know how. He knew thinking too much about oneself was dangerous. He didn't want to end up like Narcissus, the god who fell in love with his own reflection in a pool of water. He had to start thinking of others. He had to come to grips with the fact that one day he was going to be responsible for their well-being. He knew this was his destiny. But every time he got to this place he backed away from that same realization. He didn't want to be king. He did not want to end up like his father. He'd never impose his beliefs on another or tell them what to do. He could never be a politician and rationalize how his profit was for someone else's good. He could never muster the arrogance needed to say, 'I am king, so you are my subjects'. No, he would never— could never become a negative king!

The eagle swooped down and looked the prince directly in his eyes, and without telling him goodbye, he flew away.

CHAPTER EIGHT

The cave rendered the mermaid blind in an instant. It was so dark she couldn't see a thing to her right or to her left, nor behind her or above. She couldn't fathom how deep it was or how far she'd gone. She couldn't see her hair streaming beside her or the shimmering of her own skin. "UW, uuw," she mewled, but no one heard her. No one responded to her cries, and deep inside she knew no one would come, because it was forbidden to be there.

The mermaid was alone for the first time in her life. She was lost and alone in the Unknown Waters of Creation. Sedina had never been separated from her school before, so being on her own didn't feel good. It felt awful. It felt strange. Something was going to happen. She knew it. She sensed it and her fin flared and went rigid.

"Calm down," she demanded. However, being angry with herself only made her more nervous.

She wanted to send a sonar message to her family, but she couldn't do it. She felt too ashamed. She'd gone outside of the Mer ways on their most sacred day. What if someone got hurt trying to help her? She'd have brought trouble to another. She could never bear that. It was a difficult predicament to be in, calling for help or continuing forward. Neither felt natural to her. Until now, she'd instinctually lived her life. However, all animals lived by instinct; what was difficult was to purposefully choose doing the right thing. She'd never been given a choice in such matters. She simply went forward through her day. She moved as one with her school. She had isolated moments with friends, or times basking on the rocks looking up into the sky, but she could always feel her family's presence nearby.

The mermaid's thoughts were becoming as dark as the cave she floated in. It was so quiet—too quiet. She tried to merge with the black abyss, but its vastness overwhelmed her. Nevertheless, her instincts kicked in and she began to listen to the quiet. She felt a murmur of life in the invisible waters surrounding her and the sensation reminded her of the beauty of being again. She felt like a star brightly floating in the night sky.

Sedina decided to keep swimming. She slowly glided through the water until she reached the cavern's wall, and then she carefully backstroked until she touched the other side. As she swam, she counted. She was trying to measure how far it was from one side to the other. However, every time she reached one side, the other side seemed further away. It wasn't working. Each time the count got longer. She assumed she was either drifting, or the cave was growing, but how could a cave grow? Nothing made sense and the lack of logic made her uneasy, so she tried swimming again. Although swimming somewhat quieted her heart, she still felt weird. She felt sad. She had not listened on the day of the Sacred Pilgrimage.

She wanted to apologize (needed to) but to whom? No one was there. She decided to ask her mercestors for forgiveness in hope they would understand, but even after praying to her guides and ancestors she didn't feel any better. She tried singing. Singing always lifted her spirits. She began singing the Life Song she inherited from the ancient ones. It was the first song her mother taught her. It was her family's most important song.

> *Trust your heart to all matters.*
> *Embrace your wisdom, mer-friend.*
> *And light will return to greet you.*
> *For with love you're connected within.*

The mermaid sang with all her heart as she circled the dark abyss, and on her ninety-ninth lap a dim light bounced off her tail illuminating the grotto. She felt dizzy, so she stopped and waited for her balance to return.

When she began feeling steady again, she saw beyond the cave into the unknown waters and it was beautiful.

She immediately swam toward the opening. She couldn't wait to get out of the confined space. Lifting one spine of her fin at a time, she counted every adventure she planned on having. She would find wonderful seashells to make a new belt for her mother. She would harvest some of the exotic waters' seaweed to take to her father. She'd bring sand from the new shores for Oola's castle. Then in the distance the weird light flickered again.

The mermaid quickly darted toward it, but as if it sensed her presence, the glittering light grew still. She still continued toward the eerie glow. She didn't care what might be there because to her life was simple—relax and hum then all will become one again. She resumed singing. Her voice echoed through the darkness. "Trust your heart to all matters," she sang. As she sang her body lit up like an eel and she saw everything.

She began exploring the new seas. The fish were small but fat. This made her happy because it meant seaweed and plankton were surely nearby. Sedina hadn't realized how hungry she was until then. She needed to eat something, so she quickly made her way toward the water's surface, but it was further away than anticipated. However, she spied a small school of fish and began following them. She ate the bubbles of air from the fat fish first to make sure they weren't toxic, and when she knew they would not harm her, she caught some. She ate three then tucked a couple into her hair for later. Now she could concentrate all her attention on the sunshine coming through from above. She made her body sleek like a rudder and propelled herself upward toward the sky's light.

When she surfaced she found herself in a pool of clear mountain water. "Ooaah!" she gasped. She was directly in front of the clump of seaweed, spreading the most beautiful rainbows ever. She slowly approached the sparkly matter, never taking her eyes off the glint of metal nestled inside the ray of light. Once there, she patiently began untangling the jumble of plants until it was finally freed. When it was released, the bauble started sinking, but she quickly dove and caught it. Grasping it tightly between her fingers, she sat down in the water and took a deep breath before carefully opening her hand. There resting in her palm was a ring of amazing brilliance. It was a starfish-shaped diamond, surrounded by tiny sapphires and on the golden band was deeply etched, '*With love we are forever connected. M.M*'.

Sedina was stunned. She read the inscription again and again tracing each word with her finger. "Thank you, dear Great Spirits of the Unknown Waters. Thank you, for your lovely gift," she sweetly said as she slipped the ring on her finger. The mermaid was also grateful for having found her way through the Sacred Mountain, so she thanked the spirit of the mountain too. She thanked her mercestors who protected her and lit her way, and she thanked the Mrage Manulir for his guidance along the way. She thanked her parents for teaching her the Life Song, which always renewed her courage. She even thanked the water's currents for bringing her to that exact moment and place. With deep appreciation she continued to thank everyone and everything, and on her last thank-filled breath she was yanked out of the water onto the shore above.

CHAPTER 9

The sky grew dark above the mermaid. She tried focusing her eyes to acclimate herself, but she was having a hard time doing this on land. As she flipped back and forth on the hard surface, she coughed and sputtered. "Oowe, oowehle!" she cried. She tried calming her pounding heart, but a strange sound bellowing in the air made it worse. When she finally adjusted her eyes to see through the bright sunlight, there was a hairy two-legged, Hu-man standing directly above her.

"Oye, ancestors of heaven, what is this you have sent me?" asked the Prince with a thunderous laugh. He was nervous.

Sedina went numb. She stared at the furry beast with eyes like a tiger fish and long, tightly knotted hair that resembled evening coral. His body appeared to have been sculpted of burnt copper and it stood out against the blue in the sky. He was handsome for a Hu-man. His face had a calm expression even in the midst of his surprise.

The prince stared at the strange woman-fish caught in his net, and he became still for a good long moment. He took an offering of *mealie* and some cowry shells from his sack and sprinkled it on the sea creature. Then he raised his arms up and prayed. "Dearest Mother Amma, blessed as I am, you continue to give to me. Thank you," he said, and then he studied her in silence. Afterward he laughed aloud once more. The prince was sincerely grateful for this day's catch.

Sedina watched the huge sienna colored Hu-man drop shells and pollen on her. She didn't know what else to do. If she tried diving back into the water the net would surely return her right back to where she was.

Then she remembered there was a knife in her sack. Maybe she could cut through the twine, but it would take too long for the silt to subside for her to find it. She had to think of something else.

"Please put me back in the water. I beg you," she implored. "And please don't touch me. Your stories of us are false. I will not harm you." The mermaid had lost her sound. Her voice was choppy and disjointed. She was afraid. The only thing Sedina knew about Hu-men was they believed mermaids to be witches that would harm a sailor at a moment's notice. She had to convince this man she would never offend anyone.

The prince quietly pondered the mermaid's request. It was a confusing one. How could he put her back in the water while staying away from her at the same time? However, after a careful moment of consideration, he gently hoisted her up and carried her back toward the pool. As he neared the water's edge he saw the ring on her finger and he dropped her on her tail and stomped away. She was just a few feet away from the lake. She could crawl to the water, but he returned. Then he stormed off again, and he repeated his back and forth pacing, growling like a trapped animal the entire time.

Finally, he approached her. "Where did you get that ring, my lady?" he defiantly asked. "I've been looking for it for years. It belonged to the woman who gave me birth and died the day I came here."

Sedina could not believe her ears. This man spoke like her kind. He rhymed, and his sound resonated beautifully with the water. So why was she cowering in the woods like a gnome? She'd imagined this moment many times in her childhood. Every mermaid did. Meeting the beings you shared half your form with was like finding out you had stepsiblings somewhere in distant waters. She'd tell him what happened. He'd be upset with her at first for not leaving the ring where it was, but that was simple to resolve. She'd give it back.

The prince was furious. The mermaid had brought out all his issues with people stealing resources from his continent. She also reminded him of the beautiful women overseas who tried every trick in the book to conquer him. Now here he was finally at home where common sense and honor were the most cherished values, screaming at a thieving she-fish.

"How dare you come upon this land and pillage like a base colonial. I will not take this disrespect from you, even if you are beautiful!" he screamed. The prince released three years and two months of rage on the strange being made of colors he'd never seen before, and then he began pacing back and forth again.

Sedina felt awful. Worse, she felt guilty. She didn't mean to take anyone's ring. She thought finding it was her divine fate. Why else would the ring attach itself so perfectly to her? But this was not her ring. It was his heirloom. She knew she had to give it back and give it back immediately, but when she tried to remove the ring from her finger it wouldn't come off. She struggled with her hand as the Hu-man stood there watching her. He was making her nervous.

"It's not yours, my lady," ranted the Prince.

Sedina kept trying to remove it from her finger but her hands kept slipping off the metal band like two magnets of the same polarity. No matter how hard or how gently she tried, the ring sparkled and stayed exactly where it was. Her finger became swollen and it started to throb. She had to get the ring off her finger, and now.

The sun was brutally beaming down its noon rays, and its vibrating heat acted like a prism. It reflected the ring's inscription onto the prince's body and he froze dead in his tracks. Reading the words dancing on his skin, he fell to his knees and covered his face with his hands. "Enough!" he mournfully complained. "Amma, enough," he sobbed.

Sedina became quiet and looked out onto the horizon. She wanted to give the man his privacy. She had seldom experienced sorrow in her life, but she'd had great experience with compassion. So, in a soft compassionate tone she commanded her finger to release his ring, but it still would not budge.

The prince finally composed himself. He knew it served no good being angry with one's personal guardians. He had to make peace with everything. He had to accept where he was and who he was. He had to let go of the past and forgive everyone or it would make him a nothing of a man. He'd vowed he would never be a negative king, but never was a negative. Thus, here he was, already what he wished he wouldn't be.

The mermaid's body had begun to weaken from sitting in the dirt, so he stood up and reached over to help her. He had to put her back in the water, but now the phrase danced on both of them, *'With love we are forever connected'*. When the she-fish propped herself up with one arm, the prince grabbed her by her waist, placed her other arm around his neck, and lifted her slippery form. He mindfully avoided her piercing stares. As he carried her toward the water's edge, he looked directly ahead. He had to locate the only place shallow enough to walk into the pool. Plus, he was ashamed at how he'd behaved. He could still feel his blood racing in his veins. He breathed in slowly and then slowly exhaled. He didn't want his heartbeat to tell her stories about him. Finally, when he felt the water was deep enough, he returned her gaze, and gently released her back into the bay.

"Are you better now?" he asked, startling the mermaid.

He surprised her. She hadn't noticed him paddling beside her. As she rinsed the dirt of her body, she waved her head from side-to-side gesturing 'yes'. She was perfectly fine. However, in Librebe a side-to-side gesture wiped things away. It meant 'no'. Now the prince was confused. "Then how can I help you?" he said. The prince was worried. If she was not better as her side-to-side gesture inferred, did it mean she felt offended? Had he been too harsh with her? Maybe he'd hurt her feelings. Now he was truly perplexed. Was it not his ring to defend? Then again, hadn't he used the adage 'Finder's keeper—loser's weeper' in his youth?

While treading water, the strange pair watched each other. They were completely curious about one another; a man made on earth and a maiden created in water. Sedina couldn't stop looking at the Hu-man. His heart beat as hers. He communicated in similar patterns, but he was very serious. So, she encircled the Hu-man with her tail and dunked him like a tea bag. This surprised the man so much he accidentally gulped a large mouthful of water, which he quickly gurgled before spitting it out. The mermaid laughed so hard tears filled her eyes, which in turn made the Hu-man laugh too.

"There that's better," she said. "Thank you for sharing joy."

The prince and the mermaid played like two otters in the sea until the sun appeared like a painting on the horizon. Their time together was coming to an end. They both knew it. The prince was getting cold. He had to get out of the water soon. He needed to get warm before his muscles tensed up and he drowned, but he didn't want to say goodbye, not yet.

Sedina sensed the Hu-man's discomfort. He was out of his element. She felt him getting tired. She also felt his pride. Some men would drown before they'd stop a desire. She had to help the Hu-man care for himself, so she began drifting toward the shore.

The prince knew the leaves from the sacred tree would irritate the mermaid's delicate skin, so he stopped her before she reached the flotsam. He stood up, neck high in the water and bowed with respect. "I know you have to get home now," he said.

This made Sedina smile. She'd never seen anyone bend before. The Hu-man had disappeared into the water then emerged again with his hand over his heart. She responded by encircling him with her body and touching his chest with her hand as he had done.

The prince was in awe of her. The mermaid made him feel so peaceful. He decided to give her his mother's ring. Not because the ring wouldn't release itself, but because he wanted a part of himself to remain with her. He knew he'd been blessed by her visit. Being graced by a water-goddess was a miracle of the highest order, but it was time. It was time for them to say goodbye.

In one clean stroke the mermaid lifted her arm and waved her ringed hand before plunging into the water and disappearing from view. The prince calmly watched the spot where the mermaid had been, and his mind went completely blank. It was as if she'd washed away all worry and fear of being different. All his self-created earthly woes were gone. Once again, Amma had taken over his upbringing. He'd be the king he was meant to be, because as unique as his experience had been; it was as normal as he felt right now. In this moment, the prince was simply a man who had just spent an afternoon with a woman of water.

CHAPTER TEN

Sedina was shocked at how quickly she'd made it back to the cave. The sun was still filtering in off the horizon, so she sat on a ledge and watched the afternoon play out in her mind's eye. Her eyes gently floated back and forth. Sometimes she stopped and smiled at the images, but then her smile would leave as her eyes returned to watching her life. Once she looked down at the ring as she quickly replayed the afternoon's events. When her eyes finally turned outward again it was night.

"Oh my," she quietly exclaimed. The entire southern hemisphere of stars twinkled above her. She watched the full moon rise and take its place in the firmament, lighting her way back through the cave.

"Uuuhmm," she whispered as the current pulled her along. She enjoyed rolling in the brisk water. "Ooom," she contentedly sighed. When she relaxed onto her back she heard her oooms echo back. She knew she was getting near the opening because the smell of the air had changed, and all sound rebounded in half the time.

"Ooommm," she hummed. And again an 'oomm' was heard floating in the air. She loved the water. She started to think of the Hu-man again, then she felt a shift in the current. She was getting very close to the opening now. She flipped herself over and pulled her arms tightly beside her. Next, she closed her eyes for a moment then opened them again to adjust her vision to the change of light. When the opening of the cave came into view, she collected her hair and propelled herself toward the archway, and like threading a needle she made it through. Back through the cave of the

Unknown Waters into Mer oceans the mermaid went but came back out again.

The current was so strong it carried the poor mermaid past the reef and clam beds bordering her realm, back toward the entrance of the cave. Sedina flung out her arms hoping it would slow her down however the current's pressure was so strong it bent her arms back in a most awkward position. "Mahhhlllloo," she shrieked. "That hurt!" Next, she tried angling her arms to make the cross towards Mer waters, but again the turn eluded her. She even tried using her backstroke to guide the water by pulling it from behind her toward her, but it only made the water swirl like an eddy. It took her under then spat her up in the center of the vortex where she had to fight her way back out, all over again. On and on the mermaid tried navigating the spinning waters, and over and over again she ended up right where she started. She was getting tired. She was getting really dizzy too. She tried resting and going with the flowing water, but it just spun her around like a starfish.

"Eeeennnnuuff," she screamed.

"Who's there?" A voice replied.

And before her head completely disappeared under the swirling water once more, the mermaid moaned, "Meeeeeee!"

"I see. I see. I see," nodded the sea horse, and off he swam. Then he returned with an entire herd of seahorse brethren. The little seahorses all bobbed outside the cave watching as the mermaid circled and disappeared then reappeared again. She stopped saying "Me" and began giggling "Whee!"

"I see. I see. I see." saw the seahorses.

The littlest one who had found the mermaid explained, "She's been at it for a very long time. If we don't get her out of there she will get sea-sick."

"I see. I see. I see." they all agreed. So, they all lined up and together they tried rescuing her.

"Now on three!" commanded the little seahorse. "One – two – three!" he shouted. But they couldn't hook the mermaid. She was spinning too fast.

"Me wheeeeee…" she hollered before vanishing again into the water.

The little seahorse was determined he would not be beaten, especially by the sea. The sea was his home and home was a safe place, so if the sea was not comforting then how could it be home? Of course, the others saw what he meant, so once again, and on three, the little seahorses turned in unison hooking their tails together, and on the mermaid's next turn exiting the cave, they grabbed her trailing hair and pulled her into calm waters.

"See! See! See!" cheered the seahorses.

"See you are safe now," heralded the little seahorse.

Sedina was still swirling from her experience. She looked at her seahorse saviors and immediately threw up.

"Uuughh see," groaned the seahorses.

"I see!" snorted the first seahorse.

The next morning Sedina awoke on a lovely bed of fresh algae. She stretched her arms and extended her tail and greeted the day. She cooed as she combed through her hair and smoothed her fins. She looked at her reflection and satisfied with her appearance, she slipped into the water to find the seahorses that saved her.

"Who's there," someone asked? It was a familiar voice. One she remembered hearing.

"Oh, it's you!" Sedina happily said. She had finally found him.

"My name is Equoo. I saved you from spinning," said the proud seahorse.

"I see," she joyfully said.

"Me too!" said a happy Equoo.

When all the seahorses heard the mermaid was awake, they rushed in and began to dote over her. The entire herd surrounded her and began working. It was hard to see what they were doing because they created so many bubbles it clouded her like a curtain. They whispered while they worked very quickly and efficiently.

"Whooooaahm!" the oldest amongst them said. They were finally done, so they all stopped and bobbed away. There before them loomed the mermaid. She was dressed in crystals and shells, pearls and gemstones, and they completed her regalia with a lovely crown of purple coral.

"Oh me, I'm *mervalous*," gasped the mermaid.

Sedina turned ever so slowly to the left, then ever so slowly to the right. She was trying to see her reflection in its entirety. She wore an abalone breastplate that shined like a rainbow over her bodice and her hair was braided with pearls and small opalescent shells. She was crowned with a gorgeous piece of purple coral that accentuated her rose-lilac locks perfectly. She was so ornate she blushed at her reflection.

"They even painted my body!" she cried and regrettably aloud.

"Of course, we did. See!' Someone yelled back. Then the little seahorses gathered together and blocked the ray of sunlight illuminating the mermaid, and like a dancer at a Mariner's ball, she glowed in the dark sea. She was fluorescent!

When the other seahorses had bobbed away, Equoo tilted himself to the side and presented his tail to Sedina. He was so proud. No one in his herd had ever caught anything this large or beautiful before. "You'll be my date," brayed Equoo.

"I see," said the amused mermaid. "I am most honored, Equoo."

The odd pair left together to meet the rest of the herd convening by the reef but when they found them they were all deep in conversation.

"You do it."

"No, you tell her."

"No, I think little Equoo should. He knows her better," neighed one of the seahorses.

They continued discussing among themselves who should tell the mermaid about her condition.

"Then Equoo must do it!" shouted someone in the herd.

"Here they are now!" screamed a seahorse.

"You must tell her, little Equoo!" snorted another.

Equoo did not look pleased at all to hear this. "I see! I see!" he defiantly replied. "You want me to do the hard part!"

Sedina cautiously watched the others. She was truly puzzled. Could they not see she was right there? "Tell me what?" She asked. "What?" She asked again.

The herd immediately grew silent. Then a little portly seahorse emerged from the crowd and floated before her.

"You are full of child. And your people have migrated. And the current won't let you follow them," said Equoo's mother.

"And you are too big for us to feed!" someone in the crowd yelled.

"I see. I see. I see," mumbled the mermaid as she floated out of the sea corral into the current again.

CHAPTER 11

The prince was not ready to return to his village. He'd had a most perfect day, so he didn't want it to be disturbed by the politics of tribal life. Since his return from the colonial's school, everyone kept staring at him. First there was his auntie sighing and fawning over him at every opportunity; and then there was his father, who could not stop comparing their tribal ways to the colonial's ways, and always deciding their way was best, plus there were the women of the village. They would not leave him alone. Was there no other man in Librebe!

The prince took his time and leisurely prepared for the walk back to his village. He wondered if the mermaid was thinking about him. A pink forester butterfly flitted past him followed by an aggressive *drongo* bird. "Go get 'er, my friend!" shouted the Prince. He thrust his foot into an empty knot of the fig tree and ran up the side of its trunk like when he was a boy. From there he had a bird's eye view, so he watched the butterfly evade the advances of the black bird. After they both flew away he grabbed a branch and hoisted himself up, then he lowered himself down and hoisted himself up again and then lowered on the inhale once more. He repeated the action until sweat poured off his body. It felt good. The prince felt everything was delightful today.

"Stop it," someone gently said.

The prince immediately fell to the ground and rolled his body into a standing position.

"Who said that?" he demanded. "No one tells me what to do!"

A gentle laugh replied, "But you stopped."

The prince rose to all of his height and strutted from one side of the huge tree to the other looking for the culprit. He walked through the twining roots to the other side, but no one was there.

"Only a coward would speak to me in such a way and then disappear," he yelled. "And I have no time for cowards!" The prince waited to see if his harsh words would make the scoundrel reveal himself, but no one appeared.

"You must be the only coward here," replied the voice.

Now the prince was livid. He was so angry he couldn't breathe. He pounded his chest. "You find this funny! I am no one to toy with!" he screamed.

Then the voice compassionately replied, "But yet you play like a child in the trees."

The prince's bronze skin turned red with anger. He wasn't angry about the intrusion or even the intruder's insults. He was angry for having his lovely day finish on such a sour note. Then he realized if he was going to play with a trickster he must be tricky. "I like to play in trees. Yes, I do. Why does that bother you?" the Prince replied feigning compassion.

The air became very still and all sound ceased. Next all the leaves on the tree began to vibrate and rustle. The prince didn't like this. His hair rose up at the nape of his neck and the little coils on his chest tightened closer to his heart.

"How did you do that? Are you a witch-man?" he cautiously asked. "How can you make the leaves rustle when there is no wind?"

All became silent. Finally, the voice replied. "Try thinking."

The prince turned purple with rage. Not only was this voice mocking him, it was insulting him now too. Still he refused to let the villain see him off-center again. He had to be strong and calm. "Okay I will accept your challenge. Who can make the leaves move without wind, you ask? Are you a god?"

"Good god, no," answered the voice.

"Are you a demon?" asked the Prince.

"I don't believe in devils and demons," laughed the voice.

"Aha!" the Prince exclaimed. "You did not answer the question!"

"No, I am not a devil or a demon or a bad entity or a mother-in-law," the voice calmly said. And all the leaves giggled at the voice's bad joke about one's in laws.

The prince began to understand. "You are a tree!" he happily answered.

"Really," mocked the tree. "Yes. And I am the very one you have been pulling on. So, stop it."

The prince laughed his huge guffaw. Everything was magic today. His people always knew this was a sacred tree, but no one knew it could talk! Today he felt as if he had walked through a portal into another world. He sat up against the tree's base and felt its strength and wisdom and began talking with it like an old friend.

"I met a water-goddess today. But she was not rooted like you, dear ancestor. She vanished. How do I find her? I mean would she even want me to find her is a better question." The prince had whittled a dead tree branch down to a nub.

"You are not completely stupid for a man. And I meant that as a compliment," the tree said. "First you guessed my identity and now you have had the good sense to think of her feelings too. Not bad for one so young."

"Don't move," the tree directed.

The prince, who was mounting an upper branch, immediately stopped and got still or as steady as he could. He was having a hard time holding his balance because he had one foot on the ground and the other up the side of the tree. As he slowly moved to commit to one position or the other, the tree's leaves began to quake.

"Stop, a snake!" warned the tree.

The prince froze and there before him was a green bush viper ready to strike. CRACK! A huge dead branch split and fell from above catching the viper right behind its head, which was in the middle of striking. Grateful for its life, the snake scurried off into the undergrowth.

"Thank you," sighed a relieved Prince. "Excuse me but what is your name, dear ancestor?" he respectfully asked.

"Tree, I am a tree. What is your name?" asked the tree.

"Man, I am a man," said the humble Prince.

"Some call me Edinkira although I do not call myself that," the tree confided. "I believe the name came from some unrequited love story. I seem to remember centuries ago a woman who came and sat beside me and cried for a long time, but that was when I was young and beautiful and there weren't as many people, so I became known as the place to be. But I am older now." Then the tree trailed off and was silent for a good long moment.

"I always have fruit so many still come. A lot of stories have been created about me, although not as many as in the old days," the tree quietly said.

The prince sat talking with the tree for hours, but it was getting dark now. He had to say goodbye and make his way back to the village. It'd been a most amazing day. He had met a water-goddess and a grand, Grand-elder of the earth, called Tree. When he heard the drums in the distance calling all to dinner, he quickly dug up his gut sack of fresh fish from the cool soil. The prince gave the tree a warm hug. "Goodbye my friend," he said. Then he secured his gut sack across his shoulders and headed toward home.

"I'm going to be late. I know it," he said to himself. Then he stopped. "What am I doing? So, what if I am late," he declared. "I was already nearly bit by a viper. If I keep up this pace, I will end up as someone's dinner myself." After that, the prince slowed down and focused his eyes and stealthily made his way through the forest into the clearing to Librebe.

CHAPTER 12

The prince arrived at the village just as everyone was sitting down in front of the communal bowl. He tried to make himself small and disappear into the crowd, however two young hunters spied him entering and jumped up to greet him. They began playfully fighting over who'd help him with his gut sack of fish. Seeing their young Prince-Guardian had returned, the young women gracefully arched their backs and seductively slid over and made a space for him to sit beside them.

The king closely watched his son to see how he'd handle all the attention, but the queen gracefully stood up and took the prince by the hand. His aunt had been coming to his rescue since his first day of birth. The day her sister-in-law died.

The Fire-Tender acted as if nothing out of the ordinary had happened. He simply smiled and threw another log on the fire and then swept the ashes to one side. While all the women put on their most loving expressions and talked in their softest voice, the Fire-Tender read their ashes. The embers told him what the people were really thinking, and the embers never lied.

Then something out of the ordinary happened. The Man-of-Medicine, and the Fire-Tender's daughter, Adisa quickly turned their heads toward the fire. They alone had seen the hot coal roll off the top, down the mound and into the pit before the Fire-Tender immediately swept up the coal and replaced it on top of the burning mound. It was the young prince's thought, and the Fire-Tender was bound by duty to protect the Guardian family's thoughts from invasion. However, when the Fire-Tender swept the prince's thought back into the fire, the thought put the fire out. The entire village collectively gasped. Even the Fire-Tender thought it was strange. He immediately borrowed some embers from under the cooking pot and started the fire again. As he stoked the new flame he could feel the community come back to life. The villagers let out a long sigh and returned to eating their dinner.

Adisa watched her father with great interest. As well as being the most beautiful girl in the village, the Fire-Tender's daughter was also the brightest of the young women. She had secretly learned how to read the fire, but no one in the village suspected it because it was forbidden, especially for women, to read fire. Adisa knew what was going on in the minds of her tribesmen. She had knelt beside her father while he worked since she was a child. She felt the changes in him as he tended the flames. She could tell what he was thinking by his gentle sighs or the way he tugged on his beard, or if he got really excited about something he looked away from the fire and scratched the earth. She learned to read the fire because she learned how to read her father. That's how she knew she was the one most likely to be chosen to marry the prince, and it was how she knew it was the prince's thought that doused the fire.

Adisa easily read the Man-of-Medicine too. He thought the young prince was enamored with her, and being he was shy, he stopped his thought from exposing this secret. It was mostly true. The young prince was shy but not because of her. He was shy because he was different. No one had ever been to the colonial's schools and come back. Most men who left, left for good. Also, the young prince's color was too fair to hide his emotions. He blushed.

The queen placed the prince's tribal cloth beside his father. She too had seen how the prince's thought had put out the fire. Before guiding the heir to his real place of honor, she clasped her hands in prayer and gave praise for the Fire-Tender, who remained staring at the ground in front him. Next, she clapped twice, and the women of the village immediately began to ululate. "Lleulleuleleueleli!" they cried in unison.

The prince was again the center of attention, so he quickly sat down in the place his aunt had set for him. The queen smiled with satisfaction as she returned to her spot on her brother's other side. Adisa lowered her eyes and watched the fire. The prince fixed his eyes on his bowl. The king, and the queen, kept their eyes locked on the young couple, and the villagers never stopped watching everything and everybody. But the Fire-Tender never took his eyes off the man sitting across from him with his eyes closed, the Man-of-Medicine.

As the Fire-Tender swept the ashes and fed the spirit of the fire, he watched the Man-of-Medicine gently throw a piece of fat from his soup onto the ritual fire. This was not good. No one was to look into the flames yet throw an object in there. It was considered most disrespectful.

The Man-of-Medicine was sure he went unnoticed. The Fire-Tender was no threat to him. He could easily deal with him. He was certain of that. The medicine man simply needed time to process the information in the fire. What made the fire go out? Was it the young heir's thoughts? Was it Emadi, the Herb-Woman's jealous daughter? The entire village knew she couldn't tolerate the thought of the Guardian-Prince choosing Adisa. Or maybe it was the Fire-Tender himself. Maybe he didn't want anyone to have that piece of information, so he intentionally put the flame out. As the Man-of-Medicine gnawed on his bone his mind became clear. It was the Fire-Tender. Satisfied with his answer he threw the fatty gristle into the fire.

Adisa lifted her long graceful fingers to her face and lowered her head so no one could see her. No one disrespected her father. She felt her blood flooding her face, so she quickly looked over at the prince to divert her true thoughts. She'd always been leery of the Man-of-Medicine, and now she was positive she didn't trust him, but she couldn't let him see that. He was a most powerful and dangerous man.

The women in the village giggled. They thought Adisa was pining for their Guardian-Prince. Emadi, the Herb-Woman's daughter, did more than laugh at the young beauty. She sucked the air through her teeth in disapproval. She wanted Adisa to feel shame. She believed having beauty and keen intelligence, plus a father of noble position to be too many gifts for one person. Emadi felt Adisa was too entitled, and she believed Adisa willed it so.

This was good. Adisa was happy for the petty women's judgmental stares. She needed time to collect herself. She needed time to think. What did put the fire out? She knew of only one thought large enough to eclipse all others—love. The prince was in love. But who made his heart so liquid with love? Who was he in love with?

The prince was happy for the drama going on around the fire. It meant no one was looking at him. He could relax now. He felt so comfortable he ate two bowls of stew and could have eaten a third. He couldn't remember the last time he felt this hungry. He welcomed his rumbling stomach. It kept his mind in a safe territory. Not even the fire would begrudge him the desire to eat. However, he couldn't go on this way. He was going to have to choose a bride and soon otherwise the anticipation would destroy the village.

Meanwhile, the Fire-Tender tended his fire.

<h1 style="text-align: center;">CHAPTER THIRTEEN</h1>

Sedina was in shock. She tried to swim but she couldn't coordinate her movements. She tried floating but her emotions made her tail sink. She eventually slowed to a stop and took a long deep breath. It was beautiful there. Rays of light penetrated through to the ocean floor in long triangular slices. "To sit in the sun," she humbly thought. She wanted to rest, but her head was still spinning from the whirlpool outside the cave. Now there was news of a child. She spotted a ledge engulfed in sunlight directly ahead and she darted towards it. As she curled up on the rock shelf, she toned, *"I am a mother. I am with myself. I am healthy. I can find food. I am funny. I am inventive."* And she continued counting her assets until she said, "I'm okay."

The mermaid began studying the illumined water. It was going to be winter soon. She had to find a comfortable place to nest if she and her baby were to survive. She poked out her nose and felt the direction of the current and then she turned over onto her back to feel which way was warmest. The current responded with an emphatic warm rush that streamed over her tummy just below the diaphragm. "Then that's the way it will be," she decided. So, the mermaid began preparing for her migration north toward the equator.

She slowly removed the jewels and shells the seahorses had given her and wrapped them in an old seaweed sack. Next, she collected some rich blue algae, tiger lotus, blue water lilies and some water hyacinths. Hyacinths were her personal favorite. She didn't want to waste time foraging later.

She would need the time to find a place to nest for the baby's sake. When all was done, Sedina took a final look around.

"Thank you, dear waters, for taking care of me once again," she quietly said.

"You're welcome," replied the sea.

"Who's there?" she cautiously asked.

And camouflaged in the seaweed was Equoo. "You see, it's me!" he said.

"What are you doing here, Equoo? Won't you get in trouble with your herd?" asked the concerned mermaid.

"I found you, so I should be with you," he answered. "Yes, yes this I see. I must help you birth your baby." The little seahorse spoke so sincerely it was as if he was making a vow to himself.

"I see," the mermaid quietly said. She was secretly happy not to be alone again, so the mermaid and the seahorse rested on the ledge and enjoyed the final rays of sunshine.

Sedina slid off the ledge and began scouring the area. She scavenged a good-sized mason jar and filled it with as many small crustaceans as she could find. She added a bit of algae, some rocks and shells and placed the pearls the seahorses had given her inside as well. Then she poked some holes in the top and tightly closed it. It looked like a magical shrimp theater. Equoo was very happy to see the shrimp aquarium. Seahorses were very proud beings that only ate live food.

The mermaid continued foraging for their journey. She found more shrimp and sea-flowers and a huge piece of silk some Hu-men had lost. She wrapped the jar around her body and secured it with the stray piece of parachute.

"Look at you. You are already learning to be a mother," Equoo said.

Sedina smiled at her reflection. The pouch of shrimp did indeed look like a nestled baby.

"Shall we be going?" she asked.

Equoo bobbed his head. He was ready.

The mermaid gently lifted the seahorse and placed him inside her seaweed sack. "We will make better time if you ride with me," she explained.

Equoo found it funny that a horse of the sea would be riding a mermaid. "Hi ho away we go!" he gaily shouted. And off they went.

CHAPTER 14

The next day the prince returned to the spot where he'd met the water-goddess. He was hoping to continue their dance from the day before. He believed she would be a lovely partner to share his life with. His people called this union, the Dance of Life. It began when they entered this dimension via the Sun only to end when they exited through Earth's door.

His people were born sons of the Sun. That was why they were created in so many beautiful colors. They were baked for one lifetime until it was time to hibernate in the Earth and this cycle continued over and over again until they learned how to be so light-hearted they married the sun for eternity, like the stars. Being called Sunny was the biggest compliment ever in his village. It did not matter if you were a girl or a boy if you were sunny you were perfect.

As the prince fished he thought about the day before. However, he pondered a lot more than he fished. He hadn't moved his pole in more than an hour. He was secretly waiting for the mermaid to return. "Why does this watery woman sing within me so?" he asked himself, but the prince did not get the answer he'd wished. His mind reminded him that thinking of the past was creating stale thoughts in the present, and that was not good. He was next in line as King-Guardian, so he had to be aware. He had to be present.

At the meeting with the Elders that morning he could barely think of anything but her. When his father called upon him, he didn't answer. He hadn't heard him. The others laughed and asked if he knew his name. The prince felt embarrassed. Not only had he not been present, he'd shamed his father too. His father had called him Sunny, the most endearing term of his people. He rarely called him that. On those few occasions when he had called him this, he always followed with telling him how important the term was to him. Now he, his only son, had not heard this valuable and rare compliment. He also noticed the Man-of-Medicine had been watching him the entire time. This was truly not good because the medicine man was a judgmental man who could come to a wrong conclusion. He could come to a bad one, something other than he was simply thinking about a water-goddess.

The prince decided to draw his own conclusion. He was a man of the earth and she was a woman of water and they lived a day's dream together. That was that. Still in the back of his mind there was a gentle, tinkling, waterfall of an image—the image of the mermaid. This would not do. The prince knew he had to stay focused. He had to clear his thoughts and he had to clear them now.

"Oye!" someone cried. "Oye, Prince-Brother, where are you!" yelled Adisa.

"Here, over here," the Prince replied.

Adisa bent her knees and slowly made her way down the sloping cliff where she spied the young prince fishing. He was standing on the edge of a natural quay in the deeper part of the bay. It was slippery there, but he stood completely balanced on the mossy stone. She was impressed. She steadied herself before moving forward. As she made her way toward the prince she thought about the years she'd known him. He'd been a loyal friend and he was always a compassionate hunter. He was also a good student, but then she remembered him as a child. He used to be a whiny boy. It was true; however, she immediately came to his defense. She thought most men of privilege were whiny when expressing themselves. It was as if they had to speak for their entire lineage every time they opened their mouths. At least he didn't do that. He always spoke from his heart.

"Give me your hand. There is a lot of moss here," the Prince said. Adisa took the prince's hand and allowed him to help her out onto the rock.

"I've been looking all over for you. I should have guessed you were here," she said. She immediately wished she hadn't said it. It implied judgment and she wanted him to feel comfortable around her, so she explained herself. "Isn't this where the boat took you north?" she asked.

The prince adeptly switched subjects. "I hope it wasn't too much trouble finding me," he said, and respectfully waited for her reply.

"No trouble at all," she said. "Auntie asked me to find you. She's looking for you," she explained.

The prince looked out to sea with a quizzical look on his face. "Do you know what she wants?" he asked with reserve.

Adisa looked out to sea and answered, "To try on robes, I believe."

The prince sat down and baited his hook and gestured for her to sit beside him. "We have time. Those robes are for the harvest festival and it's the beginning of summer," he joked.

Adisa smiled at the good-natured way the prince critiqued his aunt. He returned her smile.

"Do you fish?" he asked.

Adisa didn't know what to say, so she said nothing. The prince took her silence as a yes and presented her his fishing rod, so she gently took it and cast the line far out into the cove.

"You're a pro with that," said the Prince. "Here." He gave Adisa some mealie to add to her bait. "They love it," he teased.

The Fire-Tender's daughter kept taking long deep breaths to calm her body. She didn't want to appear too anxious to be sitting beside the prince, even though she knew it was what the queen had intended.

Then the Prince said, "They are all waiting for me to announce our next Queen, aren't they?"

This sent a shiver down Adisa's spine. It wasn't because of the question about choosing his bride. It was because he did not look at her when he asked it. He looked out to sea.

CHAPTER FIFTEEN

The mermaid made it back through the Unknown Waters and she was not only alive, she had more knowledge than she had upon entering. She had learned nothing, not one single thing, could hurt anything connected to all things and she had learned this from a land animal. She'd also made a friend—well, two friends. She had met the mountain Hu-man and now Equoo.

The mermaid opened her sack and smiled at the sleeping seahorse. She felt blessed. She had ventured there and was still here, plus she had a lovely ring to prove it. Everything she was told about going beyond Mer waters was not true. The cave of the Unknown Waters didn't lead to non-existence. It expanded her awareness and her physical body too. Her tummy was getting very round now.

Where was her school? She wanted them to meet Equoo and tell them about the Hu-man and his ring. The little seahorse fell asleep whenever she began telling him. He had never met a Hu-man so he couldn't imagine the story even when she described it. She hadn't thought about this before. How was she going to describe something to someone who couldn't imagine it happening?

She began practicing telling her story to others. "Oola, I met a man with two legs and he gave me this. It has the song of our people etched on it. What do you think?" As the mermaid played her part and smiled at her invisible schoolmate, her smile turned upside down. "They will think I am ill, or worse, crazy," she thought. "But I have proof. I have the ring. They have to believe me," she silently argued, but there was no one there to argue back. She continued her imaginary conversation with her school. She had the ring. It mattered. The ring proved her story, but Mer-ones did not live in the land of matter. They lived in the sea, so none of her story would matter much to them.

Sedina continued swimming and musing and wading and pondering and listening to imaginary-comment after imaginary-comment from someone not actually there. Then she finally looked out and noticed no one was there. She was alone again for the second time in her memory. Nary a soul, being, fish, or reef was there. She had been musing so deeply the sound of her thoughts pushed all other life away.

"What is it?" Equoo asked.

The mermaid felt better. Equoo was still there. She was beginning to understand why her family feared the Unknown Waters. She'd never known doubt and now here she was worrying like a two-legged, landlocked being. She immediately stopped and sat down. "Flow, flow still," she thought. So still she became.

"Where did everything go?" Equoo asked.

The mermaid didn't answer the seahorse. She resumed swimming. The sea was vast. The emptiness had nothing to do with her. There probably was no one there to begin with, but with every excuse she gave herself for the vacant waters the mermaid became more frightened by the dark void.

"When I was little, very little indeed, this happened. We all looked up and all was gone," said the seahorse.

"Then what happened?" asked the mermaid.

"We drifted and followed the sound," Equoo said.

"What sound?" She asked.

"That sound!" Equoo excitedly said.

Then the mermaid heard a gentle roar. Arrruuugh, and the sound grew, *Uuurrghhhhhhhhh*. Sedina stopped and adjusted her eyes to the darkness surrounding them and saw a huge waterfall come into view.

"Wow!" whistled Equoo.

"I agree," said the mermaid in awe. "Shall we follow it?" She asked the seahorse.

"Sounds good to me," agreed Equoo.

"Get ready!" she said.

They jumped off the ledge into the water falling deeper into the sea. Sedina took the waterfall as a good sign. Waterfalls held water nymphs, nixies, selkies and others like her. Maybe they could help her find her family. She became hopeful. "I will find my family, and then I will be whole again. They'll know how I feel and that is all that matters to me." On that thought, the mermaid dove deeper into the waters looking for the path of silvery bubbles carrying the spirits of her kinsmer.

CHAPTER 16

It was the night of the third eclipse, thus the village was a little nervous. Eclipses always brought huge change. The last time there were three eclipses within one moon's journey the old King-Guardian had died, plus there had been the long drought that killed so many others. The Man-of-Medicine was sure the colonials had manipulated the weather, so the rain would not come, and the people would die. The Herb-Woman believed it was beings from another world that stole the rain. She saw them as dim in spirit. She thought the rain stealers were so dull they were gray. Whoever stole the rain returned it fifteen years later, but it brought a sickness that ate one's blood. However, that sickness never hit Librebe, so they were going to celebrate by honoring the ancestors for sparing them that indignity.

The villagers solemnly surrounded the fire in their ceremonial robes. As soon as they were all settled a huge Bateleur eagle screeched overhead and everyone jumped. Then an ember exploded in the fire and everyone jumped again. An audible gasp was heard from around the circle.

"Silence!" demanded the King.

The Fire-Tender immediately tried reading the eagle's message but to no success. The Man-of-Medicine secretly fondled his divining bones. He was trying to make sense of it too, however it was the Herb-Woman who saw the meaning behind the visit.

"Look!" she cried.

There in the fire was a huge bird dropping in a true heart shape. There was no widow's peak in the middle, like a symbolic heart design. This was a real heart shape that curled softly to the right at an angle.

"Sit! Everyone, sit please, my children," the King compassionately demanded.

Everyone sat down again, but they never took their eyes off the heart dropping in the fire.

The king quickly motioned for the ceremony to begin. "It is with gratitude that we have been visited by the great eagle," he began. "Especially today, the day of the ceremony honoring our good fortune in the fields and at home. We must be humble and honest to purge all fear from entering our village," said the King. "We must be pure."

When the king ended his speech, the Herb-Woman mixed the ceremonial drink and poured it into the communal gourd. As the bowl of bee pollen and milk was passed, the Fire-Tender circled counter-clockwise and smudged the heart-of-the-mind of everyone in the circle. It was a point in the center of the forehead just above the eyes that formed the triangle of life—the earth, the sky and the product of it, the community.

The Man-of-Medicine sat in his place of honor beside the Prince-Guardian, casting the divining bones. The bones would foretell if danger would elude them for another year. However, every time the bones fell, one would fall on its side invalidating the reading. The shaman called over Emadi, the Herb-Woman's daughter and had her wipe his fingers with the gizzard of an albino crocodile, but still the bones would not fall flat on the ground. He tried a third time and this time the bone popped up and landed in the prince's lap. The eagle screeched again, and no one knew whether to laugh or cry. In one moment, all signs pointed toward prosperity, and in the next, some unknown element entered the picture.

The prince sat with his eyes downcast looking at the bone in his lap. It was strange. He couldn't pick it up. He was too frightened. Not because the bone fell sideways three times or because the last time it fell in his lap. He was afraid of this particular bone. The prince was afraid of the bone shaped like a fish's tail. And the eagle cried for the third time that evening.

"What is happening?" shrieked the Herb-Woman.

"Someone is messing with us!" said her daughter, Emadi.

"Jealousy, I am sure because we've all been well," cried someone else.

"I don't understand," muttered another in the crowd.

"Silence," said the King. "Silence, I say! We are a respected and very ancient group of people, not some new tribe filled with superstition!"

The king was not happy, but he tried to keep the emotion from showing on his face. Never in all his years of life had a ceremony been shat on. He watched over the group until the communal bowl finally reached the lips of the last person and then he motioned for the drums to begin. As the drummers brought their instruments into the circle, the young prince picked up the bone and handed it back to the Man-of-Medicine and the entire village became silent for a good—long—moment.

Finally, the prince sat forward and addressed everyone in a soft voice. "*L'oboto* everyone, night's greeting to you all," said the Prince. "Tonight, we have been blessed with the prayers of an eagle. A most honorable creature that flies very close to Spirit." The prince continued comforting the crowd. "He, or she, has spoken to us not once, but three times."

The women giggled when the prince included them in the eagle's song.

"Like our honored Man-of-Medicine who has also played his part three times," added the Prince.

The crowd quickly looked at the Man-of-Medicine to see how he was handling the prince's words.

"But now, this third time it has landed in my lap. Why? What does this mean, we all ask ourselves," he said. Then the prince paused and finally lifted his eyes and looked out into the crowd.

The queen sat so still she could have been made of wood. The king's left hand twitched as if he was preparing to throw a lance in his son's direction to stop his chatter if it took a wrong direction. The medicine man looked relieved to have the spotlight taken off him. Everyone else simply looked hopeful that the prince's words would explain the events that had just happened. Even the Fire-Tender looked at him with anticipation. Adisa was the only one that did not look at him, but this gave him courage because it was her eyes he did not want to meet.

"The great eagle mates once in its lifetime," the Prince continued. "It is one of a handful of Spirit's creatures that know how to be the sole mate of one being happily and faithfully."

Now the prince had everyone's attention. He knew what they were expecting. He knew what they were all waiting to hear. They believed he was finally going to do it. He was going to announce his wife, their next Guardian-Mother. He could feel their anticipation. The prince had to tell them. He knew he had to give them his answer tonight.

"So, under the supervision of the loyal, one-for-eternity wisdom of my brother eagle, I wish to be honest with you all. I do not know whom I shall wed. I am still finding myself after being away for so long. So, I humbly ask all of you to give me a sun's cycle, one year to learn all there is to learn."

The prince couldn't look at his father. He already felt his disapproval. He knew he was upset because he didn't consult with him first before openly speaking to the people. He knew his aunt would be upset too because she wanted grandchildren to give her purpose after her brother stepped down. He also knew Adisa was crestfallen. He could feel her disappointment. She hadn't looked up since he mentioned the mating habits of eagles. He also knew her father, the Fire-Tender, would watch his every thought for the entire year, looking for the answers behind his behavior. But mostly he knew he couldn't get married right now because he was in love with another.

"I humbly ask you to give me one more year of being a son, so I may learn to be as perfect a father as my own has been to me, and to all of us." Then the prince fell silent, and he let his head gently fall toward his chest.

He didn't hear his father give permission to the drums, but they were beating, and everyone was loudly singing along. There was a lot of music, but there was no harmony in it. The village sang from its head, not its heart. It was not until the eagle lifted its stocky body and extended its wings and flew away without a cry, that all became quiet. All one heard was the heavy flapping of its wings against the air.

The prince listened as the eagle lived his dream. He wanted to fly away with the great Bateleur. He wanted to go on as he had before, fishing and hunting and exploring life. He didn't want to govern a people or wed a woman chosen for him. He simply wanted to float in the ocean with his mermaid. He couldn't give up this dream yet. He had one year to find her. What if he did not find her within that year? He would happily marry the Fire-Tender's daughter he answered himself.

CHAPTER SEVENTEEN

It'd been just under a year since the mermaid and the seahorse had nested in the northern waters near the equator, and since two months of that time was taken making the journey, the maiden was ready. She was really ready to give birth now.

Equoo had worked endlessly foraging the waters for things to eat and stray jetsam to keep the cold current from entering their cave. They'd been lucky to find the recessed geode filled with so much crystal it stayed light the entire season, but he had to work to keep the seaweed growing around the entrance, so the large predators didn't smell them. He had grown quite fond of the mermaid. She was truly pleasant company. She never criticized him or complained about his snoring. She never wrinkled her nose at his smelling of shrimp. She never cursed or called him names or added *little* in front of his given name. He hated being called Little Equoo. No seahorse was large, but if they had one scale of height advantage they all galloped around braying about it. "What asses seahorses can be," he said to himself.

The current changed. Feeling the water flow differently, Equoo quickly turned and watched in horror as the mermaid pivoted her body and stood on her head. She was trying to scratch some dead scales off her body near her dorsal fin.

"No, no, no," he yelled. "Don't do that!" Equoo bobbed over as fast as he could and helped the mermaid return to a prone position. "What were you doing?" he asked. "I have had millions, no trillions of babies and never, ever did I do that upside down! Trust me," he whinnied.

The mermaid looked at Equoo with great compassion. It was true. The males of their species carried the eggs and gave birth in seahorse culture. "I'm itchy, Equoo. Please scratch me," she pleaded.

"Oh, I see. I see," said Equoo. As he scratched the mermaid's back he began to sing a song from home.

> "I see, I see," said the seahorse bride.
> To the reef, to the reef, where the shrimp reside.
> And she wiggled and ate 'til she burst at the sides,
> And her eggs she did place in her husband's insides."

It was a strange song but a fitting one for a seahorse midwife-husband. Equoo continued scratching Sedina and singing to her until all he could do was hum.

Sedina was now in full labor and with every contraction she screamed the refrain from Equoo's song, "and her eggs she did place." She never made it to the end of the stanza *in her husband's insides* for the pain was far too great. In fact, she almost smashed poor Equoo with her tail during one horrendous cramp, however after four minutes and twenty-two seconds the mermaid gave birth to a baby-mermaid-girl.

Equoo stared at the baby with alarm. "Ewgh! What was the father, a striped bass?" Equoo asked.

"What do you mean?" inquired the mermaid. "I think she's beautiful," she said as she cooed to her daughter.

The baby was large. It looked like an overgrown mudskipper. It had big eyes and a long, chunky, tadpole-like body. It scrunched up its face in the weirdest expressions and it had the strangest amber red hair ever, but that wasn't the worst part. It had little tiny feet hiding underneath its little tadpole flippers, that when touched retracted like a slug into its shell. The baby looked nothing like her mother.

"Well you can't go home now!" exclaimed Equoo. "They will surely kick you and your mutant baby out of the school."

Sedina burst into tears upon hearing the seahorse's judgment. "Well, look at you. You are very funny looking," the mermaid angrily replied. Then she grabbed her baby and disappeared into the back of the cavern.

"Oh me, oh me, oh me," cried Equoo. "I've upset my friend." Equoo leaned against the seaweed divider covering the entrance and tried to think. He knew she missed her family and he was all she had, so he had to behave like family and tell her the baby didn't look that bad. Then he thought maybe he should say something nicer than that, and he finally came up with something to say. "What a baby!" Equoo proclaimed. He was happy he had found the right words. It was a perfectly honest thing to say, so he continued rehearsing his comment, but with different inflections. "What a baby! What a baby. What A Ba-by." He repeated until he was satisfied with the sincerity of its delivery. "What—a—baby."

Mermaids can't hold anger for long so Sedina immediately returned to the front of the cave again. Her little one was already swimming behind her, following her bubbles.

"What a baby," Equoo gently said. "She is still wee. She has all the time in the world to become beautiful like you." The seahorse truly didn't want the mermaid to feel bad about her strange looking offspring. The big baby was kind of charming in its own weird way. It never stopped giggling. Maybe the odd pair of appendages tickled it. Then the little tadpole mermaid swam over to Equoo and grabbed his tail and flung him out into the open water.

"Tesi, sili hi he li," she giggled.

"No, my love, we must be gentle!" said the shocked mermaid to her daughter.

Equoo slowly bobbed back in and went directly to the rear of the cavern.

"I'm sorry, my dear little Equoo. She did not mean to offend you," Sedina said.

But Equoo did not hear her, because he was still reeling with rage over her calling him "little". Now that she had her baby he had become Little Equoo! He was not going to tolerate this at all. "I'm going home," he announced from the back of the cave, but the mermaid did not hear the seahorse because his little voice was swallowed up by the sound of the sea.

Equoo did not sleep well that night. Between the baby's mewing and the mermaid's cooing all he could think of was being home and pregnant too. He remembered all the babies he'd had in his youth, but now he was getting older and nobody asked him to hold their eggs anymore. Poor Equoo began to cry. He felt truly miserable. He was stuck in a cave being bullied by a big baby that looked like a sea-monster. Well maybe it wasn't that bad. Equoo always exaggerated when he was angry, but he still felt the baby didn't look good. "I see! I am not blind," said the frustrated seahorse.

Then through the darkness reflected by the quartz, two huge eyes appeared, and they disappeared when a big pink mouth opened. "Galumm," said the baby mermaid as she swallowed the seahorse.

Sedina could feel the draft on her right side so she bolted upright and looked around. Where was she? Then she saw the pink opening illuminated by the crystals and she knew what had happened.

"Spit, little one! Spit him out, I say," demanded her mother. Then she took both her hands and placed them on either side of her daughter's mouth and squeezed.

"Boulorum," gurgled the tadpole mermaid and out popped a very disgruntled Equoo.

"That's it!" Equoo cried. "I've had enough. I'm leaving!" Equoo bobbed once again to the back of the cavern, and as he packed he ranted about this sacrifice or some challenge and all the obstacles he'd endured and then he raged on about this and that some more. "I have given my all to you and your selfish baby. And she is disrespectful!" he screamed.

"Dearest little Equoo, please don't leave us," Sedina pleaded.

She tried to apologize, but before the words had barely left her mouth, Equoo screamed, "I am not little!" Then he grabbed his bag and bobbed out of the cave.

"Oh my," mused the mermaid. "He must feel terrible," she thought. "We must go after him," she said to her daughter. "And you must apologize." Sedina lifted herself up and stood on her tail and shook her finger at her Mer-child. She wanted to make sure her point was heard and taken seriously.

The baby simply stared at her mother in awe and said, "Merma!"

Sedina melted at hearing her first word. Her mer-child had just called her mother.

CHAPTER 18

The prince came every day for almost a year to the place where he first met the water-goddess. He had finally made peace with losing his mother but now another loss haunted him. When each new morning came he packed a lunch of millet, mangoes and ginger beer in a sack and left before anyone awakened. It was his three hundred and fifty-seventh consecutive day of visiting the mountain cove. It was on this day the water-goddess returned.

The mermaid snuck into the bay swimming silently under the water. She immediately knew the man was there because she could smell his earthy scent. Then she saw him. He sat on a rock dangling his feet in the water as he quietly fished. She thought he looked more like a merman than a mountain Hu-man. She swam directly underneath him and nibbled on his toes. She wanted to get his attention, however it tickled the prince, so he quickly removed his feet from the water. Next, she tried using the sun's reflection and their ring to pull his focus into the water, but the prince grabbed a banana leaf and shielded his eyes from the aggravating glare. The mermaid was excited to see the man so her failed attempts to attract his attention truly frustrated her, thus she leapt from a stone out of the water and quickly snatched the leaf from his eyes.

The prince was astonished. It took him a moment to realize what had happened. She was back! With a huge smile he dove into the lake, however his exuberant body made such a splash it created a huge ripple, which pushed the mermaid back out toward the deeper part of the pool.

Sedina burst into laughter and said, "Before I approach the water's edge you must calm yourself for me."

The excited prince forced himself to be still and patiently tread the water. It was the hardest trial he'd ever been put through, but he calmed himself and waited for the mermaid.

As the mermaid gracefully swam toward him, she slowly began to explain her return. "I have been gone now for almost twelve moons only nourished by the sea. I never found my original joy, my mermaid family. But then my belly swelled with love, the love of you and me, so now you have a daughter, a beautiful child, half earth and half sea."

The prince was shocked by the mermaid's words. He immediately knew he should marry her. He would marry her, and he was ready to say it out loud to her or anyone else that was listening, but the mermaid lifted her fingers to her mouth and silenced him. Then she began speaking again.

"And she has grown her land legs now and wishes to be with thee." Sedina then took her daughter out of the seaweed sack secured on her back and released her into the water. She was a girl. A shimmering, honey-tinted child with amber hair that flowed like twisted seaweed, and her eyes were the color of a deep green sea. The mermaid-tadpole grinned and swam straight toward the prince dog-paddling near the rocky shore. When she reached him, she stopped and pushed her nose forward like an otter and smelled her land-father. The prince was so in awe to find out he had a daughter, he forgot to paddle so he immediately sank into the ocean and disappeared from view.

Without missing a ripple, the toddler mermaid dove down after him and came nose-to-nose with her furry father. He never noticed she was there because his eyes were tightly shut. He was still trying to navigate his liquid surroundings. As his faced puffed up, the wee mermaid mimicked him with compassionate curiosity.

 The prince was ashamed of himself. He knew he was flailing. Flailing indeed he was. He demanded his eyes to open, and to his surprise his daughter stared back at him, so he motioned for her to rise and they both glided up to the water's surface.

It was late afternoon now and the sun had just started to make its way under the horizon. As the mermaid watched her daughter drink in her new surroundings, she knew their time together was ebbing away, however she released the thought like the sea released the tide. She was enjoying their family reunion even though she knew the water would soon become too cold for a man of earth. Their child was made from both of them, so she was able to be on land or at sea for as long as she wished. She loved watching her daughter play with the man. The entire time she carried her she had wished for this. She wanted her to get to know her father. She wanted her to experience all the elements she was made of and every part she had come from.

"She can stay the winter and spring with you, if you like. The sea is too cold and harsh to play in the winter. Then she could come home in summer and fall when the land is too hot and dry to sustain her humid ways," the mermaid said to the prince.

The prince stared at his child as he soaked in this new knowledge. He immediately knew nothing would give him more pleasure than to be her Guardian-Father. He would protect her and teach her the sacred ways of his people. He would. But how would he do this? He was a man.

"How will I… Is she able to…?" The prince tried to verbalize his concerns however they were too concerting to speak aloud.

"Please don't worry," the mermaid said. "After drying in sunlight her legs will fully protrude and her scales will easily exfoliate with sand," she said. "She only returns to her maternal lineage when she is in Mer waters." She watched the two-legged man with great interest. She could feel his heart constrict the way the people of earth did when an unsure thought entered their minds. "She is a child like any other," she said.

The prince had not thought about any of this. The responsibility of being a father or becoming a father in one afternoon made him downright anxious, plus the thought of being a father of a mixed elemental child (not to mention her being a girl) simply overwhelmed him. What would the villagers say? He knew the women would take offence. Not because he had sired a child that was not of his world—their world, but because he was next in line as King-Guardian. There had never been a king who had sired a water-goddess-mothered child before. There had never been anyone who'd done this in his village. He knew these women. They would be jealous.

Now Sedina felt a constriction in her chest. Had she brought trouble to this kind man's life? She had lived at sea for centuries and although she'd watched the two-legged Hu-men from afar, what did she really know of their life or how they felt? The mermaid's skin started to appear dull and scaly and this worried her even more. Her empathy was taking its toll on her. But when she looked at her daughter who was so excited, her faith returned. "All will be alright. I know this," mewed the mermaid to her daughter. Then she spoke to the Hu-man. "You will be perfect. You're perfectly thee. You'll see." On that note she gently lifted her arm and made her way back toward the deeper part of the pool where the eddy would take her under once again.

As the mermaid slowly swam away she saw her child and her father floating in the water before her. Her daughter being half-sea never looked back. The idea of being apart did not exist for her. Her daughter was like a drop of water in her personal ocean—nothing could separate them. Sedina knew this, but she still did not like leaving her. It felt like she was swimming against the tide, not with it, but she never let the man, or her daughter see the sadness enter her eyes as she swam away.

The prince quietly watched the mermaid float away. So far away again it was to be, although this time he was not alone. He had a daughter. The prince became afraid again. He didn't know why being a father scared him so much, and that frightened him all the more. This time he was sure it had nothing to do with the villagers. They would always be upset about something or another. It was their nature. He was afraid his daughter might not take to him as her mother had. What if she found him boorish and brown and earth-like?

The young mermaid began to watch her father with great interest. She didn't understand the emotions rippling through his body or why he spoke so sadly to himself, although she liked the way he smelled. He smelled like fresh air and coconuts. And she absolutely loved the little copper springs of hair that coiled on his chest. She asked if she could play with them, but he didn't hear her through his thoughts. She tried to mimic his mewing. She began to scrunch up her forehead and sway from side to side, and he finally heard her.

"What is the matter, young one?" he cautiously asked.

The young mermaid lit up with great delight. Now her father was present with her. She got so excited she hadn't noticed how hungry she'd become, but before she could vocalize her desire her tummy gurgled.

"Are you hungry? Is that it?" he asked.

The young girl thought, "*Why yes, let's eat!*"

"Okay, then eat we shall," her father happily agreed.

The prince was happy to have a chore he felt capable of accomplishing. He motioned for his daughter to follow him to shore and with each stroke of his arm his heart pounded. He was alone with a child for the first time in his life. He tried to remember what her mother told him. He was to let her dry and then rub her down with sand.

The prince took a long breath before stepping onto shore. When he finally turned he saw his tadpole daughter flipping around in the shallow water. He quickly bent down and grabbed her little arms and held her close to his chest. She felt like a newborn baby, but cold. Her little body was so cold he almost dropped her. He walked over to his sack and got a towel and began drying them both off, but the little Mer-girl began to whimper. The rough towel hurt her fragile skin. The prince panicked but then he remembered she was too dry in the sun, so he dipped his daughter in the water to soothe her irritated skin and then he placed her tiny body on his chest. When the sun had warmed her frame, she began to peel, and two perfectly formed legs appeared.

"Dear Amma," he thought. The prince was truly in awe. He had never in all his years seen a transformation up close like that. Once he'd seen a pupa open and a butterfly emerge, but this topped that by a long shot.

As his daughter's land legs took solid form she scratched them. She wiggled her newly formed toes and whispered that she was still hungry.

The prince took some sandy earth and gently rubbed the remaining dead skin off.

"Is that okay?" he asked. "How do your legs feel?" The prince was truly curious.

The little girl smiled at him and patted her stomach, which had begun to grumble quite loudly, so her father reached into his bag and pulled out his last mealie cake and a small but nicely ripened mango and presented it to her. The little girl smelled the mango and smiled then immediately bit into it.

"No, no, wait!" yelled the Prince. But unfortunately, it was too late. The youthful mermaid had already swallowed it. The prince could tell what she thought of the fruit by the strange expression on her face.

"Noolea," she told him. Or did she for she still had a mouthful of mango rind. Then the prince heard the strange word again "*Noolea*". The wee mermaid pulled the rind out of her mouth and stared at the two-legged Hu-man she now called father.

The prince felt like an idiot. He gently wiped her face and gave her an apologetic smile. Afterward he took the mango and peeled the skin back. He then showed her how to scrape her teeth across the rind to get at the fruit. Upon tasting the pulp, the wee mermaid let out a big giggle and smiled at her father and the prince swooned. She had her mother's smile. As the little mermaid sat eating her mango the prince tried to make conversation.

"What does 'noolea' mean?" he asked.

As she expertly stripped the mango of its fruit she explained. "*Noolea means it tastes neither sweet, nor sour, but in between and it tingles in your ears. My mother taught me to read stories in your language. I am not sure of your tales of us because it doesn't match what I know. I think the Little Mermaid should sing in the book, but I can't hear her.*" Then aloud, in a voice vibrating from inside out, the puerile mermaid said, "I'm finished."

The prince was reeling. He had heard of some medicine men or *Sangomas* who could talk without speaking and hear the same way, but he had never seen or heard anyone actually do this. Now his child—a mermaid, was standing in the sand on her own two feet silently talking to him! Maybe he'd imagined the entire day. Sometimes the men working on boats did this when they had been out at sea in the sun all day. He needed to be sure he wasn't hallucinating so the prince pinched himself. "Ayyye," he winced. He wasn't asleep.

The young mermaid began to cry. She couldn't understand why her father doubted her sound. Maybe in earth ears it sounded funny. Maybe her tone made him hurt, but why would he hurt himself? Oh no, if in earth waves her voice sounded like being pinched no one would ever want to talk to her.

The startled prince jumped! He not only heard his daughter's thoughts, he heard the sadness and worry in them too. "There, there little one, I hear you and you sound beautiful," he softly sang. He closed his mouth and thought, "*In my culture we speak very loudly so your silent ways shocked me is all.*"

This made the little girl laugh out loud. She found it hilarious that quietly listening to each other would shock anyone. On the contrary, she thought it was the exact opposite. Using loud sounds and pinching oneself to express how one felt, seemed far more shocking. She decided to name her father Eel-Popah. It meant my shocking eel father. This sent the little girl into peals of laughter.

The prince didn't know whether to laugh or cry, but he finally agreed that Eel-Popah was a fitting name for a father younger in wisdom than his daughter. He would have to rely on her to explain her ways. He didn't even know his own daughter's name, but enough thinking or talking or whatever one called it. It was getting late. They needed to make their way back to the village before the nocturnes began hunting. He began preparing for the journey home. He scanned the site for anything they may have left and as he stood looking over the area, he felt his daughter's small hand slip into his.

"*I love you, Popah, and I will only call you Eel-Popah when we are alone. It will be our secret,*" she thoughtfully toned.

The prince said nothing. He looked into his daughter's teal eyes and smiled. He was beginning to see the advantage of her silent ways. He was also beginning to feel his heart expand in a quicker pace than even her mother inspired. He knew in his soul he would protect and love this child for all time.

"Your love is my protection, Eel-Popah," she thoughtfully giggled.

The prince could not resist her laughter. He lifted her onto his shoulders and made his way toward the village. Now they were both giggling with delight. As they walked inland the little one began to talk aloud and very quickly.

"I like the mango's insides very much, Popah. And the color is very pretty. It's pretty on the outside too. Look at this part. It looks like my eyes and over here it looks like your skin and it's smooth too. Feel!" she chattered.

When the two passed a rain puddle the little girl squealed with laughter. "Look, a little sea, Popah!" Then she threw a piece of the mango's rind into it. "Popah, it floats! It is just like us. All the colors and tastes are mushy and soft and hard and sleek. Call me mangoes, Popah! What a nice name that would be, yes?"

The little girl kept talking as the prince proudly listened. Her voice comforted him. She was not his little silent child of the sea, but a very happy noisy child on his shoulders. She was a lovely combination of the mermaid and him. She was strong and courageous like her father, and smart and charming like her mother. She constantly wiggled like a fish, but she tapped his chest at his heart center to get his attention just like he did when he wanted to make a point. The prince already loved this child more than his own life. He felt complete as if he'd given birth to her himself. He decided to name her after the mermaid and himself. He would name her 'me and she', but before he could say it aloud the little girl stopped chattering and said, "Mianshe! Well I like that very much, Popah. Mianshe. Then Mangoes can be my secret name like Eel-Popah is yours!" she said.

The prince laughed. Mianshe was now formally Mianshe. They continued on their way down the path with Mianshe sitting on his shoulders, happily narrating everything she saw. As the two grew small in the distance, one could still hear her asking him the names of things she saw along the path until they finally disappeared into the bush.

Then all of a sudden, as loud as one's own voice, was heard, "With love we are forever connected." Sedina said. "*I am forever connected to thee!*"

BOOK II

LANDING HOME

CHAPTER 1

The entire village sat in a circle with their mouths agape and stared at the prince when he entered carrying a chattering Mianshe on his shoulders. They went completely mute.

"Well hi there!" chirped the excited girl upon seeing the villagers sitting around the fire. Then she quickly added, "I'm sorry." Mianshe thought she had interrupted their supper since they all sat with their mouths wide open.

The prince and the young mer-girl hadn't expected such a quiet reception, although the villagers hadn't been completely silent. They'd gasped; however, the prince and his daughter hadn't heard their shock when they broke through the vines bordering the town's center. The barking dogs announcing their arrival had masked the audible part of their reception. "Aiyee!" and "Heavenly ancestors," or "Oh my, Amma!" where the phrases the people used most to express themselves. The silence didn't appear until after the child said "hi there" or something to that effect. The odd stillness continued which made Mianshe laugh, so the prince took her hand and placed it over his mouth, and the giggling girl stopped giggling. She'd never felt him communicate in this way. He was serious, so serious that no thought dared run through his mind. Finally, a true silence was heard, and it was quiet for a good long moment.

Mianshe looked at the crowd to see if they knew why her father had gotten so somber. They were all seated. They sat around a pot. They sat in a circle. They all wore different robes, some with fish like tails and others with two separate columns. Some wore nothing on the top, while others wore metal and mesh and seeds and shells for tops. Some had no hair while others were very hairy indeed and they all sat with their mouths open. Mianshe finally understood. They could not breathe.

"*Breathe*," thought the Prince, so he inhaled deeply before opening his mouth. "Good evening, my family." The crowd finally closed their mouths.

Mianshe felt this was the perfect time to introduce herself. "Hi, I'm Mianshe," she said. Just then a mouse ran out of the communal fire into the woods. "Look, Popah, a fire mouse!" cried the mermaid-girl with delight.

It may have been on the word Popah, or when the little girl's red hair fell forward in a heap, or perhaps it was a mouse coming out of a fire that made the crowd gasp again, however it was definitely on being called Popah that the prince stopped looking into his father's eyes before gently floating out of his body into the starry night sky.

Mianshe felt her father escaping so she quickly followed him into the darkness. It was pitch black. Nothing was in the sky but the quick twinkling of far off stars. Her father sat quietly in thought. He was trying to figure out what he to say to the village.

"*Well you already said, Good evening, my family,*" toned Mianshe. She was trying to help, but her father continued to sit in the sky deep in thought. After a bit, Mianshe got bored. She decided to go explore a little star not too far off, but when she got there it was too bright to see anything. The bright light made everything disappear. "Wow!" She delightfully said.

"*Wow,*" thought the prince as he rested in the cool night sky. No matter what he said (the truth or any version of it) it was going to frighten the people. He wondered what they were wondering right now.

"*Then ask them what they think,*" thought Mianshe. And off she went again chasing another shooting star.

Upon hearing his daughter's voice, the prince was plunged back into his body, and he stood there dumb-founded by the dumb-founded crowd before him. But then he remembered his daughter's words. "How are you this evening?" he implored. As soon as the words left his mouth the young mermaid's spirit plopped back into her body jiggling his shoulders. The prince was mortified but he tried not to think about it. He didn't want to worry his daughter, so the prince stopped thinking altogether. However,

Mianshe found jiggling to be great fun, so she smiled. This made the little boy peeking from the tree in front of her smile. When the young mermaid realized the young boy was smiling at her, her toes wiggled.

It was all too much for the queen, so she promptly passed out cold and fell forward in a heap directly underneath the dangling feet of the young red-haired girl sitting on her nephew's shoulders.

∴M∴

CHAPTER 2

The next morning the smell of Sandal, Wenge and Blackwood incense wafted through the streets. The entire village was in prayer. They were afraid of the strange red-haired creature that giggled. Her sudden appearance mortified them. They were terrified of how she had enchanted their prince, and they were furious that she called their soon-to-be-king, *Popah*. So, what if the term of endearment for father in Librebe was *Bba*, they could tell from looking at her what she was saying. But their worst fear was the child's mysterious mother. Mothers never leave their children. It was unheard of in their culture. Who was this woman that would leave her child? Was she a witch trying to take over the land? Was she a mad woman that would come rushing into the village ranting and tearing out her hair, or the hair of those that had stolen her baby? Or maybe the child was sick and would bring her sickness into the village like the colonials brought theirs. Whomever or wherever this mother was, it was not good. It was already affecting the community because now all they could think of was how could a marriage take place with an alien mother on the loose.

In order to quiet the anxious villagers, the king placed a communal silence over the land. No one was allowed to speak for three days until the moon rose completely full, and even then, they were only able to voice their opinions when holding the *talking stick*. However, the king never stopped voicing his opinions of the girl to the queen. He grunted and groaned and gestured and gesticulated and mimed and grimaced and then began the series all over again.

The queen could no longer take the king's fussing, so she went into her quarters and closed the door between their chambers. She was truly done with communicating in any way, shape or form for the evening. Fainting in front of her people was bad enough, but to have a son that did not confide in her was worse. "Enough," she thought as she got into bed, but as soon as the queen began to slip into a nice slumber she was awakened by her brother's tossing and turning.

"I will send him home to his dead mother!" threatened the King as he slept. "Ugh, stupid! I'm not dumb, stupid boy." The king continued muttering to himself until he managed to fall deeply asleep, thus allowing the queen to do the same, although the peace did not last long because the king began to snore most thunderously. "Aaaarrrrrrgggnnnfffff!" snored the king thus waking the queen.

The queen rose before dawn. She couldn't sleep. She washed her face and then her torso and her more private areas before purifying the centers of her feet. Next, she cleaned her teeth and scraped her tongue of last night's toxins and then she got dressed for the day. She was now ready to say her morning prayers to her ancestors. After her morning ritual she let out a deep centering sigh before opening the door to her brother's quarters.

It was quiet. The birds were still sleeping. Even the insect family had ceased cricking. The sun wasn't even up yet. The queen sat on the edge of her brother's bed and enjoyed the brief peace and quiet. She knew it was only the calm before the storm. Thus, she took another centering sigh before pulling a little twig from under the king's mattress and tickling her brother's nose.

The king bolted upright. "What!" he asked? To which the queen replied by taking his hand and leading him to the breakfast table.

The king was grateful to have a little time to gulp some tea. Afterward, he quickly put his robe over his pajamas and exited into the morning sun's first rays. What a rude awakening. Normally sunrise would bring him such joy his eyes leaked, but today it only brought light to the fact that this was going to be a very difficult day. It was already a disaster. The sun wasn't even completely up to see him being dragged by his hand through the village by his sister. Shame! Even the roosters were crowing and laughing at his cuckolded state.

Since no one could talk or gesture or write or busy their mind in any way, they sat on their porches smoking their pipes and playing dominoes into the wee morning hours. They could not wink or draw in the dirt or point or communicate to each other, so they slapped down tiles and counted their scores in their heads. This made the Men-of-Learning very happy for they had been asking the people for years to read and write and play counting games. The only ones allowed to communicate were the innocents (the babies and toddlers) and they only saw the humor in the situation anyway. As if they knew they had the power to say anything and everything they wished, the children of the village never stopped mumbling and muttering and giggling and laughing and gurgling and clicking their tongues. Mianshe adored this. It made her feel like she was underwater listening to all the creatures in the sea. She believed her father's village was the most magical place on the face of the earth.

The villagers outside in the courtyard looked at their feet as their King and Queen passed them on their way out. They were too afraid to lift their heads and look at anyone. They were sure their eyes would give away what they really thought about last night's affairs, so they walked around as if the earth would crack or dissolve underneath them. Some of the villagers wouldn't even walk. They stayed seated, or worked in their gardens or went hunting, or sewed or did anything they could think of, so they didn't think about what was happening.

However, the king never stopped voicing his opinions as they walked into the rising sun. He would look at his queen-sister and gesture how unhappy he was with their son. He finally got tired of miming and gesturing. He needed to express himself. His motions of burying his only male child in the sand until the ants chewed him up into tiny teensy little pieces or tying him to a Baobab tree until the birds plucked his eyes out, or even throwing him into the sea with the mystery quartz until he'd learned his lesson, didn't satisfy him. He needed to hear his thoughts out loud to come to any conclusion or possible solution, so he mimed his last communication to his son's auntie-mother-queen. 'This way!' he gestured.

The queen knew her brother well. She knew when he touched her face he was happy, and if he touched her back he was concerned, but if he grabbed her arm he was angry. The king was tightly holding his sister's arm, so they picked up the pace and walked swiftly into the forest without saying a word.

The king used his official staff to push aside the vines. He was watching for snakes and other predators. As they hiked, he thought over all the questions he had about the previous night. He tried to phrase each inquiry in a positive light. When did his only heir sire a child? Is this child of his to be a princess of theirs? Was this so-called princess of unknown origin of royal lineage? Maybe she was of a lineage higher than his. The king pushed that thought away and filed it deep into his subconscious, along with the thought that perhaps his son had slept with one of Amma's wives and that's how the bastard came to be there. She was almost five-years-old! And the thought returned, what if the gods did not want a child sired with an earthly human? Maybe they thought humans were the lowest form of animal in the universe. Maybe they thought his son was an ape with a tail between his legs like the pictures the pale foreigners drew of them. Maybe they thought the bastard was his banana, a monkey's banana! The king stopped. He had to quiet his mind. He had just called his own son a monkey and that was not good. It was not a nice thing to say, but if a man plays like a monkey, he must be a monkey. The king could not forgive his son's monkeyshines.

The queen quietly walked behind her brother. She too was anxious about the strange child's presence. Some days earlier, when she had secretly visited the Herb-Woman to ask about the prince's upcoming wedding, the roots woman told her she saw a storm coming. She saw a huge storm that would delay the marriage. However, storms come, and storms go so this didn't worry the queen, but the other warning did; a warning about a woman from the red sea who would drown the prince's desires. A man without desire was worse than a zombie. He was no longer a man. If that man became king then the woman of the red sea would rule and if the woman of the red sea ruled, where would that leave her? The queen stopped. She had to quiet her mind.

The king stared at his sister with agitation. He was holding aside the panther's hide that covered the opening to the Sacred Cave of Reckoning. The skin of the panther was to deter intruders from entering their tribe's most secret chamber, but it wouldn't be secret for long if his sister stood outside daydreaming. He couldn't wait any longer, so he pushed his sister inside.

"Aiyee, King-Brother, patience!" exclaimed the Queen.

This sent the king into a tizzy. He was not used to being corrected or advised by anyone, and especially not by a woman. However, it was his sister. The woman who raised him after his father brought home his sixth wife. They called her the wench-wife because she would not talk to any of the king's other wives and she tolerated their children even less. After her arrival the only time they got to see their father was during ceremony. This made the king angry all over again. Then his heart softened. He was not going to allow that to happen to him and his son, but then he remembered he already had. He allowed his fourth wife to separate him from his children, but he was in mourning then and not thinking straight. He knew he was making excuses for himself. He had to work things out, so he could share the rest of his life with his only male child.

Now the queen waited while her brother contemplated. She didn't want to interrupt his thoughts. She didn't want any negative ideas or mean energy to get absorbed into the earthen walls. That was why she had stopped before entering—to clear her mind of worry.

"What?" The King asked. He was irritated all over again.

The queen erased her observation from her mind and smiled. "Just here, Brother-King," she sighed. "Just here with you."

Now the king was furious. She had put *brother* before his title of *king* and that was unacceptable. He never understood women, especially his sister. Her way of saying just enough to make you wonder if she was saying more, but two could play that game.

"Since we are here," the King smugly said.

"Yes, we should get started," said the Queen, saving her brother from further embarrassment.

Now the king was fit to be tied. He was truly upset. He could not understand how the ban on women's thinking had been lifted. There was a time when no tribal business could be handled in front of a woman. Their delicate natures and tendency towards drama would have rendered the meeting completely useless.

The queen feigned a small cough, immediately grabbing the king's attention.

"With blessings in all directions as above so below and within and around…" began the King.

And the queen gently closed her eyes and waited for the ancestors to come and give them their blessings, but when the king and queen were summoning the spirits, the panther's hide moved, and the sun came pouring into the cave.

"Who is there!" demanded the King. And there before them two eyes stared directly at them.

"Ayeii!" screamed Two-Eyes. Then he turned and ran, but as if by magic the king's arm reached over and grabbed the boy by his ear.

The king was beside himself. The queen was forlorn, and Two-Eyes was scared—truly frightened. No one knew he lived in the Sacred Cave of Reckoning. Up until now it was the perfect place to be because no one ever came there. The boy guessed they reckoned everything was fine.

"What is happening, dear ancestors!" cried the Queen. "First the red-haired child and now the child of no one's womb!" Then the queen returned to pulling at her braids and digging her toes into the damp soil.

"I need to think!" screamed the King. He couldn't think with children and women around. He found the loose emotions distracting.

Two-Eyes didn't know what to do. He was hungry. He had a guava and some cold mealie and a soup bone in the corner but if he did not get to it soon the ants would surely make a meal of it instead.

"Sit down, boy!" yelled the King.

However, it did not sound very kingly. The boy thought it sounded kind of shrill and girl-like. Still a king had to have a kingly yell. It went with the name, so Two-Eyes squeaked, "Okay, sir," and then he saluted him.

This sent the king into a rage. Colonials and warmongers saluted people. He remembered the Frenchman that saluted him with his drinking vessel. He made a sort of click-clack and then he drank. The Frenchman downed all the liquid in his vessel and sneered at the king. The king tried being polite. He tried drinking the sweet blood that smelled like soursop but drinking the entire mug at once seemed greedy. He should have known then the strangers would try to take everything from his people, but it wasn't until he caught the man trying to steal the green stones from the quarry-basket that he became sure of their intentions. So, the king sent the Frenchman to his ancestors by way of a red anthill. When the man left his body and exited back to his elders in the sky, the king lifted his glass and drank to his health, 'salute'. Even though the Frenchman was a thief, the king preferred his salutation of clanging his cup over the colonials' popping hand-smack to the head greeting.

The queen watched the exchange between her brother and the child. She tried to remember the day the boy came to the village or ran into the village. It was a day like any other. The women were tending the fields and grinding meal or airing the night covers. The men were pretending to prepare for the hunt, while the king amused them with exaggerated tales of honor. The children ran about harassing the goats. The young people hid under the trees watching the sunset as they tried to steal an affectionate touch from one another. It was in the shadow of the setting sun when the little boy ran into the village and into the hut of the Mending-Woman. The Mending-Woman was putting cowry shells on a kente cloth for an upcoming wedding ceremony and… The queen did not finish her thought because it brought her right back to where she started. They were being plagued by unnatural acts.

The boy looked exactly the same. He hadn't grown a bit since he came to the village some twelve moons and three eclipses ago. That was the real reason no one would take in the child. He had appeared right after the moon swallowed the sun. That plus he ran into the village followed by a very large lion. The only reason they didn't kill the child was because they killed the lioness instead. She was amazingly tender meat—an auspicious sign. That's why they could not decide whether the boy was a good or bad omen. They even took a vote and it was even. Half said a good omen, and the other half said he was a bad one. The only person who could have broken the tie was the Mending-Woman and she would have no part of the boy who ruined her cowry adorned kente ceremonial cloth, so they did nothing.

Outside of the lioness' meat the strange boy never ate with the community again. He came and went as he wished. No one schooled him, or dressed him, or gave him shelter, or brushed his hair. No one taught him their customs or did ceremony with him. In fact, outside of the lion-kill ceremony, no one spoke to him after that at all. Maybe that was why the village was having all this bad luck. They hadn't included the boy in the community.

This made the queen sweat. She started to defend her actions. "But we did not exclude him either," she muttered to herself. The villagers left food out and clothes and firewood. No one yelled when he listened in or ran through the village catching butterflies. No one complained when he slept by the warm embers after the community meal was over. In fact, no one paid any attention to the boy at all. It was as if he was invisible.

"No," thought the Queen, "This is worse." It was a kind of no man's land. He belonged neither here nor there, so he belonged nowhere. He was just like the other child, this new child—the child of watery eyes and amber hair, the child of their blood but not of any ancestor's blood. All this new information was too much for the queen to handle so she sat down on the cool earth and filled her pipe with tobacco.

The king solemnly pulled the flap aside and looked up into the sun. He was testing the gods to see how they felt, but he couldn't test them any longer. His neck hurt. When he lowered his head and realized he still had his sight he sighed. "Aahhh," he sadly said. Amma had not blinded him so she must have been happy with the way things were going, but he still had no idea why the boy interrupted their conversation. The king decided to ask the child.

"What are you doing here, boy?" asked the King.

Two-Eyes was shocked to hear the king speak directly to him. He was truly shocked to have anyone address him at all. No one had ever spoken to him before. The boy looked at the king and shrugged his shoulders. He did not want to get the answer wrong, so he decided it was better to say nothing at all.

The king stared at the child and waited—and he waited some more. When he asked a question most people responded. Sometimes they lied but they answered all the same. No one had ever challenged him in this way before. The king was unsure what to do next. After getting no response to his question the king and the boy stood in front of each other looking down at the ground.

The queen watched her brother interrogating the child as she finished her pipe. She could not believe he thought asking would get him an answer. She knew children and their ways. She was not going to give up as easily as her brother.

"Are you hungry, child?" the Queen asked. It was working. She noticed a flicker of light cross the boy's eyes as his head darted to one side before returning to a downcast stare. She opened her sack and pulled out a small clay pot and a pone muffin. She drizzled some honey from the pot over the corn bread and offered it to the boy. When he still stood motionless like a statue, she carefully hoisted herself up and approached him. "Here, eat," she cooed.

The boy badly wanted to eat the muffin, but he wanted to eat his meat and mealie first. Putting the honey on his muffin made it a dessert, so eating it now would spoil the sweet impact it would have later. He looked deep into the queen's eyes and gently took the muffin and ran to the corner of the cave.

"What impudence!" the Queen said, and then she threw her hands into the air and deferred the next move to her brother.

The king looked as bewildered as the queen by the new development of the boy running away with the honey bun, so he mimicked the boy's response and shrugged his shoulders too.

The queen was ready to strangle them both. She was truly frustrated. Nevertheless, she remembered where she was, so she fell to her knees and began praying. She closed her eyes and began. "Dear Great Spirit of all Spirits," she implored. Then she looked up at her brother and motioned for him to kneel down and pray with her, but her brother was looking elsewhere.

There in the corner of the room the boy had set an amazing table. It was dressed in banana leaves and orchids and was illuminated by a small clay bowl of sheep fat. He had divided the muffin, his mealie cake and the small bits of meat from the ox bone into three portions and he stood beside his makeshift table like a fine maître d'hôtel.

"Oh, my Amma!" exclaimed the Queen.

"The Creator is truly trying to talk to us right now," sighed the King.

"Dinner is served," said the proud boy. He was emulating his cousin Jean Noelle who worked at a fine restaurant in Kinshasa.

As the strange tribune sat eating their meal, the afternoon sun started to warm up the cave. "How long have you lived here?" the Queen asked. She was sure to keep a gentle tone when talking to the boy, so he would feel comfortable answering her, but the boy only looked down at the ground each time she tried to engage him in conversation.

The king ate. He was hungry. When he finally sucked out the marrow from the ox bone he stood. "Thank you," he said to the boy. "Thank you for that most delightful and informative meal."

The queen was suspicious now. What on earth was her brother talking about? No one had said a word of information to anyone. They were no closer to understanding any of today's events or yesterday's affairs than they were before they placed the ban on the village. They couldn't return without something sensible to say to the people. The queen wasn't sure her brother understood the seriousness of what was happening. The people were scared, and they needed a strong king that could bring order out of the chaos. This man could not get a child to answer his pleas and thanking the boy for his strange ox bone (which was on the edge of being spoiled) was not helping matters one bit.

The king sensed his sister's rage and it excited him. Now she would have to wait to hear what he thought. Normally it was the other way around. She would hem or haw and pretend to answer him but give him riddles instead. Now she was the one sitting there with a puzzled look on her face. Yes, what a wonderful meal it had been indeed. He had figured out a way to solve two problems with one action. Yes, he was a genius, indeed he was. Maybe he should remain king. The village wasn't ready for him to step down yet. He knew his fish mongering, woman-hiding son wasn't ready to fill his sandals, but all was going to be okay. He was sure of this because the gods had blessed him. They had blessed him with not one child, but two. They had blessed him with twins!

CHAPTER 3

As the trio made their way back to the village, the boy turned and looked at the Sacred Cave for what he believed to be his last time. He was sure the barking king and his tobacco-smelling queen were going to finally string him up and leave him for the lions, and when the lions had devoured him, the boy was certain these people would trap the lions and eat them too. Lions were sacred animals. They should not be eaten. His people loved lions, especially a female lioness because she warned them of anything bad that was going to happen.

That was exactly what happened the day he met the king and queen, and their strange village of fire worshippers. The lioness was chasing him. She was trying to tell him not to run into town, but he didn't listen to her. He wanted to meet the white man that gave away sweets. His cousin Peeta assured him if he smiled and made his knees click when he danced the snake dance from their manhood ceremony, the man would surely give him two sweets, maybe three! But he never got to see the man because the lioness rushed up and told him "No!" She chased him away from town straight into the village of fire worshippers, and now he was going to join his lioness ancestor in the cooking pit, covered with savory leaves, crushed peppers and yam roots.

The king quickly walked down the mountain and onto the path that led into Librebe. He felt invigorated. He'd eaten a small but lovely meal. He had solved his problem and he'd silenced his sister all at once. The gods were surely smiling down on him. This was going to be a good day!

The queen was desperately searching her mind for an anecdote to whatever poison she was sure her brother was about to give everyone. The last time he was so happy about a solution was when he gave away the rights to the canal that divided the two territories. He gave it as a wedding gift to the doddering old Queen of Fermemi. She had to be over three generations old already. Here she was over sixty, forcing a young man of seventeen to lay with her, and her brother (another doddering old fool) honored the union with the only advantage Librebe had over Fermemi—the waterway to the ocean. Enough, this was not the time to think of her brother's past mistakes. They were over. What was done was done, although she was beginning to understand the Fermemi queen. One doesn't mind a foolish young man as much as an idiotic old one.

As they crossed the gateway into the village the king pushed out his chest and slowed down his pace to a most contrived strut. The queen tried not to do it, but she sucked the air through her teeth all the same. Upon hearing his sister's discontent, the king slowed down his pace even more. The young boy thought this purposeful walking was some custom of the village, so he slowed to a snail's pace too. He decided he would walk as slowly as humanly possible without actually stopping, maybe it would please the limping king, but it was difficult to do. He had to slowly balance on one leg then slowly inch the other out, until he slowly placed that leg down while he slowly lifted the other leg off the ground and he went on like this until he bounced off of the queen's butt.

"Ayyyee, boy can you not see I have stopped!" screamed the Queen. Then she amended her tone and gestured for the boy to walk ahead of her.

The king stopped walking when he heard the ruckus and started watching the boy and his sister as they dosey-doed around each other like owls on a tree limb. The queen finally pushed the boy in front of her with her feather fan.

"Are we ready now," asked the King in a slow judgmental tone, almost as slow as his walking. The pair nodded and silently continued slowly following their king into the streets of Librebe.

The entire village was awake now and going about their day, however you would never have known it because it was so quiet there. It felt like nothing was happening at all. It was as if everything was moving in slow motion. The king, the queen, the boy and the villagers were all moving to some strange internal rhythm. If it weren't for the fact they were all alive, one would wonder if they were moving at all. The king continued his gallant slow marching all the way to the royal enclave and with one final slow deliberate step he entered and closed the door behind him.

The queen and the boy stood outside on the porch wondering what to do next. Should they wait for the king to return and tell them his brilliant plan? Was he expecting them to enter behind him? That didn't make sense because it was his personal quarters and no one, except the king and his son ever went in there. On extreme occasions (like this morning) the queen was allowed to enter but only through the family hallway and with an appointment. Even the prince had to be announced first but given there was a ban on communicating until tomorrow's full moon that was not an option either, so the queen went into the courtyard and sat down on the stairs. The boy followed the queen and sat beside her, but on a lower step. From the side it looked like he was under her skirt. All you could see of him was his bare feet, but when standing in front of the odd pair you could see the boy was sitting next to the queen's legs.

He was extremely bewildered by the rolls of scaly netting around the queen's ankles. He tried not to openly stare but the strange, odd colored, flaking skin looked like a molting python. It smelled like it too. He gently turned his head to the side and tried to escape the foul odor, but it found him nonetheless. Outside of the rolls of dead skin-like-netting, she was not too different from the women elders of his village. No matter how beautiful or ugly women were, when they became old they started to smell like it. It was the same for men too, but they smelled more like beer and cigarettes. That was it! The queen had the authority of a man, so it made her smell like one too. "*Interesting*," thought the boy.

The queen filled her pipe and stared at the boy. She wondered what he was thinking that made him so quiet she couldn't feel his thoughts. She thought he was handsome for a foreigner. His deep brown skin held high cheekbones and large eyes that looked like chocolate drops. He'd have no trouble making babies when he got older. The queen returned to thinking about her present situation. What now? What were they to do now? They could not sit on the stairs for the rest of the day waiting for the moon to rise. The queen resolved herself to the fact that nothing could be done until her brother decreed it so, so she got up to leave but the boy stood up with her. The queen motioned for him to sit down. Now satisfied he understood her, she exited the courtyard into her living quarters.

The boy sat and tapped his head to clear all the strange, fearful thoughts circulating inside. When the queen passed him, he tried not to look at her toes, which looked like a vulture's talons. What if she saw him looking at her claws and that was why she left? He began tapping his forehead again. He tapped in the same direction his mother would tap when he got headaches. First, he tapped the center of his forehead between his eyes. Next, he tapped both sides of his forehead. Then he tapped the place behind his ears and massaged his eye sockets where the aliens attached their eyes. He wondered why the aliens put those things over their eyes. Maybe the queen knew, but he was too afraid to ask her. He was afraid she would laugh at him or worse tell him they were their eyes. Those strange mirrors in colors frightened the boy. Maybe the strange foreigners that took their eyes off-and-on might steal his good eyes. The boy had forgotten where to tap next, so he decided to tap everywhere on his face and as many places as he could simultaneously. As the boy tapped away his aches and fears of contact lenses, one of the doors in the rooms surrounding the courtyard opened.

The queen exited her quarters with a sleeping mat and pillows. Two young women quickly followed behind her. The older of the two carried a tub of warm water. The younger held some clothes and plate of food. The queen walked over to the boy and stood behind him. The first woman set the tub down beside him and began to undress the boy. Two Eyes jumped up and opened his mouth, but no words came out. He was afraid the woman would steal his only shirt, so he clutched it tightly with both hands. The queen took her hand and placed it on the boy's forehead then looked deep into his eyes. When the boy became calm the queen stood erect and motioned to the women to continue bathing him.

The queen's attendant gently removed the boy's shirt and washed his torso with horsetail root. It tingled and made his headache disappear. The boy smiled at her and then took off his pants and let her wash him from head to toe. When she had finished bathing him, she presented him with a clean pair of khaki trousers and an old bootlegged Reebok t-shirt with the words, *I am that I am.* Now pleased with his appearance the older girl cleared the dirty bath water and then served him his plate of food. The younger girl mimed washing his old clothes before gathering them up in her apron.

The boy did not know what to say. He wanted to thank the women who'd shown him so much kindness. It had been over a year since he'd felt a woman's touch. It tickled, but he made sure he did not laugh or even smile. He didn't want the women to feel he was unappreciative. He was truly grateful for his shiny new pants and the shirt with symbols all over it. He was sure it must have belonged to the king when he was eight, because he felt quite regal in it.

The queen watched the women prepare the youth for whatever was getting ready to happen. She prayed her brother was not going to sacrifice him and make him the scapegoat for all the strange affairs that had recently happened in the village. She was beginning to like the little fellow. She enjoyed how present he was. Without even knowing a ban had been placed he immediately fell into their rhythm and held his tongue. He was also very clean. Even before being bathed she noticed there was no leaves or debris in his hair and his body smelled like verbena root. She had to be careful not to grow too attached to the little one. She wasn't ready to have their fates meet in any other way than what had already transpired.

The boy was waiting for the queen's blessing before he began his meal. He'd been watching her for some time before she felt his eyes upon her. When she motioned for him to begin, he took his glass of water and drizzled some drops onto the ground. He thanked his ancestors for taking care of him once again. Next, he took a few morsels from his yam and cabbage and placed them on a leaf in honor of his plant relatives who had given so much so he could survive until tomorrow. As he placed his first bite into his mouth he heard, *"What does that taste like?"* The boy missed his face completely and dropped the entire mouthful into his lap.

The queen sucked the air through her teeth and retracted her thought about the young man being present. He was as dense as the rest of the youth his age. As she sat gently shaking her head back and forth in thought, she noticed her attendants scurrying off behind the house. She wondered what was agitating them until she saw exactly what it was. The little red-haired being had come into the courtyard and was smiling at them like a madwoman, or mad girl.

Mianshe toned to the boy again. *"What does it taste like? Tell me."* But the boy simply sat starting into his lap. The young mermaid focused harder on being heard. She smiled very sincerely this time, and with all her heart, she closed her eyes and toned. *"Does it taste like mangoes? It has the same color."*

The young boy heard the little girl's words split through the silence in his head and it felt strange. Stranger yet, it didn't make his head ache. How could she think into his head without making it ache?

"Why would I want to make your head ache? Just eat another morsel of the orange one and tell me what it tastes like, please," she toned. Then she walked over and stooped down and laid her head in his lap, so he had to look at her.

The little boy pushed the mermaid's head off his lap and immediately stood up. He lifted his hands in an X shape across his chest to protect himself and thought with all his might. *"It is mushy!"* he screamed to himself or to her or in his head somewhere. *"And it is sweet,"* he added.

"May I try?" Mianshe quietly asked. She wanted him to understand he didn't have to scream when being silent.

Now the boy truly had no idea what to do. If he gave the girl some of his food would he anger the queen? What if the strange little girl was not welcomed in the village as he had been only moments ago? Or maybe the yam wouldn't agree with the girl and she got sick, what would he do then?

But, what if she was hungry (as he had been many times in the past) then he should surely share his portion with her. They had given him a week's worth of food. He had plenty to share and as the boy continued to create scenario after scenario of what could or may not happen his hand reached down and gave the girl a hunk of red yam.

Mianshe sat down beside the boy on the step and ate her yam. As she chewed the boy stared at her with anticipation. She knew he was waiting to hear her reaction to the new food, so she chewed all the more slowly, making every morsel count. When she'd finished her piece of sweet potato she turned to the boy and kissed him on the cheek.

Happy she was happy, Two-Eyes returned to eating his meal. He would give the girl a bite and watch her eat it, and then he'd eat his bite. Then he'd give the girl another bite and he'd taste it vicariously through her, and then he'd take another bite for himself. The pair went on sharing their meal until all that was left was a sliver of skin from the potato, which the young girl took and placed on the plant-people's altar.

The boy stared at the little girl with fiery hair and he smiled, and she smiled back at him. She had blue-green eyes that felt familiar. Years ago, his mother read his palm and told him about this girl. She said a little girl with a big heart would make him a king, but then soon after she would break his heart. She would travel far away by sea and leave him alone. The boy stopped smiling and looked closely at the little girl with garnet yam hair and gem stone eyes. He liked her.

The queen had never in all her years of life felt so much energy pulse through her. She could not discern if she was afraid or amazed or disgusted or in awe, as she watched the spectacle of the two children intertwined like weeds in the nightshade. She slowly backed away, further down the porch until she reached her brother's quarters and quietly escaped behind the door into his room, but the door opened again, and the king's hand ushered the queen out of his chambers, and then pointed right toward her own quarters.

The queen could feel her energy rising in her body. She heard her heart beating in her ears. She felt her pores open and push out water like a hot kettle released steam. The queen had lived more angst in the last day and a half than she had lived in her entire life. If she didn't get control of herself immediately, she would end up cursing creation itself. So, the queen slowly closed her eyes and walked past the children into her house.

CHAPTER 4

The moon appeared on the horizon. It was time to get ready for the ceremony that had no name. The queen took off her robe and aired her body in the cool night air. As she unraveled her long braids she watched herself in the mirror. She rubbed cream on her high forehead and examined her plump face. Even the fat that accumulated after the change from woman to crone couldn't help her eyelids from sagging. "Mother you can be so cruel," she said to no one. She pulled the drooping skin around her eyes from side to side.

Why didn't she marry him and move to the city? She had asked herself this question every night for the past thirty years, so she was well aware of the answer. If she had survived the tribal genocide in the cities she'd have ended up the subservient to a man who would have surely given her the sickness of the blood. He was not the type of man to be monogamous. Even as a young woman, she knew that. She had to be satisfied that she knew him when he was invincible and still had love in his heart.

After the queen finished oiling her scalp she took some shea butter and massaged it in between the folds of her belly. She would never have a child, but she would always be the village's Guardian-Mother and that was enough to keep her happy. So far, her royal responsibility had been her purpose in life and it had been a good life, so far.

The queen sat on her bed surrounded by a multitude of skirts and head wraps. She couldn't decide which one to wear. Every ritual had its own wardrobe so normally it was easy to pick out something. One wore goldenrod yellow for the sun ceremony honoring the reaping of crops.

You wore indigo when someone was going on a spiritual quest. You wore red for the announcement of marriages and white for the birth of one's first child. Blue was for solstice and black for business, but no one had ever told her what color to wear for a ceremony for chaos. The queen thought of the young foreigners who wore all the colors at the same time. She smiled in the mirror at herself, "This is good," she said. At least she hadn't lost her sense of humor.

The drumming started. It was going to be a serious gathering. Normally wood pipes accompanied a full moon. It was a more ethereal sound and more fitting for a luminescent orb, but now the drums were pounding out a long steady rhythm that would summon the dead. The queen chose an indigo, star-patterned robe with a violet headdress. It grounded her and helped balance her emotions, so she remained neither here nor there but would stay exactly where she was supposed to be. She was ready.

The king was calm. He didn't doubt what he was going to do, because it was the right thing to do. He was more concerned with presenting his idea clearly. He wanted to be sure he had the authority of his heart, not his mind. He didn't want to impose any idea upon his son or the others that they didn't wish to follow. He had to be very aware of the way he presented his solution, so all would agree to it. Being a king was not easy, but it was expected of one. He had to have clarity and a quick return to normalcy, and he knew he must do this without imposing on the people too much.

The king drew a circle in the earth with his cane, then filled a glass with water and approached his altar. In a loud voice resounding within him, he affirmed, "We are one and no one can separate us!" Then he thought, "No two can separate us." He was ready, so he quietly walked out the door into the courtyard.

The prince stood by his door. He was dressed and ready to go. He looked magnificent. He wore white pants with a simple white shirt he'd gotten at the Hindu man's stable at the market place. He'd washed himself in scented roots and had oiled his hair. He had pumiced his feet and wiped off his sandals. He was ready, but Mianshe was a mess. He didn't know what to do about his daughter's appearance. He stood searching the room for something to dress her in. He didn't want to ask the women for help because he had no idea what they would find under the ripped parachute that hung over the little one's body. What if she had little fins under there? And her smiling at him like he was the most perfect person on the face of the planet didn't help much either. Especially since he felt like the village idiot.

Mianshe was in awe. She was sure her father was the most handsome man on the face of the earth. He glowed and shined and radiated so much beauty and power, and confusion. Confusion? That was a strange thought. Then the wee mermaid spied herself in the looking glass and she understood her father's predicament. She looked awful. She looked like flotsam on a beach after a hurricane. Her clothes were ripped, and her hair was in knots all over her head. She began to understand how important water was in taming hair.

The young mermaid immediately went into action. She went to a basket of clothes in the prince's closet and began to sort through them. He tried to see what she was doing, but she moved so quickly he was not able to make any sense of it at all. She grabbed his comb and an old copper wristwatch, which no longer kept time. Next, she pulled off her tattered clothes and covered herself with coconut oil. Then she massaged some oil into her hair and piled it on top of her head. Afterward she grabbed a shirt given to him by a classmate and began ripping it up. She put on the hand-tailored, multi-colored, tie-dyed t-shirt with a peace sign symbol and it fit her little body perfectly. But the frayed bottom of the torn shirt curled up like a little hat brim around her legs.

When Mianshe presented herself to the prince all time stopped. The odd pair just stood there staring at each other. The prince tried desperately not to smile. Now he understood why her other dress was so frayed. He looked at his daughter. She looked remarkably like an ice cream cone. It was a strange analogy given the ice cream topping of red hair was plopped atop an inverted cone of rainbows, but it was still the closest description he could come up with. She also made you smell bubblegum whenever you looked at her. Which made him wonder if she had ever had a piece of gum before, and before you knew it, the prince was smiling with great delight at his strange looking offspring. He was truly happy. Not because her odd sense of dressing delighted him, but because when she had disrobed he saw she was a completely normal little girl. He was truly relieved. Now he could ask the village women for help.

Two-Eyes waited. He didn't know what else to do. So, he sat on his mat and played marbles with the pebbles he found in the dirt around him. It took him a while to find enough stones to play the game. Even the dirt in the royal courtyard was clean. There were no animals, no leaves, no beetles or cow dung, no bird poop or candy wrappers, no old clothes or tissue paper—there wasn't anything there. He was happy the chickens were somewhere else. Chickens were smelly. Nevertheless, the sun had set and the moon was rising, so he could no longer clearly see the small rocks in the dirt anyway. Therefore, he waited.

The drums picked up their pace drawing the people to the center of the square. The ceremonial fire was already in full blaze and the Fire-Tender was in complete regalia. He wore his fire-ant headdress and all his tools were oiled and neatly lined up in rows beside him. Adisa sat to his left in a simple beige dress that made her look like an earthen angel. The Fire-Tender listened to the drumming and enjoyed his moment alone with his daughter. He admired her. She was his greatest treasure. He enjoyed watching her quietly pray. It gave him great peace.

Adisa felt her father's eyes upon her so she quickly finished her meditation and attended to him. He was fine. Everything was in its place. She had stacked lots of good hard wood for the fire at a perfect arm's reach away. All of his tools were in ceremonial order. He had a calabash of water ready for use and a full bucket nearby. She had dug a place in the earth and buried his amulet in case he needed it. She had placed a small bowl of figs and a jug of well water nearby to remedy his sweating. Everything was ready, so she knelt and humbly waited for the ceremony to begin.

Emadi, the Herb-Woman's daughter was the first to enter. She quickly walked in and hovered over Adisa while she waited for the others. Emadi had chosen a plain teal kitenge that she tied with sacred sweet grass and cowries. It softened her muscular frame. She had wrapped her short locks in a violet headdress that made her eyes look enormous, so much so that she looked like a purple crayon drawing of an E.T. The rich violet color suited her. She looked handsome.

The Herb-Woman gently smiled as she entered and saw her daughter blocking Adisa's spirit. She knew jealousy. It was the cruelest of emotions. It was a thief that stole the joy from both sides of the coveted equation. Adisa tried to bow her head lower as Emadi puffed out her chest and gathered any energy coming her way. The Herb-Woman humbly took her place in the southwestern corner and tried to covertly apologize to the Fire-Tender for her daughter's behavior, however all the entering villagers kept crossing in front of them, interrupting their private conversation.

The Man-of-Medicine quietly walked into the circle and sat at his place in the west. He was completely dressed in black. Some would say it was because of his western position. The west honored the Black tribe in the vision of mankind as a whole, however the Fire-Tender who sat directly opposite him, knew the color was meant to scare his enemies and camouflage his intentions.

As the rest of the village meandered in and took their places, the drummers picked up their pace. The drums rolled, and the king entered holding the queen's arm. They were followed by Two-Eyes in his bootlegged, Reebok knock-off with the words *I am that I am*. Next, Mianshe entered and she got a muted but audible, "Oh my!" reaction from the crowd. The prince quietly followed his daughter. He was so humbly proud of her that the entire community felt pride for him too.

The boy sat beside the king. The queen sat on the king's other side. Mianshe sat beside her great-aunt, the queen, and the prince sat down beside his daughter. The drumming stopped. In unison, everyone looked up into the sky and held their breath. The moon was almost at its apex. As it cast its silvery light onto the communal circle, the women began singing.

Oh wondrous moon fully bright
{Oh wondrous moon fully bright}
Smile down on us, give us sight
{Smile down on us, give us sight}
Bless we with wisdom and great might
{Bless we with wisdom and great might}
As we sing in full delight
{As we sing in full delight}
For we are all beholding.

When the women finished their song the king slowly rose to a standing position, and he stood there for a good long moment. Then he lifted the sacred talking-stick above his head and signaled for the ceremony to begin. He then took the staff and passed it to the Fire-Tender.

The Fire-Tender watched as the ceremonial stick went around the circle towards him. When it finally reached him, he smudged it with the fire's smoke. After purifying the staff, it was sent again, via the circle, to the Herb-Woman who sprinkled the wand with blessed water and then she passed it along to the Man-of-Medicine. He took the stick and oiled it with the fat of the lioness—a special request from the king.

The medicine man had no desire to touch the foul lard, but the Herb-Woman was watching so he made it look like he'd been entrusted with the more important task. He was more than a roots woman (a simple cook of herbal recipes) he was a Man-of-Medicine. Thus, the medicine man took the staff and smeared it with the lion's fat plus he kept his face relaxed while doing it. Lion fat had never been used to anoint a ceremonial object before, so the medicine man carefully worked his magic. He didn't want the people to think he was making things up as he went along, which was exactly what he was doing. The people were in awe of the new ceremony, so his having endured the rancid smell was well worth the stench. When he was finished he passed the foul-smelling stick to the king who begrudgingly took it from him.

As the king stood up he secretly took the piece of cloth used to house the sacred tool and he wiped off the excess fat. Then he cleared his throat and addressed the moon. "Dear Grandmother-Moon, thank you for illuminating our hearts and minds this evening. Thank you for reminding us how blessed and full of gifts we all are. Thank you for bestowing us with many talents. Thank you for keeping our bellies and our souls fed. Thank you for filling this evening with divine wisdom. I look to you to guide our words tonight. I look to you to shine the truth in your light." After that, the king sat down and passed the staff to the queen.

The queen did not expect to be the first one called upon to speak. She had no idea what to do about having not one, but two children born of no one's womb living in their village. She was not pleased with her brother using her to deflect the seriousness of the situation. What was she supposed to say? Her brother had made it clear on many occasions how he felt about women interjecting in governing affairs. Also, the prince was her nephew, not her son, so she had no say as to how he was to be guided in life. She was there to encourage and support him. That was it. That was the answer!

"Good evening, my brothers and sisters and children of Librebe. I am very happy to be here with you this evening. I am also very proud of you for honoring the three day fast of silence with such allegiance. It has given us all time to think, has it not?" The queen continued. "I have thought of nothing else. I see living here before us a child, two children of no Librebe woman's womb. What should we do with these children the spirits have blessed us with, you ask? Well, so do I," said the Queen. "And when I've heard from the community, and the children of course, I will have a better idea. Until that point, I am here to encourage and support this village in any way I can. May the moon illuminate us with its divine wisdom. I am your queen." And on that note the queen sat down and passed the staff to the prince.

The prince was slightly put off by the queen passing over Mianshe. He tried not to show it, but his hand thrust the staff toward his daughter exposing his point of view, but the stick got caught in her hair.

Before her father panicked over the prospect of her hair being let loose again in front of the crowd, Mianshe calmly dislodged it. Like a twig from a bird's nest the staff came out, along with a clumpy oiled tress of hair. The crowd tried not to look like they were staring at the strange little girl holding a hand full of red hair, but the fact no one blinked made it very obvious they were mesmerized. Mianshe placed the large stick on her lap and shoved the tress back into the middle of the blob of hair, and as she did this she smiled at everyone watching her. She continued smiling at the anticipating crowd as she silently communicated with her father. *"Popah, what am I to say?"* she asked.

The prince was still uncomfortable with communicating in this way. He was wondering if she could hear him, could the others too? Mianshe heard his worry and assured him their line of communication was secure, so the prince told her to speak from her heart and tell them the truth. Then he added it was better not to mention her mother just yet.

This confused the mer-girl for she was her mother. Her mother and she were one. How could she explain herself and not mention the person who had the greatest part in that self? She decided to go with her father's first suggestion. She decided to speak from her heart and to speak the truth.

The prince heard his daughter's thought process and he panicked. If she mentioned being sired by a mermaid the village would throw her in the fire and eat her like a fried fish, but before the prince disassociated from his terror, Mianshe began addressing the crowd.

"I have a song to sing," she said. "Trust your heart to all matters. Embrace the wisdom within…" As she continued singing the *Song of Life* of her people Two-Eyes began to hum along with her. This made Mianshe very happy, so she slowed down so the boy could more easily harmonize. This made Two-Eyes so excited, that he hummed louder.

The crowd was spellbound. Even the Fire-Tender looked up at the strange spectacle. Only one person at a time was to speak, and only when holding the talking-stick. Although the boy hadn't really spoken. He hummed. The mer-girl felt the judgment oozing from the crowd so she took the stick and stretched her arm across her grandparents and held it out for the boy. The boy grabbed the other end of the stick and the odd duo finished their song together.

You could've heard a pine needle fall on a leaf it was so silent around the circle. Then the king let out a huge laugh and grabbed the stick from the children. "Well, what a beautiful song! And so full of goodness, don't you think?" declared the King. Then he looked out onto the circle and waited for a reply before realizing he held the stick, so he was the only person who could voice what they were feeling. "My son, what have you to say," asked the King as he passed the staff to the prince.

Mianshe turned and stared deep into her father's eyes. She was trying to console him as she silently implored him to speak from his heart and tell them the truth too. She wanted him to tell everyone about her mother, but the prince would not look at her.

The prince sat with his eyes closed and silently prayed for the right words, but as he prayed he felt more agitated, so he stopped praying and listened to his heartbeat. He looked out into the crowd and tried to feel what they were feeling. It seemed everyone was either enjoying his torment or panicking with him, everyone except Adisa. She was smiling at him, encouraging him to tell his story, so he looked into her eyes and began speaking. "Good evening, my King and Queen, my ancestors." Then the prince remembered to address the eyes of the others in the circle. "Good evening, my honored family. Three days ago, I came into the village with the greatest gift Amma has given me yet, other than you, my father and my aunt and of course our community. That gift was this little one here."

When the prince looked at Mianshe she smiled and giggled then waved to everyone in the circle. The people found this behavior unbecoming for a stranger. She was to remain silent and humble until she was asked to speak, and she absolutely was not supposed to sing. The people had never seen such behavior before in their lives.

The Fire-Tender kept staring at the fire for answers however it was as if the fire itself was waiting to hear the story before formulating a conclusion. The fire wasn't burning down or getting hotter, it remained the same. It stayed put and quietly glowed, just like the villagers and their thoughts. Everyone was trying not to think or say anything until they heard the opinions of the others and the fire reflected it.

The Man-of-Medicine believed if there ever was a time to take control of Librebe it was now. But did he want the position? Being king was an all day and night job. He, a medicine man, came and went as he chose. He also had the king's trust and could get him to do whatever he wished already, so why take on the tedious details of day-to-day governing. He was secretly enjoying watching the village come undone, and what he found especially amusing was it was being torn apart by a wee, little girl. Maybe being a king was to be his divine fate. When they needed him to deal with all the chaos, he would make his move. Satisfied with the way things were going, the Man-of-Medicine sat back and watched the show.

The prince continued, "Mianshe is my gift. Her name is Mianshe." Then he became shy. He could see all the questions regarding how she came to be sitting in the circle of one of the greatest tribes to maintain their culture, or that is what he thought they were thinking. He looked at his daughter and then to Adisa and he felt how selfish he'd been. He knew what he must do. He had to tell them the truth. "Mianshe is my daughter. Her mother…" The prince stopped in mid-sentence when he realized he didn't even know his daughter's mother's name. Oh, this was not going as he expected at all.

"*Sedina,*" Mianshe silently informed her father. "*My mother's name is Sedina.*"

The prince was afraid to look at his daughter, so he continued looking at Adisa, which made Emadi furious. Even with the catastrophe of a bastard child in the circle, Adisa still came off smelling like a rose. Everyone, even the colonially educated prince found her beautiful.

"Her mother's name is Sedina and she lives in the sea," explained the Prince. "When I was looking for my mother's wedding band, I found the sea goddess instead. We spent one day together that is all. I did nothing improper. I swam and jumped waves like a child with the woman of the sea. But this woman was unlike others, so in my excitement we sired a child. Mianshe is my joyful thought between her mother and me. Between me and she, the mermaid called Sedina." And then the prince passed the stick to the boy.

This changed everything. How could the king implement his plan of twins when his son had just told the entire community he played with a being from the sea, a being not of their world? "Who raised this boy!" the King silently screamed. "Was I nowhere to be found?" The king continued beating himself up over the strange turn in events until he no longer could, because the boy was getting ready to talk now, and only Amma knew what the boy would say.

Two-Eyes stared at the talking-stick with pride. It was the only thing Librebe did that they did at home too, but mostly at school. When the teacher gave you the stick you answered the question, or you got to ask one. He had so many questions to ask the community. The first being... "Why do you eat lions?" asked the boy.

The king grabbed the stick from the child and demanded everyone to be still. It was an easy request for the village to handle because no one had moved since the prince said, 'her mother's name is Sedina'. The king remembered his sister begging him to simply have the prince initiated in the old ways, but he had insisted his child be versed in all ways. That was coming back to haunt him now and royally.

"Listen, my family we have been blessed as my son has pointed out. This is a gift, not only for you, my son, but also for the entire village. We have done a bad thing by not including this boy in our lives. There has never been, nor do we even have a word for what others call an orphan, yet we allowed this child to feel like one. That was wrong, my people, but Amma knew we did not know what we were doing, so she sent us another child, a twin, the twin from the seed of creation itself! We all know that twins mean prosperity and balance but twin elements, my children, are the most important twins in life. We have the son of a fire lioness and the daughter of the water-moon here together in our village. We will take them in as family and honor the great spirits that sent them to us. This is a most fortunate event for this village, my people. So, my son will raise the children of no Librebeing's womb as his own, and they will teach him how to be a man. They will help him choose his bride. They will bring prosperity to this village. They will be our spirit-appointed oracles of divine fate. We are blessed, my children. So, from this moment we must let all worry and separating thoughts go! For we are one! We are a community. So, I drink to Mianshe and…" the King finally stopped speaking. He had no idea what the boy's name was, and he didn't want to ask because he was afraid of what the boy would say.

"Verité," said the boy. "My name is Verité."

Adisa smiled when the boy spoke. Not because he wasn't holding the stick or because the king did, but because his name meant truth. This boy spoke French, like the missionary women who came to teach them how to use the machine that sewed. This little boy must have traveled a long way by himself. This was one strong little boy. He would surely be able to teach the prince how to walk on his own.

The prince was in shock. He tried to act as if his father's words hadn't affected him, but he could tell by his daughter's face he was not successful. He smiled at his daughter but the drops of sweat now staining his white shirt was proof he was not comfortable with the idea.

The king watched his son process the information with a strange sense of delight. He was sure his boy would now become a man. He held the stick forward into the vast abyss of the circle, offering it to anyone who wished to comment but no one made a move toward it. The people vacillated between awe and total confusion. The more innocent of them were relieved that something positive was coming out of the strange events leading up to this moment, while the others were completely leery of it working at all. The pessimists in the crowd were sure they were doomed. Twins were a big omen in their culture, but twins meant the same and these two children were far from being alike. The questions from the silent crowd circled around the fire like a tornado.

When Emadi stood up and took the stick from the king's hand the fire began to crackle and burn with such fury it lit up the entire circle like the morning sun. "How is this going to work, King-Guardian?" Emadi asked. "That boy is of land and that girl is of sea. We have no idea whose child that boy is and where the mother of that girl lives. What if they come looking for their children? What if they accuse us of stealing them?"

The crowd gasped. They hadn't thought of anyone wanting the two children before. They had no desire to harbor the strange pair, so they assumed no one else would either. They were already on shaky ground with the neighboring tribe over the rights to the small canal that connected their villages. What if the tribe heard of these things? They'd believe the children had bewitched the village and refuse to trade with Librebe anymore. Where would that leave them? There were many practical issues to address but the people were too afraid to bother the king with their concerns, so they all looked at Emadi and then to the queen and then back to Emadi.

The queen sensed the fear running through the communal circle. Worse she felt it. Everyone's energy had made her hands clammy, so clammy she almost lost her grip on Mianshe's hand and as soon as the thought entered her mind, her hand separated from the girl's with an audible, 'Ppuk!' The queen gracefully rose to standing and took the stick from her brother's hand. She had no idea what she was going to say. She was simply covering up the fact that her hand had slipped, and the circle of energy had been disconnected.

"Dear children, please do not worry unnecessarily. No one from the bordering realms even knows these children exist. This is a good solution. Maybe these children will change our luck. Maybe that is why Amma sent them to us. For now, I will not question the Creator's ways. I will embrace them as my grandchildren and right the wrongs I have caused in my life." The queen gave the stick back to her brother and sat down.

Mianshe was so proud of her grandmother that she jumped up and hugged her, then she hugged her grandfather-the king and she finished by kissing Verité on his forehead.

Verité didn't know how to respond so he folded over and placed his forehead on the ground and sent all the good energy into the earth. He felt that was the least he could do since the community had invited him to dinner for the second time in twelve months.

The fire went wild. It crackled and burned with such zeal that Adisa had to assist her father with it. As soon as she grabbed a log and presented it to him, the fire burnt it down to ash. She ran to the fire stack and found the biggest log she could, however as soon as she got comfortable again the wood would be burnt down to one smoldering ember winking at her.

The Fire-Tender kept sprinkling water on the fire. He hoped to appease it, so it would burn at its normal brilliance and not scorch the people. He was working so hard he had already drunk his jug of water and it made him sweat all the more. He brushed and raked and sprayed and tended the fire as best he could, but with so many thoughts circulating he forgot an opinion as soon as he read the symbolism of another comment. This was the most talkative fire he ever tended.

Everybody's face was beet red. The villagers were hot—too hot. They shifted back and forth, trying to find a shady spot, but the fire was so large it glowed past the circle out into the woods. Even though it was considered taboo to hide when in the communal circle, some were trying to scoot back away from the fire. They were trying to find refuge in each other's shadows. They really wanted to lie down on the cool earth where they could escape the rising heat, and no one could see or read how they truly felt but there was no escaping it. The only solace was it was happening to everyone. Thus, they all made peace with their situation by competing with who could take the heat the longest and with the most grace.

The king could wait no longer. He was not letting his son get away without responding to his idea. His son needed to publicly accept his challenge. He wanted him to literally feel the heat. He was the one who swam in the cool sea with a mermaid. His son never had to sweat it out like he did, or the people had. He never had to take responsibility for making a home or raising a family or take on the woes of the community. He played. Well today his son would take the heat for everyone. Today his son would prove to the people what kind of king he was going to be and so with great force the king thrust the stick into his son's hand.

But Mianshe grabbed the stick out of the air and said, "I am from Mer. Where are you from?" Verité was unaware she was talking to him. He was still bent over with his head on the ground. Neither he nor Mianshe saw the king's face twisting in animated rage, but the prince did. He tried to take the stick away from his daughter, but he didn't get there in time. Mianshe had already tapped the boy on the shoulder, finally getting his attention.

When the boy felt the end of the staff touch him, he bolted upright and answered, "I am from nowhere, and everywhere. We travel the sand and sea and mountains. We follow our Mother's cycle. We are the people of no land and all lands. We are nomads." Then he solemnly said, "And I have no idea where my family lives now."

Then adding an even greater insult to the community's injury, the Man-of-Medicine sucked the air through his teeth and laughed. "A migrant and a mermaid what shall we harbor next!"

CHAPTER 5

It was morning and the embers from last night's ceremony were still burning, therefore the Fire-Tender still sat by the fire spraying water on it. It was taboo to douse a fire. It had to go out on its own but after last night's strange ceremony with no name he didn't dare leave the fire while it was still alive. Who knew what could happen with all those thoughts still ruminating in the ashes. In all his years of life he'd never seen a fire continue to grow like this one. He brushed it and stoked it and patted it down like a newborn baby. He was tired. He needed this fire to burp out its passion and go to sleep.

He found symbols he didn't understand in the fire. He was sure those were from the little girl. A mermaid in a fire created the weirdest ashes. They were long and stringy and curled up like the bottom of the little rainbow dress she wore to the ceremony. What a strange night it had been. Even though the ban on talking had been lifted, no one spoke. He wondered how long the village would remain silent.

The sun had already crept over the mountain. It was getting late. Adisa slowly approached her father and gently placed a hot cup of bush tea in his hand. She could tell he was worried. In all her years she had never successfully snuck up on her father. He would always call her name before she reached him. Sometimes he would feel her approaching as soon as she left home and it was on the other side of the camp. He would laugh and confide that he'd felt her shadow. That's how he knew she was coming. He tried teaching her how to do this and she did very well, but she was never as good as him. Her father could feel someone's shadow coming towards him from the other side of the courtyard wall, but today he did not tease her in his friendly way or call her by her pet name as she approached. Today he thanked her for the tea. Her father sipped his tea and watched the fire, so Adisa sat down and watched the fire with him. She wanted to hear what he was thinking, but he never talked while tending fire.

No one was moving around the village. They all stayed in their homes and talked between themselves. Adisa needed to talk. She was tired of hearing her thoughts fade like smoke in her mind. It felt funny. She imagined the fire must have felt like that too—all excited one minute and teary the next. She still had last night's image of the prince in her mind. She still saw him confessing about uniting with the woman from the sea and she still felt his eyes upon her, waiting for her judgment. It was funny. Most men would sleep with a goat if it held a lingering look and it would come back to haunt them in the birth of an unwanted child, however the prince hadn't even touched the mermaid, but he wanted his child more than he wanted his position of king. That was what his eyes were telling her last night. That is why she felt so much love for him this morning. Adisa wanted to discuss this with her father, but her father sat in silence sipping his tea, so she decided to sit with him and think of her question. The fire would translate her message.

"Be careful of giving your heart away too soon, my daughter," said the Fire-Tender. "The Prince's fire will not go out, no matter how much water I pour on it."

Adisa was shocked by her father's words. No matter how many times she'd been privy to his wisdom and the power invoked by the fire, it always surprised her when the message came through. She wished she'd brought a cup of tea for herself. Her mouth was as dry as the Sahara. Even if she wanted to respond she wouldn't be able to get her words out. Adisa was pulled out of her reverie when she felt her father's cup tap her arm. He was offering her some of his tea. Again, she was impressed by her father's wisdom and as she drank from his cup she wondered if it was half empty or half full.

"Have hope, Adisa. Hope is Amma's remedy for anything ailing you," he said.

Adisa finished her father's tea in one gulp. She couldn't look at him. She was too embarrassed by how much he knew about how she felt. "I'm sorry, Bba. I drank the rest of your tea. I'll get you a fresh cup," she said, but before she could make her escape her father took her hand and held it.

"It's okay. The fire is out," he said.

Adisa massaged her father's legs before helping him rise to a standing position. She avoided looking at him as they walked out into the open air. She needed time to recover from the advice he'd given her. While walking home Adisa peeked at every nuance in her father's expressions. He was tired, and his body was sore. He'd been sitting by the fire on the hard ground for almost twelve hours. Her father was old and tending fires was beginning to take its toll on his body. Any time she'd mention taking on an apprentice, he would smile and tickle her like he did when she was young. It made her laugh. It was funny how men were always in denial when it came to their bodies.

Then her father's mood changed drastically. He smiled and lifted himself up and started walking like a young man. The only time she'd seen him do this was when the South African dance troop came to town. When he saw the red-brown woman with the black lipstick he pushed out his chest and lowered his voice. They went to every neighboring village to watch her dance. Granted she was a good dancer but after seeing the same dance ten times it grew old. Plus, they spent all their money for crops, so they had to eat with the Herb-Woman and her daughter for many months. It was embarrassing. Adisa was only ten years old then and it was only two years after her mother had drowned.

When her father brought the woman home for dinner the woman pinched her on her cheek. She was nice and easy to be with. She even taught her some steps from her Xhosa initiation dance. That day her father was acting so differently. She wondered if this new woman was going to be her mother, but that evening when she played dress up with the woman, her father got angry. The dancer had dressed Adisa in a flowered sarong with some pink plastic shoes and had painted her mouth with berries. The Fire-Tender saw red and didn't speak to the woman for weeks. Since her father would no longer talk to her, the South African woman decided to leave with the others. After that her father's eyes were always bloodshot and his breath smelled of yeast. Adisa made her father drink bush tea with yellow flowers until his eyes finally brightened and he started to smile again. Then things went back to normal.

"Look," her father said.

Adisa didn't understand what her father was referring to. At first, she didn't see anything but when she lowered her eyes something moved and there she was. The little sea-girl was standing by their house waiting for them. She was drawing circles in the sand with a small stick. When she felt Adisa's eyes upon her she waved and started to run towards them. Or was it skipping? She was unsure what to call the mermaid's cadence. It was a little hop, then a skip, then she slid and did a little hop-hop. It was very strange and very musical. Adisa couldn't take her eyes off her. She was so transfixed by the exotic child she didn't notice she was now standing in front of her.

"Hi, can you help me with my hair? Look," Mianshe said, and then she lifted her arms and took the ribbon out of her hair, but her hair stayed exactly where it was. It was a tangled mess.

The Fire-Tender gently sidled around the girls and quietly snuck into the house, or he would have if a ribbon hadn't been tied to the pull string on the cottage door. Hanging from the string was a package. It was wrapped in the comics from an old newspaper and had red crayon marks on it. The man slowly untied the string and opened it up. It was sliced mangoes slathered with honey and flower petals. It was definitely from the little girl. As he opened the door to slip inside he saw his daughter smiling at the prince's child as the door closed behind him.

He sat the mango package on the table and went to wash his hands, but the wrapper still floated on his other hand. It was stuck to his fingers like fly paper. He rinsed one hand with the left-over water in the teakettle before attempting to unglue the sticky paper from his other, but when he went to rip the paper off his fingers he noticed the red crayon marks. It was a little map of mermaid symbols. It was her thoughts drawn out for him and she was one happy little girl. The Fire-Tender did something he rarely did. He laughed.

Adisa smiled at the little girl. "Wait right here," she said and quickly entered her house. She returned with a wide toothed comb, a brush and a pot of coconut soap. "Let's go to the river. Wait! Does the Prince-Guardian know where you are?" she asked.

"Why of course he does. He sent me here before going off with King-Popah," Mianshe replied.

This made Adisa happier than she'd been in months. The prince trusted her. She was the person he had sent his most prized possession. She would clean and comb and brush this little girl's hair to brilliance and then she would present her to her soon to be king. She took the prince's daughter by the hand and they hopped then skipped and slid out of the yard down the path toward the river.

Mianshe chattered the entire way. She asked about the red ant and why it had to work so hard. She wondered why the people didn't build cool homes in the earth like the ants did. She was curious of what the big animals did during the day and where they slept at night. She was concerned about the lonely sounds they made. She didn't care much for bats because they squeaked, and it hurt her ears. Then she began describing the townsmen. She thought the entire town must be very smart to be called Librarians, and she wanted to know how many books Adisa had read. She liked the Fire-Tender very much because his name suited him. She thought he was a very tenderhearted person indeed. He reminded her of a dolphin. She liked the way the Herb-Woman's body bobbed and jiggled and the sounds it made. She looked like a seahorse bride in an underwater waterfall, but mostly she loved all the colors in the village. Orange was her favorite.

Adisa had no trouble understanding why the prince was so in love with this child. She was truly lovely. She found pleasure in everything, the swirls in the dirt and the puffy clouds, the mist in the night air and the colors of sunshine. She saw colors in places Adisa could not see. She couldn't answer Mianshe when she asked her the name of the color of the angry smoke. She did not know. Her first response was gray, but when she showed the little girl something gray she assured her that was not the color she saw in the fire. She told her she must have boo-boos for eyes. This worried Adisa because boo-boos meant a small hurt that ached, and she didn't want the little one to think her eyes hurt or worse, that she had old eyes. However, the little girl informed her that a boo-boo was the little bulb on seaweed and it got its name because when popped it sounded like a boo-boo or it sounded that way under water. She suggested on their next trip they should go to the shore, so she could hear the boo-boos talking. Adisa agreed.

It was strange seeing things from another person's eyes. For example, to the girl the end of the eagle's tail made traces in the clouds. When Mianshe described how she saw the energy of an eagle in flight it was exactly how Adisa saw the clouds that brought the ancestors home. They swirled like dandelion fluff in the sky, like a brushstroke using white water. Mianshe adored the word dandelion and wanted her to call her that, but just for the day. So Adisa and Dandelion went down the path and into the river, roaring with laughter all the way.

"Guess who's here!" shouted the newly named Dandelion.

"Who?" Adisa giggled as she slipped her dress off and walked into the water.

"Me," replied Verité as he emerged from under the water with a fish in his hand. "Are you hungry?" he asked.

The girls clapped with delight upon seeing Verité. Adisa knew it was going to be great fun seeing the two in action. Then she thought of her prince again. He was a very private man, so she was sure he was having a difficult time being with others all day long, although there was nothing more endearing or humorous than watching a father parent his children.

It was time to tackle the little one's hair. Adisa walked the girl into the river and cooed gently to her as she lifted her head back into the water, and the little one immediately slipped out of her hands and started gathering more fish for Verité.

"Here. Oh, here's one too. Here's another one!" she cried throwing the fish from the water onto the shore.

Adisa had to stop her from catching so many fish. She was breaking Verité's heart. The only reason he was hiding in the water was to impress his little sister and here she was trying to impress him. Adisa wondered how the sexes ever got together long enough to couple. They were always in competition, especially if they liked each other and these two little ones were already in love.

"Mianshe, I mean Dandy-lioness shall we begin doing your hair?" Adisa asked.

"Okay," said Dandelion-Mianshe. She rushed over and sat between Adisa's legs as if she'd been doing it all her life.

Adisa breathed deeply as she tried to comb through the knots and tangles in the mermaid's hair. It was difficult. Her hair was not like any hair she had touched before. It was more twisted than a jungle vine and just as strong, but it was silky too and slipped through her fingers like a dragonfly. Plus, the little girl had a hard time sitting still for long periods. As soon as she would untangle one lock the girl would ask to run off to see what Verité was doing but she always came back when called.

Verité was building a fire. He dug a hole in the sandy earth and put some dry pieces of driftwood he found around the area inside. Then he gathered some leaves and mixed it with the wood. Afterward he went to the river to get the fish he'd tied in a cloth and left dangling in the water. When Mianshe saw him get the fish she begged him to bring it to her. She apologized for not coming herself but Adisa had a good strong hold on a tress of her hair. The braids were so tight they started to make Mianshe's eyes slant.

This made Verité frown. He was sure she was in pain. The comb was pushing all her face to one side and he didn't like that at all. "You are hurting her," he quietly said.

Adisa tried to explain. "The braids will loosen soon enough, so there is nothing to worry about."

Mianshe wanted to see what they were discussing, so she pulled her braid through Adisa's fingers and ran to the water's edge. Verité ran after her with Adisa trailing behind them.

"See!" exclaimed the boy. "You look like a Chinese man."

Mianshe had never seen a Chinese man so she didn't know if this was a compliment or an insult. She looked at her reflection with great intensity.

"If I don't braid it tight it will come out and get all matted again," sighed Adisa.

Mianshe wanted to tone a question to Adisa. She wanted to ask her if a Chinese man was a good compliment or a bad insult, but she didn't want to scare her like she had her father. Land beings liked noise. They were afraid of silence. She didn't want to go to that scared place with them again. Even Verité acted as if he was punished when she toned a conversation. Just like the day she silently asked him for a piece of his sweet potato and his response was, well he had no response. He was too terrified to respond. How was anyone to have a private conversation in this place? She didn't care if she hurt Verité's feelings or not she needed to know if looking Chinese was nice or not nice.

"Do I look like a Chinese man?" Mianshe asked.

"No, dear child, not at all. You look like an Ethiopian princess," cooed Adisa.

"I look like a Ittipopan princess!" shouted Mianshe. "So there!"

"I still think you look Chinese," Verité said, but very quietly.

Adisa was having a marvelous time. The two children were funnier than the funny papers the sewing women brought her, but as Adisa was enjoying the performances from the children she failed to notice how quickly Mianshe's hands were moving. In a split second, Mianshe's amber hair was floating like dandelion fluff in the wind again. Verité thought it was a great improvement, so he went over and kissed her on her forehead.

"How do I look now, Adisa?" Mianshe asked. The little girl stood as straight as she could as she waited for Adisa's judgment.

Adisa knew she would win no favors with the prince if she returned the little girl with her hair in almost the exact same shape as before. Maybe she was exaggerating a bit. The girl's hair wasn't piled in a cone on her head anymore now it was flying around her face like a lion's mane, catching everything airborne in its wake.

"You look like a roaring lion," she said. "And although it is a truly regal look you may scare people because the lion is very strong, very strong indeed." Then Adisa sat down and folded her hands in her lap.

Verité put the fish back in the water. He could see it would be a while before the women were ready to have lunch. He thought about Adisa's take on Mianshe's hair and she had a point, a very good one. This tribe was afraid of lions, especially lionesses. He didn't want the tribe to eat his only friend, so he decided to have a different opinion.

"I like the Chinese man in the market. He would always give me some vegetables if I helped him. He smelled like licorice." Then Verité looked at Adisa and smiled and then he sat down and folded his hands in his lap too.

Mianshe was furious. She knew when people were being untrue. They were trying to appease her. They were being condescending. She didn't like when people said one thing and felt another. It made her heart weak. So, she ran to the river and grabbed a fish and bit off its head. She then ripped open its belly and removed the insides until all that was left was a little piece of smelly string. She plunged the fish into the water and ripped the intestinal cord clean out. Next, she wrapped the string around her mane until it became a tail.

"There!" she exclaimed.

Mianshe looked like a genie emerging from a bottle. The wrapped part protruded from her head and the tail cascaded down her back and made a copper halo around her face. She looked gorgeous.

"Wow!" cried Verité. "Look at you!"

"Nicely done, little one," Adisa affirmed.

"Let's eat," said Mianshe. She calmly ripped the fish into three pieces and gave one to each of them. "Eat. Its better when it's fresh," she said.

The land duo didn't know what to say or do. Mianshe was watching them so they couldn't throw her gift away which is what they both wanted to do. Verité slowly put the fish in his mouth and bit it and then he gulped. His brow furrowed but afterwards his lip curled. He liked it, so he ate another bite and another until it was finished, but he didn't want to waste his work, so he got some rocks to place over the fire pit. "We can use it for wild yams," he said, before running off into the forest again to forage.

Adisa took a tiny nibble and grinned. She tried to make her smile look sincere, but it was hard to do with a cold wet slimy lump of fish in her mouth. She decided it wasn't horrible tasting, it was just horrible feeling. She didn't like the texture. It felt like someone had already eaten it and that was not a good feeling. Adisa had already had a taste of the girl's wisdom so she knew she had to tell her the truth. Even if she wanted to bend her story to make her feel better, she knew it would only make her feel worse plus she would never trust her again. She had to tell the mermaid that on land things are better when they are cooked, but she had to say this in a kind way.

"You don't like it do you?" inquired the girl.

"Well it's not as good as sweet potatoes, or as nice as a cup of honeyed bush tea, but it's not as bad as lion's meat or sour milk either. I'd have to say it is somewhere in between." Then Adisa added, "But it is my first time trying raw fish. Maybe I could get to like it. I'll try it again later."

Mianshe smiled at Adisa. She liked her. She was honest, gentle and kind and her sincere reply made her very happy. "You are a true friend. I love you. I will always be your Dandy-lioness. Where did Verité go?" And off she went looking for her land brother.

Adisa was truly touched. She'd never had any female treat her with such compassion and respect before. This little girl was more woman than most women she knew. Adisa had lived without a mother for as long as she could remember so sharing her feelings with another person of her own sex felt odd. This was what had bonded her to the prince. He too had little knowledge of female nurturing. Granted he had his aunt, but she was more about business than tenderness. Now the prince had Mianshe, the little girl who could touch your heart.

It was late afternoon. Adisa didn't want to go back to the village just yet. She was having too much fun watching Mianshe and Verité explore everything they saw. When Mianshe pointed out a red ant trying to carry off a huge morsel of yam, Verité enacted the red ant's dance by trying to walk with the largest boulder he could find. Then a dragonfly flitted by and warned him about the heavy load he was trying to carry, and the children went off listening to dragonfly wisdom, but when the yellow-headed lizard ate the scarlet dragonfly, Mianshe began to cry.

"Oye little one, don't cry," cooed Adisa.

"The lizard was hungry," explained Verité and then he ran off into the forest.

"Are you better now?" Adisa asked. Mianshe smiled at her and then she ran off to find Verité.

Adisa couldn't help but remember her time in these same forests playing with the prince. They would run like goats in a pasture after everything they saw too, and the prince was as sensitive as his daughter. One time, when they had snuck up on old man Ousman slaughtering a pig, the prince cried.

The sun was now touching the horizon. It was getting close to dinnertime. They were going to have to hurry to get home in time to eat with the others otherwise they'd have to fend for themselves. Adisa went off into the woods to find the children. As she slowly walked deeper into the forest she could hear them giggling. When she stopped walking, everything became silent. There before her was the most beautifully ornate spider web she had ever seen. The children had decorated it with flower petals and butterfly wings, old cocoons and sweet grass, paper-thin shells and animal fur and then sprayed their artwork with water so it glistened in the red glow of the sunset. It was absolutely otherworldly.

Adisa stood studying the web art for a good long moment. She had no words to express what she was feeling. It'd been a long time since she'd felt the purity of innocence and it was overwhelming. Being initiated as an adult was not all it was cracked up to be. No one made art or went for walks or sang gibberish or ate raw fish. No one told you their secrets or patted you on the back or gave you pet names or laughed until their sides ached. Everyone she knew was responsible and boring. It was like adulthood was a curse condemning oneself to endless days of doing the same thing over and over again. Today was a gift she would never forget, and she would gladly take this knowledge with her into tomorrow. She promised herself she would find something new to do every day. Even if it was something as simple as putting her clothes on in reverse order. This made her giggle, and the children who now stood beside her unnoticed giggled, startling Adisa back to the present moment.

"We should be heading back children," Adisa quietly said.

Mianshe wrapped her arms around Adisa's waist and squeezed her. It inspired Verité to wrap his arms around Mianshe's waist and then the odd trio skipped, then hopped and danced and laughed and giggled all the way back to the village.

/\\.\\/\\

CHAPTER 6

The prince was worried to his breaking point. He paced back and forth in his room with his hands tightly clenched behind him. He was afraid to release his wrist for fear of leveling anything breakable. He'd lost his children and it had been less than twenty-four hours since they were entrusted to him. He refused to ask his aunt where they were because she would give him her self-satisfied smile then turn the question back at him. He couldn't bear that. It always made him feel like a child himself.

"Where are they?" the Prince screamed. The sound of his own voice startled him. And his emotion carried into the next room where his nanny was working.

"Prince-Guardian are you okay?" she asked.

"I'm fine. I lost a button. I'm okay now," replied the Prince. He was never very good at lying.

"Shall I help you?" inquired Leboya from the kitchen.

"No!" he said in a curt voice. He was a little ashamed of his tone. He loved his nanny and would never want to offend her, but anger is not easily controlled. It always evades one's senses and slips out at inappropriate times before running amok.

The prince had to calm himself before people began to doubt his ability to master his emotions. They already looked at him from the side of their faces, and when he caught them doing it, they would look down at his crotch. What were they expecting to find there, a mermaid's tail? This time he managed his thought in silence.

The prince forced himself to sit down. He needed to calm himself, so he decided to tie some fishing lures. He went to his tackle basket and got some wire and elephant hair and red bird feathers and began tying them all together. He tied and tied, and he tied some more. He was so absorbed in his work that he didn't notice Leboya enter with a pot of yellow tea and some soda crackers. Yellow flower tea was the perfect remedy for calming one's nerves. This totally infuriated the prince. The old woman had judged his concern for his children as nervous tension.

Nanny Leboya tried to leave the room without being noticed but the prince's mood was denser than the elephant hair he played with. She'd been the prince's nanny since his mother died. She suckled him. The queen begged her to leave her own children to care for the motherless royalty. She sent bribes too, baskets of vegetables and meat, corn and mudcloth. The queen even fed the young woman helping her rear her own children.

"Why on earth does Amma keep sending me children," she thoughtfully asked herself? She had already raised ten—the four she birthed, three of her dead brother's children, Little Moopti's child after she got the sickness and now the prince. "And princes never grow up. They don't have too," she muttered under her breath.

Leboya couldn't remember the last time she enjoyed a private conversation with someone her own age or touched a person that wasn't sticky with sap or smelled like goat's milk. It wasn't the company of men she missed either. Some women got an itch that lasted their entire lifetimes even after the Goddess of the Moon told them to stop. Leboya didn't care if she saw another male member again in her life. In fact, if Amma asked her if she missed her husband she would answer honestly. "No dear Amma, I don't miss the man at all. He was too big and too needy." Leboya quietly but very clearly said.

This wasn't only because her husband farted and snored that she didn't miss him, or that he cursed and whined and bragged too. It was because in all their years of marriage he never asked her about herself. He never asked about what she dreamt or what she felt. He didn't know her favorite color or what sound made her happy. He couldn't buy her favorite pomade or scented oil or any present for that matter. The man simply told her what he liked, and they'd been married twenty-eight years.

Nanny Leboya hated when she thought bad things about her husband, so she tried to think of something nice to say. She did not want Amma to send her some bad juju. Her husband never hit her, and he always told her she was doing a nice job, but the man tried to work her to death and he would have had he not died first. Now the queen was trying to work her nerves. Leboya didn't mind doing her share. She was born a solid brown woman with big hands for holding life's sorrows, or joys (in her case ten of them) but sometimes she just wanted to let go and smoke a pipe on the porch too, but she couldn't stand the way a pipe made her teeth feel.

Leboya set the cup down a second time. She wanted to get the prince's attention before the tea got cold. Cold tea was worthless. But the royal boy never looked up. He just kept busy doing nothing. He was as tense as a jembe drum, so nanny gingerly made her way around the room. She was sure the lures he was making were worthless. They were too thick and would surely sink to the bottom of the ocean.

"Afternoon, my Prince," Leboya muttered as she made her way out of the room.

"Bye," grumbled the Prince.

Leboya gently shook loose the thought she'd been carrying since the king cursed his son. She gave the boy three months before he ran back to the colonial's schools, away from all the responsibility of traditional village life. These were modern times so the young were pretty useless when it came to the old ways, but enough thinking about the politics of today's entitled youth. She needed to get back to her kitchen to prepare the evening meal. When Leboya opened the door leading into the courtyard the sound of the children returning entered the room.

The prince quickly jumped up, overturning the tray of tea and crackers and he ran through the spilled snack, crunching every fallen cracker on his way. When he saw Mianshe and Verité skipping into the village square he began to breathe. Until that moment he had no idea he'd been holding his breath.

Verité slowed down when he saw the prince watching them from the porch. Mianshe sped up and ran ahead to greet her father. Adisa grabbed Verité's hand. They were not sure how to read the prince's expression, so they lingered a little behind Mianshe to see how he would react.

"We went to the river and I got my hair washed and I saw the lizard eat the red fly and Verité made yams and Adisa taught us how to make music with blades of grass!" Mianshe exclaimed. She was so excited. She told him about the web they decorated then she ran over to Verité for him to confirm it. Afterward she ran back to her father's side and showed him the treasures she'd amassed, and while she talked she'd skip over to Adisa and hug her or pull on Verité's fingers. Mianshe continued running back and forth, and forth and back, until she had described in detail the entire afternoon.

Verité and Adisa listened as they waited in the courtyard for the prince to acknowledge them.

"Nanny Leboya!" screamed the Prince. "We have company for dinner."

The prince stood to the side of the door and gestured for Adisa and Verité to enter. Mianshe had already run inside. Verité was not sure what to do, so he hid behind Adisa.

"Boy, come!" yelled the Prince. "Come on. You live here now so you may as well start getting use to the idea."

But Verité would not come from behind Adisa's skirt, so Adisa slowly reached behind her and stroked his head. "Come, sweet Verité, come and show Prince-Guardian what you found in the forest," she said. Whereby the boy simply took his free hand and clutched the other side of her skirt.

The prince watched the pair with cool curiosity. He was trying not to take the boy's refusal personally, but it was difficult not to. Now all he could see of the boy was his balled-up fists clutching Adisa's skirt.

Adisa had to think fast. She knew how sensitive the prince could be and she could see his feelings were getting hurt. "Verité, please escort me into the Prince's quarters," she said. "I am a single woman and cannot go alone without an escort. Please consider chaperoning me." Then she waited.

Verité slowly released her skirt and stood beside her. He looked up into her eyes, then back at the prince and frowned. "I am not hungry," he decided.

This was not good. Adisa knew she had to get the boy to approach the prince and quickly. They were beginning to draw attention. They were standing in the square as if they were about to be executed. Plus, the prince was becoming jealous of the attention the boy was giving her. This truly was not good. Adisa bent over and whispered something into the boy's ear and he began smiling. "Ready," she said.

"Yes," replied the boy and he took her hand and marched up the stairs past the prince into the house.

The prince was stunned. If it weren't for Adisa's apologetic expression, which helped defuse his anger, he would have left the scoundrel in the yard. But he caught himself before he got too carried away. He was acting exactly like his father and he didn't want to act like that, therefore he calmed himself and used his senses. The boy was new to the village. He himself had recently returned from foreign lands, so he knew exactly how it felt to be a foreigner. Plus, since his return he hadn't shown this young man any attention at all. He'd never introduced himself, nor smiled in his direction. He never inquired about his people. He never even asked his people about him, so why should the boy take kindly to him now? Also, this boy knew it was his father who had commanded him to be his guardian. This boy had no choice in his fate. Neither did the prince for that matter. Hence the prince decided he would treat the evening as if it were their first-time meeting. He would make the boy feel comfortable and he'd get to know this child. Satisfied with his decision the prince entered his home.

Finally, the eavesdropping villagers let the curtains fall back over their windows, covering their smiles from view.

CHAPTER 7

Leboya set the table with four bowls. She decided to place Mianshe's orange cushion beside her father's, so the boy could sit next to the Fire-Tender's daughter. Normally she would have placed the children on one side and the adults on the other, but these were far from normal times. When nanny heard the people quietly closing their windows she knew the prince and his guests were on their way inside. She had to hurry if she was going to be ready. She rushed and got a basin of water to wash the dust from their feet and placed it by the door. She then took a wrap she found in her cedar box and placed it on a chair. It had been given to her years ago and she'd never worn it. Now she was too big to fit it. It was a pretty blue—the color of a sky filled with the promise of water. It was a good color for a young woman hopeful of becoming a bride.

"Nanny!" shouted the Prince. "We're all here." The prince hoped his announcement didn't sound like a reproach for the boy's delay in the courtyard. He didn't mean it that way. He'd never want Adisa to think he was an intolerant man.

Mianshe skipped around the house in a circle before taking a seat in her father's reading chair. She loved this chair because it spun around. She did one complete turn then hopped out of the chair and motioned for Verité to take her place. Verité was in awe of Mianshe's spinning chair. He he'd never seen anything like it before, except perhaps at a fair, but never in a house. He wanted to ask the prince if he was allowed to sit in it first, but he couldn't take his eyes off it long enough to ask. However, when Verité looked at the prince to ask his permission to take his chair for a spin, the prince was staring at Adisa. So, the boy did what he had to do. He allowed himself to be pushed into the chair by Mianshe, and she pushed and pushed and pushed him until he circled into an imaginary outer space.

"Thank you for your help today. Her hair looks very nice," said the Prince.

Adisa looked to the ground before confessing what it was like dealing with a mermaid and her hair. The prince laughed after hearing how her hairdo was her own doing. "As was her wardrobe for the full moon ceremony. Maybe she will start a new fad in the village," he said. Adisa laughed with him even though she had no idea what a fad was.

Nanny Leboya entered with a hand towel draped over her shoulder. She slowly stooped down next to the basin of water and proceeded to wash the prince's feet. This embarrassed the prince. He grabbed his nanny by the arm and pulled her up to standing. Then he bent over and took the tub and knelt before his children. "Shall we wash the dirt off and return it to the forest, little ones?" he asked the dizzy children.

Leboya couldn't believe what she was seeing. The prince did fancy Adisa, so she grabbed Adisa's arm and took her into the back of the house. She motioned for her to use her washbowl and oils to remove the ashy look from her skin, and then she gracefully presented her the blue robe. "Here, child, put this on," she whispered.

"Oh, Auntie, I can't!" Adisa graciously protested.

Adisa was in awe of the fine blue silk, as well as the love in which Leboya presented it. What was going on today? Here she was for the second time in one day, receiving nurturing, unconditional love from women. It was really the third time. Mother Earth herself had started the day off with all these blessings. Adisa fell to her knees and began praying.

"We don't have time for that now, child. Get dressed," demanded Leboya before going outside to tend to her stew.

Adisa quickly stood up and oiled her body. She cautiously put on the robe. It was a bit much. She felt like a peacock. The silky blue was so blue she felt she could blind an eagle in flight. It was really blue. Adisa took a deep breath and then another before firmly telling herself, "If you are sincerely humble and show enough wise beauty the prince will surely forgive this dress."

The prince wiped Mianshe's face first and then he rinsed the cloth and presented it to Verité. The young boy took it and wiped his own face and gave the cloth back to the prince. The prince rinsed the cloth and lathered it with soap and washed Mianshe's arms and legs and rinsed the cloth again and gave it to the boy. Verité lathered and washed his legs and arms and then rinsed the cloth and gave it back to the prince. Next, he sat Mianshe on his lap and wiped her feet and Verité's eyes grew huge in his head. The prince waited for the boy to take the cloth and wash his feet, but the boy did not move. He continued staring at Mianshe's feet. So, the prince rinsed the cloth again and soaped it up and bent down to wash the boy's feet. However, when he bent over some water dripped onto Mianshe's feet and a tiny little mesh of flesh began to wiggle between her toes. Verité jumped and covered his mouth with his hand.

The prince was in shock. He wasn't sure what he'd seen but he'd seen something, and it was growing between his daughter's toes, so the prince rinsed the cloth again, but this time he did not wring it out all the way. He left it sopping with water. He took the cloth and wet his daughter's feet and lo and behold her little toes began to grow together. He dropped the cloth and it made a big plop when it hit the water. He had to know if she would revert completely, so he lowered his daughter into the tin tub and as she stood looking at him and her brother her feet slowly developed a web of meshing connecting one toe to the other. Verité took his other free hand and covered his mouth even more.

"Maybe we should keep this between us," said the Prince to his children and then he made a mental note to ask nanny where she got the water.

Verité nodded and silently agreed to keep their secret.

Mianshe stood in the tub of water wiggling her webbed toes. She had no idea what all the fuss was about. "I'm hungry now," she quietly said in the most secretive voice she could muster. She was trying to sound like them.

The two women were busy setting the table for dinner. Leboya sat a huge bowl of mutton stew in the center and then she cleared some space. Adisa quickly followed behind her, swishing and swirling in blue silk, carrying nanny's couscous. She placed it in the spot beside the bowl, so it was readily available to soak up the stew's gravy. Happy that everyone could easily get at her food, Nanny Leboya pinched Adisa's cheek and left the room.

Adisa immediately sat down and waited for the others. She tucked as much of the dress as she possibly could underneath her and the table. She even rolled the fabric from the puffy sleeves into little columns so less of it was exposed. She didn't want to look like a blue flycatcher or worse a pompous kingfisher every time she raised her hand to her mouth. That bird was so bright it upstaged the sun.

"Children we are ready!" shouted Leboya. "You must eat when it is hot."

Mianshe rushed into the room and slid into the table. She was not used to wearing socks, so she hadn't mastered their slippery texture. Also, they looked funny to her. She felt like an elf from the middle world. Sometimes the elves and gnomes would peak at her from their caverns when she would ride on her mother's back in the sea. Thinking of her mother calmed her, so she stood by the table and closed her eyes and toned, *"Hello Merma, I'm okay. I wear socks now.'* When she opened her eyes, she saw the most radiant sight ever. She saw Adisa covered in a sea of blue. "Look, Popah! Look at how beautiful Adisa looks!" she exclaimed as she ran out of the room to find her father, but she didn't have to run far because the prince and Verité were entering just as she was leaving to find them. Mianshe tried to stop but her socks didn't respond as she'd wished, so she slammed into Verité sending him butt first to the floor.

"Ouch!" exclaimed the boy.

"You must learn to calm yourself, Daughter," said a slightly frustrated Prince.

Mianshe was embarrassed. Her father had pointed her out in a most unflattering way. "I do not like these socks," she said. Then she took a toe in each hand and pulled them off.

Verité gasped. The prince covered his eyes. And Adisa finally let go of her elbows and laughed aloud.

"Ahhaha, little one! Socks are very strange indeed, plus they make your feet sweat. I agree with you. They can be quite useless when walking," Adisa said. The she reached over and helped Mianshe to standing but without actually standing herself. The thought of standing up made her, well—blue.

"Okay. Is everyone okay?" asked the Prince. "Good," he quietly replied to himself as he sat down and waited for everyone to settle in.

Mianshe was so hungry she sunk her arm into the stew and lifted a handful and immediately plunged it into her mouth. Then she spat it onto the floor. Verité laughed, not so much at the starving sea-girl he now called sister, he was laughing at the expressions on the grown-ups' faces. They looked horrified. He could almost read Adisa's reaction. She had a how-can-the-face-of-an-angel-turn-into-a-hyena-so-quickly, look on her face. And the prince, well no words could explain his expression, and this made Verité laugh even harder. But when the shamed Mianshe looked at him with her sad teal eyes and toned, "*Duduju*", Verité pulled the meat out of his mouth, pushed his bowl to the side and rested his head on the table. Verité felt awful. He knew Duduju. Duduju was his cousin Je-Jean's pet baby lamb, and now it was all grown up and thrown up on the floor.

Adisa grabbed Verité by the hand at the very same time the prince picked Mianshe up in his arms and they all rushed outside to get some air.

"Stay here. I'll be right back," said the Prince.

Adisa and the children sat on the stairs and waited for the prince to find some dandelion leaves. They had no idea what sickness the children had gotten in the forest, but they were sure the leaves would purge it from them. The prince was tired. The last thing he wanted to be doing was foraging at night. He had spent his entire day worrying and now here he was still vexed. Whatever this duduju was he was going to rip it up so no one would eat any more of it. He wondered if he should mention it to the village in case they accidentally ingested the foul duduju, but he decided against it. He was too embarrassed to admit he didn't know what it looked like, much less its properties. The prince harvested some dandelions and decided to keep the entire incident a secret. With each step he made he tried clearing his mind of the belief that being a parent was going to be an endless night of vomit and mucous-ridden emotions.

"How do you feel, young ones?" Adisa asked.

The children didn't hear her. They simply stared into each other's eyes. Adisa felt their foreheads to make sure whatever was upsetting them hadn't gone viral. They were fine but Nanny Leboya wasn't. She could hear the old woman huffing and puffing and muttering away inside the house. Her food was still sitting on the table uneaten. Adisa couldn't blame Nanny Leboya for feeling hurt.

"Aieee!" hollered Nanny Leboya.

When Adisa heard Leboya scream, she rushed up the stairs and into the house. Nanny stood by the table barefoot in a regurgitated puddle of stew.

"How do you know Duduju?" Verité quietly asked.

"I just ate him," Mianshe sadly said.

"I know, but how do you know it was him?" he asked.

"He told me," replied Mianshe.

"Was he sad?" wondered Verité.

"He was not happy. He was scared," cried Mianshe.

"What did they do to him?" asked Verité.

"They hit him on his head," Mianshe whimpered.

"Where was my cousin? Where's Je-Jean?" Verité demanded.

"He is not here," Mianshe replied. She was confused by Verité's question.

"*I know that,*" toned a frustrated Verité. "*Can you find him? Ask Duduju where he is,*" he silently screamed.

"Duduju is dead, Verité," Mianshe calmly explained in the most heartfelt voice that one couldn't tell if she was thinking it or saying it aloud.

Verité stomped down the stairs and began kicking the dirt up in big clods. Mianshe followed him into the courtyard.

"Verité, I'm sorry. I can only hear those I can feel." She hoped that made sense to her angry and sadly desperate two-legged brother.

Verité was upset. Not because he'd eaten lamb and that lamb was his friend, he missed his family—all of them. "*What do you care? You bit off the head of a fish!*" he angrily thought. Sometimes toning didn't allow one to censor their thoughts.

"I said a prayer, Verité. Plus, I promised to elevate it to a Mer-one!" Mianshe tried defending herself and her people's ways but the lonely two-legged boy stood his ground.

"What's so good about being a mermaid? That fish was happy as it was," he coldly said.

Verité's comment made his sister burst into tears. He didn't care. He was tired of having to think about everyone's needs before his own. What about his needs? What about Duduju's? That lamb would smile at him and follow him everywhere. But Verité was not naïve. He knew each species relied on another. He just hated that one felt they were better than the other.

That's not true, Verité. I was just honoring the little fish," Mianshe calmly said as she wiped her tears away. "And Mer-ones don't feel like they are better than anyone else."

Verité finally calmed down. He took his little sea-sister in his arms and gently rocked her even thought it was really him that needed nurturing. He missed his family and he missed his mother most of all.

Mianshe cupped Verité's face with both hands and softly toned, "*I love you, Verité. You are my brother.*" And the two children sat on the ground and stared into each other's eyes for a good long moment before entering the house.

After having some dandelion tea, Leboya helped the children get ready for bed. She laid two grass mats right beside each other near the hearth in their room and watched as they crawled inside and immediately fell to sleep. It'd been years since she'd taken care of little ones. She'd forgotten how quickly they could drop in and out of slumber. She loved how their scent and the sound of their voices could make her heart grow, so she sat down and waited for their breath to deepen, assuring her they were in that other world where their spirit guides would take over for her.

"The children are asleep," said the Prince as he slowly sat down on the stairs beside the Fire-Tender's daughter.

Adisa smiled. She was exhausted. All she wanted was to take off Leboya's slippery dress and crawl onto her sweet grass mat and sleep until the sun kissed her eyes awake. She had to watch herself. Being tired was the perfect environment for saying something stupid like "being kissed awake". She was not some young girl who had the luxury of believing in fairy tales. No one ever came and saved your day. She knew this. Truth being, this was the complete opposite. The prince needed her. She couldn't leave yet because he needed someone to talk to.

"What happened, Adisa? They were so happy one moment then so sad the next," said the Prince. He was truly bewildered. "Was it the food? Was I too hard on them? I literally bent over backward to please them today," he said.

Then the prince stopped talking. He was silent for so long Adisa believed he'd gone to sleep, so she quietly stood up and began to creep down the stairs, but as soon as she thought she'd snuck away, he spoke.

"I don't know," he said before trailing off into silence once again.

"Ah Prince-Brother be gentle with yourself. Today was one day and tomorrow you will have another," she said. Then Adisa addressed him formally. "Guardian-Prince, I must go tend to my Bba now."

"Yes, yes I understand," said the Prince. "Please excuse me, I have taken up so much of your time today. Please know I am most grateful for your help."

Adisa nodded and smiled and then made her way down the stairs. Now she felt a little melancholic. Their conversation ending in formalities made her feel sad. This day hadn't turned out exactly how she thought it would.

"Adisa," called the Prince.

"Yes, my Prince?" she quickly replied. He startled her.

"Blue is a very befitting color on you. I agree with my daughter. You look beautiful," he said. Then the prince rose to standing and smiled.

"Thank you," she quickly replied. "Good night." Adisa didn't know which form she should use when addressing a compliment from one's prince, so she smiled and waved goodbye and continued on her way.

What a perfect day she thought as she ran out of the courtyard and into the pasture toward home. It was a waning full moon, so the evening light was full of shadows. It was late, too late for a single woman to be out unescorted. Adisa was going to have to be careful if she were to get home without being noticed. When she finally made it to her house, she was so grateful she hadn't been seen. She took off her slippers and tucked them under her arm. She didn't want their smacking sound to wake her father. Next, she slid one bare foot into the slightly open door, and then turned her body to make sure no moonlight entered. She carefully gathered the yards of blue silk and gingerly began inching her way through the small opening.

A sliver of moonlight had divided the Fire-Tender's daughter in two. Half of her screamed like a peacock and the other half hid in the darkness like a chicken. The Fire-Tender had to blink several times before recognizing it was his daughter. His first thought was of the South African dancer. He thought she was coming to beg him to take her back, but this was no showgirl, this was his daughter.

"Adisa?" said the bewildered Fire-Tender.

Once again and for the second time that evening, the sound of her own name startled her. Adisa immediately dropped the dress and covered her legs. "Yes, Bba?" she replied.

She followed the sound of his voice until he came into view. He was standing by the fence looking out toward the sea. His shadow loomed forward and met her before he could complete his turn. She waited, but he said nothing more. Then she began to understand. Her father was upset. "It's Nanny Leboya's dress," Adisa meekly said. "It's a bit loud."

"Very," he said.

"Yes," said Adisa and then she shut up.

The Fire-Tender had never hit his daughter or even touched her without a father's love in his heart, but today all he could think of was ripping that dress off of her. "Maybe you should change," he said. Then he turned, taking his shadow with him and he walked into the dark pasture.

"Yes, Bba," she said before escaping into the house.

Adisa's heart was beating like a bat's wings. It fluttered between fear and excitement. When she thought of the prince she'd get so happy her heart danced, pit-a-pat, pit-a-pat, but when she thought of her father her heart would pound in her belly and move around as if the bat was fighting to get out. She took off Nanny Leboya's dress and wiped it down with a damp cloth. Afterward, she misted the dress with rose water and wrapped a sheet around it and hung it as far from the ground as she could. Her father hadn't returned yet and this frightened her. He rarely got upset but then he rarely had reason. She was a good girl. What a strange day it had been. There had been so much love but a lot of anxiety too. It was like the prince describing his children—so happy one moment, so sad the next. Adisa lay down on her mat and watched her heart moving beneath her skin. She was waiting for her father to return to give the final judgment on a most unusual day.

CHAPTER 8

The rooster announced the morning for the second time and this time the prince heard it. Needless to say, it still surprised him, so he jumped up and knocked over his breakfast tray. It made such a clamor that Nanny Leboya rushed in ready to lodge her complaint.

"Now if you had a proper grass mat on the floor your feet would stay still and maybe then you'd have noticed that tray beside you!" she said with a great deal of frustration.

"Yes, yes, I know," said the Prince as he helped her put everything back in its place. "Where are the children?" he asked as he removed his pajama bottoms and wrapped his cloth around his waist.

Leboya was always uncomfortable around naked men, even her husband. When she consummated her marriage, he had to sneak up behind her. He put his hands over her eyes before turning her to face him, so they could formally embrace as husband and wife.

"The children felt fine this morning, so they went fishing," she said.

"What!" said the Prince. "Who gave them permission to do this? They will come home sick again, Nanny!" he cried.

The prince stomped out of his room straight into the queen's arms.

"Greetings, Son, where are you going in such a rush?" the Queen asked in her good-natured way. "Leboya, please bring us some tea," she added.

Nanny gave the prince an 'Oh well' look and off she went into the kitchen to fetch him another breakfast and the queen some tea.

The queen went to the prince's small desk and sat down. "Sit," she said.

The prince resigned himself to the unannounced visit and went over and warmly embraced his aunt. It was unusual for a woman to take tea in a man's sleeping area—especially a queen. "I am fine, Auntie. And how are you today? You look well," he said. He wanted to get all the civilities out of the way as quickly as possible.

"I am blessed," answered the Queen. And with some trepidation she asked, "So where are your blessed children?"

"They've gone fishing so I'm all yours, Queen-Mother," he replied.

Now the queen was worried. Her son had resorted to using formalities. He wanted her to leave. Or maybe he wanted her to stay to help with his parental duties. Either way this was going to be a most amusing morning.

❖ /.\ ❖

Verité sat on the shore pouring water on Mianshe's feet. He quietly watched as they grew together and then separated when they dried. It didn't bother Mianshe at all, in fact she didn't even notice. She was too focused on making her father a boo-boo necklace.

"Listen," she said. She pressed the algae until it popped with a bloop-bloop sound. "See!" she giggled. "It talks!"

"It does not talk it makes sounds," said Verité as he poured more water onto Mianshe's feet.

Mianshe gathered her feet to her chest and kicked the boy so hard he rolled over two times. Then she pounced on him and the odd pair rolled straight into the water. Mianshe was angry and this upset her, and Verité for that matter. As they sank into the bay, the young mermaid's curly hair stretched out behind her like a red vine. She grabbed Verité's shirt and with open eyes began searching the waters for a fresh patch of seaweed.

Verité was dying. Mianshe had been towing the boy underneath the water for thirty-eight, thirty-nine, forty seconds and counting. He had to do something and quickly or he was surely going to drown. She kept pulling him under toward the algae beds, so he grabbed a hunk of her hair and yanked it as hard as he could, and she finally released him. Nevertheless, Verité did not release her. He made his way to the surface and onto shore with the hunk of her hair still in his hand.

"I just wanted you to hear the boo-boos!" she screamed. Mianshe was so full of rage she ripped up her father's boo-boo necklace and began to weep. She cried, then sobbed and wept, and continued wailing all the more.

"You are nuts! You're a mean crazy, *folle*, stupid, crazy girl!" shouted Verité. Then he began to silently think, in the loudest silence he could muster, every mermaid insult he could come up with, accompanied by the meanest ugly-faces he could possibly make to punctuate his point. When he caught his breath, he stood up and wiped the sand off of his pants and ran up the sacred fig tree.

"Not again," sighed the tree. "You must belong to the Prince," said the tree to the boy.

Nothing in Librebe could shock Verité anymore. Not talking trees or angry mermaids, or lion-eating kings and queens, or people who didn't speak to you for a year and then decided to talk your ear off for hours, not sweet one minute but mean the next little sisters, and especially not a big old talking tree with skin thicker than an elephant's. Nothing could shock the boy anymore!

"I understand," said the tree sympathetically, and then the tree respectfully said nothing at all, until the boy finally relaxed and fell deeply asleep.

The moon was almost at its highest point in the evening sky. As it rose, its light shined down on the tree, illuminating the hunks of seaweed strewn around its base.

"Little boy, little boy," the tree said again. "Everyone is looking for you. Look!" And sure enough, there were lit torches bobbing up and down in the woods.

"What time is it?" Verité asked.

"It is late enough that one needs to light a torch," said the tree.

"Am I in trouble?" asked the boy.

"With whom?" the tree asked.

"With the Prince," replied the boy.

"Oh, him," said the tree.

"She tried to drown me!" exclaimed the boy.

"Don't get angry with me," said the tree.

"But it's true!" cried Verité.

"I know that, young one," the tree gently said. "And she is very sorry."

"Oh, what do you know," said the boy. Verité was angry all over again.

"I know you are a great deal like the Prince. I know he will not hurt you. I know he is worried sick, and I know she is truly sorry for what she did," answered the tree.

"Mianshe! Verité!" screamed the Prince in the distance.

"Oh no, he is going to kill me!" said Verité.

"He will not kill you," said the tree with great compassion. The tree remembered being young hundreds of years ago, and then he erased the thought from his consciousness. What good would an old tree's memories do to help a young boy up a tree?

"Where is Mianshe?" asked the boy with great trepidation.

"She is still sleeping," answered the tree.

"What!" exclaimed the boy? Now he was truly terrified. "Oh no, he is going to kill me for sure," he said, but before the tree could speak, he ran up its limbs further into the night sky.

"Mianshe! Verité!" hollered the Prince again.

The prince was getting frustrated. Since having children he'd lost them twice, been vomited on and ridiculed by the community and he had slept less than when he was studying for his final exams at university. He had no privacy and worry had become his constant companion. Raising children was difficult.

"Children answer me now!" screamed the Prince. He was truly getting angry.

The Herb-Woman was having a hard time keeping up. Her body was not created for walking up and down. It liked to sway side to side, but the prince insisted she come with him in case the children had eaten duduju again. She'd never heard of the vile substance, but she wasn't going to let the prince know of her ignorance, so with a smile she grabbed her sack of remedies and followed him out into the woods. She was sure that no matter what the children ate, a good tablespoon of oil would slide it right out anyway.

"Mi-an-she!" screamed the Prince once more, but no one answered. The prince sat down and tried to calm himself and the plump and extremely grateful Herb-Woman collapsed right beside him.

"Thank you, my Prince," she panted. "This is a good place to wait for the children," she said between gulps of much needed air.

However, the prince sat in complete silence. He was in thought and this thought excited him. "Of course!" he said, and he jumped to his feet in one hop.

The Herb-Woman groaned and slowly made her way to standing, but by then the prince had sat down again. The woman became even more exasperated. She'd had enough of searching high and low and jumping up and down and screaming and hollering. She was tired, and it was getting late. She should be home having tea on her porch and enjoying the rest of her romance novel, but here she was in the woods being eaten by bugs. She wished she owned a pair of pants or boots like the missionary men. The forest was no place to be in a housedress at night. Your house was where you should be in a housedress, but the prince needed her, so she leaned against the tree and inched her way back to the earth and sat by him once more.

"*Mianshe, wake up,*" toned the Prince from behind his closed eyes.

"*Good morning, Popah,*" toned Mianshe in return. "*Verité and I had a fight and I cried,*" she said before bursting into tears again.

"*Enough, this must stop!*" toned another. "*I am not a fan of salt.*"

"*Who is there?*" the Prince silently demanded. He was not happy to have his thoughts intruded upon.

"*It is I, mountain man. Have you lost another woman?*" toned the tree and with much sarcasm.

"*Popah, make Verité talk to me,*" cried Mianshe.

"*Where are you, little one?*" thought the Prince.

"*She is drowning my roots at present,*" the tree toned.

"*Keep her there with you, my friend. I am on my way.*" And then the prince stopped toning and began to panic. Where was Verité? The prince now knowing something of children, knew this evening's trauma was just beginning. He had to calm himself or he would be of no use to anyone.

"I am not a migrant. I'm a nomad, and nomads are not rude. I don't hit girls!" said Verité and quite loudly. Especially the fact that he did not hit girls, that thought was screamed with such force it made the leaves shake and fall to the ground.

In the quietest, most soothing voice possible the tree silently told the prince to come and get his children.

When the prince arrived, he stopped and bowed to the tree. This created some concern for the Herb-Woman. She loved plants and all things green and growing in the ground but never in her life had she bowed to a remedy. Having children was truly taking its toll on the young prince. As she watched her prince fawn over a tree, she smiled. After seeing all this, she was sure he would pay her well tonight.

"There she is!" exclaimed the Prince.

"Yes," sighed the Herb-Woman.

"Hi Popah," said the miserable little mermaid. "Verité is mad at me!" she cried holding the word 'me' for so long and in an octave so high that the leaves on the tree started to curl back toward their branches.

"It's okay, little one," the Prince consoled. "Where is Verité?" His daughter slowly lifted her arm and pointed up toward the top of the tree. The prince, the mermaid and the Herb-Woman, even the tree tried to convince Verité to come down, but he refused to descend.

"What are you going to do now?" asked the Herb-Woman.

"We can't leave him there," cried Mianshe.

"Verité, please, I am sorry," said the Prince. Then he muttered under his breath that he wasn't sure why he was sorry, and this sent the boy scurrying further up the tree.

"*Listen, little boy, you will surely bump your head and fall,*" said the tree. The tree was losing patience with the entire affair.

When all became quiet, Verité stopped moving. Even the Herb-Woman ceased panting. It was an eerie silence, the kind of silence that preceded a storm or a bomb or a horde of locust. Then a voice came through different than any voice he'd heard before.

"*Apologize,*" it quietly but resoundingly said. Everyone heard it. Even the leaves on the trees heard the still quiet voice demanding an apology.

The prince began. "I'm so sorry, Verité. I know you are not a migrant. You are my son, and I am proud of this, and I am proud to be your father."

The Herb-Woman apologized for not knowing how to cure duduju. However, she did say she was sure she could heal all tummy aches the children might have.

The tree quietly toned an apology for scaring the boy and assured him its leaves would gently break his fall.

Mianshe begrudgingly apologized to her mother. "I'm sorry, Merma. I did not mean to punch him, but boo-boos do talk!" And then she shut up, but the wind began to blow in from the sea. It was a strong gale and it was electric! Mianshe grew pale and started to whine. She left her hiding place and rushed and hid underneath her father's armpit.

"*You must not spoil her!*" said Sedina's voice in the wind.

The prince fell to his knees and looked out to sea. He wondered what he'd done in the past to be haunted in this present moment. He looked his daughter in her eyes and demanded an explanation. "What did you do?" "Why is Verité risking his life to get away from you?" he asked.

Mianshe burst into tears again, which made the tree groan and the Herb-Woman suck the air through her teeth.

"I ..." began the young mermaid. "Verité, I'm sorry I pushed you," said the girl.

"*And,*" toned Sedina deep within the sea.

"And I'm sorry I pulled your ears," she said.

"And," said her perturbed father.

"And I'm sorry I held your head under water for so long," yelled Mianshe up to the furthest branches where Verité sat listening.

"Is that all!" said the Herb-Woman in astonishment. She couldn't believe a young girl from anywhere would beat up a boy. The idea was outrageous. "She could have drowned him!" said the Herb-Woman to her

Prince. She thought at the very least the child should be spanked, but she kept that thought to herself.

"*Mianshe*," toned her mother with a sound of disapproval.

Mianshe gathered her courage and looked up into the tree. A warm glow of sincerity and peace washed over her face and she spoke. "Verité you look just like you did when I met you." Then she laughed, but she stopped laughing when Verité pointed out to sea. On the horizon a huge burst of water gushed up like a geyser, then another and another until the bay looked like a million volcanoes had erupted.

"And I love you, Verité! You are my brother and I will love and protect you always," shouted Mianshe. She was scared.

"You're just scared. You're not sorry," Verité shouted back.

Then the sea became still. The prince and the roots woman and even the tree seemed to look at the juvenile mermaid in anticipation of her response.

"Dearest Verité, I need you. You must teach me how to be gentle and kind like you. You were right, I was putting words in the boo-boo's mouth." she said and so sincerely that the monkeys and lizards and even the small animals of prey came out of hiding to see who was speaking.

"Okay, I'll come down," Verité said. He turned around and placed his foot on one branch and then another, but the third branch was very far away. The tree tried to stretch its limbs to meet the boy's foot, but it was a good foot short of its mark, thus Verité slipped and fell.

Mianshe screamed! The prince rushed toward the tree and the Herb-Woman opened her bag and frantically began mixing medicines. The tree stretched its trunk and rustled its leaves and called an abnormally large Goliath heron, which rose into the air and grabbed the boy by his shirt and gently carried him to safety.

Mianshe rushed toward Verité but she caught herself and stopped on her tippy-toes and clapped. "Yeah, Verité! You were so cute when you were falling," she gleefully cried.

The prince picked the boy up and held him tightly. "Are you well? Did you break anything?" he asked with great concern.

Verité had never had a grown man hold him before. In his village only women showed emotion, but since the prince's touch felt nice and sincere, the boy wrapped his arms around him and patted him on his back.

"Look!" said the Herb-Woman.

Everyone turned and looked. The rising sun had created numerous rainbows everywhere the water sprayed.

"Thank you, Sedina," said the Prince as he tapped his heart. "*And thank you, dear tree for taking care of my children,*" he silently toned.

"*Yes, yes of course,*" replied the tree. "*Now you must take them home and wash them or they will be itchy for weeks.*"

Mianshe smiled at her father and tapped her heart center too. Then she rushed over to Verité and covered him with kisses.

"Calm down, Mianshe," Verité said as he smiled.

The prince lifted Verité onto his shoulders and laughed. "Shall we go," he said.

Off they went. Mianshe led tapping her heart all the way and giggling at the vibration it created in her chest. While the prince proudly walked behind her holding an equally proud Verité on his shoulders. The Herb-Woman panted and clutched her bag in her arms like a baby as she plodded along behind them, trying to keep up.

The prince's daughter disturbed the Herb-Woman. It was not because she had the gall to fight a boy or that she came from another element; the roots woman couldn't understand how someone born only a year ago, could look six years old today. If she grew six times faster than their people, the mongrel girl would be as old as she was in six years! Children weren't meant to be equal to an adult. That was why they were children. If an adult could be made in six years, it would change the face of nature forever. This was not good. The Herb-Woman quieted her mind. She was afraid the water-goddess would hear her and drown her in the ocean like her daughter had almost done to the young foreign boy. These were strange times, she thought before ceasing to think at all.

∙∙∙ ⋀ ∙∙∙

CHAPTER 9

The Herb-Woman sat on her porch smoking a pipe of mullein leaf. Being out in the forest had congested her lungs so she used the medicinal herb to agitate the mucous and push it through. She was pondering last night's events. She was impressed with how the prince handled the stress of being a father. She was also astounded by the young boy's determination for justice, but she was furious at the water child's odd behavior. If she had been successful she would've killed the boy, and the membrane that grew between her toes was disgusting. They didn't know she'd seen it, but she did. It grew and connected one toe to the other whenever water touched them. If she transmuted every time she mixed with water, who's to say what kind of beast she would become? What if her totem was the shark!

The woman had gotten herself all riled up again. How could a water-being cohabitate with land-beings? Librebeings were lamb-like people. They did not start wars or sacrifice blood to gods. They did not banter to solve a problem or send plagues. They did not colonize or enslave one's will. They did not mutilate their women or scar their men. They followed the sun and were cleansed by the rain. They learned to dance like the wind, and they listened to the wisdom of the fire. They were people of the earth—strong, brown, rich and fertile. They were ancestors of the star people. They were all kings and queens. They were not beasts!

The Herb-Woman felt anxious. She wanted to talk with someone about all she'd seen but whom? Who could she confide in? The Fire-Tender and his daughter were so blinded by loyalty to the royal family they would never discuss it. Of this she was sure. Plus, the possibility of Adisa becoming queen meant they wouldn't tolerate any warnings regarding the prince's alien daughter. They would deem her words as unkind. Not to mention they were important enough to discredit her in the eyes of the community. She knew telling the elders wouldn't change anything either. The elders were sheep. They wouldn't take action even if you set them on fire. The only person who would take her warning serious would be the Man-of-Medicine.

The roots woman hopped up and ran in a circle three times to the left and then three times to the right. "Aye yee!" she muttered to herself over and over again. She remembered something. She remembered the reading she did for the queen that said a woman from the red sea would drown the prince's desires. She was told the marriage would be delayed. It said there would be a great storm.

"Oh, no!" sighed the Herb-Woman. Now she knew what she must do. She had to take the medicine man as her confidant and reveal what she saw if she was going to stop the deluge that was sure to come.

⚜ ⋀ ⚜

The Man-of-Medicine went into his back room and began organizing all his tools. He smudged his bowls with sweet grass and copal and arranged them by their elemental uses. He oiled his cobalt bowl so the water wouldn't seep in. He took the lava stone cup and burned it in a cast iron pot and placed it in the east to catch the morning sunlight. Next, he picked up the conch shell and blew into three times before setting it on top of the altar near the open window so it would sing with the wind. Finally, it was time for his favorite tool. The one he inherited from his grandfather. It was a red clay urn, centuries old and seasoned by medicine men of great reputation. It was this urn that poured the waters and shook the seas thus stopping the colorless men from invading the village. Its strong medicine carried the slave traders back to their hell. Thus, with great respect he took the urn from its resting place and went outside. He sat on the cool earth under the moonlight and buried it facing west.

After looking over his sacred lodge one last time, the Man-of-Medicine closed the door and went into the yard. He placed a kettle on the fire and brewed himself a cup of English tea. He'd never been fond of the colorless men, but he found their use of spices and distilled spirits to be most exhilarating. He sat down facing the entryway and sipped his Earl Grey. The mole that burrowed into the straw matting of his bed told him she was coming. Now all he had to do was wait.

✷ ⋀ ✷

It was waning into the Scorpion new moon cycle. The Herb-Woman knew there would be no better time to uncover and reveal the truth. If she understood what was going on, she'd have a chance of finding its remedy, but she had to be careful, even with her own daughter. She wouldn't want anyone to think she was conspiring with the Man-of-Medicine. Everyone in the village was secretly afraid of him. They'd seen what he was capable of, so they knew to stay on his good side. The king thought he had the villagers respect, but they revered him with a mixture of fear and awe. It was a bad mix because it gave the medicine man too much power and power always distorted the truth.

Emadi waited for her mother to address her before pouring her tea. Her mother was a stickler for it being hot. She liked it so hot it scalded the roof of your mouth. Her mother had developed resilience to boiling water. Emadi imagined it was like the fingers of the Senegalese women in town who used the Marcel irons to straighten hair. They could heat those copper irons until they were molten and then they would comb through it while holding the burning tress until it moved like corn silk and they did this with their bare hands.

"Pour, chile. I'm ready," said the irritated Herb-Woman.

"I'm sorry. I was just…" said Emadi, but before she could explain herself her mother took the pot from her hands and poured the tea.

"What? You were just daydreaming again?" she curtly said. The Herb-Woman hated to belittle her child, but she needed a reason to leave the house and it had to be a reason where she wouldn't want to follow her to clear things up.

160

The next step was going to be difficult. The woman knew her daughter. She knew the tea was going to be piping hot. She also knew she was going to have to hold that hot tea in her mouth long enough to prove to her it was tepid. She knew it was going to burn but it wasn't going to hurt half as bad as hurting her daughter's feelings.

The Herb-Woman quietly exhaled and then gulped the boiling liquid. She swished the tea around in her mouth and then spat it out on the ground. "You think that's hot!" she said scolding her daughter, and it was a hard ruse to pull off because when she opened her mouth to complain the steam from the hot tea exited like a speeding locomotive.

"I ask for one thing, girl and that's for my tea to be hot!" she said. And then she stomped off the porch out of the yard and onto the path toward the medicine man's hut.

The Man-of-Medicine was just about ready to give up. He wondered if maybe he should throw the bones again but decided against it. It was never a good idea to doubt one's medicine. The medicine man went inside and got a clean nightshirt. He was going to bed. He never liked sleeping with the day's energy soaked in his clothes, so he always changed into a clean shirt before retiring. He knew it was a luxury and a waste of good soap and water but when he didn't do it he didn't sleep well. As he was putting on his blue and white striped linen pajama top he got on his last birthday from one of his sons, he heard footsteps outside.

"Bba Temne," the Herb-Woman quietly said. Then she waited.

The medicine man smiled as he buttoned up his shirt and made his way towards the voice. He was right. It was a woman the animal spirits saw visiting. He took a deep breath and centered himself before opening the door.

"Good evening, Mma Ellen," he replied using the same honorable greeting she had bestowed upon him.

"Oh, Bba, I am so sorry you were getting ready for bed," she whined. "Excuse me."

"No, it's the perfect time. Please, come in," he said.

"I promise I won't keep you up for long," she said. Although she knew this was a conversation that needed finessing and careful diplomacy and that was going to take some time.

"Can I get you some nice hot bush tea?" asked the Man-of-Medicine. He knew how much the woman loved a good cup of tea or should he say, a good hot cup of herbs. The Herb-Woman wouldn't drink anything that didn't come from the woods around the village and as she got older her preference narrowed to those things she grew in her own backyard and she would never mix her infusions with milk or sugar.

"Please make no fuss on my account, Bba," she replied.

"Well it's no fuss at all. I would love a nice cup myself. I even have your personal favorite, your homegrown mint tea." The medicine man filled his teapot with the fresh mint. When the water had come to a rapid boil, he steeped the herbs until their scent burst open, filling the room with its stimulating aroma. Then he began pouring the hot tea into one glass and then the other until ribbons of steam surrounded both of them. Satisfied the mixture was just perfect he gave her a glass.

"Here's something for tomorrow morning. It's my special blend," said the Herb-Woman. She lifted her mature breasts over her taunt belly and pulled a small package out of her pocket. It was a lovely array of Kinkeliba bush tea mixed with hibiscus and cardamom.

"Thank you, Ellen. Shall we have this instead?" asked the medicine man.

"No, Temne. That is for you and you alone," she said.

The medicine man could feel the love she'd put in the package. It was so strong that Ellen's image in her yellow flowered dress came to mind. She could have had any man she wished in her life, but she stayed in Librebe to take care of the king. What a waste of pure feminine energy.

"Have you eaten, Mma?" he asked. "Can I get you a little something to soak in your tea?" The medicine man sweetly smiled at the woman and waited. He knew if she accepted, the sugar would have its way and he would have all the information he needed. The sweet would also make her excited and then things would go much faster.

"Thank you, but Emadi has just fed me to bursting. Ah, this tea is good and hot, perfect for digesting my daughter's meat pie," she said.

The man wished he'd made English tea. He could see this was going to be a long evening and the stimulant of the black leaf would have been very helpful to him.

"How is Emadi?" he asked. He was stalling, or better yet priming the proverbial pump before starting. All mothers loved talking about their children. It made them feel worthy and nurtured themselves. "She has grown into a very lovely lady," he added.

"Thank you. Yes, she is a good woman and she does good by me," she quietly said.

The Herb-Woman had to erase the last image of her daughter from her mind. She could still see the pain in her eyes and feel her shame at being chastised. Emadi was a sensitive girl and did everything in her power to please her so she wouldn't have to endure the humiliation of being criticized.

"Children are our riches. They will take over all that is left when we leave. And they will take our memories into the future," she said with such sincerity it sent a shiver down the Man-of-Medicine's spine. "Do you trust the children to do a good job?" she asked.

This was not going where the man thought it was going to go at all. This was deeper. The Herb-Woman believed something was ripping at the core of not only the community, but the entire tradition of the Librebe people. She'd seen the destruction of their lives from the ancestors to the children yet to be born. If he'd been a fearful man, he would have been scared right now.

"Yes," he replied but with none of the sincerity that the roots woman had when asking him. "On the whole I think the children will carry on as we've been carrying on since we entered Amma's womb." Then he stopped talking. He knew his words didn't come from his heart. He was trying to solve things with his mind. Things were changing, and they were changing fast.

"Maybe," said the woman. The Herb-Woman didn't have the old

shaman's confidence that things would go on as before. She felt it changing. She knew exactly when a change was coming from within nature. In only a few hours after coupling, she could tell by a small vein on the side of a woman's neck that she was with child. Life changes everything and the change she was feeling was in the belly of Great Mother herself. It reached from the bottom of her oceans to the heights of Father Sun. This change was not coming from nature. It was coming from behind the veil of nature. Did he not feel it? The Herb-Woman took another sip of tea and calmed her mind. It had never occurred to her that she might be the only person feeling the seasonal change that included the entire heavens, but that was a lot more than she could address over tea and after sunset.

"Uncle, if you don't mind too much, I would love a biscuit," she said. She was stalling.

"Of course, Auntie, of course," he replied as he went into the back for the tin of cookies. He felt uneasy. Whatever the woman had seen or dreamt had changed her so much she felt everything was going to change. What kind of premonition upsets tradition? The Man-of-Medicine continued thinking and arranging the cookies on the plate over and over again. Now he was scared.

The woman sat as still as a church mouse in her chair and watched the medicine man arrange the cookies on the tray. Most people would simply pull the tin off the shelf and present it opened for the guest to take as many or as little as they wished, especially if the visitor had dropped by unannounced. This was different. The Man-of-Medicine was anxious. Why? Just moments ago, he was his most confident, albeit arrogant self but now he was acting like an apprentice.

"Here. They are ginger. They go nicely with the mint," he said.

The Man-of-Medicine placed the plate on the table in front of the woman. If she picked a cookie from the outside he would wait until she felt comfortable to tell him what was truly on her mind, however if she chose one from the center, he would get his bones and put an end to all this suspense.

The Herb-Woman reflected on all that had passed since her arrival and it came to her. The medicine man was worried too. As she considered how she should proceed next, the woman reached for a cookie. Enough beating around the bush, she thought, as she took a bite out of the ginger biscuit from the center of the pile.

The Man-of-Medicine slowly stood and went into his back room. When he returned the Herb-Woman was standing as well.

"Is everything alright?" she asked. "Shall I be going?"

"No, you should stay. Please stay and tell me what is really in your heart. I too feel a change coming. Now whether it is a good change or a bad one has not been decided so I went to get the bones. Do you mind?" he asked.

"What a brilliant idea. I knew I should come to you," she said. The Herb-Woman was relieved.

"Shall we?" he asked as he sat down on his ceremonial rug. When the roots woman had settled down beside him, he smudged them both with sacred copal and frankincense. Afterward, he sat with his eyes closed shaking the bones between his cupped hands for a long time.

While the medicine man incanted the ancestors, the Herb-Woman covertly moved her crystals around inside her bra until they formed a heart shape over her breasts. She still didn't feel comfortable working with the powerful shaman, but she would do it for the sake of the village. She silently called on her personal spirit guides and asked them to protect her. What if together they uncovered the source of the shifting and made it stable again, would the medicine man use the opportunity to push her out? Would he take all the credit for uncovering the real story behind the strange children? Yes, he would do this and more because his only loyalty was to power. She knew this. All medicine men were this way otherwise they were ineffectual. You needed a huge ego to take on the out-of-body, or possessed or demonic spirits inhabiting the other worlds, and if they made it into your world, you had better be absolutely deluded into believing you were the only one able to send them back.

The medicine man mustered up all his power and focused on one thing. What is creating the doubt present everywhere? It was the most diplomatic way he could phrase his question so everything would be revealed. As he threw open his hands another doubt entered his mind. Why hadn't he felt the shifting before? He had a small inkling when the villagers panicked about the water child, but he hadn't felt the actual thread ripping them from their ancestors.

As the bones fell they clattered like dominoes on the earthen floor, and when each one dropped it stuck immediately. It was a strange pattern. One the man had never seen before. It was as if each bone was going in a different direction even though they made little clumps here and there. He used eight bones. It was a technique he inherited from his father who had inherited the way from the star people. Eight was their most important number.

The first bone, which was a piece of driftwood found inside an alligator, looked like a finger pointing due north. To its left and moving west was a flat bone that looked like a scapula. It was alone by itself too. Next, two bones landed together in the southwest, underneath and to the left of the others. It was a frail connection where the two bones met, but it formed an impressive shape. They looked like they were pulling away from each other. Only their ends touched. They formed the shape of a cauldron but with only one leg. It was a total oxymoron—a bold shape formed by a weak union. Next (and the oddest one of all) was a small bird shaped bone. It went flying out, far away from the rest. It went hurling up and to the right of the others. It looked so happy and free. However, it looked as if it was moving away from the other bones' formation, further from earth or beneath it depending on which direction you sat. This bone troubled the medicine man.

Finally, the last three bones that fell east of the others but remained one unit. One bone was flat and resembled a stone with a plant like fossil imbedded on it. It was the bone that represented all life. It was nestled between the feminine bone that resembled a woman's entryway and the male bone that protruded forward in two directions—one end went south and the other shot upward toward the heavens. But the female bone was on the right of the life-stone. This was not good. The female energy always rested on the left, toward the moon but in this casting the male sat on the left and the female on the right.

"What does it mean?" asked the Herb-Woman.

"I don't know," answered the Man-of-Medicine.

The man tried to explain to the best of his ability how the bones seemed to be spiraling upward. It was as if they were ascending. They were all following the small bird-like bone that flew off to meet the sun in the east. It was such an exotic pattern that the man was frightened to read what he saw.

"Things are changing more than we ever thought. We are going upwards towards the stars now. We are going to meet the Sun."

"What? What does that mean? Is it a bad thing? Will we all be burned? Is the anvil coming down on us?" shrieked the woman.

"No, dear sister, we are going to meet the anvil. We are going to return to Nummo!" he quietly exclaimed.

"Nummo! Nummo is the water god that comes from Amma! We are going to return to water! How do we do that? Water cannot be separated. One drop is equal to all others. To become water, we must merge with it and that means drowning, Temne!" said the woman with more fear than she'd ever felt in her life.

Librebeings lived in the mountains above the shore. They migrated there because the savage coastline protected them from the slave traders and pirates, but the deep rocky coastline meant they couldn't travel to sea, not without a motorboat with a strong engine. Granted Librebeings were fisherman, but they were not divers. They never ate the fish in shells that lived on the bottom or those that attached themselves to rocks. Those they left for the other fish. Plus, the wild coastline made entering the bay almost impossible. The current was so strong it brought the boats in too fast and threw them against the rocks. That was why the canal had been so important to their people. It allowed access to the beach where they wouldn't have to carry their supplies up the rocky crag.

The Herb-Woman tried to remember all the stories the fishermen told her about their relations in the oceans, but only the bad stories came to mind. Those stories of floods and waves so high they erased all life on earth. She had to tell the medicine man everything she'd experienced with the child of water. This was not the time to be silent. She had to warn him of the water-mother and her power to move the seas. It was time to reveal all she knew. If they were to survive, they had to stick together; maybe even become one with the Fermemi community. She had to think realistically now and tolerate differences so they would live.

The Herb-Woman waited until the man went through his personal memories before speaking again. She gently touched him on his arm and began her story. She was finally explaining why she'd come. She told him of the sea-child's temper and of her mother's powers and how they spoke to each other without talking. She even mentioned the bad, duduju the children had eaten and how it made them sick. And then she said the thing she never wanted to say aloud. "She has enchanted our Prince, and when he becomes king she will rule, I am sure." Then she stopped speaking and began rocking from side to side.

It was a long time before the Man-of-Medicine responded to the Herb-Woman's story. He sat looking up at the moon before turning his eyes toward the woman. "It is late. We will not solve this tonight. Please go rest now and I will pray on these things." The man stood up and escorted the woman out into the yard.

"Ellen, please let this be between us for the moment," he said.

"Of course, Temne, of course," she said before covering her head with her shawl and secretly making her way down the path toward home.

◈ ⋀ ◈

CHAPTER 10

As he waited for the kettle to whistle, the medicine man poured out the rest of his mint tea. He needed to think and to do that he needed to be awake. He had a couple of hours before his quiet time when his ruling planet passed overhead. It was the time he was born. It was his personal time, the perfect time to summon the ancestors. He needed to ask them for clarification on the bone reading. He had no idea what it meant but he felt whatever it was; it was going to be monumental. The Herb-Woman thought it was a message solely for the village. That was good because he knew this message was a lot larger than that, much larger.

The kettle screamed before hissing and the sound made the shaman drop one of his favorite tools. This wasn't a good omen. An eagle feather should never touch the ground. He picked up the feather and went outside to smudge it in the smoke coming off the fire. The fire was almost out and its hot embers cast an orange hue over everything. It was eerie, truly strange but the man couldn't look away. Then something moved in the fire.

"Temne," it softly called.

The medicine man stood transfixed by the dying flames. He heard it say his name. He hated being tricked, and he despised being confused even more. Today he'd not only been baffled by the Herb-Woman's visit, the strange bone reading had stumped him too. Now a fire was summoning him!

"It is not the fire, Temne. You are not of the Fire-Tender's lineage," it crooned.

The medicine man stood completely still. Not only did this thing he could not see talk to him, it talked about him. What was this entity? What kind of spirit dared enchant a medicine man? Did it not know he had his own powers and gifts?

"Temne, listen to me. I am that you are. I am whom you've been calling on all these years. I am a part of you so old it has seen what you are searching for. Ask me your question," it said. Then the last flame subsided, and all that rested was a small clump of bright orange embers.

The medicine man started to feel uneasy, so he planted both feet hip distance apart and grounded himself in the earth. He didn't like anyone telling him what to do much less a strange fire spirit who hid in orange ashes.

"L o o k," it said, so slowly the word seemed to extend to the ocean.

The Man-of-Medicine did not look. He had no time to speak with precocious entities. He took his black tourmaline crystal from his medicine bag and raised his clenched fist high into the sky and circled counter-clockwise around the fire six times. As he silently prayed in all directions, he made sure to cloak his thoughts from the strange intruder in the orange flame. When he was finished with his rite of protection he grabbed the kettle and went back into the house. Enough, he thought. He'd had enough mystery and warnings for one day. He needed to do some research. He had to chart the sky and follow the lineage plus now he'd have to prepare some protection amulets.

The Man-of-Medicine remembered he hadn't eaten in quite some time, so he went into the pantry and got himself a hand full of nuts, a couple of biscuits and some antelope jerky to get him through the long night's work ahead. Pouring everything inside a small gourd he resumed making his tea. He opened his cupboard and pulled out his Brown Betty teapot and the strong black tea from England the prince had given him. As he was adding some milk and sugar an orange streak of color ran past him. "What the…" but the man never got to finish his thought before being stunned into silence. There before him was the oddest thing he'd ever seen. It was an orange lizard standing on its hind legs and it had a large and quite erect webbed mane circling its face.

"You may close your mouth now," it said. "I am you and you are me and I am called Frill Lebo."

The Man-of-Medicine was in shock. He had no idea what was going on but today was like no other. "How dare you use the name of our first ancestor, demon!" screamed the Man-of-Medicine, but when he went to strike the strange reptile everything stood still, including his raised arm.

The medicine man was transported into the night sky. He floated far above his home with his rigid arm still in a mid-swat position. He tried to scream but no sound came out of his open mouth. While the strange lizard that called itself Frill Lebo hopped from one star to the next until it had hop-scotched itself in front of him. He stared at the strange being with great trepidation. He was terrified. Who was this spirit that could pull him out of his earthly body and hold him suspended like stardust in the sky? He was frozen. He was incapable of any movement whatsoever. The only thing he was able to do was to think. He watched the lizard and tried to implore his compassion through silent looks, but the lizard didn't relent to his pleas.

The shaman had never met any being incapable of feeling compassion. He relied on the emotions of his adversaries when dealing with them. Without compassion or pride, or anger and jealousy, or pity and hatred, or any other grandiose reaction of the ego, how was he going to manipulate an outcome? Then the lizard did something even more bizarre. He jumped up and kicked the man three times on his forehead, and once on his crown and then it bit him in his crotch. "Ayyyeeeee!" screamed the medicine man.

The Man-of-Medicine bolted awake. "Ahhhmma," he groaned through clenched teeth. He surveyed his surroundings. He was home. It was almost noon. The sun was high in the sky, but he was shivering. His nightshirt was soaked all the way through and had stuck itself to the mattress cover. He was shaking under his blanket as he looked out his window onto a beautiful sunny day. He tried to use his teeth to scrape the night's toxins from his tongue, but he couldn't open his mouth to do so.

Since his body was still in shock, he tried thinking instead. "What happened last night?" was the first thought that entered his mind. He tried reconstructing the evening's events in full. He remembered making tea but when he went to get a cup, the fire smoldered and streaked like badly dyed clothing. "But there is no fire pit in a cupboard," he thought and aloud. And as if on cue, the orange lizard came back. He hopped down from the medicine man's nightstand and bit him on his forehead forcing his memory to return. Then the strange entity spoke to him again.

"I am Frill Lebo. A snake ate me when I came into this world. I have traveled many universes to talk to you. So listen!" it said.

Now the medicine man's mouth would not close. He tried shutting it, but he was too in awe of the apparition to manage it. The orange lizard was directly in front of him, standing on its hind legs and with a hop it jumped up and vomited symbols into the medicine man's wide-open mouth. Some of the symbols he recognized but others were foreign to him and the odd symbols tasted bitter. As he swallowed Frill Lebo's regurgitated message he watched his mouth fall down to the floor, and then up and down all over again. His jaw pumped like a bellow and as quickly as his mouth chewed the exotic forms, it just as quickly pumped them back out all strung together like clothes on a line. It was most strange indeed. It read:

> As we rise to the occasion
> The lake shall swallow the sea
> And all our relations
> Will be wed for eternity

Then moving his lips like a drawbridge, the old shaman's mouth slowly began to close but before his bottom lip touched the upper, Frill Lebo bounced eight times and jumped into his shrinking orifice and for the first time that day (or the evening before for that matter) the medicine man's mouth was completely closed.

The shaman was fully awake now and he felt truly nauseous. He wanted some nice mint tea to calm his belly, but the smell of mint made him remember the entire evening all over again and his stomach tightened even more. He didn't have time for stomach troubles. He had to keep his vision fresh. He was entrusted with a most important message and he couldn't lose it like a hunk of biscuit dunked in a hot cup of tea.

"Remember," he vowed. "I must remember the message." The medicine man got up and grabbed a handful of soup beans and began recreating the cryptic message on the dirt floor. As he reconstructed the strange symbols to the best of his memory, he recited aloud the verbal message Frill Lebo had given him. "As we rise to the occasion," he mumbled. He didn't understand what the weird little lizard was trying to tell him, however he was sure if he repeated it enough times, the message itself would tell him what he needed to know. But each time he said the double couplets of verse his stomach would cramp. Finally, he gave up and collapsed on the floor.

As he lay on the cool earth he continued reconstructing the bone reading from the previous day's visit with the Herb-Woman. He cautiously crawled around the room. He had to clear his mind to keep his drawing intact while keeping the lizard's regurgitated symbols separate. But circling around the room on his knees while thinking about lizards made him feel sick all over again. He needed medicine and it had to be something strong.

Making sure to use the eastern door, he crawled into his granary and dragged himself around the circle. He started wide and ended up in the center of the lodge. It seemed to take forever to manage the twenty-five-foot spiral to the middle of the room, however he made it. Once there, he began digging. He dug until he found what he was looking for. It was wrapped in the caul from his birth. The thin membrane of his mother's birth sac did not break when he was born. It stayed with him into this world, enabling him to see into other worlds beyond. He peeled back the casing of dried skin and looked at his most precious amulet. It was a little drum made from a lizard's hide. He inherited it from his first ancestors. But why was their first ancestor haunting him now?

He took the drum and played the first word the Nummo gave them. The Nummo were primordial spirits. They were watery pure beings that brought order out of chaos. They gave his first ancestor the little lizard drum that made a big sound. The sound rang out like morning thunder and sent out its warning of a storm that was sure to come.

⋙ ⋀ ⋘

CHAPTER 11

Mianshe didn't understand why she couldn't sleep, but she couldn't. She had apologized to her land brother and she'd been most sincere; so sincere that he slept deeply on his cot undisturbed. She wanted to wake him up and tell him about her dream, but she was afraid of how he would react. Having one's dreams interrupted was never very nice. Even if one's dream was scary, it was always better to see it through to its end. Equoo told her that and he was one wise seahorse. She missed him. She missed her sea family. Maybe that was the reason she couldn't sleep. Maybe she was seasick.

Mianshe slid out of bed and walked through the quiet house. Her father was in bed asleep on his side. He looked funny. His lopsided face emitted a tiny stream of saliva and his tongue twitched. She wondered what he was dreaming about, so she sat on the floor beside his bed and listened to his thoughts fly in and out his mind like little kites. He was watching her mother swim away. Now he was asking himself how got pregnant from his loving thoughts. Then Adisa entered his dream dressed in blue and her image froze there. Mianshe immediately stood up and scurried off into the kitchen. She wasn't sure if spying on her father while he slept was such a good idea. There are some things that were better left unknown, especially concerning a land father.

"What are you doing up, chile?" asked Nanny Leboya. The wee mermaid had startled the old woman sitting at the kitchen table drinking tea in the moonlight. "Don't you feel well? Are you scared?" she asked.

"No," replied Mianshe. She didn't mean to sound impertinent, but she just didn't have any other answer for that question. She really had no idea why she wasn't sleepy.

"Me too," said Nanny. "I can't sleep either."

After that the old woman's voice trailed off so Mianshe took it as a sign to disappear too. She quietly slipped out of the kitchen and returned to her sweet grass mat on the floor near her brother. He was deeply asleep, and he was smiling. He was dreaming of camels. Mianshe didn't think it was a pleasant dream. It didn't make her smile in the least. She thought the camels smelled awful and they had those big eyes that followed you around while they chewed. She was imagining them eating her when she felt another pair of eyes on her.

"Stop it," said a sleepy voice. "I can see you," said Verité as he slowly sat up on his elbows.

"I can't sleep," she said in her loud whisper that sounded more like a hiss.

Mianshe didn't know what to do so she grabbed her blanket and went out onto the porch and sat down on the steps. The night air was cool, and it felt good. She spied a little field mouse building a nest in a pile of old sticks, so she watched it for the longest time. It comforted her. He didn't think, or maybe the mouse was a she. When the little mouse rolled onto his back and laughed at the idea of being a girl, Mianshe got truly irritated. She was not fond of being laughed at, so she threw a rock at the little rodent and sent him scurrying into the woods.

She didn't understand. What was wrong with being a girl? She liked being a girl. Her body made circles and her voice could reach octaves beyond. Her hair grew where it was supposed to grow, and she could cry and rinse bad thoughts away whenever she wished. In fact, she was crying right now.

"What's wrong?" asked Verité as he sat down beside her on the steps. Then he yawned and asked, "Why are you crying?"

"Because I can," she said in between sniffling. But when she talked at the same time as she cried a piece of mucous got caught in her nose and made her sound like a duck. "Don't you laugh at me!" quacked Mianshe.

Verité wasn't laughing. He felt sorry for his sister. "Here," he said. "Blow." Verité pulled a wad of tissue from inside the sleeve of his pajamas. "Blow," he repeated.

"Blow what, through what? I am not a whale, brother," chirped Mianshe.

Verité took a little piece of the tissue and pressed it against his nose and blew but nothing came out. "Here. Now you do it," he said.

"Why?" Mianshe asked.

"Because there's something in there," said Verité.

"What?" she asked in alarm.

"That," he said pointing to a little lump hanging from her nostril.

Mianshe took her finger and dug the little morsel of clumped mucous from her nose and stared at it. "Why is that there?" she asked with great curiosity.

"So, it's not in there," Verité said with a touch of frustration. He was tired, and he didn't feel like educating his sister about being human. If he had felt like teaching at three in the morning, he probably would have started with whispering had zero, if anything at all to do with hissing, or that spying on people while they slept was truly rude. What if he was having a conversation with his personal guide or his angels or an old ancestor had come to tell him how to find his way home, or someplace without whining mermaids.

"What do I do with it?" she asked as she stared at it in the moonlight.

"Throw it away," he sighed. He could not believe she was still holding it. "But it's mine," she replied.

Verité couldn't believe his ears. Not only was he awake having this ridiculous conversation, he was awake at three in the morning in his pajamas on the front porch still looking at the booger in question. "Keep it if you wish! I don't care what you do with it. But people will think you are a dirty girl!" he said, making a point to hiss at her like she did and frequently.

"Why?" she asked. Mianshe was in shock. Why would anyone call her a dirty girl? Where she came from that wasn't even a possibility.

"I-don't-care-what-you-do-with-it," said Verité as he calmly punctuated his words.

Mianshe thought about this for a moment. Then she did what most children do. She flicked it. "There, dirty boy!" she hissy-fitted at him. She was happy that the issue was finally resolved.

"Shhh, you are going to wake everyone up," he said. It was slightly louder than he'd wished so he placed his hand over his sister's mouth in case she decided to answer back.

Mianshe felt odd. She felt like someone else was there, and this someone had a strong smell. The smell was so intense it made her see orange.

"*Someone is watching us,*" she toned in a soft voice.

"Who?' asked Verité. He released his grip on his sister and quickly looked around the square to see if the neighbors were up watching them from behind their curtains.

"Not who, what. It's large and it smells strong like blubber or oil glands, but it's not fish." she said in the most curious voice.

"What!" exclaimed Verité?

The lights went on in the prince's bedroom and in the kitchen and around several other houses in the village as well. Verité grabbed Mianshe and rushed into the house and hopped back into bed, before noticing his sister's blanket was still on the front porch. If they went to get it now, they would surely be caught so he lifted his cover and pulled her inside. As he pulled her towards him, he made sure to keep his hand over her mouth the entire time. He could hear the prince and nanny discussing the noise and with every step he heard approaching their room, Verité rocked his sister in his arms.

Mianshe tried to clear her mind of all thoughts. She had to calm down. She didn't want her father to hear her heart beating, so she thought about rainbows. She imagined all kinds of rainbows; the circle ones in soap bubbles, snowflake rainbows, and the rainbows in quartz crystals, teardrop rainbows and heat induced rainbows, oil slick rainbows and of course the rainbow that comes after rain.

The prince quietly entered the children's room and smiled at them nestled together like an old married couple. He could tell Verité was trying to avoid Mianshe's fish breath as much as she was trying to avoid her brother's sweaty armpit. Satisfied all was okay the prince returned to his room and immediately fell back to sleep.

Grateful for their narrow escape, Verité toned a thought to his sister. *"Are you awake?"* he thought.

"Yes," she replied.

"Did you have a bad dream?" he quietly implored.

"No. I just woke up," she toned back. *"The stranger isn't human."* Then she added, *"I'm sorry I watched you and your camels."*

"What camels?" He quietly asked, as he smelled the air around him and tried to remember if he'd seen any unusual tracks in the earth lately.

"The ones in the field with the big eyes," she answered.

"All camels have big eyes, Mianshe," he said as he yawned and gently started drifting back to sleep, but not before he wrapped his thin arms around his sister and whispered, "Don't play with boogers. They are not good for you. They catch all the dirt in the air. That is why we blow them out."

Mianshe smiled and toned, *"Thank you."* She liked having a big brother. Even though he laughed at her, he didn't want others to mock her. *"I love you, Verité."* she toned before falling peacefully asleep.

As Verité felt his sister's heart beating, he smiled and fell deeper into slumber, and he continued smiling as he listened to his sister confess her love for him over and over again until she slowly sank into a dark abyss where a huge tsunami washed her and the entire village away from view.

CHAPTER TWELVE

Sedina gasped. Her body went rigid and thrust itself upward into the dark sea.

"Whoa, silly. Wait!" screamed Equoo. The poor seahorse was not used to such a rude awakening. Only moments ago, he'd been peacefully sleeping in her hair. Now he was being shot out into the open sea like octopi ink. Of course, it was a silly analogy because octopi squirt more than shoot, but it was the perfect description from a seahorse being catapulted awake. However, the mermaid hadn't awakened yet. She was still asleep and darting around the ocean like a deranged jellyfish and Equoo was having a terrible time holding on.

"Sedina, wake up!" he screamed, but the screams of a seahorse don't carry very far, especially in open seas.

Equoo had to wake her up and quickly before they entered hostile waters. They were headed directly toward the area where the large vessels sailed, and the large ships had torturing devices. They had machines that sent out sounds to confuse you, so you wouldn't be able to distinguish a net from a reef. The noise drove you insane until you beached yourself in agony to get away from the hideous screech. That sound could split your ears in two. "Well in four," thought Equoo. Being one has two ears, but why was he lecturing himself on math right now. If he didn't wake the mermaid soon, they were going to end up at some Hu-man's fish fry. Hu-men were unethical lazy creatures that would love a mouthful of dead mermaid they didn't have to hunt down. How could they eat dead matter, for that matter? Equoo couldn't understand anything Hu-men did, and he was pretty sure they didn't know why they did the things they did either.

"Sedina! Please wake up!" he screamed, as loudly as seahorse possible.

Sedina darted and bounced off a sand dune and then she ricocheted into a reef. Crack! A huge piece of coral the size of a manatee broke off and began sinking. This was serious. A coral reef took years to grow an inch, yet six feet. The seahorse was truly worried now. His beautiful mermaid had become a Hu-man wrecking ball. He had to do something and fast.

"Silently," he said to himself. "I must intervene in silence." He knew the only way to communicate with someone asleep was to enter that state with them. But what if he forgot what he wanted to say? What if being asleep made him forget his purpose? He had to be able to enter her dream state without forgetting the intention he made when he was awake. Equoo curled himself into a little ball and rolled around her hair as close to her scalp as was possible. Next, he began to clear his mind of all thoughts but one. "Wake up before you get us killed,' he quietly thought. He imagined being caught in the net of a drunken sailor's boat early in the morning and it was a horrible vision.

Sedina woke up a mere hundred feet away from careening into an outrigger trawler and the sonar beep of the fish locator went wild. "What in oceans! Whoa!" she screamed. The mermaid furiously back-paddled as hard as she could. The high-pitched squeal of the sonar device made her heart race. She darted back and forth. She was desperately looking for a gap in the netting before it slowly closed in on them. She had to get out of there and now! The constant drone of the machinery kept pushing against her ears like a terrible migraine and she started to faint. When she blacked out her body began drifting toward the engine's propellers. As her lifeless form began to sink her hair floated upward toward the motor's wake.

Equoo didn't know what to do so he let his instincts shut down all his senses. As they floated toward the blades of the propeller the little seahorse became entangled in her hair like a piece of seaweed. The motor churned. The propeller turned, and the net slowly dragged the unconscious mermaid and seahorse toward the ship.

When all was prepped to haul them aboard the Hu-man's boat the motor stopped, and a low humming sound began. Neither Sedina nor Equoo were aware of the pandemonium going on, on deck. They couldn't see the men rushing about the winches and tightening the main. They'd sunk too far to feel the boat burse from one side and then the other. They'd no idea the aluminum mast holding the rigging had cracked and the large metal spear was now hurling like an arrow straight down into the water. But before they were impaled, a huge pod of humpback dolphins pulled back the trawler's net and dragged them out. Whereby they bounced the mermaid from one snout to the next. The rest of the pod circled around and guided them safely away from the Hu-men's machinery.

Equoo didn't know if he was alive or dead. All he could sense was a constant stream of silver light and the most delightful sound he'd ever heard. He concluded he was dead because he'd never heard such heavenly music in all his years of being. He simply wanted to float in that silvery light and listen to its sound forever. If they had live shrimp there, he was sure he would be the most loyal fan of the Creator from now until eternity ended.

Sedina felt sick. She couldn't understand why she'd taken to such gross displays of nausea, but she seemed to be hurling a lot of late. Maybe she was pregnant again and then she heard it. It was amazing. It was the most peaceful sound she'd ever experienced. She remembered reading a book she'd found that described the angelic realm of Hu-men and in it there was a section on the Seraphim. Those angels could sing so beautifully their Creator surrounded itself with them. That was how the mermaid felt—like she was in the center of angels.

"Wake up. You are not out of trouble yet," cooed a voice.

Sedina sat upright immediately. She opened her eyes but saw nothing out of the ordinary. There was sand on the floor and seaweed floating everywhere. It was cold, but in a comfortably chilly way. Her hair was in a knot above her head and there was beautiful music everywhere. That was when she knew something was wrong.

"Good, you are awake now. That was a very close call, dear mercestor," toned the voice.

Sedina wanted to turn to see who was communicating with her but her neck would not move. "Ooootz!" she cried. "That hurt!"

"*Yes, you have been injured. That is why my family is sending you the healing tones,*" toned the voice. "*Do not fight it. Allow the sound to wash over you and cleanse you of all pain. Unfortunately, the knot on your head will remain for a little while,*" it hummed.

Sedina slowly tilted her body and floated around until she saw the source of the kind voice. It was an unusual sight. It was a silvery dolphin-like fish but with a humpback like a whale and it had huge growths, like a witch's warts all over its body.

"Yes, we are new. We've had to adapt to survive with the Hu-men," he said.

"Hu-men!" screamed Sedina.

"Yes, I understand your reaction, especially since they almost decapitated you and dragged you in a net to filet for dinner later."

"Hu-men!" she screamed again.

"Yes, humans. They are not as bad as you can imagine. Some are even fairly healing individuals capable of great love," said the humpback dolphin.

"Equoo!" Sedina fearfully cried.

"Yes, or no I have never heard them called etkoos before. Hmmm…" thought the humpback dolphin. "I will ask my family if they have heard that name."

"Equoo!" screamed Sedina. She was worried. Had she killed her best friend? Sedina began hunting through her hair for the tiny seahorse. She tried to calm down so she didn't squash him in her search, but the agony was too worrisome.

"Oh, yes, wash it out. Yes, wash that bad experience from your mind and restore yourself to harmony. How wise, dear mermaid. How wise," the humpback dolphin admiringly said. "Oh, my name is Dolph. I know not very original," he said. And then he began to laugh, and it was a most melodic chuckle.

"Stop it! I can't hear!" screamed Equoo.

"Equoo!" Sedina cried. She was so delighted to hear him complain.

"Stop interrupting the music! Where is it coming from? Better yet, who is singing?" Equoo asked. "I love it!" he delightfully cried.

"Wow!" said an amused Sedina. "I have never heard you say you loved anything before."

"I am not a female. I don't have to tell my emotions to every whale, shark or, whoa! What is that?" he asked.

"That is a …" but Sedina said nothing further. She didn't know what to say. She'd never seen a more unattractive dolphin in her life. Dolphins by their nature were elegant glorious beings of great intelligence and wisdom, but Dolph was big, really huge and ugly. Then she corrected herself. He was unique.

"Yes, I am different. I'm a little larger than most," he said with a smile.

Sedina hoped he hadn't heard her thoughts. He wasn't monstrously huge. He was large like a whale and extremely weird like a manatee or worse. Oh no, what if he heard her say that! Well, people mistook manatees for mermaids all the time, so there. Mermaids can't be all that beautiful if people thought they looked like that. "*Stop thinking, Sedina,*" she told herself. "*Be present and feel!*"

"You are so sensitive and kind! Thank you for saving us," Sedina said. "Thank you so much," she said again. "Tell Dolph thank you, Equoo," she firmly said.

"What happened to you?" Equoo inquired.

"Oh yes, that, hmm, how do I explain? Okay. A few thousand years ago…" he began, but before he could get good into his story, Equoo interrupted him.

"Oh, no we don't have time for that. Get to the part where you developed a head like a buffalo," he said with disgust.

"Equoo," warned Sedina. She tried to tone to him to be nice, but her head hurt too badly to have her thoughts in there too.

"Yes, that, yes, it happened when a tanker spilled some oil and some chemicals, and I think they dumped some old light bulbs that were glowing in the water for fifty years or so. Yes, that's when my head grew, and my testicles shrunk but my voice got really soothing," he said with delight.

"Okay, right, I see and where were you living when all this happened?" Equoo asked.

"Listen!" said Sedina. She sat down and listened to the new species of dolphins crooning overhead. They were magnificent. She'd never heard such a serene sound in all her life and mermaids were known for their voices.

"You should try out for the Meriads! They would love you!" she giggled. "My family has the revue every other winter's season, and everyone travels from all over the earth's waterways to attend. It is the most anticipated event in the sea!"

"Yes, that would be fun. I will ask the others if they would like to do this, but for now I must be going. They can't circle around all day, you know," said Dolph, and he bellowed his huge laugh again.

As the school of humpback dolphins swam off in unison above them, they made a heart formation before singing one last song.

You are who you are to be
Beauties of the wondrous sea
May graceful joy grow deep in thee
My mermaid-seahorse family!

Sedina had to lie on her back to see her new friends off because turning her head still hurt. As their bodies formed the shape of a heart, the mermaid felt such love. She was again humbled by the way the sea always sustained her. This wasn't the only time she'd narrowly escaped death, but it was the first time she'd been saved by a new species. The polluted waters had made them hard on the eyes but soft as sponge on the ears.

"Speaking of ears, how come they didn't faint from the hideous sound coming off that boat?" Equoo asked.

"You are getting good at toning my friend," said Sedina. "You heard me thinking."

"Yes, we have gone deaf now from all the noise pollution, but we hear better because we feel more now. We hear in the great one way," Dolph said from out in the marine ethers somewhere, before trailing off in a mystical sound of glory.

"He heard that!" said Equoo in amazement.

"One way, or another, we are all going to have to adapt, I guess," Sedina sadly said.

"Are you awake now?" asked Equoo. "You could have killed us! But that was not a complaint, it was simply an observation."

Sedina did not know what to say. What could she have said? She had no memory of the events that happened. All she remembered was a man in a dog suit (a jackal's hide to be exact) was pouring water into the wind, and the water curled until it rose up like a mountain and washed her weeping daughter away.

CHAPTER 13

The last waves of sound from the lizard drum washed over the medicine man and he felt better. It had been a most interesting and strange evening. First there was the arrival of the Herb-Woman and then the odd entity that called himself Frill Lebo. Lebo was the name of his first ancestor and he was as important to his people as Adam was to the colonizers. Lebo began the earth settlement. When Amma, as Creator, flung the pellets of primordial clay creating the sun and moon, the earth was born. Amma baked earth into being using her light thus ending the chaos of unformed eternity. Amma loved her creation so much that her need to express this love was overwhelming, so she procreated with her creation, but it was a defective union. Instead of the intended twins that were to bring balance into the world, one single being came into existence—the jackal. Thus, the origin of trouble on earth was born.

Amma tried procreating with her creation again and this time the intercourse proved successful. Amma's feminine semen watered the earth and twin spirits were born. They were called Nummo and they were born perfect in every way. Each Nummo had both male and female capabilities just like Amma. The Creator was happy, so Amma brought the Nummo to the celestial home and taught them the language of creation.

But the jackal was left behind. It also wanted to possess speech so it too could manifest creations like his twin siblings, but he was not given this knowledge so the jackal became resentful. He was jealous. He wreaked havoc all over the earth until he became lonely and inconsolable and when he grew up, he became incorrigible. Thus, he plunged himself into his Mother, the Earth and the incestuous act defiled the planet.

The Nummo twins knew if the lonely jackal continued raping and pillaging earth, Amma's creation would return to chaos and her light would go out, so they returned and spoke the light-language of creation and the warm vapor from their mouths formed rivers and lakes and oceans. They brought plants from heaven and they moistened them with their watery natures and the earth flourished and came into its green and blue form. The moist luminous nature of the Nummo purged the jackal's errant abuse of the earth. They continued doing Amma's work and with each word they uttered, the earth evolved, enabling them to tame her wicked son—the jackal.

As the medicine man silently recited the creation story he felt stronger within himself. He filled his ceremonial pot with spring water and added some of the sacred Iboga plant. He wanted his mind to drift to the part of the story after Bba Lebo died and was returned back to earth via the snake. He knew the lizard wanted him to remember this leg of the journey. He sensed this part would hold the key to the symbols the orange reptile had placed in his mouth, so he drank the hallucinogen and waited for a message from his guides.

As the drug started to shift his awareness, the medicine man started to see the drawing of the bone reading with new eyes. He cleared his mind of all judgment and previous knowledge, so its truth would reveal itself. The first symbol looked like a backwards E, with its outer horizontal limbs pulling away from one another. It made the medicine man uneasy and that agitated him. It resembled an arrow flying down from the heavens with amazing force. Worse it reminded him of a trident. The trident was a powerful symbol of the sea but as the medicine man stared at his drawing he saw the symbol change colors. "Ayee!" he screamed. "It's the blue comet returning home!"

This sent a shiver down the man's spine. Eight years ago, at the secret meeting of the world's shamans, a man with long hair who came from north of the equator mentioned a shooting star that would herald the end, so all could begin again. He didn't understand the man who called himself Hopee, however he could feel his heart and it filled him with hope. The medicine man couldn't remember anything else the Hopee elder said. The only other detail that came to mind was his desire to study with this man and learn his ways. It would have been good medicine to add to his own.

The Man-of-Medicine reprimanded himself for allowing ambition to cloudy his thoughts. "Desire will be the death of mankind," he said and aloud. The shaman reprimanded himself for a second time. He knew better than to speak his thoughts out loud. Words had great power and he had no desire to end mankind's journey with a bad word. Especially since it was speaking aloud a sentimental thought that had begun the journey to begin with.

That was it! Lebo was the first to die a mortal's death! He descended into earth and was reborn through Great Mother's womb via the snake. Ever since that day, men have been placed on earth to find their way back home. Amma needed proof of our loyalty to creation. But why was Amma sending the comet? Only a zombie ignored Amma's calls. What was Lebo trying to tell him? Maybe the second symbol held the key.

The wind began blowing through the cracks of the granary walls, chilling the shaman to his very bones. The medicine man went into the house and got a blanket and his pipe. The Ibago plant had made him restless so he wanted some tobacco to ground him. Maybe then the ancestors would tell him what he needed to know.

The second symbol looked like a hand with eight fingers. He knew this was going to be an important clue. The number eight was a very important number. It was central to his ancestor's philosophy. It meant completion. But how could the second symbol complete a story with six chapters left to read?

"Focus," he thought. "I must focus."

The second symbol was a hand with eight fingers. Only Amma could have created such an appendage, therefore was Amma herself throwing the blue star to earth?

"Uncle are you there?" shouted Emadi from outside. She was waiting in the courtyard.

The medicine man jumped up and turned toward the door and his foot slid, smearing the seventh symbol drawn in the dirt. He tried to remember what had been there, but it was already lost to him.

"Who is there? What do you want!" demanded the medicine man.

Emadi backed away from the shaman's steps and centered herself. "It is my mother, Uncle. She is not well, and she asked me to fetch you," she cautiously said.

"Give me a moment," he yelled. He was trying to sound normal, but he was feeling far from it. Nothing was normal anymore. "Please, Emadi, go and tell your mother I am on my way. I must wash and prepare first. I will be there soon," he said.

"Yes Uncle, I will let her know," she replied. But she did not know which direction to cast her voice. She stood at the Man-of-Medicine's front door, but his voice returned to her from his granary. No one rested or washed in a granary. It was a sacred place, a place for rituals and prayers but there were no festivals or ceremonies in the near future. It wasn't even the time of a full or new moon, so why had the shaman locked himself in his lodge. Was he sick too?

"Thank you, Uncle. You are a blessing," answered Emadi as she descended the stairs with a head full of questions.

CHAPTER 14

The Herb-Woman could not stop perspiring. She felt like she was detoxing bad meat, but she hadn't had meat since the last community circle and that was days ago. She was tired, plus the roof of her mouth hurt. But that was her own doing. The hot tea had burned her more than she'd liked to admit. She needed to wash the bad smells off her body before Emadi returned with the Man-of-Medicine. She decided against it. She didn't want to erase the very symptoms that held the answers to her cure before he could diagnose her. Still, she made herself get out of bed anyway. She should at least wash between her legs before seeing him.

As she watched the kettle come to a boil, she thought about their last meeting. She studied the memory watching the man's face the entire time. She hadn't noticed his eyebrow raise slightly on the left side of his face when she mentioned the young girl's toes growing back together. She watched again as his mouth curled upward in a shy grin of satisfaction when she recounted what the mermaid child did to the alien boy. Why did that awful story make him smile? "Yes, I see," she said to herself. Then she giggled and turned around in circles.

"Well, you seem to be feeling better," said Emadi upon entering the room. She was surprised to see her mother dancing in her nightgown in the kitchen. Her mother would've had her hide for a handbag if she'd found her doing the same thing. She would've been afraid she'd knock over one of her medicine jars or that she'd stir up spirits in the house, or some other nonsense. Emadi renewed her vow to never get married and have children. She wanted to be free. She was going to get herself a little storefront and do hair, but naturally. She was going to bring back all the old designs of braids, knots and sculpting her ancestors had worn. As soon as she saved enough money for her license she was off to the city.

"I was just trying to release the shape of the pillow from my back," her mother said. She was lying. It was true she needed a pillow to hold the space between her rear end and the bed. Her butt was so big it made a gap between her and the mattress, so she shoved a pillow in between to fill the space. She'd been sleeping that way for years and she always woke up right as rain. That wasn't the reason she was doing pirouettes in the kitchen.

Emadi was confused. Why was the medicine man pretending to be well when he clearly was not, and her mother pretending to be sick when she clearly was well? Something was going on. She made a mental note to watch the Man-of-Medicine and her mother very closely. If something was the matter, then she needed to know how dismal the matter truly was. Maybe her mother was having romantic feelings for the old shaman. Emadi reached into the cupboard and got a mug and two teacups for her mother and the medicine man.

"Are you staying?" her mother asked and immediately wished she hadn't. She could see her daughter was suspicious. She'd just found her dancing in the kitchen. Now she would never get rid of her.

"Why of course, Mma. I'm your daughter and I live here. I wouldn't want to leave you unattended with a man. What would people think?" she said with a slight tinge of sarcasm.

"Oh, I see. Thank you, Daughter. Cause this ole widow would hate to have…" But the Herb-Woman would have to wait to cap her daughter's sarcasm, because the Man-of-Medicine was headed for their door. "Oh, I must get a gown on," she said. The roots woman was nervous.

"Mma, you're already wearing your gown," Emadi said.

"Are you going to keep trying every nerve in this old body, chile" quipped the Herb-Woman. Then a knock was heard, saving the women from saying something else they would regret later.

Emadi happily escaped her mother's last remark by quickly rushing to the door. When she returned with the Man-of-Medicine, she noticed her mother had grabbed her nicest shawl and had thrown it over her shoulders. She was bewildered by the old woman's behavior. Her mother was already sweating like a pig so why drape herself in a heavy, hand woven shawl? Maybe she was planning on using it as a towel. Emadi continued rationalizing her mother's behavior as she pulled out a chair for their guest. "Greetings, Uncle, here she is. Here, sit please," she said.

Emadi was nervous being in the same room with her mother and the medicine man. She knew of their ongoing rivalry. She'd heard her mother's true feelings on many occasions. The air being sucked through her teeth and then exhaled with an audible "Hhump" always expressed it best. She decided to prepare the tea for their meeting. It gave her something to do. As the tea steeped she presented the shaman with their nicest teacup and set their best honey on the table before gracefully stomping out of the house. She grabbed the nearest chair in the yard and positioned it to the side of the door, so she could see into the kitchen. Then she plopped herself down.

"Well it seems I am not the only one feeling badly today," said the Herb-Woman apologetically and just loud enough for it to carry outside to her daughter's ears.

"Please sit and rest, Mma. I am here now," said the Man-of-Medicine. He continued speaking in his most soothing tone. He was trying to smooth the ruffled feathers in the hen house. Two grown but single women living together was always a recipe for disaster. The thought made him smile.

"Yes, Bba, I should sit down. I am tired," said the Herb-Woman before making a great display of slowly lowering herself into her armchair.

"Please, here. Sit here so I can examine you easier," he said.

As the Herb-Woman moved to a stool closer to the medicine man, she peered out the door at her daughter who quickly looked away.

The medicine man was having a hard time concentrating. He was still nauseous from the night before and the smell of a menstruating woman and an aging menopausal one was not helping in the least. No wonder these women didn't feel well. If he had a hormone revolution in his house, he'd be feeling like cow pies too.

"You are fine, mother. What made you believe you were sick?" he asked with complete neutrality.

The Herb-Woman thought he would have made a great diplomat or politician. "I cannot stop perspiring and my tongue feels like ash," she sweetly said.

Her voice was so intimate in nature that it shocked her eavesdropping daughter. Emadi nearly fell out of her chair, so she repositioned it, so they couldn't see her through the screen door.

"Open your mouth," said the shaman. "Yes, I see," he sighed. "You must stop drinking your tea so hot. Cool it off a little first," he said. "Blow on it," he added.

"Yes, I know how to cool tea, Bba, but what about this sweating," she firmly said.

"Yes, you are becoming a wise crone now. It is an honor. Congratulations are in order," he firmly said.

But the Herb-Woman was not to be dismissed and especially by a man who had just inferred she was old. "What of this rash, Bba," she said, and she pulled back her nightshirt and exposed her chest.

When the Man-of-Medicine saw the woman's chest he let out an audible, "Oh my Amma!" There on the Herb-Woman's chest was the exact design he'd drawn in the earthen floor of his granary. The design Frill Lebo had given him!

"You see! I told you. Now even you don't feel well!" the Herb-Woman intently said. The roots woman was happy. She had made the Man-of-Medicine gasp. She finally had his attention. Her body recorded the changes of life and all nature's changes. She was not a hysterical woman. She was a roots woman in alignment with great Amma. She was the one she chose to deliver Creator's message. She was the winner!

CHAPTER FIFTEEN

"So, are you going to tell me?" Equoo asked.

"Tell you what?" replied Sedina.

"What your nightmare was about," said Equoo.

"Oh, that," sighed the mermaid. "It was awful."

"Go on," coaxed Equoo.

The mermaid began recounting last night's dream, the dream that nearly killed them both. It started out as all her dreams did, in a peaceful radiant blue light that usually went to white at the end. But this dream went black after the blue and the seas rose like cement walls and the walls formed a round room and in the room was a long black man that turned into a jackal. Around the jackal-man was a fire circle that danced until the fire froze. Then the fire flared opened and stood up like a paper fan and an orange dragon appeared. The dragon danced around the fire while the jackal-man spit water into the wind.

"What does it mean?" Equoo asked.

"That's not the worse part," she said. "During the dream that seemed to go on forever, I heard Mianshe crying!"

"Oh, no, Sedina!" said Equoo.

Equoo never called the mermaid by her name. She was far too regal of a lineage to talk to in such a casual manner. Granted he could be himself around her, but he never forgot who she was. She was always going to be a Mer princess.

"It gets worse. She was crying out the Life Song and it was filled with so much pain, Equoo," cried the mermaid.

"Oh, please don't cry, dear friend. Please don't," he whispered. "It was only a dream."

"But dreams come true, Equoo. And this was no ordinary dream. I traveled to see this!" she shouted and then she began to sob.

"So that was why we were moving so fast," said Equoo. He was trying to make sense of it all, but his good sense told him it was a warning. "How did it end?" he sadly asked.

"I don't know. I woke up and the rest you know," she calmly said.

Equoo stared into the mermaid's eyes for a good long moment. "Well it ends with beautiful music," he finally said.

"Yes, and we will learn to adapt," Sedina said. She was smiling again.

Equoo loved how easily the mermaid recovered. No matter how stressed or how desperate things got, she always found something in it to smile about. "You are amazing," he said. "When I grow up I want to be just like you." He was trying to make the mermaid laugh, but she didn't find his little pun very funny.

"Mianshe is in trouble, of this I am certain, but I don't know how to help her," she softly said. "And I couldn't help her even if I wanted to."

"Why?" Equoo asked.

"Because we must never intervene upon someone's path without being asked. We could ruin their flow and set them back in life," she affirmed.

"No, that would not be good," said a thoughtful Equoo. "That would be very bad indeed." Then the seahorse had an idea. "What if we ask Dolph to listen in and let us know what is happening on land? It was no coincidence that ugly pod of humpbacks showed up. And I say that with the greatest awe," he humbly said.

"What a perfect idea, Equoo!" cried the mermaid with delight. "Now you are thinking like a Mer-one," she gleefully said. "Except for the ugly remark, we would never have said that," she said with a smile in her eyes.

"Oh, that, well, yeah. At least I'm truthful," he said. Of course, it was a gross rationalization. Even Equoo knew that.

"Yes, that you are," replied the mermaid.

"You know, I almost thought you were going to let that remark slip by," he added.

"Equoo, you must erase the word ugly from your vocabulary. Okay?" And then Sedina rose up before him and waited for his reply.

Equoo loved when she used all of her body to express herself. If he had her immensely beautiful body, he would have done the same thing.

"Okay, you're on, my beautiful mermaid. And the unattractive know who they are anyway," he said with a wink.

Sedina laughed. She had no idea what Creator was thinking when she created the male species, but she liked them. She liked them a lot.

Sedina never let on to Equoo that she was still upset by her dream. She didn't go through the porthole home like in a normal dream. She went beyond the familiar to witness this. She went beyond the ocean, beyond the universe even. She went beyond space to somewhere else. It was somewhere before any of this mattered. Even more bizarre was the only presence that felt familiar, was the jackal-man. It felt as if they'd been traveling together for a long time. But where had they known each other, and when had they met? Was it in this life or another? The only thing Sedina did know was she did not trust this animal-man. Truth be told, she feared him. Not because of any powers he may have, or because he chose a horrible beast to emulate, she feared the jackal-man because he wanted to hurt her daughter. He wanted to possess Mianshe.

Sedina remembered hearing the horrible mewls of her kinsmer when caught in a fisherman's trap and it was the exact sound her daughter made in her dream. It was the cry of someone desperate and in excruciating pain and tired of being that way. It was like someone had been siphoning her daughter's life force and had left her with little more than agony.

Sedina had never veered from universal law. She'd always gone with the flow that encouraged life. She could never harm anyone or thing, ever, but if she caught a jackal, especially a cruel one harming a child—her child, she would put it in a lobster crate and take it to the lowest point in the sea, and sweetly sing the Life Song until it was blue in the face.

"Okay, we must go now," she quickly said.

"What? Where to?" Equoo asked with surprise.

"To find my elders," she answered. "I am not well," she said, as she tucked Equoo safely away in her pouch.

"Is it the bump on your head? Do you have a concussion?" asked a concerned Equoo. "Being part Hu-man is weird, eh?" he asked. Equoo could never stop talking when he was nervous.

"No, I'm having bad thoughts," she said. Then she darted out into deep waters.

"But you have no idea where your family is. Stop, please! Let's think about this a moment," pleaded Equoo. "Here we go again," he mumbled.

Sedina stopped and sat down on a rock. "You're right. I am moving faster than my heart. Let me get still then I will summon Dolph and have him find my family."

"Okay," said Equoo with resolve before saying nothing more.

Sedina hummed herself into a trance and toned a note to Dolph.

Dearest kind Dolph of true beauty through
Please help me protect my dear one who
Is a young innocent from my seed
She is a mer-girl called Mianshe
Listen to those who say that name
For there are those who wish to gain
From harming her and nature's reign
To end the world for private gain
Thank you grand being of music and light
True protector of our watery rights
May your lovely sound purge worry and fear
We are humbly grateful for you, Dolph dear!

When Sedina finished her toned plea, she opened her eyes. "We should forage some food for our journey," she said.

"You didn't ask him about your family," the seahorse said.

"One favor at a time, Equoo. I don't want to impose myself on the very being that saved us only hours ago," she replied.

"Then I will ask," Equoo haughtily replied.

"Please, Equoo, I must know that Mianshe is okay first," begged the mermaid.

And as the pair bickered over the etiquette of sea favors, a huge ripple of water made its way toward them like a mushroom cloud from a nuclear bomb. The strange liquid was as quiet as a shark and as inspiring as a bubble in a quartz crystal. It silently engulfed them like an embryonic sac until they were caught inside it like snowflakes in a snow globe.

Sedina immediately grabbed Equoo and placed him in the hidden slot inside her sack. She collected the little sprigs of seaweed and krill and other live matter floating around her and quickly put it in her bag and snapped it shut. As the wave circled her, she closed her eyes and tried to ground herself into the earth underneath the sea floor. She visualized her tail extending to the center of the planet and she anchored herself there. She didn't like being in closed spaces. She grew up in the open seas with nothing in her peripheral but sky or water, so boundaries truly addled her. After calming herself She started to hum. She was hoping she could penetrate the jelly-like shield of water, but to her amazement, the water began receding on its own until it became a beach ball sized bubble. Then it began to spin, and the sweetest sound emanated from it.

Oooh la da la oooh
Oooh la da la oooh
Dearest Sedina we've heard your pleas
Floating so sweetly over the seas
We have listened and watched and have found
Many wish Mianshe buried in the ground
They are plotting dreadful things to come
They are smart and won't let us see anyone
But don't worry I've informed your Mer-family
And they are coming to you now on calm seas.

Then the bubble burst, and so did Sedina. She cried so long that all the water around her appeared opalescent.

"This is very bad news about your daughter," Equoo said. "But it's very good news about your family," he quietly sighed. Equoo was worried. He knew how cruel Hu-men could be, but he also knew how snobbish Mer-ones were. Would his mermaid throw him away like a fish skeleton when her family came? Would they mock him and call him little and treat him like a child? He was old, so old he couldn't remember how long he'd lived in the sea. He was one of the few seahorses to escape being eaten or crushed by a whale's tail or any one a myriad of things that can happen to one so small in a place so large. Equoo knew he had to stop this line of thinking and trust what was to come, because these sad thoughts were making him miserable. If he were to be happy he had to have hope.

"Yes," contemplated the mermaid. She was still listening to Dolph's message about the jackal-man wishing to harm her daughter. She hadn't heard Equoo's musings, however his anxious sound finally made its way to her ears. "My family is going to love you, Equoo. My father will try to give you a whale's mouthful of krill for saving me," she added. "That seems so long ago, doesn't it, my friend? Oh my, look what traveling with me has brought you," she sadly added.

Equoo was thrilled. He loved being needed and his mermaid still desired his company. He vowed to always stay by her side. He would protect her. His name would go down in history as the seahorse that saved a mermaid princess! He felt happy again.

"Don't worry, dear friend, we will save your daughter. I will never let any harm come to you, you know that. We are a great team! Between me and you, and the Mer-ones, and those huge dolphin-humpback thingies, that jackal doesn't stand a chance on land or in the sea!" he vowed.

"I believe you, my dear Equoo," said the mermaid. "Because you always speak the truth!"

CHAPTER 16

It was twenty minutes before sunrise and the prince was the only one up. He wasn't quite sure what to do. He didn't know if he should wake his nanny or meditate or go fishing. He wondered if he should go to the market place or just go back to bed? He had no idea what to do. What he did know was he was craving a hot cup of honeyed bush tea, so he got dressed and went into the kitchen as quietly as he could. Nanny Leboya normally made breakfast so he was having a hard time finding where she kept the kettle or the kindling to start a fire.

He didn't sleep well last night so he was grateful for the strange noises outside because it gave him a reason to get out of bed altogether. Then the prince's thoughts went in another direction. His father hadn't visited him in days. Nor had his aunt for that matter. That was odd. Even though his father was an anti-imperialist, was he secretly using their tactics now? Was he trying to use reverse psychology on him? He'd been using foreign tactics a lot since he returned. His father wasn't happy unless things went his way. But in his defense, all kings were like that because they always got their way. That was what being a king was all about. They ruled.

Then the prince's thoughts went back to his earlier observation. Since having children, no one stopped by anymore, not even Adisa. What if he visited her today? The prince's heart leapt at the idea of visiting the Fire-Tender's daughter. He wondered if he should take the children with him. He could say they wanted to see her. They wouldn't mind. They were very fond of her. But what if Mianshe felt she was slighting her mother? Now there was a thought. But he had to be realistic. How was he going to live underwater with a sea goddess? Unless she had the power to enable him to breathe liquid their relationship was surely doomed.

Since the prince had become a father of two he'd become extremely practical. His father probably knew this would be the outcome. That was why he was avoiding him. He wanted his son to bond with every emotion being a father brought. Not only the pain and agony of worrying for one's children but the profound sense of being alone that went along with it too. Was that it? Was he simply lonely and that was why he was craving Adisa's attention? The prince didn't want to think his body ruled his actions. He refused to believe he was a dog, a simple canine that humped its anxieties away. No, he was a man—a very sensitive man, so he'd go to Adisa's house and court her like a gentleman. He needed a gift. He needed to take her something besides two children from two different mothers and another father. It couldn't be anything too extravagant otherwise the Fire-Tender would think he was trying to buy his daughter. He needed to take her something personal, something from his heart.

"Nanny!" he yelled.

Leboya heard the prince yelling for her so she turned over on her side and placed a pillow over her head. She had no idea how anyone got to be twenty-two and still not know how to make their own breakfast. Didn't he learn anything overseas? They were always dropping their instant milk and cereals all over the continent. You'd have thought he'd grown accustom to fast flying food by now, but, no, he still measured how much milk to put in dry cereal. Who thought of that anyway? Not even horses liked their cereal dehydrated by an oven and then remoistened with another's milk. What nonsense life had become. He could at least boil water and she knew he could make a fire and hunt too, but he would be completely useless after that. He'd probably bite the furry animal and being proud would go yummy as he pulled its hair out of his teeth. Now she was angry, and who can sleep when they're angry, so she pulled back the covers, placed her feet on the ground, grabbed her robe from her sitting chair, and promptly stomped into the kitchen.

"Good morning," said the Prince. Then he pulled a chair out for his nanny to sit.

And there before Leboya was a hot pot of tea and a bowl of grits so runny you had to use a spoon to eat them. The tea was good, and his mealie pie was perfectly crispy, a little too crispy in some spots but nothing a little honey wouldn't hide. Nanny Leboya was so proud of the prince she couldn't eat. She stood up and gave him a big hug then took a sip of tea and repeated the process all over again.

"Sit, Nanny. Please sit or it will get cold," said the Prince. He was laughing too. It gave him such delight to see her so delighted. "Now eat," he said again.

And nanny looked at the soupy bowl of grits that even when cold did not congeal, and she hopped out of her chair and hugged the prince all over again. "I must wake the children. They must see this," she said, but the prince caught her before she could leave the room.

"Let them sleep, Nanny. I would like to talk to you alone," he said.

The last time Leboya heard this tone in the prince's voice he was getting ready to run away to the northerners' schools.

"And I did not cook you breakfast this morning just, so I could impose on you. I just got up early," he said.

Nanny Leboya meekly smiled. This was serious. The prince was thinking things through. The grits were still soupy. Well so much for a good morning, she thought.

"I would like to take the children to visit Adisa and I'd like to take her something besides my children. What is an appropriate gift?" he asked. "I don't want to leave a bad impression, you see," he added and then he stopped talking.

"I see," said Leboya, as she took a teensy bite of mealie. After many years of living with royals, she'd learned to think before she spoke, and what better way to give her a little time to think than a nice mouthful of mealie and honey. The grits were still a liquid.

"More tea, Nanny?" said the Prince as he filled her cup.

Leboya gently blew on the steaming liquid then sipped it ever so slowly. She was trying to surround each grain of corn with tea. She wanted to see if it were possible to make grits a soup, like the prince had done. Leboya had finally found the answer she was looking for.

"Your honey, my Prince. Take Adisa some honey! You took care of the hives. Or take her something else you've made yourself. Take her something you have made with your own hands that is useful," she said.

It was the worst thing she could have said. The prince was an intellect. He was not an artisan. He made nothing. He hunted, yes, but he couldn't take her an antelope. Presenting a young woman dried meat was definitely not romantic, and taking her fresh honey was downright suggestive.

"Okay," said the Prince with some hesitation. "Maybe. Let me think on that," he added. "I really wanted something a little more personal," he shyly said.

"I can make her something," yelled Mianshe, scaring the prince and her nanny out of their wits.

"My word, child!" was the only words Leboya could muster.

"Mianshe, please," was the Prince's response.

"But I can!" screamed Mianshe. She had completely missed the point of the prince's pleading.

"Child, you are loud," said Nanny through her yawns. She was tired.

"Good morning," said Verité.

And being her brother was the only person who loved her no matter what, Mianshe pushed Verité aside and stormed out of the kitchen.

"Okay, I've had just about enough of this," said the Prince. And he stomped out of the kitchen after the young mermaid.

"What's for breakfast," yawned Verité.

"Gritty soup," Nanny Leboya said. Then she yawned again. "I'll be in my room."

She was already tired, and she'd been up for less than an hour.

Verité enjoyed the silence. He went to the cupboard and got the pumpkin-shaped mug. It was his favorite. He filled it to the top with hot milk. Then he took two forks and made a makeshift pair of tongs. He grasped a piece of cold mealie pie and shoved it in the fire like a marshmallow.

Next, he released one fork and speared the charred mealie and dunked it in the pot of honey. It was so good it made him sing—and in French!

"Bon, bon, bon! C'est tres bon? Est-ce bon? Oui vraiment bon!" he sang. It tasted very good to him.

The prince went out onto the porch and watched his daughter furiously pound the earth with her feet.

"Young lady, you must learn to control your emotions. You nearly scared your nanny half to death," he calmly said.

"But she is still alive," said Mianshe just as calmly.

"Listen, little one, sassing one's father won't be tolerated. Please give me the respect of being the elder or else…" but the Prince did not know what else to say.

"Or else?" Mianshe haughtily asked.

The prince snatched the young mermaid by the back of her nightgown and lifted her from the earth and placed her small body face down on his lap. He lifted his arm and swatted her bottom. It was not as hard as he would have liked, because his hand would take no part in the punishment. "Dear Amma!" cried the Prince.

The prince was livid and sad all at once. He didn't want to hurt his daughter. Hurting never did anything for anyone except hurt them, but he had to teach her to respect others. He remembered the Nordic tale about a bratty princess who laughed all the time and how she was taught to be somber. They made her cut onions—bushels of them, so that is what the prince decided to do. Mianshe was going to clean the dishes, toilets and slop pots until she learned how to be a lady.

The prince pushed the shocked little girl off his lap and stood over her. He was not going to be swayed by teary eyes or pouty mouths or bouncing hair. He was a father now and she was going to act and respond accordingly, but when he lifted his hand and pointed his finger in preparation to lay down his sentence, Mianshe pulled the most amazing little clay doll out of her pocket.

"Here. It's Adisa's present," she cried. She then took some of her tears and molded a bow for the dress she had formed from Librebe clay. It was a darling replica of Adisa wearing Nanny Leboya's blue dress. "Now she will feel how mean you can be!" she screamed.

The prince had no idea what to do next. He thought the doll was a darling idea, but its creator was far from being cute. He grabbed her by the arm and pushed her into the house.

"Nanny!" he yelled.

Leboya rushed in and with one look at her kitchen screamed bloody murder. "On Amma's grave!" she exclaimed. It was a most disastrous cry because Amma was God and gods could not die thus a grave was completely unnecessary. Nanny found Verité asleep with his face resting on a slab of mealie. He'd drunk two pots of mint tea, eaten an entire pot of honey plus all the mealie pies except the piece he now used for his pillow and the few grits that were left were still runny.

"You ate those nasty grits too!" said Nanny in amazement.

The prince was none too happy to hear that. In fact, he was downright furious. He was furious with his daughter, his son and his nanny. "That's it!" he screamed. And when he heard his neighbors giggling, he screamed again. "I am the Prince! I will not be disrespected by man, woman, or child! Does everyone understand this?" he yelled with great force and absolute control.

"Yes, sir," saluted Verité. And then he stood at attention.

"I apologize, Guardian-Prince," Nanny sweetly said. And then she curtsied and kept her eyes on the floor.

But Mianshe just stood there looking at her father like he was the vilest creature to roam the earth.

"Mianshe," demanded the Prince.

"Yes?" she coolly replied. She really had zero idea what she was supposed to do.

"You will stay here with your nanny and clean this kitchen until it sparkles. Verité, you will sweep down the porch and shake out all the rugs," instructed the Prince.

"Please, Prince," whined Nanny. Leboya couldn't understand why she was being punished with the presence of the children, but she caught herself before she said anything more.

"And Nanny you will make sure these things are done to our satisfaction! Does everyone understand this?" he firmly asked.

"Yes, sir," said Verité. He hadn't moved an inch since the prince said 'that's enough'.

"Yes, of course, my Prince," Leboya meekly said.

Mianshe looked at Verité.

"Your brother cannot help you now. You will do this, or I will tan your hide and tie you to the sacred tree with the words *Bad Girl* taped to your heart!"

Mianshe gasped! It was the most tragic insult she'd ever heard. Bad was bad and she was not a bad girl. She was a very good girl. Mianshe walked past her father into the kitchen and began cleaning and she did it in silence.

"Go, my Prince. I will take over from here," said Nanny.

The prince was happy to escape the strange looks and the eerie silence oozing from his children. He grabbed a piece of muslin and a strand of ribbon from nanny's sewing box and started wrapping Mianshe's clay doll, but his angry fingers couldn't make the present, presentable.

Leboya felt sorry for the prince. She knew how he'd been raised and having responsibility was never one of his chores, but he was a good man, so he trained himself to take on the burden of being spoiled. That is why he ran away to the colonial's schools, so he could learn how to take care of himself.

"Here, my Prince, let me do that for you," Leboya compassionately said.

"Thank you, Auntie. I could use the time to wash up some. Thank you," he muttered again. Then he gave Mianshe's doll to Leboya to finish wrapping and escaped into his room.

By the time Leboya had made a care package for the prince to take to Adisa, the children had over half of the house cleaned. Verité was fueled by finger dips from what was left of the honey and Mianshe by her anger with her father.

"I want to go home," she said every time she passed Verité.

Verité collected the rugs and shook the dust and the girl's comment out the back door. He was not going to let her get him into any more trouble than he was already in.

"I'm going to tell merma and then she will come and get me," she said. But when Verité didn't respond as she wished, she embellished her threats even more. "She's going to come riding a whale, a big blue whale, no a shark!" she said in the highest pitched hissy fit she could muster.

Nanny could feel the children's frustration, so she did what she always did when children were frowning. She made bread pudding, but not just any pudding. This one was made with fresh cream and eggs, cinnamon, clove and cardamom and a lot of raw chocolate. She added raisins and peanuts too. Then she applied a fine layer of raw cane sugar to the top and caramelized it so when one put the spoon in, it cracked and released the creamy contents.

"Children come!" she yelled.

Verité jumped when he heard her call out for them. He wondered what Mianshe had done now. He knew his sister was going to have a rough time living in Librebe if she didn't thicken her skin a bit. Librebeings could be very difficult to win over. He was a good boy and it took him over a year for them to find him a family. Mianshe was not even from this land or any land for that matter and had been in trouble on an average of twice a day.

"And my uncle Equoo will beat him up," said Mianshe as she crawled on all fours wiping the dust off the floorboards.

"Isn't Equoo a seahorse?" asked an amused Verité.

"You stop listening in on my thoughts!" yelled Mianshe.

"Children come in here right now!" screamed Nanny. She couldn't believe the little heathens could not smell her prized pudding sitting on the table.

As the children slowly made their way into the kitchen, Verité stooped down and whispered into Mianshe's ear. "What did you do now?" he asked.

"Nothing and I didn't do anything before either," hissed Mianshe.

"Come in and sit," Nanny sweetly said.

Verité marched into the kitchen like someone about to be executed. He stood by the door with his hands folded and his eyes closed. Mianshe followed so closely behind him that you couldn't see her at all.

"Sit down," Leboya said. "Here." She gave each child a nice steaming bowl of hot pudding.

Verité held his bowl in his hands and smelled it for a good long moment. Bread pudding was one of his favorites.

Mianshe secretly watched him and did exactly as he did, although she couldn't understand for the life of her how he smelled the pungent spices for as long as he did. Maybe he was praying. So, she silently prayed that the spices did not make her sneeze and blow boogers into the fluffy soup.

"It's not a soup. It's a pudding," said Verité.

"Of course, it is," answered a confused Nanny. She was completely unaware that Verité was responding to Mianshe's thoughts.

Mianshe decided she wouldn't say anything, or even think a thing ever again, because no matter what she said or thought it turned out to be wrong anyway. "Are we allowed to eat it?" she asked.

"Of course, child. I truly wish you would," Nanny answered. She had no idea why the children kept sniffing it. "It's perfectly good pudding," said an exasperated Leboya. She was getting irritated.

Mianshe ate a small spoonful of nanny's pudding and smiled for the first time that day.

"Well, thank you Amma, Jesus and Credo Mutwa!" Nanny said with glee. "I finally got a smile."

Verité took a huge mouthful and began his song again. "Bon, bon, bon. C'est tres bon. Est-ce bon? Oui, vraiment bon!"

CHAPTER 17

As the prince neared Adisa's house he began walking slower and slower with every step. He wondered what he would say or maybe she'd be the first to speak. He was sure his presence on her doorstep would produce an audible exclamation of some kind. Perhaps she'd say, "Oh my, Amma" or "Prince!" or something. Finally, he stopped imagining what she would say. She was far too poised and collected to shout out some schoolgirl inanity anyway. Now he felt silly. Here he was having an argument with himself. He didn't understand why he was feeling so unsettled, so he tried settling down by noticing every nuance in the forest. As he approached Adisa's road he stopped. He heard the sound of the waves crashing against the north shore and it scared him. Why?

The prince sat down under a tree and said a silent prayer. When he felt his muscles begin to relax he reached into his gut sack and pulled out Adisa's gift. He slowly untied the ribbon making sure he didn't soil or rip it. He simply wanted to look at it and see if he could see it from Adisa's perspective. The small pot of honey that Mianshe's doll now held glistened in the sunlight and its golden rays radiated over him warming his heart. He knew this was right. Adisa was the brightest person he knew plus she was beautiful, but more importantly, she was kind. He was certain he would not find a better wife anywhere in Africa.

And the waves crashed against the hillside again and the prince shuddered once more. He knew loving a mermaid was a doomed adventure. She wouldn't be happy on land and he could not survive in the sea. He was not an unreasonable man. He had to live with someone from his world if he were to reach his potential. He couldn't be a king with two foreign children and a mermaid wife too. The villagers would not stand for it. He needed Adisa. He continued his debate with himself.

"Good day, Prince," said the Fire-Tender.

The prince was startled out of his reverie. He immediately wondered how long the Fire-Tender had been watching him. He felt ridiculous sitting on the ground brooding in front of the man who would soon become his father. "Good day, Uncle," he said, quickly lifting himself up to greet the Fire-Tender, however when he did, he shifted his weight and the doll, and the honey slid off his lap onto the ground and shattered. One of the figurine's arms flew into the brush and the other cracked and got stuck in the dripping honey. The head of the doll slowly rolled down his thigh. The prince gasped. He quickly tried to catch the walnut sized head before it fell, but in his effort to grab it, he slipped. His knee immediately landed directly on top of the clay head bust and it all happened in front of her father.

The prince was crestfallen. Today was not a good day and as he was listing his reasons for coming to that conclusion, something moved in front of his face, stopping his train of thought. It was the Fire-Tender's hand. He was so distraught he forgot Adisa's father was still standing over him.

"Here, my Prince, let me help you," said the Fire-Tender.

The prince took the Fire-Tender's hand and allowed him to pull him up to standing.

"I'm sorry you lost your present," said the Fire-Tender, "but it seems the ants are happy with the way things went."

However, the Fire-Tender wasn't staring at the hundreds of insects devouring the honey. He was staring at the little ball of red dirt resembling the face of his daughter. He was transfixed by how the face had remained intact while the back of the head had been pushed all the way into the earth by the prince's knee. Was this an omen? Would the prince try to suppress his daughter's will? Or maybe he was only interested in her face and had no interest in her mind. His daughter was bright, smarter than the prince or himself for that matter. She'd learned to read the ashes very quickly, although she didn't know he knew this, but he did. His daughter was remarkable, and he felt no shame in boasting this fact to anyone. She was instinctually intelligent, but supremely naïve. She would be no match for a man who slept with water nymphs and English women.

"Mianshe made it for her, Uncle, for me to give to her," said the Prince.

"Are you courting my daughter, Prince-Guardian?" the Fire-Tender asked, and he asked his question with so little emotion one could not tell his intention or the sentiment behind it.

The prince didn't know what to say. If he said yes, then he'd appear rude and disrespectful. To court in Librebe you had to get the permission of both the mother and father, and since Adisa's mother was dead it meant he had to be twice as responsible and extremely respectful of her father and he hadn't been either respectful or responsible. He hadn't asked her father first before visiting her. But if he said to her father that he wasn't courting her then he would be guilty of toying with her affections. The prince was truly between a rock and a hard place. He had to say something. He'd been asked a question—a very serious question.

"I know this must look very forward of me to be bringing sweets and toys to your daughter, sir. The children made this package and were to be here with me, but they got into trouble with Nanny, so they are home doing chores. I promise you I will make my intentions known before I approach your daughter with any behavior other than as her prince or childhood friend, Uncle," said the Prince, then he shifted his weight to his other foot.

The Fire-Tender was truly suspicious of the prince. Not only hadn't he answered his question; he had deflected it and used his authority as prince to stop any further questioning. Plus, he had used his children as an excuse to do it. It was a politician's tactic not a king's! The Fire-Tender was not a naïve man. He'd worked alongside the prince's father and had been the tribe's Fire-Tender since he was fourteen and no one, not even from the beginning of his journey as the Tender, had ever doubted his position. Everyone was certain he was up to the task. Even the king was happy to see him take over for his father. Granted it was more because of his father's cataracts clouding his eyesight than his being ready, but he still held the confidence of the king. The Man-of-Medicine, who was five years his senior, knew he was destined to be a great Tender too, and fire tending was not his only gift either. He could also tell what was in a man's heart by watching the light dance in his eyes. He'd seen the prince's eyes staring out into the distance. The prince was still seeking the company of another. Why else would he sit down only a short distance from his destination?

"Do you miss your daughter's mother, son?" asked the Fire-Tender. He was risking everything in that moment, but he had to know. He had to know for his daughter's sake.

The prince was stunned. Not just by the Fire-Tender's brazen bluntness but by his calling him son. He wanted him to feel little and confide in him. "Why do you ask, Uncle?" said the Prince calmly. He had to keep his wits about him.

The Fire-Tender stood to the side of the prince. He purposely chose his position. It was a stance of equality and togetherness, plus it directly blocked the path to his house and to his daughter. "I asked," said the Fire-Tender, and then he paused for a moment and slowly pointed to where the prince had been sitting. "Because you were drawing waves in the dirt," he said.

The prince was shocked. He was unaware he'd been drawing the tide in the earth. "I didn't notice. I was listening to the wave's crash," he confessed. And then the prince trailed off into silence. How could he respond to the Fire-Tender's question when he himself did not know the answer?

"My daughter is a strange and wonderful creature, Prince," he gently said. "She is both wise and naïve, and her heart is both courageous and timid," the Fire-Tender said and then he stopped. He wanted the prince to feel his words.

"She is pure, Uncle, I know this," the Prince quickly replied. But it was too quick a response so the Fire-Tender misunderstood it.

"I am not speaking of physical matters, Prince," the Fire-Tender firmly said.

"Neither was I, sir," said the Prince in his defense. "I meant pure of heart. She is kind and she is nurturing and…"

"And," said the Fire-Tender.

"And she is your daughter," said the Prince. "I have watched Adisa from the day she was born. Auntie brought her to the ceremony the same night. She laughed at me, Uncle. No one had ever smiled at me before. Everyone felt sorry for the motherless prince, all but baby Adisa. She laughed and made faces at me, Bba." Then he corrected himself and called the Fire-Tender by the more colloquial name of uncle.

The Fire-Tender watched the prince closely to see if he was sincere or not. He was. The prince was an honest man by nature. He never lied or tried to rationalize his behavior. He never bragged or made a big deal about his position. He was always authentic. He too had a pure heart, but the Fire-Tender was still not convinced. He had to be sure the boy didn't want to marry his daughter to appease the villagers, or to have a mother for his children, or because his flesh cried out to be touched. He needed to know he loved her, truly loved her and not like a sister or a nanny or like the mother he never got to know. He needed to know he loved her because his heart wouldn't have it any other way. He owed this to his daughter. But the design in the sand told him differently. The prince couldn't let go of the mermaid, and the Fire-Tender would die before he allowed his daughter to be the wife of a king who had a sea goddess mistress.

"I see, my Prince, I see," was all the Fire-Tender could say without exposing his anxiety over the issue as a whole.

"Thank you, Uncle," said the Prince. "May I join you on your walk home?"

"I was going fishing," he said. "Why don't you come with me?" asked the Fire-Tender.

This was not how the prince saw his day going. He thought he would give Adisa her present and she'd be delighted with it and they would talk the day away. Perhaps she would've given him insight on how to discipline his children in a kind manner. He even thought she'd allow him to embrace her before leaving, but now he was going fishing with her father who did not trust him. He knew the Fire-Tender would be doing his fishing inside him. He was still fishing for the answer to his first question. He needed to know whether or not he was still in love with the mermaid. Was he in love with Sedina?

"Yes, I would love to, but I don't have anything to fish with, Uncle," replied the Prince.

"You have an empty gut sack now, so your guardians must believe you will catch something, my Prince, and I'd love the company," said the Fire-Tender.

The prince couldn't refuse him. He would appear rude if he did. "Of course, I would be honored to join you," said the Prince.

The Fire-Tender cringed at the word honored. No man who wanted to become a son should say this. "Delighted" or "I'd love to," or even "I could use the company too," or simply "Lead on, Bba" would have been better. Because when you say 'love' or 'Bba' you have honored them! The Fire-Tender had to control his emotions. He couldn't let the prince see how angry his reply had made him. He resented having to wear a mask. He was old enough to know that a man without the freedom to be oneself was a most dangerous man.

"Wonderful, shall we go? The tide is perfect now and I have two of my daughter's fine meat pies just crying to be eaten," said the Fire-Tender.

The men turned and made their way down the hill toward the shore. The prince looked around the countryside, searching for a long pliable stick with a nice grip to tie a line. The Fire-Tender searched the prince's face for answers. He couldn't stand the dread he felt regarding the prince courting his daughter. Only weeks ago, a union between them was all he wished for, but now he wasn't so sure. After he caught his first fish he would offer to cook it and then he would read the prince's ashes and if the ashes answered his question like he thought it might, he would permanently return the prince to his mermaid himself.

The prince found the perfect stick to tie a line to. It was strong but supply enough to handle the larger deep-sea fish that occasionally entered the bay. He masterfully stripped the bark off, exposing the moist red-brown wood underneath, then he took the string that had held Adisa's present and wove it through the crack at the top where it had been separated from the tree by lightening.

"That's impressive," said the Fire-Tender. "You are good at this."

"Thank you, Uncle. I have spent most my childhood fishing on these cliffs," the Prince replied.

"Yes," answered the Fire-Tender. Then the two men ceased speaking and cast their lines into the bay.

It was the Fire-Tender who got the first bite, but he let it go unnoticed. He was trying to join hearts with the prince, thus saving himself from all the distrust and anxiety he felt. He was impressed with how the young man accepted his fate and settled in to this new change of plans. He would make a good king and a just one. He didn't attach himself to things and he was adept at living each present moment. That was important. However, the bad side was he didn't attach himself to things easily. The Fire-Tender was thinking of his daughter to whom he was incredibly attached.

"Uncle, may I ask you something?" asked the Prince.

"Yes, of course. What is on your mind?" replied the Fire-Tender. The prince's tone made the Fire-Tender nervous. It was a young man's voice. A voice filled with uncertainty. A voice he'd never heard from the prince before.

"May I court your daughter?" the Prince shyly asked.

The Fire-Tender had been waiting for this moment for almost two years. He had anticipated it with delight and pride but now it felt empty. He felt as if he'd forced the prince to take a stand when he himself was unsure of the direction his heart was taking. Also, he never answered his original question regarding the mother of his daughter.

"I want to say yes and wholeheartedly, my Prince, however I am still unsure of your relationship to your daughter's mother, my son," he said.

The prince thought this was a good omen because the Fire-Tender had called him son. He was a good father and that was another reason why he wanted to marry his daughter. Adisa came with so many gifts plus having this wise, compassionate and strongly caring father was a perfect dowry.

The prince had to be most sincere, and perfectly honest in his response to receive the Fire-Tender's blessing.

"Bba, I will always have feelings for my daughter's mother but not as a woman or a wife or a mistress but as a messenger from Amma," said the Prince. "She found my mother's ring and placed it on her hand that day. The ring wouldn't come off. It was like my mother had come home to me. That is why I was filled with so much love for her and I believe that is why my child was born." Then the prince paused. He had to gather his thoughts for his next words would decide his fate with the Fire-Tender's daughter.

"But I do not breathe water, Bba. I breathe the sweet grass scent of your daughter. I always have. I am more myself with her than I am by myself. This has little to do with her being soft on my eyes or shaped in the body, Uncle. This is because she sees things I cannot see. She would be an amazing queen. Not only can she feel the hearts of the people, she can hear their thoughts," said the Prince. "She scares me sometimes, Bba." Then the prince became so quiet the fish ate freely of his bait.

The Fire-Tender laughed so hard he scared the greedy fish away. He was so delighted he was beside himself. Now he knew the prince loved his daughter. He was absolutely sure of it. Because love was the most frightening adventure a person could take, and the prince was afraid of his daughter.

"My Prince, nothing would give me more pleasure than for you to court my daughter. This has always been my wish," he said with more pride than he'd felt at his own wedding. "Now I think we had better eat her pies, because it does not look like we'll be having fish for dinner," he said.

And the Fire-Tender took the prince's rod from his hand and handed him a sun warmed, meat pie lovingly made by his daughter.

The Man-of-Medicine didn't remember his walk taking so long. He'd made it to the Herb-Woman's house in no time, but now the distance felt a lot farther away. As he mentally looked over his visit his body recoiled. He hated the suspicious looks her daughter gave him and her mother's competitive nature unnerved him too. Nevertheless, he was thrilled when she presented him with the lost symbol from Frill Lebo.

The medicine man stopped and breathed in as much air as his lungs would hold. He didn't feel well. The last few days had taken its toll on his body. He was sick. He could tell by the phlegm on his tongue and the whooshing sound of his heart trying to release it. He had to take care of himself now. He couldn't appear vulnerable in any way, especially to the Herb-Woman. He could hear Emadi's questions just by looking into her eyes. However, he was impressed with how the Herb-Woman handled it. She spoke so gently and in such soft tones that their meeting appeared more intimate than business in nature. She knew her daughter would never reveal a mother's possible crush on a rival.

The Man-of-Medicine and the Herb-Woman had always jockeyed for the king's attention. If one couldn't remedy the problem the king always brought in the other. However, he had still solved more cases than she, but not by much. That's why the medicine man wasn't bothered by the herbalist's glee at seeing him off center. Her gross display was amusing. She was like a card player who still had a trump to play when all the other players thought they were gone, but now he'd seen the ace up her sleeve and it suited him just fine. She'd given him the missing piece to the puzzle.

The medicine man pulled up a couple leaves of dried mullein and rolled them together. He walked off the path, into the forest and sat down and lit his herbal cigar. He slowly inhaled its smoke deeply into his lungs and released it the same way. The first draw of mullein left him gasping. His lungs felt like they were on fire. He took a second pull from the cigar and the smoke expanded into the small capillaries and vessels in the lower lobes and the mucous began to move. He heaved a small egg-shaped ball of green phlegm onto the earth, but when it hit the ground it splattered like water and was absorbed by the dirt.

The medicine man stood up in shock. Someone was watching him. He could feel it. His heart started to rapidly beat. He looked in every direction, even up in the trees to see if there were any signs of an intruder, but the forest was still. How could he belch up a solid but spit out a liquid? He knew whoever was trying to scare him was also afraid of him, so he relaxed and got back on the path toward home.

When he finally made it through the gate he fell to the ground and turned onto his back. He reached his arms and legs out as far as he could. He needed the earth's energy now. He dug his hands into the soil and stared directly into the setting sun. As he aligned himself with nature he made a vow. "I will erase those beings who have polluted the land. I will restore our people to their natural pure state. I will strengthen the earth, so it never needs to crack open again. This I promise you, dearest Amma. For I am king now!" he quietly said. And then the man rolled over and crawled into his granary.

As he entered his lodge he circled eight times to the left and then eight to the right. The knees of his pants were filthy and caked with red dirt. He pulled his legs toward him and brushed off as much soil as he could, before removing his pants altogether. He sat bare bottomed on the earthen floor. He took off his shirt and sighed. He knew what he had to do but he didn't have the strength to do it. He had to make a sacrifice and no chicken or any other animal but he would do.

The medicine man rose to standing and lit the lamp in the eastern quadrant of his lodge. He then went to the western corner and washed himself with spring water. Next, he went south and lit some Wenge incense and then he faced north and blew twenty-two sharp tones into the ceremonial flute he'd made from the breastbone of an eagle, and a strong gale came through the cracks in the wall extinguishing the candles and the lamp. All became quiet. "It's time," he said.

The shaman lifted his arm toward the sky with his fingers outstretched revealing his wide-open palm. He took a sharpened tooth from his medicine bag and sliced open his raised left hand at the base of the index finger. He dropped the tooth and quickly drew a square into the earth as he made a fist with his left hand. He slowly brought down his arm and pointed into the center of the square, and he let the blood run down his finger until it made a perfect red spot. "Dearest ancestors, I am Temne. Wash the beasts from our lands. Burn our enemies in the fire and mark those traitors to our cause. Restore the primordial flow of life so the First Being may take dominion of this earth! So it will be, for it is as it should be!"

The medicine man fell to his knees in front of the smeared diagram of symbols the orange lizard had given him. It was exactly the same pattern as the blisters on the Herb-Woman's chest. There were eight symbols that spiraled like a conch shell and they rose like a ladder into nothingness. They were an abstraction of the strange bone reading. In fact, the strange symbols were now appearing everywhere. Why hadn't he seen this before? He began to chant. His voice was so steady and gentle that the sound blended perfectly with the stream that ran the length of his farm.

"Ahm ma ka mer ka ba ba am ma ka mer ka ba ba am ma ka mer ka ba…" he droned. And he continued chanting well into the night. When he stopped, he opened his eyes and saw a pool of water surrounding him. It was already three inches deep and it covered the entire floor of the granary. "The vision!" he screamed.

The medicine man grabbed a piece of charcoal he used to cleanse the colon and began drawing the symbols on the walls of the lodge. Frantically sloshing through the water, he managed to recreate four of the symbols before they were washed away and disappeared into the mud. The small piece of charred wood was worn down to a nub. He had to save the rest of the vision exactly as the lizard had presented it to him otherwise he knew his judgment would taint their pure message.

He began pouring out the contents of every jar in the room so he could place the empty containers over the bean diagrams, but it didn't work. The beans simply floated inside the glass like little aquariums. He cursed his guides and whoever was trying to destroy his world, as he knew it only yesterday. He had to remember Frill Lebo's directions on cleansing the watery evil from Librebe. He believed that was what he came to tell him. He felt it in his bones. His bones!

The medicine man quickly gathered his divining tools from the earth and placed them high up in the dry corners of the granary. His heart was pounding. He had to calm himself. He grabbed a handful of poppy seeds and slowly chewed them until he eyes focused on what was, not what had been only seconds ago. It was a mess. It was total chaos. The oracle had begun. All was upside down and spilled on the ground. All his medicine was poured out on the table and mixed together. The flowers and herbs were now moist and beginning to mold, and his little drum from his first ancestor was floating like flotsam in the muddy water. It circled creating an eddy-like effect, making him dizzy or maybe it was the poppy seeds making him feel ill all over again.

The Man-of-Medicine began to laugh a hysterical cruel guffaw. "Do you think you can scare me!" he screamed to no one and everyone. "I am Temne! I accept your challenge. I am king here!" Then the shaman began to chant the numbers that held the world together and the water began to recede. He mumbled them so fast it was indiscernible in any language.

"Onesixninefoursixeighttenzerozerooneoneeleventwentytwoeight nine…" he recited at break-neck speed and he continued reciting them over and over again. He demanded his mind to stay clear and not question why this was happening, but like the myriad of numbers he spoke, a million questions entered his mind. Then it stopped and the poppy worked its magic. Now the shaman felt peace. He looked around his medicine lodge and saw the pattern forming. "Things have changed, my friend," he quietly said to himself.

The man didn't need a vision or premonition or omen or even a summoning to tell him what he must do. The earth had called on him to do what he must. It wasn't the watery spirit of the Nummo he was to avenge. He was to correct the imbalance Amma herself had created. The children had simply been the messengers. Why hadn't he seen that? Those little ones the queen defined as "of no one's womb", were indeed someone's children. They were as elemental to their story as he was to his own. They were here. They'd been created and found their way here. They were not evil to be eliminated from the village. They were the elements that would make the village stronger. They were challenging him to become that which he was meant to be.

The Man-of-Medicine knew there was no right or wrong in nature. The lizard ate the fly and the snake ate the lizard and the eagle was the predator of the snake and it went on and on until fire itself purified it all. "Or water," he thought. Yes! This was an elemental story. This was a fight to the end for the love of Amma herself. If he was to save this earth, his home Librebe, he had to correct the creation of it. He had to avenge its first inhabitant, his true first ancestor. He had to avenge the jackal!

BOOK III
FIRE ~ DIRT ~ SEA ~ BREATH

CHAPTER ONE

"Listen! Listen, listen. I know you're excited and a little frightened too, however let's simply listen to the message again before imagining its meaning," said Manulir.

The mob of anxious mermen calmed a bit however their dorsal fins still twitched and trembled, agitating the water around them.

"It's okay, my friend, I'll take over from here," said Sedina's father upon entering.

The Mer-king floated to the right side of the Mrage and began centering himself for a conversation he was not ready to have.

Manulir hid his annoyance at being interrupted by the king but his disappointment of not seeing his queen was obvious, and it didn't go unnoticed. "Thank you, Mer-grace," he replied before floating back among the coral behind the consul table.

The Mer-king was tired. He felt like he was being drained of his life force. The message clearly stated his granddaughter, a child he hadn't known existed until just moments ago, was being preyed upon by two-legged mammals. Why was all the feminine energy he loved most being stolen away from him, one mer-one by mer-woman? "I agree with our wise sage," said the Mer-king. Let us all listen to the new species' message again."

As the school settled, Manulir guided the gelatinous orb toward the spinning vortex and with amazing care he placed it into the eddy. The jelly-like blob slowly slid into the spiraling waters. Then it separated like the white of an egg from its yolk. When the law of gravity completed its

task and released the albumen-esque message from its silvery container, a
gentle *Boom* was heard, and the message began.

> *Oh my, dear mer-ones, of the sea*
> *I have been asked to appeal to thee.*
> *Your lost mer-one, Sedina, travels nearby*
> *Accompanied by a seahorse, far and wide.*
> *She needs your help to save her innocent mer-baby*
> *Who lives with her father upon land in Librebe.*
> *The earthen ones are not fond of the mer-girl*
> *For she was born of water and not of their world.*
> *The love of their prince for a mermaid made illegally*
> *Inspires hatred and is spreading well into the sea.*
> *Fueled by the first mammal created from vapor and earth.*
> *This jackal wishes vengeance for his disgruntled birth.*
> *But in three days your Sedina will come back to thee*
> *And together you must save her daughter, Mianshe.*

"*A daughter with a Hu-man!*" toned someone from the school.

"But Sedina is of pure lineage," muttered another and aloud.

"Please, I hear your concerns," said the even-tempered Mer-king.
"May I hear the message again," he asked?

The entire school listened to the message over and over again. The
Mer-king submersed himself so profoundly into its sound that the crowd
finally subdued their anxious toning. On the eighth time of playing the
humpback-dolphins' message, the Mer-king had an epiphany. "Eight," he
said with awareness.

"Yes, eight," said Manulir in agreement although he was unaware of
what he was agreeing to.

"If the message is on point, my dear ones, we have three days before
Sedina returns. So, let's try to be as prepared as possible for what is to come.
Now I bid you all get some rest and if perchance your dreams illuminate
something in the message, please include me."

The Mer-king signaled Manulir to follow him and the two majestic mermen darted out of the hall toward the king's private cavern. As they swam by, a strange silence surrounded the crowd until their water's wake no longer rippled around them.

"So much opposition," sighed the Mer-king.

"Yes, binary," inferred the Mrage. "Land and earth, fish and Hu-man, jackal and mermaid. It's the jackal reference that baffles me most. Why would a jackal desire a mermaid? Are they not land scavenger creatures?" asked Manulir.

As the Mer-king and Manulir settled into a bed of soft algae, a young mermaid attendant entered with conch shells filled with water hyacinth tea. The Mer-king took a sip and toned a compliment before continuing his conversation with the wise merman.

"I have no idea of the habits of a jackal or of two-legged men for that matter even though I have inherited half their genetic ladder. Sad isn't it. So, my wise friend, maybe we should familiarize ourselves with their culture," said a solemn Mer-king.

"I could not agree with you more, my heart," said the Mer-queen upon entering. "It seems our granddaughter hails partly from a small country off the Lumerian waters called Librebe. They are an ancient culture with Amman roots. Their creator nurtures balance between the genders."

"And their creation myth?" asked Manulir. He was so excited to see his queen. He wished he'd left a space for her to finish her thought before introducing his question, but he had to ask just then. He had to look into her eyes and he had to do it immediately. It was nothing he could control. The best he could do was to keep his thoughts of love as pure as possible.

The Mer-king bristled at the sage's tone. No matter how equable the question he still felt its arrogance. No one's creation was myth! "Ah, my friend, you are either here or not. There is no myth to it," said the Mer-king. The king didn't understand his need to point out the obvious to Manulir, but when the auric field of the waters surrounding the sage merged with his queen's when their eyes met, the Mer-king understood all too well, and it made his point all the more valid.

"So, my love, they honor balance. This is good given our granddaughter is half them and half her mother," stated the Mer-king.

"But their creator Amma's first creation was born out of balance. She bore a solitary jackal," the Mer-queen quietly stated.

"The jackal, is that not a dog? I was under the assumption dogs were Hu-men's most loyal fans," said Manulir.

"But dogs are pack animals, my friend, and this one was alone," said the Mer-king.

"Thus, he masturbated using the earth, his mother as his passage," said the Mer-queen. Her dorsal shuddered at the reality of her last thought.

"And?" asked the Mer-king.

"Chaos," answered the Mer-queen.

"Why?" pondered Manulir.

"To begin the spiritual journey," said the Mer-king finishing everyone's thoughts.

"So, in summary, we have a misanthropic male dog from Hu with abandonment issues who wishes to avenge his Mother's creation, thus himself, so he can return to his father, his source?" asked an incredulous Manulir.

"Yes," the Mer-king sadly said.

"Incredible," the Mer-queen quietly replied.

"Who is the father," asked the Mer-king.

"It isn't clear being Amma was both male and female. Amma's second attempt at creating outside of itself was the Nummo spirits and for some reason they sound very familiar to me. They too have both male and female capabilities and can birth forms into matter singularly, each by itself. They are watery and use vibration and sound to create. Their moisture made the land regions green like it is today." Then the Mer-queen became silent.

"So, we have an orphaned dog with a carnivorous nature but with no other animals to feed it nor another of his kind to procreate with. Ahh, charming," said Manulir.

"With a grudge against his siblings who are exactly in their creator's image—both being male and female entities, watery and fluid, with the secret of changing vibration into matter. Most interesting," said the Mer-king.

"And your granddaughter, my king, is watery in nature and has the ability to speak loving truth and could inherit her father's kingdom, given her status in birth," and then Manulir stopped speaking.

"Yes," said the Mer-queen. "My granddaughter is in a great deal of danger."

The Mer-king's head was splitting. Everything was. His school was not happy about taking on the burden of a stray princess who had shown no attention to one of their own. Those that wished to be of service, did so blindly, or to gain the attention of the royal line. The Mer-king's head ached. He had no idea if his daughter left of her own accord. He used to believe she was jetted away by a strong current or possibly eaten by a blue whale and had just made peace with those answers. However, his daughter would be home soon to answer the question herself.

The Mer-king's head truly hurt, and it continued to throb. Why? This was not the time to address his emotions. There were more important issues to deal with, like the anomalies going on around them. The toxic waters were splitting their DNA. It had already created humpback-dolphins. Now a jackal wanted to devour his granddaughter and create a discordant movement on land against the sea. Nehtoon's heart was breaking for his family. His poor unknown granddaughter would be torn apart by having to choose an allegiance to her mother or to her father. It was an unnatural choice for any child. It would create division and malice between Hu-men and peace seeking Merfolk. His soul was being shattered because all this had to matter more than the merman standing beside him holding the hand of his beloved.

"First, we must arrange a celebration for our daughter's return, something comforting and humble in nature. No fanfare or ornate displays, this must feel soothing. Familiarity is what she needs now. She needs her family," said the Mer-king.

The Mer-queen looked at her mate with admiration. He was a most remarkable merman. A true king almost god-like in his desire for truth and love in all he did. There were times all she wanted to do was to listen to him tone. He brought understanding and consolation to even the water surrounding him. She adored her king.

"Yes, my daughter has never been fond of public recognition. She is a stargazer," said the Mer-queen. Then the queen remembered her last conversation with her daughter and her gracious smile flat-lined. The memory rose up in her, chilling her down to her bones. "Oh my!" exclaimed the Mer-queen.

The Mer-king and the wise merman quickly swerved and faced their queen.

"The day before we left for the Sacred Ceremony she asked me about a prophecy. She asked how something that had been created could disappear and exist no more and I didn't take her question seriously," the Mer-queen said.

"What prophecy," asked the Mer-king? "We need to speak with the one who had this premonition."

"Yes, of course," said the Mer-queen. "Upon her return, I will ask her at the appropriate time."

"This jackal wants to wipe out the lineage of his watery creator siblings," said Manulir.

"But he is a part of that lineage," said a confused Mer-queen.

"He wants to be king. He wants the mutants to rule," the Mer-king concluded.

Then the triumvirate said no more.

CHAPTER 2

The medicine man opened his eyes and immediately stood up from his prone position. He felt invigorated, strong and alert. He scanned his lodge and could see at once the chaos surrounding him. It was exciting. He could distinguish between corn and split pea, or black-eyed peas and small grains. He could tell which seeds were soaked through from those that were damp and beginning to mold. He could feel the skin on the little lizard drum tightening from the rays of morning sun spilling through the thatched roof. He could hear a mouse scurrying from left to right, trying to hide behind an upturned basket. It was trying to find an escape route into the woods, or was it trying to hide itself from the medicine man's gaze. This amazed him. Now it was so easy to take everything in all at once, while keeping all the information separate.

"Hah!" cried the medicine man. He could see like the eagle and it was exhilarating. His sense of smell was keen too. He could decipher which bean was spoiled from the ones that had begun to sprout.

"Ha, dearest Amma. Thank you!" he screamed.

His voice had changed. His tenor had become a baritone. This was good. He believed depth in sound reflected a more profound understanding. People would not only hear him they would feel him talking. He wanted to explore his world with his new eyes, but first he had to clear the old one.

The man lifted the spilled basket and grabbed the mouse by its tail. He went outside and flung it far into the woods. He picked up some kindling and added it to the ashes from last night's fire. Next, he took some salt and nuggets of copal incense from his pocket and threw it onto the stack of wood. Then he lit it and with one long deep baritone exhalation he slowly breathed life into the fire. "Aaahhhhmmmmaaaah," he said with intention, and the fire bristled and raged its appreciation in dark crimson tones. It excited him. Even the elements were doing his bidding.

The man quickly walked into his granary and sorted through the debris. He adeptly collected the medicine that was still of use and discarded the rest. When the basket was full he threw the entire contents onto the fire, repeating his mantra honoring the Creator. "Aaahhhhmmmmaaaah," he groaned. He did this until his granary lay beautifully bare, adorned only by his most powerful artifacts.

In the east was his lava stone mortar and pestle, which he filled with copal, frankincense, wenge and myrrh. In the south he buried the lizard drum in the earth and then stacked his ancestral red dirt bowls in a basket over it, however the crystal bowl he used to honor the waters of the west was broken so he dug a hole and pushed all the black stones he could find into its form. It looked like a mosaic basin of tourmaline and onyx, lava stone and obsidian, shungite and black abalone. Afterward he filled the ebon fountain with spring water that was so clear he could see his reflection, and he screamed.

"Ughaaaah!" cried the medicine man.

There in the water his hairy face and yellow eyes were mirrored back at him. The man now had a week's worth of growth on his face and the whites of his eyes had turned an amber hue. When he raised his hands to examine himself, he noticed the downy tufts of hair. It extended the length of his arms all the way down to the backs of his hands. "Amma, what is this?" he growled. However, when he demanded an answer from his creator he saw his teeth had grown, making his jaw appear longer.

The man fell to all fours and began exploring his body from head to toe. Had he died and been reborn? It seemed the only answer for such a transformation. His senses were keen, way keener than ever before. His hair had turned coarse and wiry and it had grown up the back of his neck. He now had hair on his hands and over his toes. His incisors were longer and slightly separate from the others, and his legs and hips opened and closed and lifted and lowered effortlessly. There was no muscular strain to his movements. It was as if his body responded immediately to his thoughts. Almost involuntarily like his eyelids did when dirt became airborne.

The man sat down and listened to the machinations of his internal organs. His blood flowed easily. His heart beat steadily. He had no desire to urinate or eat. He was simply alert, aware and erect. The man stared at himself in awe for a long moment. Then he returned to cleaning up his granary.

He turned to the north. Normally the eagle would fly in the northern sky, but it felt wrong today. He spied the eagle's feather hanging over the doorway and remembered dropping it during last night's ceremony. Was it no longer pure? He knew it was never good to doubt one's tools. It could make the medicine bad, so the man searched his granary for something new for his northern entrance. The heron was too graceful to do the job he needed. The hawk was too independent to listen to his subtle wisdom. The falcon could take his vision higher and assure its success and it would do his bidding by any means necessary. "Yes," said the Man-of-Medicine. "Yes, the falcon will fly perfectly here."

When his granary was intact the man pulled up a stool and sat by the fire. The large clump of wet beans, wood, trinkets and feathers burnt slowly emitting huge clouds of billowing smoke. The strange bonfire produced amazing light. There were so many colors bursting forth in the flames. It sizzled like the fire show the Chinese put on in the marketplace at the end of their year.

The man pulled his stool just behind the ring of light exuding from the fire. It was hot and felt good. He became sleepy. He needed to rest. He was looking forward to dreaming. He couldn't wait to see the other dimensions with his newly developed awareness. He knew Amma would explain why the spirits had blessed him. He was happy and proud to be the emissary for his creator. He would never fail Amma. He felt like the Hogons of the old culture. They were pure and untouched by earthly woes. He was sure he'd be given divine wisdom tonight. He knew a message was coming because Amma had given him his new form so he wouldn't forget or misunderstand it. His new senses would never allow it. He couldn't wait to fall asleep.

And so, the Man-of-Medicine fell soundly asleep.

CHAPTER 3

The Herb-Woman's chest was on fire. A bolt of lightning split the sky and the flash illuminated the blisters covering her torso. They were getting larger. She knew she should lance them, but she didn't have the energy to lift herself out of bed yet get everything needed to safely do it. Plus, she was out of the mother aloe vera, and the young new stalks didn't have the wisdom to do the job. She needed fresh dragon's blood too and given the storm brewing, harvesting the sap was out of the question. She had a little left in a glass jar in the cupboard but like her tea she preferred all her medicine to be as fresh as possible.

The storm was growing. There was a clap of thunder so intense it made the fluid in the blisters burse from side to side. "Aaaough!" she cried. It was painful. She had to do something to relieve her agony. She had some young cucumbers in her clay bowl. They would bring relief, not for long, but immediately.

The Herb-Woman gently removed her pillow filling the gap behind her lower back and placed it horizontally underneath her. She inched her body down until her shoulders were slightly raised. Next, she squeezed her stomach and slung her legs over the side of the bed. "Aaaaeough eee, Amma!" she screamed, and the tears voluntarily fell from her eyes. The pain was excruciating.

She wanted to call out to Emadi for help but she was too ashamed to do so. Unless she was willing to completely confide in her daughter she had to let her remain innocently angry with her. She had to protect her. She knew the medicine man was already suspicious and Emadi's questioning him would irritate him all the more. He respected her daughter's strength but if she got in his way he wouldn't hesitate to trample her like a weed. Plus, he knew she was having her moon. He could smell the fresh blood and it terrified him. A menstruating woman could absorb the power of the most powerful shaman anywhere. Men were afraid of the creative abilities of fertile women. That was why so many took them by force. They wanted their creative nurturing power for themselves. She would kill a man who tried to force himself upon her daughter, and all it would take was a kind word and a cup of puff adder-mint tea.

The Herb-Woman steadied her breath while she sat at the edge of her cot and waited to hear her daughter's gentle snores coming from the hammock. Young women had such hot blood. She couldn't remember the last time she slept in the open on a hot night. She was too old for that now. The cool air and lack of firm support underneath her body would have crippled her for the rest of the day.

She watched her daughter sleep while she regained her strength. She needed to get moving so she'd have a little time to herself. It was going to rain shortly, and the storm would surely bring her daughter rushing back into the house. She wasn't ready for her daughter's questions. She had no idea what was happening to her anyway so what could she honestly tell her.

The old woman got out of bed and walked into the kitchen like a pregnant sloth. She made it to the chair closest to the doorway and slid into it. She was exhausted. She couldn't remember the last time she'd felt this badly. She took the broom from the corner and used it to push the bowl of Persian cucumbers toward her. She was going to have a harder time getting to the knife. It was in the drawer and since the broom didn't have fingers she'd have to use it as a cane and make the five-foot walk.

The Herb-Woman took a deep breath and lifted herself out of the chair and took one giant step. Thunder was heard in the distance and then a long bolt of lightning flashed through the small kitchen window. She stopped. "Please, Mma Amma, gently please," she said to no one and everyone. She continued her hobbled walking until she made it to the counter. She gingerly opened the utensil drawer and took out her paring knife. As she turned to make her way back to the table where the cool fruit lay, another clap of thunder was heard, and was quickly accompanied by more lightning.

The woman took the round two-sided mirror from the counter and set it before her on the table. She reached in her pocket and removed the small Zippo lighter her daughter had given her from her last trip into the city. It was a prized possession the woman rarely used, especially when flint or stone was around. She placed it on the table and picked up the knife and sliced the cucumbers into thin uniformed pieces.

Again, the thunder rang out into the night air and again it was accompanied by another electric light. It made her jump. "Why is thunder coming before lightening?" she asked. Maybe she imagined it. Maybe sound did come before light. She wasn't feeling well enough to take on such spiritual matters right now. She needed to release the burning in her chest, and quickly, but before she lanced the boils she needed to put their message down first.

The roots woman was tired. She didn't have the energy to cut vegetables yet go back to her room for a pen and paper, so she flipped the mirror to its smaller view and drew the design directly onto the glass with the only thing available—her daughter's eyebrow pencil. Normally this would've upset her. Her daughter always left her hair supplies, barrettes, rubber bands, Marcel irons and scissors, lipsticks and pencils in an old coffee tin on the table. Not only was it unclean to have it near her herbs, it left her bloodline open to manipulation. A strong shaman could take your hair or nails or a tissue you used to blow your nose to blow you to smithereens. Her daughter knew this. She'd helped her cure many people from this sickness of the soul. Usually it was a lover wanting revenge or an envious neighbor coveting the joy of another. She'd yelled at her own flesh too many times about leaving pieces of herself all over, but her child was trusting—too trusting.

After recording the shape and whereabouts of her blisters the woman flipped the mirror over and studied the sores one by one. The first one had swollen to the point that it looked like a bee's butt in mid sting. She purified her needle with fire then soaked it in the cool solution of green aloe vera and witch hazel herbs. She moved the slices of cucumber nearby so they were ready to absorb the pain that was sure to come. She decided to pour herself a glass of fermented herbs in case the cucumber cooled off before the pain did. She took her broomstick and pushed the liquor jar toward her. She didn't have the strength to get a glass, so she opened the Mason jar and took a long gulp. She was ready.

A huge clap of thunder shook the house and was followed by a bright, neon-blue jagged line of light. The Herb-Woman quickly pushed the needle into the bulbous sore. While gripping the table, she screamed into the sleeve of her nightgown. She didn't see the figure in the shadows outside her window. She didn't taste the burn from the shot of herbal alcohol she'd consumed. She didn't see the bright orange mucous oozing out onto the table nor heard her heart pounding its staccato rhythm. She only felt pain. She was consumed by pain, the burning brutal pain of Frill Lebo's release.

Emadi saw it. She saw it all. The lightning entered the house and traveled into the needle. The needle sparked when her mother pierced her skin. She couldn't believe the orange orbs she saw exiting her mother's body. She felt the electricity the orange bubbles emanated as it crossed the room and entered her tear ducts. Then the orbs floated inside her throat and they made the star gland in the center of her head sparkle. She felt it all and it was awesome! But Emadi never saw her mother slide off her chair onto the floor. Nor did she feel her mother's last breath or hear her last words.

"Be careful, my flesh, stay light and rise above the rest," said the Herb-Woman as she slowly exited this world and entered another.

CHAPTER 4

"Too much!" Rose said. "That was way too much," she said again. Then she flung the covers off her body and breathed in the cool sea air. She patted the bum of the young man sleeping beside her and got out of bed. "Sleepin' like the baby you are," she quietly said.

She grabbed her tobacco pouch from the nightstand and the batiste linen nightdress she inherited from her great-grandmother and quietly made her way out the back door into the garden. She slid the soft thin fabric over her svelte body and sat down in the grass and rolled herself a cigarette.

"Too much," she mumbled again. "I have to stop drinkin' my own recipes," she lilted in that sweet southern tone indigenous to the island.

She loved the island. It was where her grandmother was born, and her great-grandmother had escaped to. It was her great grandma that took the family tree down a paler path. She'd been pushed off the little canoe they used to escape the slave ship by those bigger and darker than her, so she only slept with Indians and Creoles after that. Now all that was left was a group of yellow slaves trying to oppress each other.

"Shame, shame on me, callin' us yellow," she muttered as she blew out smoke.

She looked at the young man dreaming in her bed. He came to her three nights ago wanting her to make the reverend's wife fall in love with him. He wanted to get off the island and he was willing to take Jacob's ladder to get there.

"Little devil, you," she quietly said to herself.

Why anyone would want the reverend's wife was beyond her. The woman was the town slut and her cuckolded husband was the most pious person she'd ever met. She guessed between the two of them there was balance. But this boy had a gift. He was pure and truly innocent, plus he had the voice of an angel. He could sing. That's why she slept with him and drank her own Kool-Aid, so he'd have more experience to make that kind of decision. Asking for help from the ancestors on the other side of the veil could prove disastrous. She knew he should be careful of what he was asking for; because the preacher's wife was the darkest light-skinned woman she'd ever met. She was truly evil.

Rose stopped thinking bad thoughts about her neighbors. She really had no judgment about the wife or her lover. People would live whatever lessons they needed learning. She was just ornery because of that feeling. It always made her a touch testy. She headed to the only place where the bad couldn't get her—her rose garden. Nothing bad ever happened around sweetness. She called it her aromatherapy. She'd planted gardenias and frangipani bushes, some honeysuckle and jasmine vines, and lily of the valley covered the ground and it was all sheltered by huge magnolia and jacaranda trees that her mother's mother had planted. She kicked off her slippers and walked in the moist dirt. She'd been doing it since childhood, but she'd never appreciated it more since her return home some eight years ago.

Rose looked down upon her namesakes and smiled. "Well, here you are my sweet sterling silvers," she sighed.

She'd gotten that particular bunch of rose bushes from a president's wife that must always remain nameless. She wanted out of the oval office as much as the people wanted her husband out, so she came to Rose and asked her for assistance and she helped her for a kindly sum. It allowed her the rare fragrant Sterling Silver roses from Asia that she so adored plus the rest of her family's land.

"And there you are," she coldly said to the apparition. "Too much," she quietly told herself before fading off into a crisp, adrenaline-filled stillness.

The old woman sat silently panting in the corner under the jacaranda tree. She looked at Rose and gulped like a guppy that had jumped from a fish tank onto a shag carpet. She was not from the island. That was for sure. Her clothes alone gave that away. Rose couldn't tell if it was the sweet smell of the garden or the huge boils on the ghost's chest oozing a syrupy tangerine pus making her feel ill, but she definitely wasn't feeling well now.

"Good evening. You know where you are?" Rose asked.

The spirit woman looked at her with the blankest expression she'd ever seen but she understood the question. She could tell because the woman started looking around for the answer. She was trying to remember or familiarize herself with her present surroundings.

"I know you," moaned the old woman.

It hurt Rose to listen to a phantom talk. You heard what they said way before the echo reached your ears. If someone could replicate that sound it would revolutionize the music industry, but she had left that world a long time ago. She tried telling that to her family who came by seasonally like a parasite cleanse to beg or borrow, but not so much since she'd moved to her great-grandmother's house. They were all too afraid.

It hurt to have the dead pass through you. It was way too much information. You smelled everything they smelled and felt everything they felt, and you had the added experience of them not wanting to let go of all that information. Sometimes she prayed for Alzheimer's. She thought it was one of God's more humane diseases. You came into this world not knowing a damn thing you might as well leave it in the same condition. Who wanted or needed all those disappointments and regrets anyway.

"Your family know you're here?" Rose asked. She made sure to speak as clearly and as monotone sounding as humanly possible. No vibrato or diphthongs or harmonies or lilts to shake her up. Too much vibration could tear a new soul apart.

"I need your help, Rose," said the Herb-Woman.

Rose walked backward out of her garden and spun around counter clockwise three times. In all her years of divination (and she had been divining since birth) no one had ever called her by name. The only one that knew her name was her guide and spiritual sister, the mermaid from the

Pyrenees. She had to be careful now. She couldn't think or talk out loud or write things down until she was sure who or what this being was. For now, she had to commit her body to remembering things for her.

Rose crept back into the house and saw the man. He was still asleep in her bed and it irritated her. "Wake up!" she hollered. "You got to go! Now!" she screamed.

The poor boy had no idea what hit him. He was sleeping one moment and was being screamed at the next, but being he was still young he was used to it. He quickly got up and grabbed his things and ran out of the house taking the money he'd left to pay her with him.

"You little thief! You think I didn't see that!" she yelled.

The boy couldn't hear Rose howling into the wind as his car skidded out of her driveway and onto the dirt road that led back into town. It was a new moon night, so she was sure she'd be avenged immediately. If you weren't careful on those old country roads you could end up in a swamp smelling like oysters and being courted by crocodiles. He was a native boy, so he probably just got stuck on the shoal of Gilla Pass and then walked to ole Hub's place.

Hub's never closed. He made most of his money on the spontaneity of the drunks in the area or the many trysts going on around those parts. Tourism wasn't going to pay your mortgage. Most foreigners were terrified of the waters. Between the tales of the river passages eating boats alive and fallen civilizations coming back for revenge only those looking to find treasure or trouble came here. Then there were those like the President's wife and a few movie stars that came to see her. She didn't care much for them, but they allowed her to keep her family's land in one parcel. She owned half of the twenty-two-mile island and no one but her and old Bennie were ever allowed there uninvited.

"Okay, who the hell are you? Cause you sure don't look like no angel to me," she said to herself.

Rose remembered the woman's skirt. It had a print on it set in a batik that she'd seen before. The only other telling thing was she didn't wear earrings and had no jewelry on at all and she smelled like cucumbers. But that was probably because she was trying to take the heat out of those blisters. They were huge. Someone burned this lady. But why did she come to her now? Why wait until she was dead to come for help?

"What help can I give the ole coot now," whined Rose. "I need a drink."

Rose went into the kitchen and put the kettle on and got her French press ready. She needed courage and what better strength than dark coffee and cognac. She opened the refrigerator and took a handful of soaking almonds and ate them. As she chomped on the nuts she hummed. It was a strange rhythm she had never heard before.

Yah hoo ooohumm
Yahh hoom
Yah hoo ooohumm
Yah way oomu mu mu
Yah way oomu mu ooo

She continued humming as she made her breakfast. She peeled a mango and devoured it. Next, she poured a shot of cognac from her grandmother's amethyst snifter and downed it. Then she finished with a cup of the blackest espresso ever made.

"Yummy, I'm ready," she said.

Rose never bothered with getting dressed. There was no one around to see her naked body through the sheer linen anyway. She grabbed her big straw hat she got in Amish country but decided against it. She'd gotten that hat while traveling with a wild redheaded biker who had the sweetest disposition of insanity she had ever met. She had to admit, she loved herself some crazy men. She had to focus. She had a mournful woman in her backyard that needed her attention. She had to help her home. She sure as hell couldn't stay where she was, so she grabbed her late sister's Irish linen cloche and headed out the side door.

She made her way down to the 'y' in the river where the salt mixed with the fresh water. It was her favorite place for ritual. But as she approached the delta she saw the top of someone's head sitting on a rock and as sure as she knew her own hands, Rose knew that old coot was waiting for her so she stopped and collected herself. She grounded herself as deeply as she could into the earth. She imagined a ley-line of energy going into the center of the planet up through her spine and into the heavens. Then she divided the gold-silver ribbon into three cords and braided herself into the hem of Mother Mary and Lord Yeshua, and all the Mahavidya's robes before she took another step toward the old ghost soliciting her help.

"I'm coming now, Auntie. Here I come," she said as she made her way down the pathway alongside the river flowing out toward the sea.

CHAPTER 5

"Here they come," said the Queen.

The king sat on the edge of his bed deep in thought.

"Brother, did you hear me?" asked the Queen.

The king turned his head toward his sister, but he hadn't heard her. He was listening to something else. The sheepherders from the small green belt near Librebe were playing their strange flutes in breathy chirping rhythms. It reminded him of her. He could see the Herb-Woman walking up the path and hear her breath punctuating each step. The herders must have felt the same way because they were playing the background music to her familiar march. Everyone loved her. She gave so much of herself to everybody and anyone, and all she ever asked for in return was a cup of hot tea.

"Brother," the Queen-Guardian softly said.

"Yes, yes, I know," muttered the King.

The queen knew her brother well. He didn't have the heart to mourn another lover. He didn't know she knew this, but she did. After the death of the prince's mother his witch of a fourth-wife separated him from those he loved and as a result, he took ill. That's when the affair started. The Herb-Woman soothed him in many ways for many years. It only stopped because his son ran away from home to the university in London. After that nothing on earth could soften his heart. He was inconsolable.

"Brother, the elders are waiting," she quietly said.

"I know. Please go and tell them I will be there promptly," he replied.

"And will you be?" asked the Queen.

"Please give me a moment to just…" he said before trailing off into another silence.

The queen fell silent as well. "They are coming in from other villages," she finally said. "She was truly loved," she added, saying it more to herself than to her brother.

"Who is with her daughter?" asked the King.

"Adisa is caring for her," she replied. "Plus, I sent a few others by the house."

"Who am I to meet with now," he asked?

This worried the queen because it was the first bit of information she gave him upon entering his room. "The Man-of-Medicine, Elder Josop, the Fire-Tender and the Prince, my King," she replied, making a point to honor him.

"I see. Why are we meeting only hours after her death?" he asked. It was strange to disturb a corpse's transitioning. One should mourn until the time came for it to dance over the rainbow bridge into the arms of its ancestors.

"They wish…" and then the Queen lapsed into silence.

"They want me to see her body, is that it? Why, my sister?" he asked. His strength had returned now, and he wanted answers.

"Oh, my brother, everyone is talking. Even nature thinks there may have been foul play. That unusual storm last night, and the duduju virus no one's heard of before, even her daughter insists there was something strange about the matter."

The king immediately interrupted his sister. "The matter is death, the death of a loved one of this lineage! Excuse my tone, my sister, but this death is closer to me—to us than you imagine," he firmly said.

"I understand," she solemnly said. "We have received notice that the Fermemi Queen is coming to honor our dear friend," she respectfully added. "I can sit in for you if you like. I can delegate the funereal duties. It would give you some time to yourself," she condoled.

The king sat with his head in his hands.

"Should I hold the information that the shepherd queen is coming," she asked?

The king finally lifted his head and made eye contact with the queen. "Yes, and please listen to the elders and bring their cares to me. Then we can decide how to handle all this together," he said. "And my Queen, use the healing chamber for the meeting," he added.

"A wise choice," she replied.

"And if you could, my sister, sit across from the Man-of-Medicine for me," he gently said.

"Of course, my King," she firmly said. Then the queen embraced her brother and quickly exited toward the hall and as she walked she gathered herself and placed her vulnerabilities deep inside her bosom.

The king's body ached. He felt his leg muscles jumping underneath his skin. He ran his hands down his legs and massaged his calves. He wasn't going to be able to keep up this pace much longer, but he had no choice. It wasn't a good time for him to hand over the kingdom. The king grabbed the pillows from his bed and a cushion from his reading chair and inched his way to the floor. When prone he took the pillows and placed them under his knees and rested with his legs elevated. As he lay on the ground bolstered by the cushions he prayed. "I, King-Guardian rise above the chaos and unify all opposition, for this is who I am. This is what I do!" Then he roared in agony from the cramp rising from his leg into his groin.

The Man-of-Medicine was surprised. In fact, they all were to see the queen enter without her brother, their king. The prince rose first and embraced his aunt and offered her the chair to his right. It was the position to the left of the king's chair. However, the queen motioned for him to take that seat, and then she sat down in the king's chair facing the Man-of-Medicine.

"Good evening, my family, I am so sorry to keep you waiting. The king has business to attend to on top of his heavy heart, so he won't be joining us at this moment, but soon," she cryptically added.

The queen was a wise woman and an even more astute politician than her brother. She knew if she left the door open for her brother to enter at any time she would have a more amenable meeting. She also knew mentioning business before the rite of passage referred to a hierarchy. She was ready, but now they weren't.

"I know I am a poor substitute for my brother. I also know there is no substitute for my sister, Ellen. So, I ask you, how do we honor our unique spirit, our Herb-Woman?" she confidently asked.

The king watched the entire meeting from the gazer's round behind the mirror. It was a viewing hole where one could see the marriage between science and faith. It was built that way so they could each share their knowledge. The room not only allowed one to view a surgery, it also opened up so one could see the stars and view the seasons move. But they no longer used it because they no longer had a Hogon like in the olden days. The years of traveling to find a safe haven from the slave traders had robbed them of this great cultural gift. The elder Hogon (their tribe's most important spiritual teacher) had died on the journey to Librebe. Since tradition ruled the Hogon was the only one able to find his replacement, no one replaced him. Thus, the entire spiritual realm of their existence changed when they moved habitats.

The Fire-Tender looked at his hands. He was not used to having meetings with anything other than fire, and fire never spoke in riddles.

"Is my father okay, Queen-Guardian?" asked the Prince.

"He is in mourning, my son," she said. "I assure you, he would've preferred to be here rather than where he must be at present," she added.

"My Queen, I have faith everything is as it should be," said the Man-of-Medicine. However, it was more a question than an affirmation.

"My daughter is arranging the dama's dancers and organizing their masks and the young pure males are harvesting the wood for the ceremony's fire," said the Fire-Tender.

"Nanny Leboya has organized the women and the repast is being prepared," said the Prince.

"Emadi will bring me our sister's personal requests regarding her wishes for the day, I mean her ceremony," said Elder Josop.

"May I cleanse her body first?" asked the medicine man of the elder.

The queen simply smiled when he overlooked her and directed his question to the older male.

The king had to place his hand over his mouth to cover his alarm. It was never a question of who would clean the body. With the Herb-Woman gone who else could do this but the Man-of-Medicine, so why would he ask such an obvious question?

Elder Josop looked to the queen before responding to the medicine man's request. He didn't want to ruffle any royal feathers, especially today.

"It is not only my pleasure to grant you this, my friend, it is your duty. However, my sister's daughter wishes to be there with you when you do this," the Queen said. "The Herb-Woman was all Emadi had, so if you could allow her to share in this responsibility I believe her balance will be restored. I know my sister Ellen would have wished this," stated the Queen.

The king was astonished. Not only had his sister handled the strange insult with tact, she'd had the foresight to handle the request as well.

The prince thought it was brilliant. He knew this room. He had played here often as a child. He could feel the small but perceptible stream of air flowing in and rushing against his eyebrow. It was to the left of him in the western corner.

"Yes, my Queen. It is an honorable arrangement," the Man-of-Medicine consented and then he folded his arms into the sleeves of his boubou.

The Fire-Tender could almost taste the bitterness in the medicine man's mouth. The Herb-Woman was once again gently managing the situation. Now her own flesh would clean her for her dama—the funeral ceremony. The Fire-Tender discreetly brushed the Man-of-Medicine's face with his eyes before resting his gaze on his queen.

"Is there anything else we should report?" asked the Queen, but her tone announced the meeting was quite over. After a moment of silence, she pushed her chair back and stood up. "Oh, my dear Uncles, may we have a gentle water drum under those flutes please? Those high tones are making me a little crazy," she said with her sweetest smile.

The men all agreed with her. It was true the little pipes and whistles were most annoying.

"I will handle that, my Queen," said Elder Josop.

"Thank you, Elder," she said. And then she paused for a good—long— moment. "I will miss her," she said. Then she left the room without another sound.

The prince looked at the Fire-Tender. The Fire-Tender smiled back. The Man-of-Medicine quickly excused himself.

"I must begin preparations. Amma's blessings," the medicine man said.

The Fire-Tender turned to wish him blessings in return, but the man had already left the room.

"He is in good form," said Elder Josop with a smile.

The prince and the Fire-Tender knew the elder's words carried many meanings. The two men smiled at the old man's sarcasm, which held more truth than either wished to admit. Before the elder could clutch the table to raise himself, the prince took one of his arms and the Fire-Tender his other and they lifted him to standing.

"Between the three of us we make quite an eagle," said an amused Elder Josop.

The prince laughed at the older man's humor. As the three men crossed the threshold and exited the hall, the prince turned and looked directly at the place where his father sat watching them, until the door closed blocking both men's view.

∗ /\/\ ∗

CHAPTER 6

Someone was watching her. Mianshe could feel their burrowing eyes, but she couldn't hear their thoughts. They didn't think; therefore, they must have known who she was.

"Verité, what?" yelled the young mermaid. "Why are you spying on me?" Mianshe had given up on hissing and traded it in for outright punctuated yelling, however only at her brother.

Verité calmly continued staring at his sister.

"What?" she asked him again and in a louder voice.

"You are in trouble," he calmly said.

Mianshe burst into tears. "I didn't do anything! I have cleaned and washed and…"

But before the girl could list anything else, Verité took two fingers and clamped her mouth shut. He quickly began talking in a hushed voice filled with secrecy.

"The Herb-Woman died…" he started saying.

"Ugh bib en boo ught," Mianshe declared through closed lips.

Verité held his other hand up to his own lips to quiet the girl. "Some people may say it was duduju that killed her. I know it wasn't, but we can't tell them that. We can't tell them without telling them how we know. Stop squirming!" he said between clenched teeth. "Because if we tell them you can talk without talking to anything including animals they will be even more afraid of you than they already are."

Mianshe had enough of Verité pressing her lips together. She felt like a platypus and that was a horrible feeling. So, she took her free hand (the one which wasn't trying to pry Verité's hand from her face) and pinched him hard.

"Ow!" he cried. "*T'es méchante*, mean girl, a horrible person," he hissed.

"I didn't do anything to the Herb-Woman. I liked her and the way her body jiggled," she declared. Then she plopped herself on the floor and buried her face behind her hands.

Verité hadn't thought his plan through. He only wanted to warn his sister about how cruel people could be and teach her how to protect herself. He hadn't considered the grief aspect of his lesson. Had he known she would feel this badly he would have surely been more understanding when telling her the woman died.

"I'm sorry, Mianshe. I'm sorry your friend died," he said.

"She wasn't my friend," said a puzzled Mianshe. The young girl stood up and looked at her brother for an explanation.

"Well, I'm sorry you will miss her body jiggling," he said. He was starting to get irritated in that way he got when talking to the mermaid.

"No you're not." she sweetly said.

"You're missing the point, silly girl! You are in danger," he said, and he was truly serious. Then he pinched her in return.

"Why did you pinch me!" she cried.

"I wanted to do it when you pinched me, but you wouldn't shut up!" he screamed.

"What on earth does pinching have to do with talking, silly boy?" Mianshe laughed and made a point of saying silly as silly sounding as possible.

"Stop," said Verité. "and breathe," he told himself. He began toning to his sister. "*You are in danger. Someone wants to hurt you. I dreamt a tidal wave washed you away. I heard you crying. I want to teach you how to fight,*" and then he folded his hands and sat down cross-legged on the porch.

"Okay," she loudly said. Then she jumped up and started to dance around kicking and swatting at anything and everything.

"What is going on?" asked the Prince as he walked into the courtyard. Only seconds ago, he was pondering over how to approach his father about the rumors surrounding the Herb-Woman's sudden death, but now all his good reasoning had vanished upon entering and finding his daughter fighting with imaginary beings. "I ask again," he demanded. "What is going on?"

"Verité is teaching me how to protect myself," she said.

Verité simply looked down at the ground.

"Well, he is doing a fine job. You truly scared me," said the Prince.

After that, the prince grabbed Verité's hand in one hand and Mianshe's in his other and escorted the children into the house. "Sit," said the Prince. When the children were seated and had settled themselves, he gently looked into their eyes. "Children, do you remember the Herb-Woman? The sweet woman who came with me to find you the day you fought? Well she has passed on now," he quietly said.

"Yes, she died. Verité told me," Mianshe sadly said.

"Who informed you, my son?" the Prince inquired.

Verité was so shocked to be called son he forgot the question. But Mianshe rushed to his rescue and repeated it in tone.

"*Who told you she died?*" toned Mianshe.

Verité didn't know what to say. If he told him, the village would surely burn him like they did his grandfather, but if he didn't tell the prince, he might put him in jail like they did his parents, so Verité decided to say nothing at all.

Mianshe felt the quandary going on inside Verité. He was afraid, and she didn't like that at all. "He doesn't know the person. He overheard it," she said. She lied. For the first time in her memory she had lied and intentionally. Death plus lying definitely foretold a most horrible day. Verité was right. She really did need to protect herself.

"I see," the Prince confided.

Verité was happy he didn't pursue the issue any further. Everyone knew everyone in the village and he didn't want to mistakenly identify some fictitious person that could turn out to be real.

"Nanny is helping the ladies prepare for Auntie Ellen's dama ceremony tomorrow, so we are on our own tonight," he said.

The prince walked into the kitchen and began scouring it for something to cook. As he looked, Mianshe followed his every step, returning all the things he misplaced back to their rightful places. Verité made himself useful by starting a fire and putting the kettle on to boil. He felt no matter what the prince prepared, he was sure he could swallow it with a gulp of honeyed bush tea.

"Okay, here we go, one millet and peas with a nice turmeric curry coming up," he said.

Mianshe looked at Verité when the prince said, 'coming up' and the pair silently laughed at his choice of words.

As meals go it wasn't terrible. After Verité added some clove and cardamom and the peanuts, it was really very good. The prince was indeed happy because nothing remained on the children's plates. Mianshe remarked that maybe they shouldn't be so proud about dinner when telling Nanny Leboya, because it might hurt her feelings. Verité patted his sister on the back. She was finally getting the essence of being human. Truth was wonderful but sometimes a well-placed lie worked wonders.

Dinner was over. When Mianshe went outside to give the dishwater back to the plants, the prince called Verité over. "Verité, don't worry. I won't ask you who told you about the Herb-Woman, however if you hear anything else, or something sounds odd or unnatural, please let me know. I'm not asking you to spy or tell tales on people, I just need to know what they're thinking so I may assuage their fears. Understand?"

Verité nodded his assent. He understood a lot more than he let on. Something was not right in the village. He could feel it. It wasn't just his dream. Everything was off. People were dying. The seasons were oddly changing, and the tide was going out when it should be coming in. The birds were migrating early, and the small mammals were burrowing as deep as possible into the earth. All of nature seemed like it was preparing for something. The entire world was in survival mode. They were all getting ready for something terrible, a war or famine possibly. Whatever it was, it did not inspire hope.

"Good," said the Prince. "Thank you, my little prince, thank you." The prince patted Verité on the head and went in search of Mianshe but when he went into the back to find his daughter, he found his father instead.

"Evening to you, my son. I hear you cooked quite a tasty meal tonight," said the King. "Please don't worry, this little one here has already told me there are no leftovers. She did offer to make me some spiced bananas and eggs," he said and with much amusement.

"That is her delicacy, my father. You have been greatly honored," said the Prince.

"Mianshe, please go ask your brother to put the kettle on for tea."

"I can do it," she screamed running back into the house.

"Let your brother help you!" hollered the Prince after her.

"You are doing a very good thing here, my son. You have taken to this challenge quite nicely," said the King.

"You are a wise king, my father. You knew exactly what feat to give me," he concurred.

"Shall we go in?" asked the King.

The prince understood his father's need for privacy, so he immediately ushered him into his study. After allowing the children one banana and one egg to make a pudding, he took the tray of tea and biscuits and said a quick silent prayer for the safety of the kitchen.

The king was amused by having his son serve him, but it didn't give him pleasure for long. There were far too many things happening in the village to enjoy the moment of his son maturing through single parenting.

"So, what did you make of today's meeting?" asked the King.

It was unusual for his father to be so forward but who had time to be ceremonious. The community was unraveling at a rapid pace, so they had to hurry if they wished to mend the hole ripping Librebe apart.

"Well, so many things come to mind, Bba. First and foremost was the amount of adrenaline present because you weren't there. It wasn't like you to miss a meeting of someone so important to our village. Please know I am not critiquing you. I only bring it up because the others felt alarmed too. A sort of electricity filled the air, and as a result, it made everyone communicate more cautiously than they would have normally."

The prince took his time pouring the tea. He was just beginning to see what happened at the meeting, so he needed a moment to understand things from this new perspective. "Given we were all somewhat shocked by Auntie Ellen's passing and hyper vigilant because you were not there, things took a very different tone, but having auntie replace you was a stroke of genius. You knew the men would dismiss her and get sloppy and expose some of their true emotions, didn't you?" asked the Prince.

"Women have a way of getting us to show our underbellies, my son. They truly make the best spies. For too long they had no other way of defending themselves, other than their uncanny knowledge of others," he said.

"I wonder if that is what happened to Auntie Ellen. I wonder if she knew something she was not supposed to know and she was silenced? What a thought," said the Prince in alarm.

"I have been to look at the body," said the King.

"And?" questioned the Prince.

"And it was strange, very strange indeed. She had a pattern of blisters on her chest. And she smelled like no smell I've ever smelled before." The King became silent and looked out the window.

The prince imagined he was trying to reinvent the smell to get another shot at naming it, but his father didn't come up with an answer.

"But we get ahead of ourselves," the King continued. "Please, tell me more of what you gleaned from the meeting, my son."

"Well, father, the medicine man's strange request to wash the body. He seemed agitated and almost hung over. His eyes were tinged yellow and his body smelled. His odor was strong, almost gamey like lamb," said the Prince.

"Like lamb," the King repeated. "Well, we must be paying him too much if he can have lamb for dinner," said the King with a smile.

"And Auntie saying Emadi wished to be a part of the dama cleansing was, well..."

But the prince couldn't find the words for what he'd experienced in that moment.

"That was your aunt's genius, my son. She needed the men to show more of their hand. Plus, she instinctually felt something wasn't right and thought having another person there a wise move," explained the King.

"I see, makes sense if you will. However, well, what do you think, Bba?" asked the son of his father.

"I think there was a haint put on her and she met her ancestors in a most untimely way. I believe the pattern on her chest has something to do with it and I think we need to find a way for the Fire-Tender to read those blisters," the King replied.

"But how, sir? We've already alluded to her daughter being there which is not customary, now to have the Fire-Tender there as well. Bba, that would seem like we were accusing the medicine man of murder," said an alarmed Prince.

"And if he did?" the King asked. "Or is this a sickness brought on by the children, my son?" he wearily stated.

The king didn't wish to play chess with his son, but he had to. He had to know if the woman of the sea was trying to take over the land. He had to know if the nomad boy was a witch who'd brought a virus called duduju and he had to know what side his son would take if a war began between the elements. If all that meant throwing a friend into the fire to protect the family, well then that was the way it would have to be. The king also knew the Man-of-Medicine coveted his position. He'd always pushed to have the Hogon be the governing body of the village, therefore the royals would simply be puppets or movie stars like they were in the occidental worlds of those corporate nations. He had to be sure who to trust and who was loyal, because if a threat came he didn't want to thrust his knife into the wrong person.

"I truly do not believe my daughter, or her mother have it in their natures to wish harm on any living thing, my King. As for the boy, he's a child and for the first time in his life he's not living from hand to mouth so to choose now to become villainous seems out of sorts. But regarding your question to me, no I cannot say without a doubt that my children are innocent, because there are those who must love them as I do. Who wouldn't fight for the life of their child?" said the Prince and with great confidence.

The king was truly impressed by his son's answer. He'd not felt this much pride at his birth. Not only did his son objectively answer his question, he addressed the question of his own loyalty to him. It was an intelligent and courageous dissertation because he had let his father know that he too was a father who would defend his children to his end while asking if he'd do the same for him.

"You have truly become the man I've always wished you to be. Please thank your lovely children for an evening I shall remember forever. Now I have taken enough of your time," said the King.

However, before the king could finish his salutation, Mianshe and Verité came in with a "Tada!" The children presented the men with a clump of steaming hot banana soaked in flour and honey and every spice in Leboya's kitchen.

"Don't worry, Popah, we cleaned the kitchen. No one could tell a thing," Mianshe said. And she began eating from the same bowl she had presented to her father.

The king cringed when he heard the young mermaid's complicity. He feigned having a full stomach and excused himself from sharing the dessert made by his son's children. Then he cautiously exited out the side door, avoiding the eyes of the villagers still up preparing for the Herb-Woman's funeral.

CHAPTER 7

Emadi had no idea why she felt hopeful, but she did. Her spirits soared, but her uplifted disposition scared her. She loved her mother. She cared for her to the extreme, so why did she feel elated now that she was gone? She felt free and that felt horrible; worse it made her feel guilty. She tried to sleep and feel the heaviness that accompanied someone's passing but she couldn't keep still. She needed to move. Normally with death, the living relatives took on the dense feel of the body so the dead person's soul could fly free, but Emadi felt the exact opposite. She felt as free as a bird however her mother's spirit felt heavy and it hung over her everywhere.

She couldn't sleep, so she got out of bed and began cleaning the house. She beat the dirt out of the carpets. She stripped her mother's cot and then grabbed every dress, nightgown, shirt and underwear she owned and threw it all in a pile. Afterward she took three enormous chunks of myrrh, frankincense and copal and shoved it into an incense burner with a huge piece of burning charcoal. The house was awash in smoke. The scent was so strong Emadi covered her nose and mouth with a handkerchief.

After smudging everything in the house, she lugged the washbasin of dirty clothes into the back yard. She didn't want to walk down to the bay. She couldn't bear seeing the women of the village yet. She just didn't have the heart to play the suffering daughter, especially under the watch of pity-filled eyes. She decided to wash her clothes in the rain water her mother had collected to irrigate her herbs.

The Herb-Woman would've had a fit seeing her waste good god-water. That's what she called rainwater, god-water or Amma's water or Amma's blood. Anytime it rained her mother would go out into her garden and dig trenches. She would direct the water like a conductor directed music. Then she would dance and giggle and wash her clothes while they were still on her. Afterward she would strip naked and do her little, or rather big, butt-naked rain dance. Emadi would laugh because it didn't make sense. It was already raining. She didn't need to dance for more rain, but her mother only saw it as the abundant nature of nature.

Her mother never talked much about Father-Amma. Her mother never included men much in her conversations at all. On those occasional times when she did speak of her biological father, it was always followed by, "Bless his soul". The only thing Emadi knew about her father was that after the drought seventeen years ago he went south to make money in the mines and he never returned, bless his soul.

Emadi had finished washing and had hung all her mother's laundry to dry and the house was still billowing with smoke from the incense.

"Emadi, my daughter, are you there?" the Queen asked and then she took two rocks from the stone fence and clacked them together.

Emadi stopped dead in her tracks. She'd forgotten about the village women that would surely be visiting. She could hear their mournful wails in the distance. Now she understood why they weren't circling nearer. They were waiting for the queen to visit first. She wasn't ready for them. She didn't want to hear tale after tale about her mother and her wonderful medicines. Or about how she loved her tea hot and how they will all miss her. She couldn't take all the socializing and ceremony, especially right now. All she wanted was some time alone to remember her mother.

"Emadi, are you okay," inquired the Queen?

The queen was worried. She could see she was home. The laundry was hung, and the hearth was burning brightly. In fact, it burned too bright. Smoke was everywhere. "Oh, Amma! Please…" said the Queen as she rushed into the house. "Emadi, it's your queen! Answer me, child!" she screamed.

"I am here, Queen-Mother before you," Emadi meekly said.

As the smoke cleared the queen saw the girl's figure standing in the doorway leading out back. The sun stood behind her like a burning still life framing her in perfect silhouette.

"I'm okay, Queen-Guardian," she said. "Please don't worry so."

But when Emadi walked out of the brightness of the sun into the house the queen screamed. "My child, what have you done!" cried the Queen.

Emadi was startled by the queen's response. She had no idea what she was referring to or why she seemed so alarmed. "What, my Queen?" said Emadi with equal distress.

"Your hair, child," said the Queen.

Emadi touched her hair with both hands. She rubbed her head all the way from the front to the back and then from the back again to the front. Her braids were intact. Her scalp was oiled. Granted her hair had grown some, so she circled her braids from one side to the other toward her face. Her mother loved it that way. She said it looked like a crown. Every time she wore her hair this way her mother would smile.

"I wanted to make my mother smile," Emadi said.

The queen had never expected that answer. Of all the answers one could come up with for dying one's hair, this one took first place. "I see," said the Queen. "It is a most interesting orange. I believe it suits you," she commented, and she prayed it sounded sincere.

"Orange!" yelled Emadi. She rushed into the kitchen and grabbed the two-sided mirror. "Oh, oh mother, no!" she screamed.

Emadi's hair was perfectly orange with a touch of red. It was the color of the blood orange, but without the speckles. It was evenly orange all over. It was tangerine, a beautiful bright tangerine. To explain it was difficult. The only color in nature that replicated it was the rare frill lizard. When excited it would blow out it's cowl into a huge red-orange mane around its head. Emadi stared at herself in the mirror until she fainted.

Finally, the smoke cleared. The queen didn't know how she managed getting the girl into her room, but he Herb-Woman's daughter was now laying on her bed with a cold compress on her forehead. "Here drink this," she said. The queen watched as her friend's orange-haired child slurped her tea down in one gulp. "Do you feel like talking?" the Queen cautiously asked. "You know, I believe with a little vinegar and some burnt bark, I may be able to get your hair back to its natural color."

"Alright," said Emadi. But she was far from all right. She was stunned at how fast things were changing. Her mother had died only hours ago and now her hair was orange.

As the queen got some water from the rain barrel, Emadi undid her braids. Not only had her hair turned orange overnight it had grown eight inches. When the queen returned with the bucket of soapy vinegar water she gasped.

"Look at you!" she cried. "Look how long your hair is!"

Even being in its natural kinky state of a soft cotton ball texture, Emad's hair shined like the setting sun. It was beautiful.

"It's weird, isn't it?" Emadi quietly said. "Just like my mother's death, weird."

The queen was happy that the young woman finally felt like talking. "What happened last night, Emadi?" the Queen compassionately asked. "The king is worried. And there are rumors in the village someone hexed your mother," admitted the Queen.

"It was strange, Guardian-Mother," said the Herb-Woman's daughter. "My mother has been," then she corrected herself. "My mother had been, was acting oddly since she returned from the forest the night the Prince's children got lost."

She told the queen everything. The strange way her mother had been acting. The odd visits to the Man-of-Medicine's lodge. How the medicine man pretended he was well when he was clearly sick, and how her mother was dancing in the healing room. She described the blisters on her mother's chest and showed her the mirror where her mother had outlined the design. It was still intact. Emadi told the queen everything, however she left out the part where the orange bubbles floated in mid-air and traveled through her tear ducts into the follicles of her hair. Until she knew if it was a good or bad omen she would keep that part of the story to herself.

No matter how many times or what the queen washed it with, Emadi's hair stayed orange. Plus, all the shampooing and conditioning made it even more radiant. Her long orange tresses reached past her shoulders to the middle of her back, directly behind her heart, but when it started to dry each strand reached away from the young woman's head, creating a halo of bright orange around her face. It looked like her head was emulating the setting sun.

"Oh my," said the Queen.

"This won't do," she said. "I can't go to my mother's last ceremony looking like this!" Emadi cried.

"Calm yourself, child, please. It will be okay. We will figure something out," replied the Queen.

Emadi heard the town's women ululating before it reached the queen's ears. They were coming to wail and gnash their teeth in honor of her mother. It was their custom. "Listen. They are coming now!" she cried.

The queen quickly began braiding her hair into two long plaits and she circled them around her head again. She rushed outside and grabbed a scarf from the line and covered Emadi's bright orange locks from sight. Then the women quickly folded the laundry and put what was left of the rainwater in the kettle for tea.

"Oh, my sister! We are here!" yelled the women as they entered the yard. They came onto the porch and stood at the door and wept and hollered and ululated and screamed and pounded their chests with their fists until the tea was ready. Then the women sat on the porch and ate honey-cakes and drank the Herb-Woman's good mint tea while recounting story after story about the deceased woman until the moon rose up and rested directly above their heads.

CHAPTER EIGHT

The entire school came out to meet Sedina and her infamous seahorse. They stretched from the rock border of Merlandseia, down to the crystal caverns where her parents awaited her. The mermaids and mermen floated in silence, each solemnly holding a lily candle to guide her along the way. They lit the path with rose quartz crystals nestled in lotus leaves, which emanated a lovely pink hue across the sea floor. Sedina slowly swam through the water gauntlet and as she passed, the merfolk toned a personal greeting, one after the other.

"*Welcome back, my lovely princess,*" toned one.

"*You were truly missed, dear friend,*" toned another.

"*Sea-ing you again—all puns intended,*" toned a young one.

"*My grace, my heart is with you,*" confided a merman.

"*You are safe and that's all that matters,*" was also heard.

"*Pretty princess, nice catch,*" was giggled. It was Equoo's personal favorite.

"*Tea and cakes tomorrow?*" asked Oola.

And the Bad Watermers simply ooh-wahed in three-part harmony, "*We missed you toooo.*"

It was the sweetest, most sincerely touching homecoming ever. Every time someone toned a blessing to the princess, Sedina's heart swelled and her eyes filled-up with tears.

"You know the sea can only take so much salt water," said an amused Equoo. "Who are the triplets with attitudes? I like them," he commented after hearing the Bad Watermers.

It worked Sedina finally stopped crying and started giggling with delight with each blessing bestowed on her. However, with every greeting came a comment from Equoo.

"I want what he's eating, please," he said of a portly merman.

By the time they made it to the crystal caverns and were climbing the labradorite stairs, Sedina felt completely at home. She felt like the entire experience had only been a dream.

"Thank you so much, my dear Mer-family. I feel so loved and connected to all of you. It feels as if I never left, but I did and some of it, well a lot of it was harrowing, truly frightening. But for the life of me, right here and now I can't remember any of that! If it weren't for Equoo's chatter I would've never known time had passed at all. So now it's your turn to tell my opinionated friend what you think. And a one and a two and a ..." Sedina said with a smile.

And with great delight the entire school responded in tone and in unison to every comment previously made by the seahorse. It was a thousand voices coming in at great speed on a myriad of topics. It was so delicately loud and so singularly complex it tickled.

"*I eat my shrimp dipped in sun-dried kelp. You are cute. Gotta a big brother, handsome. Hi ho silver and away. Ride, ride that seahorse. Sedina's lite-knight, and Oooooyouequooo!*" The entire school had great fun teasing Equoo.

"Ok, I hear you," said Equoo. And as he laughed, he heard Sedina's comment come in through all the rest.

"*My hero!*" she sweetly toned.

The seahorse did something he rarely did. He cried from all the loving attention.

As Sedina made her way up the stairs to her parent's thrones, she gently placed Equoo in the recess of the bun in her hair. The Mer-queen's fins were fluttering in delight and her father could contain his excitement even less. He rose to full stature and bellowed.

"My daughter, you are here!" The Mer-king exclaimed.

Manulir gently floated down the stairs and gave her a homecoming basket of blue hyacinths and shrimp balls and honeyed clams prepared by the water nymphs. Next the entire school softly sang in unison the Life Song. Afterward the Mer-queen darted toward her daughter and covered her in kisses.

"Ooh, my dear daughter and friend, Equoo. You must be exhausted. Please, take some time to refresh yourselves and we'll all meet again in the Great Hall when you are ready," she said.

"But before you rest," said the Mer-king. "You must know we all missed you and are ecstatic that you have returned and we all offer our services to our granddaughter, our youngest princess, Mianshe," her father said. "And thank you, Equoo, thank you for being such a dear friend to my daughter. My kingdom is yours." And then he held his daughter in his arms for a good long moment. "Now rest, all will be fine."

Equoo was truly touched by the Mer-king's display of affection. He smiled then quietly hid in the mermaid's hair so the mer-king wouldn't see his tears of gratitude spilling out of his eyes.

"Come dear, Equoo, I don't know about you, but a nice nap sounds perfect right now," Sedina said. She darted toward her cavern and quickly entered, but once there she was overcome with sadness.

"What's wrong," said a wary Equoo.

"I don't know," she replied. "I have been waiting for this moment for so long but now…"

"Now what?" Equoo asked. "What is it?"

"It's different," she said.

Sedina floated around the room touching everything she saw. She looked at the small aquariums and treasures artistically displayed everywhere. The strands of beads and Hu-men toys and baubles she had collected over the years were now spilling out of an old chest her mother had given her ages ago. Her airtight book viewer still rested on page four of *Re-member ~ A Handbook for Human Evolution*. It was a book she'd discovered years earlier on a canoe adrift in the Caribbean Sea. She looked at the amethyst-rose quartz chair she made when she was Mianshe's age. That was it. Her room felt like a young girl's room.

"Are you okay?" asked a compassionate Equoo. He could feel his friend's anxiety over being home after being away for so long. Once you returned it was always difficult to find where you fit in. He was small so creating himself anew was easy. All he needed was a piece of coral, some kelp and krill to call any waters home. Then he added, and one's mate. You had to have someone to share it with.

Seahorses were monogamous creatures. They only mated once and they were extremely choosy about who they paired with. They would do a mating dance every morning for ages before committing so they knew if they were going to be a good fit or not. Since meeting the mermaid, Equoo hadn't thought about Ekwine in ages and she was his perfect fit for years or had been before a blue whale gobbled her up with his morning krill. The mermaid had no idea she'd saved him too. He no longer missed his babies anymore because she brought comfort to his spirit, but now she was home amongst her own kind. He was sure some handsome merman was already floating outside the cave ready to knock him on his head so he could carry his dear friend away. But Equoo didn't care about that. Seahorses had short life spans and his was already two-thirds over anyway, so for his last part he would play the hero of the most beautiful mermaid ever.

"I'm okay, Equoo. I'm home," Sedina quietly said.

"After all you've been through it may not feel like home, that is natural," he replied.

"You are so wise, my dear friend," she said. "I think it's me that's changed. I'm different." Sedina stopped looking around her room and gazed upon Equoo. "How are you feeling?"

"Outside of my species going extinct and my not having babies in months, I'm good," he said with a wink.

"You are one of the strongest species ever, my friend. A little slow maybe," she teased. And Equoo burst out laughing.

"You've been hanging out with seahorses too long, my mermaid princess. You have mastered the art of a graceful insult," he brayed.

"What did I say?" she said feigning innocence.

"Yes, I am slow and only four inches tall but remember I swam as fast as you, my lady."

Sedina roared with laughter. "Yes, clamped to my hair," she giggled.

"Do you have any idea how hard it is to suck in shrimp going at that speed? You don't leave a stallion much time to taste his food," he laughed.

And the strange pair bantered and teased each other until they fell asleep. The seahorse wrapped himself around a strand of the mermaid's hair and the mermaid curled herself inside a shell and as they slept, Equoo dreamed. He dreamt he swallowed one of the mermaid's eggs and when it was born, it looked like a jackal. But a giraffe-seahorse is not to be bested even when dreaming.

"Who the hell are you and what do you want?" demanded Equoo as he slept.

"I am that I am and you won't stop me," said the baby sea jackal as it slowly drifted from view.

A young merman attendant blew the conch shell for the fourth and final time.

"Are you ready yet?" asked Equoo. The seahorse was fluttering back and forth. He was hungry.

"Don't you speak to me in that tone, you old nag," Sedina quickly quipped back.

"I love when you talk seahorse," he said.

"What do you think?" asked the mermaid. Sedina wore strands of lapis and tiger's eye across her torso and her hair was austerely braided in one long rope.

"Is this a trick question?" asked Equoo.

"You hate it," she sadly replied.

"No, I didn't say that! It's just, well, so dark. Who died?" said Equoo.

"Oh, I see what you mean," she said. And she quickly went into action. She released her hair from the braid and loosely wove some blue hyacinths through the trio of tresses. She took off the tiger's eye and added strands of bright rose quartz and faceted aquamarine and draped it over the teal abalone bodice before oiling the entire ensemble in whale blubber. The effect was dazzling. She glistened like an elegantly radiant mature mermaiden.

"Let's go," she said.

As the pair swam toward the opening, her mother floated in followed by the Mer-king and Manulir. "You've traveled far enough. It seemed right that we should come to you," her mother said.

"Sorry we were delayed, mother," Sedina apologetically replied.

"It's so hard to find the right outfit for talking to one's family," said an amused Equoo.

"We are going to be great friends," said the Mer-king. And then he laughed.

Equoo beamed with so much pride he appeared to be an eighth of an inch taller.

The king and the queen sat across from their daughter. Manulir remained gracefully floating by the cavern opening, and Equoo, sensing the meeting was about to begin, swam over to the algae covered walls and hovered there sucking up the shrimp and plankton floating by.

"I still can't believe you are here," said the Mer-queen. "I have been toning worldwide for a message from you," she quietly said.

Her father didn't want the conversation to become melancholic, especially with the situation as it was. "You were greatly missed, my daughter. How wise of you to have Dolph contact us. I have listened to his message over and over again and it always astounds me. Tell us about your daughter," he said.

Sedina looked at her father and began to cry and like her tears, her story spilled out of her from the beginning to the present moment. After she had described in detail her journey the family clasped hands and shared their hearts and summoned a visual of their granddaughter. Mianshe appeared to them in her little ice cream coned t-shirt dress. Her hair was braided in a myriad of tiny plaits and flew in the wind as she played. She was standing on the earth dancing with a frail brown boy. They would come together and apart and fall and laugh and then stand up and repeat the process. It was Sedina's mother who realized the boy was teaching her granddaughter the art of combat, and upon this revelation the vision disappeared.

"Oh my," said the Mer-queen.

Sedina lifted her hand and showed her parents the ring the African mountain man had given her but when her mother took her hand to look at it, the ring slipped off her finger and slowly sunk to the cavern floor.

"Oh my," the Mer-queen quizzically said.

"Oh my," gasped Sedina. "It came off!"

The Mer-king knew this was an omen. After hearing his daughter speak of how the ring would not leave her finger bonding her to the Hu-man male, its coming off in exactly that moment left an air of dread in the room.

"We will not solve these mysteries on an empty stomach," said the Mer-king. "Daughter please, why don't you and Equoo go on to the Great Hall now. Everyone is waiting for you there, and I am sure they have prepared a feast. Your mother and I will join you shortly," he said.

Sedina recovered the ring and put it back on her finger. She collected Equoo and placed him between her breasts and exited the room. When they had left, Manulir pulled the seashell drapes closed.

"Well?" asked the wise merman.

"It seems we are at war," said the Mer-king.

"Oh my," said the Mer-queen.

"Oh, my indeed," said the Mer-king ever so sadly.

CHAPTER 9

The medicine man was furious. They didn't trust him. His mind raced as he walked along the path toward home. After everything he'd done for Librebe, now they wished to intervene over his ceremonial duties! The king's disrespectful no-show only added to his hurt feelings. Would he miss his dama too? They were supposed to be family, a community—one of the oldest on earth. His people came from the stars. In the beginning the Hogan ruled over and beyond the king. Only the Hogon spoke directly to Creator Amma, but now they expected him to listen! Not only was he supposed to listen, he had to obey a woman and an English-educated prince who copulated with beasts! The only reason the queen was queen was because her brother was king! "Never!" shouted the medicine man. "The queen-whipped king sent his sister to do his bidding. Insult after insult!" he barked. He was enraged with the barren queen who sat smugly on her throne ordering the men around, and one was an elder! It was wrong. Worse, it was against nature.

The Man-of-Medicine was in such deep thought that he almost didn't notice the group of women coming toward him. "Mourners," he grumbled. As the women raised their hands to their hearts to honor the shaman and the late Herb-Woman, the medicine man made a beeline into the bush, avoiding them altogether. It was a good decision because the bushes and the few Acacia trees in the area offered some relief from the blazing mid-day heat. He made it through the patch of grassland and found himself at the outskirts of town. He'd been so upset over the meeting that he passed his own house. He was almost in Fermemi country now.

"This is interesting," he said to himself. "Why did you bring me here, Amma?"

The medicine man sat down in the shadow of a rock and calmly thought over the day. Where was the king? Why did he miss the memorial meeting? Why didn't he have his son preside over his affairs since he was next in line? Why did they want Emadi to help facilitate the cleaning? That was truly a bad idea because the girl didn't trust him, and he was not fond of the girl. The man was truly tired of women. Even the ground he walked on was called mother. "Forgive me, Amma," he said.

The Herb-Woman's passing should have been a time of celebration for him and her too. She was finally going to her great garden in the sky, but now everything had changed. "But all change is good if embraced," he reminded himself. He was an important man. With the death of the Herb-Woman, he was now the only person for any job. He alone remained to bring the message of the stars to earth. He was needed now more than ever.

"Emadi!" he howled. The Herb-Woman's daughter was being prepped to replace her and he didn't trust the bloody girl. He had to be careful now. She was at the end of her moon's cycle but she was still able to create havoc.

The medicine man looked around before picking a spot. He had to ground himself. He saw a small sidewinder snake sunbathing on a rock in the flatlands below and watched it until he saw a pattern forming. He could see the lines of age telling its history. Once the ocean lived here. The clouds moved and he saw the snake slither out of the shadows back into the receding sunlight. This was good. Now he could see the design the pattern was making in full. The oceans had been there for many years. Then the ice came. You could see the small patches of plant life imbedded in the stone. The drought came after that. That's when all became desert.

Before the albino ants came in from the north demanding the people toil or die, they gathered their belongings and left. The new land was high in the mountains hidden by a forest and built into the stone. That's why they called it Librebe because they'd escaped and were free to live as they wished. But now they had to climb down the mountain to the bay for their provisions. They had to go out to sea for food or venture into the hidden lands behind the cliffs where there was a small river for farming. It also provided some grass for their cattle. Whatever else they needed (which was never very much) they acquired at the marketplace in Fermemi.

The man knew what he had to do next. He'd go home and summon the ancestors and ask them for help. He'd bring the rising tide to shore and wash the pestilence from the land as his fathers and their forefathers before them had done. He would let the neighboring lands know about the evil twins plaguing their country. They would insist the children be sacrificed into the sea from whence they came. After that he would restore the Hogon as leader and return his people to their rightful place. They would rule over land and sea then the medicine man would be king again. The Hogan would rule. He lit his pipe and smiled and when he'd finished his bowl he made his way down the hill into the land of the Fermemi.

The Fermemi people were fat. They all sat on their porches listening to the radio and smoking tobacco wrapped in paper. The medicine man hated coming to their village and would never have come unless he had too. But he needed their help right now if he was going to restore their first ancestor to its rightful position.

"Hi, my Uncles, I am here to see your Queen," he said.

The men smiled at him and continued drinking their fermented drinks and slapping the ivory carved stones on the table. They paid him no attention whatsoever, so the Man-of-Medicine continued down the road, but before doing so he cursed the table of men. Since their games and drink were more important than the people, he told Amma to give them a desire for drink so strong and for games so deep that life would no longer be available to them. Then he walked away down the path making sure the next person he spoke with had not been sullied by western ways.

She was a poor woman with a bad leg. It twisted from one side and faced the other. When she walked she moved like a crab in the sand. He could see she was addiction free. Her skin shined like velvet and her eyes were as bright as the sheet she was hanging. Her smell was comforting and her smile was welcoming.

"Good evening, Auntie," he said. "I am from Librebe."

"Yes, Uncle," she said. "I see by your boubou you are a great man," she replied.

"You are kind, dear Auntie. I am dressed to see your Queen. A dear friend of hers from our village has passed, you see," said the medicine man feigning sorrow.

"Ayee Uncle, we have heard! Our Queen left an hour ago to be with you in sorrow. Oh, my Uncle, my heart saddens for you!" she cried.

The medicine man hated the salutations and ceremony that went with traveling. The false displays of emotions and the courting and wooing of information was exhausting to him. So, the old fool had already left. He wondered if she took her young fool with her. But it didn't matter. Everything would go on as planned. He would tell this woman his story, this naïve woman who innocently gave him the location of her queen. What if he'd come to kill her? He would have easily been able to accomplish his goal.

"Ah, my sister, thank you," he said inching his way into the family. "I had wanted to warn the Queen-Mother first but…" And then the shaman left a gap for the woman to ask him. It had to be that way. She had to ask freely for this information otherwise the intention of his words would not work the way he wished.

"Of what, my brother? Tell me and I will make sure she gets your message," she firmly said.

"Oh, my sister we may have evil in Librebe, I fear. There are two children of no woman's womb and one is not even of this earth! They reside there," he said. And his tone worked. The poor woman was terrified but wanted to hear more. Like those moving visuals the foreign men brought, she couldn't keep her eyes off the screen of her imagination.

"Oh, my brother, how? What magic is this!" she cried in alarm.

"I do not know, my sister. That is why I came. I thought between our two great nations we could rid ourselves of the intruding spirits bringing sorrow to our land. It is in memory of our dear Herb-Woman I have made this my mission today. I must rush back, my sister, before it's too late," he said as he walked backwards out of the yard, sealing the matter. Then he turned and made his way back into the bush.

As he slipped away, the medicine man heard the woman thanking him and asking him for his name. He removed his robe and folded it up, inside out and tied it to a stick like a hobo. He couldn't risk the woman identifying him. He knew all she'd remember was the decorative boubou and the only people in Librebe to see the robe were those in the meeting that morning. However, he was sure a poor crippled woman would never get up the hill to tell on him, and he was even surer she would spread the rumor of the children to everyone in town.

He took the short cut up the hill toward Librebe. He wanted to be there when the Fermemi queen questioned the king about his evil twins. He wanted to be there when she demanded no one from Librebe come into her realm while the dreaded duduju, the plague that caused blisters, was still being spread. He had to be there to see their educated prince try to explain the presence of the nomad boy and water nymph. Yes, he had to be there.

And before he knew it, he was there. He was already entering his back yard. He felt great. He didn't ache like he normally would after a day of strenuous climbing. He didn't even feel winded from quickly walking up the hill. He didn't feel dirty or anxious about the events that were surely coming to pass. He only felt relief. He felt good. He felt everything was finally in place to begin again. He got his earthen bowl and filled it with water. He set it on the ground and knelt down on all fours and lapped it up until the bowl was dry.

"This is a good day, Father Amma. One of your best," he said. Then the Man-of-Medicine rolled onto his back and howled with laughter!

CHAPTER 10

Rose was studying the air around the phantom in her garden. It shimmered. It reminded her of being in Los Angeles in the valley where it got so hot the heat would vibrate in little waves above the pavement. It seemed like the air itself was panting.

"I am not staring at you. I cannot blink," said the ghost in long deep tones.

Rose jumped and replied, "I'm sorry. I was watching the heat. You're from someplace hot, aren't you? Even hotter than here, poor thing," she quietly said. Then she picked up her lighter and lit a cigarette. She pretended she didn't notice the three butts sitting in her granny's rose-glass ashtray. That meant she was one cigarette away from her five a day limit and it was only two in the afternoon. At this rate she'd have to drive to the wharf by six.

"Help me, Rose," the woman said again.

"Okay, now you're freaking me out. Why do you keep calling me by my name? How do you know me?" Rose asked. She felt agitated. This was different. Something was very different about this woman.

"I don't know," the phantom woman whispered.

Rose muttered to herself that it probably meant their knowing each other didn't happen in this lifetime. She preferred when the woman opened her mouth to speak. It was softer than her thoughts loudly coming in at her. It was a different loud. It didn't vibrate as much as it stirred the soul.

"So how can I help you?" Rose warily asked.

"You must stop the war," said the old lady blankly staring at her.

Rose sucked her cigarette down to the filter. "What war and why do you think I can do this? How am I supposed to do this?" she asked. Rose was scared. She knew she shouldn't string more than a few words together when speaking to the dead and here she was interrogating her like a journalist. Rose stubbed out her already extinguished cigarette for a good long moment.

Rose's father once told her she was given a gift. She responded with "some gift" when he said it. She didn't think it was a gift at all. Rose called on Archangel Michael. This was not the time to be thinking about her daddy, but it was a clue, a little breadcrumb he left her. She always knew the evil man was up to something when she had a strange thought about him come in, out of nowhere like that.

"I can help you with him, Rose," said the phantom woman.

The hairs stood up on Rose's arms. "Stop calling me by my name!" she firmly said. And she stood up. She was going back in the house.

"I am an African ancestor," she calmly said with her expressionless eyes. "My daughter is your child. Her name is Emadi," said the Herb-Woman.

Rose needed a pen and some paper. She had to write this down. How can this woman's daughter be her child? This woman had been hexed and now here she was vexing her. Rose whispered *Emadi* as she scribbled the name in the earth. Next, she drew a map of Africa. And then she began quietly talking to the woman. But she wouldn't look at her. She couldn't. The sores on her chest and her vacant stare creeped her out.

"What is your name?" Rose asked in that simple and plain way she used when talking to ghosts.

"I am Ellen. I am the roots woman for my village," she slowly said in her deep voice.

Rose didn't know why but all she could think about was Nina Simone screaming, "My name is Africa!" And then the woman began talking again, and again it startled her.

"I am a Librebeing," groaned the Herb-Woman.

Rose sighed. There was nothing free or being about this woman standing under her jacaranda tree. "Can you sit, Auntie please," she said from a place so deep inside her it hurt.

The ghost of the roots woman tried to sit but her body or lack of one did not know how to make her spirit do it, thus Rose stood up and held the woman's eyes in hers and set an intention for them to sit and the women slowly sat down together.

"What happened to your chest, Auntie?" she asked.

"I burn," she answered.

"I see that," Rose said with compassion. "And I smell the cucumbers you used to cool it. But how did this happen?" She firmly but quietly asked.

"It is a map," she said never taking her eyes off Rose.

Rose rolled the last of her tobacco and lit her last cigarette. She slowly inhaled and then released the smoke in the same way. She savored every moment of the tobacco. Even the ash falling to the ground with a feathery puff before it collapsed into nothingness gave her peace. Finally, her mind was still.

"My child was your child, two times ago. She liked you," said Ellen the Herb-Woman.

Rose looked out to sea and listened. Wasn't it a given that a child should love its parents.

"No," said the Herb-Woman responding to her thought. "You are the only one, other than me that she cared for."

Rose hated asking this question but she had to. "Did someone take your life?" she quietly asked.

"*I gave my life to save my daughter village!*" she said with as much emotion as a displaced spirit could muster.

Rose didn't understand. Did she mean she killed herself? Sometimes dark magicians would sacrifice themselves to get to the higher realms so they could do their bidding there, but that was very dark and low energy. That vibration should never have been able to reach her. Yet here she was in her garden. Did she die fighting for her daughter or her daughter's village? Was this a matriarchal society of warring women? Rose continued creating scenario after scenario in her mind.

"You must help Emadi or the Man-of-Medicine will destroy the world," she clearly and calmly said.

Rose finally looked at the woman. She must have been quite a beauty when she was young. She had that deep red-brown skin that was so spicy all you could think of was making love. Her graying hair was more amber-white than silver. She probably had ash blond woven into her brown locks and with that skin she must have turned heads all night long.

"Wow," thought Rose. "You must have made Dorothy Dandridge look plain."

"The medicine man wants to hurt my daughter," she said.

"So, you came home to help her?" asked Rose. She was confused. The only reason someone would die for another was if that sacrifice brought life to the loved one.

"No, I am stronger here," said the Herb-Woman.

The coldest cold went down Rose's spine. She'd never been visited by anyone with this much power, or this misdirected. Who died to gain power?

"I can't help you, old woman," she said. She was trying to calm her heart. She was scared. No one liked to hear the word no and especially someone on a mission, no matter how bizarre that mission was. "I do not judge you, Auntie. Look at the religious wars. How many died to kill another to save someone else. It's just not my way," Rose said. And she took a hunk of Palo Santo wood out of her pocket and lit it.

"I did not die on purpose!" she declared. "I died when I became aware," she continued. "I died when I deciphered the map," she added. The Herb-Woman's spirit stood up and stared deeper into Rose's soul. "Emadi is our only hope," she said before fading from view.

Rose could not stop rocking. The woman's words had split her wide open. She began crying. She felt a thousand lifetimes swell up inside her like labor pains. She wept and cried out all of mankind's names for the Creator, one right after another until it became one long mournful wail.

She couldn't stop. She was like a compass that could not find north. There was no south or east or west either. She became a crusader fumbling with her amah's beard as she lifted her burqa because her rosary was caught on David's star and they all got tangled in the crescent moon and star symbol and all of it was strangling her. She wept and it hurt. She tried making herself lie face down on the earth. She prayed to everyone and no one. She cried until no sound came out of her. And when she woke she saw herself holding a little red-bone child with curly orange hair and she took the child and ran full force off the cliff into the sea.

⋙ M ⋘

"*Rose wake up,*" murmured the voice. "*Wake up, my love.*"

And Rose stood up and walked over a crystalline rainbow bridge into the rose marble city. It was bright. A multitude of formless stairs reached up into the sky. After climbing them she walked through the columns to the table in the middle of the room. It had been set for tea. The roots woman's spirit from her garden, entered.

"Tea?" asked the Herb-Woman as she poured the bubbling liquid into the cup.

Rose took a sip of the boiling liquid that had no temperature. She didn't understand.

"Don't worry," the Herb-Woman told her. "You are protected here. Look."

Rose looked into her cup and saw the mint leaves stuck to the bottom. It was the same design that was on the Herb-Woman's chest.

"Oh heavens," she said.

Rose didn't remember jumping into the cerulean water but there she was fighting its current for dear life. She heard herself talking. What was she saying?

"Wake up!" he said. The young man was pacing back and forth beside her bed clutching the money he'd given her. "Take it! You were right. I don't want any of this. None of it," he said. "This is yours," he said throwing the eight twenty-dollar bills at her. "Now lift this yoke up off of me!" he screamed. He looked so pitiful.

Rose laughed. She slowly sat up in bed and laughed again. "What time is it?" she asked.

"It's around four," he told her. Then he sat in the chair by her bed and wept. He told her how the reverend was waiting for him when he got home, and he'd brought the entire congregation with him. He continued recounting his story. He said they were all there at his house, eating and praising and singing for hours. He had no idea where the preacher's wife was while they were having their revival. He told her he didn't care where she was. He was through with her, so he snuck out the back door and came here. He wanted her to make them stop.

It'd been nine hours since the Herb-Woman left Rose shattered on the beach, and that was all she could think about this morning. "You'll be fine," she told him. "Now go on home."

"No!" he screamed. "Not until you…"

But Rose stopped him from finishing his sentence. She'd had enough. "Go!" I said. And take your money with you. I didn't do a thing to you or anyone else. That yoke you're feeling is simply guilt, young man," she said. Then she softened her tone. "Please go on now. Take your money and go to the mainland and sing. Okay," she said. And she tried to smile but too much had happened to make her mouth form the shape. "Please go," she said and then she kissed him on his cheek.

The young man smoothed out the twenty-dollar bills and put them back in his wallet. He mumbled some salutation of gratitude and he left.

Rose was starving. She went into her kitchen and opened the refrigerator and pulled out everything she had. She made herself a mushroom cheese omelet and devoured it. Next, she got a big pot to make some soup. She cut up all the useable vegetables and added some garlic and Himalayan salt and mixed it all up with good bottled mineral water. While her soup simmered, she got some strong chicory and mixed it with a French roast and then she added some cardamom and waited for it to brew to perfection. Next, she put a couple slices of bread in the toaster, and while she cooked, she cleaned. She watered her plants and nibbled on her herbs like a horse in a pasture. She would have eaten the horse too had there been one to eat. Finally, she'd had her fill so she poured herself a glass of pear brandy and walked back out into her garden.

It was eight p.m. She was happy it hadn't rained. She needed those notes, so she headed straight for the jacaranda tree, and the old woman was waiting there for her.

"He will fight water with water," she said.

Rose sat the glass of brandy beside the woman and smiled. "I will do everything I can, Sister Ellen, don't worry," she told her.

Then she fell to her knees and copied the drawing on the earth into her notebook. She pulled her phone out of her apron pocket and searched until she found it. It was in the cliff dwelling region of a little country in Africa. She reckoned she could use a vacation, so she called the airlines and booked a ticket to Librebe.

CHAPTER 11

Adisa didn't know what to make of anything. The Herb-Woman was gone. How could that be? She was here only yesterday. Auntie Ellen had come by to give her father some fresh mint. Everything was changing so fast, too quickly. She watched the women draw water from the well in preparation for the repast. The women gossiped the entire time while they worked. Some of them were already talking about what they were going to make for the upcoming wedding. They didn't think she heard them but she did. The Herb-Woman was not even buried yet and they were already planning the menu for the next event. Some people could be so cruel.

She loved Auntie Ellen. She'd taken them in when everyone else pretended not to notice her father's drinking. If he had lost his mind over one of their own they would have embraced him with open arms, but he'd fallen head over heels into a bottle for a South African dancer. People could be so petty.

Adisa lifted the bucket of water onto her shoulder and started walking home. "What is going on," she sighed. She knew she shouldn't curse her own people. Why was she being so judgmental? They were sad so they talked about a wedding because it gave them joy. That's all it was. Or was it?

She knew there was more to do with this death than dying. When the Herb-Woman came to the house just two days ago her father sent her out for wood. Why did auntie want a reading with him? Her father offered no explanation but he would never reveal a private conversation. When the Herb-Woman was leaving they embraced and spoke of old times like normal. But it wasn't normal and now she was dead.

"Adisa," her father said.

Adisa wondered how long her father had been standing there and then she wondered how long she'd been home herself. Her father had already hung up his hat. He was holding a towel now, so he must have already washed off the meeting and the dust from his walk home. Therefore, a good couple of hours must have passed since she got water. She hadn't realized until then how badly Auntie Ellen's death had hit her.

"Adisa," her father said again.

"Yes?" she asked.

"What's wrong?" he asked with concern.

"Did something happen to Auntie Ellen, Bba?" she inquired. "Is that why she wanted a reading?"

"Shush, child. You're in shock like we all are. She died, Adisa. That's all. We die," he softly said.

Adisa hated his answer. She hated the inevitable. She wasn't going to believe this could happen to him. Not like it happened to auntie. She believed she would be by his side and he would touch her face and hold her hand when he passed. She even believed she'd be able to catch his spirit in the palm of her hand like he did with the butterfly. She hadn't realized she was crying until her father held her face in his hands.

"Here," he said in his softest voice.

Adisa took the tissue and blew her nose. "I miss her," she cried. "And I'm scared for you."

The Fire-Tender pulled his daughter toward him and held her in his arms. He swayed their bodies back and forth while he gently stroked her hair. "Come on, now. I'm fine. You're fine. Everything is fine," he gently cooed.

He was a kind man, her father. When Adisa was little she was sure he could pet a mambo and live to tell the story. She had on numerous occasions watched him catch a butterfly in flight with his open palm only to release it outside and he never thought there was anything remarkable about it. He would laugh when she gasped in delight. Then he would smile and tell her the butterfly trusted him. She tried on numerous occasions to catch one in his way but one time she broke its wing so she stopped trying.

"Feel better?" he asked.

"Yes," she quietly said. "When is the ceremony?" she asked him.

"They will clean her body when the moon comes up, then the wake's at sunrise and we give her back to the earth at sunset," he said, but her father didn't look at her when he said it.

"I see," was all she could say.

"I know you loved her, Adisa. But we must be happy with the times we had, not wonder about those times we didn't get to share. Understand," he said.

Adisa knew he was right, and she knew she was wrong for having pressed the issue. She was going to have to let auntie go but she couldn't bring herself to do it. She couldn't let go just yet because she knew there was more to her story.

"The pie is ready. I'm going to take it over to Emadi now," she said. And she grabbed her scarf from the table and wrapped her hair.

"Alright," her father said.

Adisa couldn't control her desire to hug her father again, so she set the pie down and went and embraced him and she held him for a good—long—moment.

After his daughter left, the Fire-Tender went outside and chopped some wood. It felt good. He loved hearing the sound of it splitting apart, and he adored the smell it released even more. He needed the wood now. It appeared the dead tree knew this too. It smelled wonderful and the sounds it made were a comfort to his ears. Every log looked like a little African statue. They all seemed to cackle and stand up like little old people dying to be of service. One even looked like the Herb-Woman. The shapely log wobbled before falling next to the pile of its wood brethren.

The Fire-Tender had worked up a good sweat so he stopped. He wiped his brow with the tail of his shirt and sat down to watch the setting sun. It was going to be a beautiful night. One the Herb-Woman would have appreciated. Her spirit was all over him now. Why did she tell him that? Why now after all these years would she confess her love for him? It was a silly thought. He knew the heart had no say over how it beat, but that wasn't what was bothering him. What worried him was it wasn't true—not exactly. She loved him. That was true. But she didn't love him like a lover. It was more like a brother.

The Fire-Tender stood up and then sat down again. The fire told him the Herb-Woman was scared. She needed an ally. She didn't desire him. She wanted his wisdom, the wise ways of the fire. She couldn't say it, but he knew it. She wouldn't let on what she was afraid of, but he knew that too. The prince's children frightened her, and the Man-of-Medicine terrified her. The Fire-Tender looked at the log that resembled his friend and sighed. He wanted to cry but what was the point in that. The sun had almost set. It was hanging on the horizon like a sleepy child. No one wants to go to sleep and no light chooses to go out.

"What a strange thought," the Fire-Tender contemplated. How did the Herb-Woman die? His friend wasn't sick the day she came by. However, fear was a sickness. It was the worst kind of malady—an unbeatable one. It was a disease that could only be cured with love. The Fire-Tender let out a long quiet whistle. That was why she told him she loved him. She needed to be loved to cure the fear inside her. The man picked up the curved log and held it close to his heart. "I love you, Ellen," he quietly said before throwing the log into the dying fire.

The log immediately went up in flames. It crackled and spit out a multitude of sparks. He had to jump back out of the way so he wouldn't get burned. He had never seen a fire cry before and this one was gushing emotion. First it sparked tears of joy. Ellen was glad the Fire-Tender heard her heart, and she was thanking him for it. Next a geyser of sparks shot upward into the north. She was trying to tell him something, but what? He didn't understand its message. Then with a loud pop, a knot in the log burst forth like a bubble and the flamed turned blue and all became quiet. Then the flames died down until they became orange embers and they stayed that way. The fire warmed the Fire-Tender to his bones and it burned for a good long moment.

"Time to give you a bath, Ellen," he softly said as he slowly dug up some soil and mixed it in tamping Ellen's fire.

∴⋏∴

CHAPTER 12

"Again!" he screamed. Verité couldn't believe his sister wasn't taking him seriously. "Tell me again what you are supposed to do!"

"No," said Mianshe. She was getting angry.

"This is serious, okay," he said with tenderness. Then he took his stick and drew the map in the dirt again. "Okay, if the water starts to rise you have to use this route but if a fire starts you must head down the hill and follow the shoreline then use the old road to go up the mountain. And what do you do if the old road is blocked?" he asked.

"I climb Mr. Tree and stay there until you come and get me," she sadly replied.

"That's right. Good job now let's practice jumping from rock to rock again," he said. And he scoured the area for flat rocks she could practice with.

Mianshe didn't want to play this game with Verité anymore. Everyone was acting so weird since the Herb-Woman died and the land-mermaid had no idea why. Even her father was talking in hushed tones. Nanny Leboya kept putting rose water in everything she cooked. She probably hoped the plant's loving ways would soften everyone's mood, but all it did was scare her. But her brother scared her most of all. Verité never stopped drilling her about something. She had to know where to hit someone so they would cough and give her enough time to run away and then she had to know where to run. After that she had to learn where all the edible plants in the area were in case she had to stay in her hiding place. Next, she learned how to build a fire from sticks. Afterward she learned how to catch rainwater and keep it unspoiled. The only time her brother smiled was when he got to check swimming and holding one's breath off his list of to-do, play chores.

"I got it. I understand," she said and then she skipped away.

Verité was worried. She didn't have it and she was far from understanding. His little sister had unknowingly started a war. He knew it wasn't her fault. He knew she was only the excuse they were using to start the battle that had been brewing since the beginning of time.

"Alright. Can't say I didn't try," Verité smugly said.

"I have been trying," whined Mianshe. "I've done everything you asked, everything!"

"No, you didn't" he calmly replied.

"I am not cutting my hair!" she firmly and quite loudly answered and then she ran down the hill toward the ocean.

Verité was terrified she was going to summon her mother and that meant the sea would come with her. "Mianshe, wait!" he screamed running after her down the hill.

"No," she giggled and then she looked back to see if he was still chasing her.

Mermaids made very childish humans, so Verité decided to take another approach, one that would appeal to her innocent side. "Look!" he exclaimed.

Mianshe stopped and looked at him. "What?" she asked.

"There in the sky. It's a dolphin cloud," he said making a point of keeping his eyes upward.

The mermaid looked up into the sky and saw the bumpy cloud he spoke of. "Dolphins don't have humps like camels," she haughtily said.

"Well, it's a humpback dolphin," he calmly said, ignoring her. He was making things up as he went along.

Looking up at the sky, Mianshe sat down and pondered his idea. "It's pretty," she softly said. She didn't know why she felt the need to whisper but she did. Maybe she would blow the cloud away with a loud thought. She liked having the cloud there. It was pretty.

Verité sat down beside his sister. "Look at that one," he said. "It's a seahorse in a bowl of fruit."

"Yes!" she said with recognition. It was the first time that day they had agreed on anything. Mianshe thought maybe now was a good time to talk. "Verité, tell me what you saw that made you scared," she cautiously said. "And don't leave anything out. I want every detail, please."

In that moment, Mianshe sounded very grown up and Verité didn't know which disturbed him more, Mianshe the child or Mianshe the adult. "Well," he began, and he recounted everything in detail. The sound she made when the jackal chased her and how its eyes were yellow. The rain that looked like rain but hit the ground like gummy bears. He described how the ocean rose up then flowed to shore and dumped all its contents on the land. He cried when he told her the part where the fish were frying in the sun while the earth had not a drop of water on it. He told her everything.

"And what happens to me?" she asked.

"You, well, you," and he paused.

"Well me what, Verité? Tell me the truth. You promised," she whispered.

"You go back to the sea," he sadly said.

"Well what was so hard about telling me that?" she happily said. But her brother's face was anything but happy. "That's not all, is it?" she warily asked him. "Tell me why and how I go back to sea, please," she said in her newfound, grown-up voice.

"The jackal grabs you by your hair and ties you in a knot and flings you into the ocean. That was all I saw," he said in barely a whisper. "I try to jump in to get you but the water is curling."

"That is not going to happen," she firmly said and stared directly into her brother eyes. "Come on, let's cut my hair," she fearlessly said. "Did you bring some scissors?" she asked.

Verité couldn't believe it. One minute she was whining and the next she was the most courageous person he'd ever met. No one in his tribe would've ever let anyone cut his or her hair. It was one of the ways his people connected to Creator.

He quietly opened the little burlap sack nanny had made him and he pulled out a small pair of scissors he pilfered from his school kit. The prince had given him the box of learning tools when he saw him writing a message to his mother in the dirt. It was a kind gesture and it made the boy love his new father all the more, however his heavenly mother would have had an easier time reading the message written on the ground, than on the lined paper.

Mianshe slowly untied her hair and began taking out all the little braids that took nanny over two hours to put there. She took some shea butter and held it in the palm of her hand until it warmed up and became a slippery pool of liquid oil. Using her fingers like a comb, she rubbed the oil into her hair, tress by tress and as she did this she prayed. "Thank you, dear part of me, for protecting my head from the sun and for covering me with colors and for all the shapes you make. Please grow back for me," she quietly said.

Verité felt awful. One of the mermaid's most defining traits was her hair. Her hair made everyone ooh in awe. It was always around her like a shield. It was strong like a rope, and it was the most amazing color he'd ever seen. He liked her hair. He liked her face too. He was stalling. She would always be beautiful with hair or without. He had to do this.

"Are you ready?" he asked.

"Are you ready?" she asked. She could see he was having a hard time.

"No," he said and he cut one long lock of hair directly behind her earlobe.

❧ M ❧

The Man-of-Medicine couldn't believe how clear everything looked as he crested the hill. He was still getting used to his new eyesight. He stopped to drink some water and watch the sun settle in for the evening and saw every inch of the valley and hills as if they were directly in front of him. When he scanned the countryside, he saw them together like a little midget couple. "Oh Amma, you truly love me today," he contentedly said.

"I don't even need a plan for your plans are so clear to me." Then he fell down to his hands and knees and laughed.

❖ M ❖

Verité was almost finished. He was amazed at how stoical the young mermaid was being. There she was being shorn like a sheep and she sat there humming.

"What are you, humming?" asked Verité.

"Don't you remember? You sang it with me the second time we met. It's called the Life Song," she said. "It gives me hope." Afterward she returned to quietly humming.

Verité had to stop. He pretended he'd got a stray strand of her hair in his eye but he was crying. It hurt him to see her like this. She looked so little and frail sitting there on a rock with all her beautiful hair beside her in hunks on the ground. He didn't want her to see how upset he was. She would think she looked ugly, when it was only the reaction of his sad heart, so he hummed with her. He didn't care if he sang it right or not. He had to do something, anything other than cut his sister's hair.

"There," he warmly said. "You look cute." He wasn't lying. She did look cute and if he hadn't been as sad as he was, she would've probably looked beautiful to him.

Mianshe felt her head. It didn't take long to do. Her hand went in then out of her scalp like it did when she petted the neighbors little wiry tailed dog. She didn't know what it looked like, but she could feel how short it was. It was short.

"Are you okay?" he asked.

"Yes. How are you?" she replied.

Verité didn't answer her question. He bent over and began collecting her hair. "We have to pick this up, every strand, so no one tries to use it against you," he gently said.

"What on earth are they going to do with my hair? They can have it. I'm safe now," she replied as she skipped around gathering her tresses.

"Mianshe, they can do bad things to you with your hair whether it be on your head or off and having it in a pile like this would make it all the easier for them.

"Why do people want to hurt me, Verité? I like everybody," Mianshe said.

Verité went over and wrapped his arms around her. He didn't know what to do or say. He had no idea why people were so afraid of those they didn't know. In his small experience it was also those that knew you best that did the greatest harm.

"You're different. That's why they are afraid of you. You don't have bad thoughts like they do, and you're truthful and that scares them. Please don't worry. It's okay now. Everything will be fine. I'll protect you," he said.

"Verité, I love you. Thank you for being my big brother. Thank you for being my friend. Thank you for being there for me. Thank you for the way you smell…" she said and she continued thanking him until she could smile again.

"Feel better now?" Verité asked. He was studying her closely. Even though she smiled he could feel her heart and it was aching. He began collecting the rest of her hair. He pulled the stray strands out of the dry bushes and shoved them deep into the bottom of his burlap sack. Afterward he searched the ground around her again. He was meticulous.

"I can't go into town like this. They already think I'm weird," Mianshe said.

Verité understood how she felt so he took off his t-shirt and stood before her bare-chested. "Turn around," he said. He gently placed her little head through the opening and then flipped the shirt up and adeptly wrapped her head. She looked like a true African princess. "Now you look like your father's child," he said. "They will simply think you are in mourning for the Herb-Woman." He was finally smiling.

"So much has happened since the jiggly woman died. I should have gotten to know her better," she solemnly said.

Verité could not stand seeing his sister so solemn, so he began making jiggling sounds. And he poked his butt out and tapped it like a drum and imitated the Herb-Woman walking through the forest.

Mianshe laughed and followed him up the path toward home silently singing the Life Song the entire way. *Trust your heart to all matters. Embrace your wisdom, mer-friend. And light will return to greet you for with love you're connected within.*

❖ /\\\ ❖

If the medicine man had it in him, the two children comforting one another would have touched him but it was too child-like for him. He didn't think children should be allowed to embrace and groom each other like cats. Plus, he was convinced the foreign children had no place in his homeland, so he waited for them to leave. He sat down and filled his pipe and watched the sun journey through the sky. What a wondrous time the world was going through. Life was growing and morphing back into its primordial existence. All was becoming, as it should.

The man looked into the last rays of sun. He was tired and there was still a lot to do. The moon would be rising soon. He didn't have much time to get ready for the Herb-Woman's cleansing and the meeting with her daughter. He tapped his pipe free of ashes and focused on the little flat rock the mermaid-girl had been sitting on. There it was. It was exactly what the shaman needed in order to do what needed to be done. The long strand of amber hair was waving like a flag. It was calling out to him. 'Now you have the final ingredient,' it seemed to say. Thus, he bounded down the hill and with one fell swoop, he grabbed it.

"With this strand I will rise up and cleanse the land of humid bestial presence. I will fight for you and I will not die. I will wash you clean and restore Librebe to its pure form before the twins came into being. Thank you, father Amma!" he cried.

Then he wrapped Mianshe's hair around his finger and tied it into a knot.

CHAPTER 13

Emadi was ready. She'd had a hard time convincing the queen of the fact, but she managed it. She wondered why the queen had been so insistent. It had to be more than her hair changing colors that spooked her. She must have believed there was something strange about the way her mother died too. Nevertheless, she got her to leave. If she got the queen to have confidence in her, she was sure she'd have no problem standing up to the medicine man.

Emadi needed the Man-of-Medicine to reveal what he knew and she knew he wouldn't open up and be himself if the queen was around. Even if the queen sat on the porch out of the way, the man would still take her presence as an insult. It had to be just the two of them. It was the only way she was going to find out what really happened. It was the only way to find out if the medicine man had anything to do with her mother's death. But deep inside, Emadi was certain he had played some part.

Emadi felt her head from front to back and side-to-side again to make sure her hair was hidden. It was good. There were no loose hairs. Everything was set. She had prepared everything she needed. The kettle was on. She'd mixed some valerian in with the fresh mint. She had cleansed the house of bad spirits and created a protective grid to keep out those wishing to enforce their will upon her by mixing her morning urine in a bucket of hot water with fresh petals, oils and herbs. Then she marked her territory with it like the big cats did when preying on the small. She had to if she was going to take on the medicine man. Lastly, she baked his favorite, a cardamom sweet potato pie. Now she had done everything a dutiful daughter should do when receiving a guest with unclear intentions. It was what her mother would've done. It was what her mother taught her.

"The mirror!" she said in alarm. Emadi grabbed the mirror out of the cupboard and wrapped it in waxed paper so the symbols wouldn't smear. She placed the mirror inside the suitcase her mother had given her on her seventeenth birthday and put it on the top shelf in the pantry and as she did she kept asking herself what those symbols meant the entire time.

She stared at the small green leather carry-on and remembered the day she received it. It was the day she and her mother had their last serious fight. She'd asked her to teach her some real recipes not just the ones she used for general purposes. She already knew those. She had known how to treat cuts and colds since she was knee high to a duck. She wanted to know how to heal real sickness. Not the easy ones nature threw at you, but the hard ones people concocted. Like the disease of the blood the colonials brought to Africa, or the sickness of the heart brought on by a desire for love, or the ugly symptoms of jealousy or even worse, revenge, but she stopped her thoughts dead in their tracks. It didn't matter if her mother never taught her about the shadow side of medicine. She'd figure it out on her own. She had to. Life itself demanded it.

The timer went off. The pie was done. Emadi pulled the pie out of the oven and said a silent prayer. She felt him coming. Her stomach reacted. It tied itself in knots. She found it hard to breathe so she placed both feet on the ground and touched her mother's crystals. They tinkled against one another inside her bra. She wasn't well enough endowed to keep them silent like her mother had, but that was okay. The sound would work to her advantage.

Her mother had brought out the big guns; tourmaline and blue tiger's eye, bronzite and staurolite, pink and yellow kunzite and blue topaz. She prayed over those crystals and left them in the moonlight the night her mother died. They were the exact ones she'd found on her body. Her mother had placed a grid over her heart and soul. She didn't trust the Man-of-Medicine either, so Emadi took her mother's advice and wrapped her doubts and the crystal medicine around herself like a shawl. Her mother would protect her. Her mother was stronger than anyone gave her credit for.

Emadi began to cry. She immediately looked out the window up into the moonlight until her eyes dried. She didn't want her emotions leaking out at the wrong time. She took a long deep breath and then slowly exhaled in a light alto tone. It was her sound, her own pure sound. The sound she used to summon her guides. She pulled down her celestial body and placed its light inside her and as she did this she watched the shaman enter the garden.

"Well good evening, child," he said through the window. Afterward he bowed slightly and then he walked into her house uninvited.

Emadi was already enraged even though she knew that was his intention. She had to quickly decide if she would act like the little girl he thought she was, or if she would rise up and be the woman she was meant to be. She needed too much information to spay the dog immediately, so she decided to cry. As she gently sobbed, she silently prayed to her ancestors to stop her before she slit the throat of the Man-of-Medicine.

"Shall we begin," he said without emotion. "Oh, my dear you've been crying. I'm so sorry. I didn't mean to be insensitive," he said feigning sincerity.

Emadi hated this man but she couldn't let him know that. With eyes downcast, she took the basin of water and presented it to him. She kept her focus on her mother's body. "May I place her favorite herbs in the water, Uncle? She is beginning to smell and the weather is going to be even hotter tomorrow," she gently said, making sure he heard her sniffles under her words.

"Of course, dear child," he said. "You rest and leave everything to me."

"It's okay, Bba Temne. I am better now. I will wash her," Emadi quickly but firmly said.

"As you wish," the Man-of-Medicine sarcastically replied.

The medicine man got his drum and began incanting the spirits while the young woman washed her mother's body. He would have preferred the smell of the dead woman to the smell of the young girl. He was grateful she'd stopped bleeding, but he could still smell her hormones all the same. She was a simpleton and her entire countenance screamed it, still, he never criticized her or made any comment on what she did. It was not exactly their custom's way however it did not veer far from the tradition of their people. He understood her covering her mother. The blisters had opened and the smell alone was hard for a mourning soul to take. It was a very different smell. When she had completely wrapped her mother's body in an immaculate white gown, he took the funeral mask and placed it over her face and began reciting the words of sorrow.

They were done. They had not spoken one word to each other during the entire ceremony. The man was pleasantly surprised. Emadi was nothing like the Herb-Woman. Her mother could never shut up but her daughter worked in complete silence and she was very efficient and neat. She didn't miss one detail. In fact, she tended to details that did not need tending. She burst each blister and placed cucumber rind over it. She'd cut it so thin that you couldn't see the peel nor the sore underneath her mother's shroud. She had cleaned every inch of her. She trimmed her cuticles before scrubbing her nails. She braided her hair and held it all in place with Shea butter. She plucked her eyebrows and did a very natural make up on her face. She even spritzed her body with rose water. The Herb-Woman looked better dead to him than she'd ever looked alive.

"Beautiful job, my child," he said. He was truly impressed. "And with time to spare."

Emadi knew what his last comment meant. He was waiting for her questions. He was waiting for whatever was to come next. "Yes, it is early," she said so slowly that one could see her words float out the window into the night. "The village won't be here for another hour to say their goodbyes," she softly said. "This is good. I can use a moment to myself," she said, making a point to speak as if no one else was in the room.

"Oh, my child, let me give you some time alone before they come," said the medicine man. He was slightly confused. He hadn't expected their conversation to take that direction. The Man-of-Medicine secretly looked around the house for the answer to the young girl's dismissal and came up with nothing until he saw it—the queen's familiar mark. The queen was left handed so the chair had been moved away from the wall, from one side of the kitchen table to the other to allow her some room to lift her teacup. The queen must have said something to the girl, something that warranted her shooing him away.

"Oh no Bba, please stay. I am so grateful for your help today. You've been a gift to me. Here, please sit. I made tea and I baked a pie," she innocently said. Then she set the pie on the table in front of him. As she turned her back to get some teacups, she could hear his glands salivating.

"But the village is to bake for you, my daughter. You shouldn't be worried with that right now," he said sitting down in the chair the queen had used.

"If I don't keep myself busy I will go insane," she said, making her voice drift away like a madwoman's. Then she set her best plate before him and cut him a huge slice of freshly baked pie. "It's sweet potato and I added some of mother's herbs," she said letting the words dissolve like incense smoke.

"This was my favorite of your mother's recipes," he warily said. He wanted to add, 'but you already knew that' but he knew he shouldn't. The girl would clam up and he would never know what the queen told her.

"What did my mother die of, Bba?" she asked with tear-filled eyes that never strayed from his own.

As the man slowly chewed his pie, he stared at the young girl the entire time. He picked up his cup and sipped some tea. He marveled at how she had mastered her mother's pie but her mother would always be the winner when it came to making tea. "I don't know. I have never in all my years had to say that, but my child I truly don't know. The blisters made me think she had a fever but she had no mucous in her lungs nor did she feel hot to the touch. For a while I thought she was having a reaction due to female changes but this was not menopause," he said without taking his eyes off the girl. "What do you think?" he added. And then he yawned.

The valerian root was working. This was good. Emadi immediately looked into her lap. She didn't want her eyes to give her away. The medicine man was relaxing. She had to answer his question. She sincerely did not know what she thought.

"I sincerely don't know what to think, Bba," she said. "I think I am angry. One day my mother is here and the next day she isn't. One day she is happy and the next day she is in pain. One day I have a family and the next day I don't," and then she stopped thinking about anything. She only listened. She listened to everything the man said with his body as well as his mouth and eyes.

"I see. It must be difficult," he said. The medicine man's heart raced when she mentioned being motherless. His soul was trying to get his attention. If he planted the thought that the prince's children and the strange duduju had made her mother sick that would be the final blow. The village loved the Herb-Woman, so her daughter was definitely not without options. She would have every woman in the village ready to nurture her through her grief. She would have more mothers than she knew what to do with. If she told these caring women that the prince's strange children had left her motherless, the women themselves would throw the children into the sea. And her pie was delicious!

"You are not now or ever will be motherless, my child!" he said with false alarm. "You are of a Librebeing woman's womb. One of our favorite Librebe women! You are royalty to this village. And after experiencing your amazing work here today, I am sure you will be our next Herb-Woman for many years to come!" he excitedly said.

Emadi was terrified. His eyes were yellow with glee. He was so ambitious this man. What did he want? Why was he trying to make her his accomplice? And his slur against the prince's children was completely unnecessary. Then the thought that must have come to her mother as well, flooded her veins. This man wants to be king!

"Oh Uncle, thank you for that," she said. She began to cry. It was hurting her to hate this much. "But you cannot blame children because of where they've come from. No child is born of its own thought. They are sired from the thoughts and actions of others," she said.

The young girl's compassion disgusted the man. How was he going to circumnavigate this nurturing impulse that plagued humanity's evolution? He remembered when the first woman was told to kill her son by the wise Ibis but she would not listen. She cried and hid the vile child until he grew up and slew her. It was not until she watched her son slit her throat that she heard the bird's warning!

"You are a child of the earth, my girl. Who's to say what children are or are not when they come from somewhere else. Your mother was healthy and then she was sick. She was here and now she is not. And the only thing that passed, that had not passed a million times before was a night in the bush with those children! Excuse me if I sound angry, but she was my friend," he said. And then he went in for the kill. "Everyone thinks we were rivals, the Herb-Woman versus the Man-of-Medicine but we were friends. Good friends who challenged each other to become better healers. I adored her visits and I think she enjoyed visiting me too, did she not?" he asked staring deeply into the eyes of the young girl.

Emadi was in shock but she couldn't show it. "Yes, she enjoyed your company a lot, Bba" she said. She got up and went to the sink for a cloth to wipe her nose. As the Herb-Woman's daughter hid behind her towel, she contemplated. She had to end the conversation on a good note. "You've given me a lot to think about, Bba" she said. "The people will be coming soon. Please help me find some night flowers to adorn her."

"With pleasure, my daughter," said the satisfied medicine man. "I would love to."

"Thank you, Bba," Emadi said. "You are a gift to me."

The medicine man bowed again to the girl who called him father, and then he made his way to the front door. It'd been a good cleansing, and a better meeting than he'd expected. All was good.

The daughter of the herbalist accompanied the medicine man outside. As they said their goodbyes, she secretly thanked her ancestors and guardians because now she knew what she had to do. All in all, it had been a good meeting, better than she'd expected. All was good.

CHAPTER FOURTEEN

"Do you have it?" asked the Mer-king.

"Yes," said Manulir. The sage handed the king an oiled parchment of extraordinary beauty. "It is a detailed map of the tectonic plates and ley lines."

"How recent?" The Mer-king asked.

"The young Osholun charted it only a few moons ago," replied Manulir.

"Oh, to be brilliant and young again," smiled the Mer-king as he looked over the map. "He has an artist's eye as well as a cartographer's."

"Yes, it is good. And you are still as flexible as the water you swim in, my friend," Manulir said.

But the Mer-king did not hear the wise merman's flattery because he was too busy having thoughts about his mortality. Since the beginning of Earth, his kind has been hunted by those that walked upon it. It reminded him of their own history and the wars they had created as a young species. He was not judging his kind or Hu-men, but life itself. The nature of growth was destructive.

"It has its purpose too," said the wise merman. He had heard his king's thoughts.

"Yes, but we must learn to master the struggle if we are to truly grow. Not all life forms with the ability to reason are created equal. They immediately think in terms of better or worse," said the Mer-king. He was trying to understand the necessity of hierarchies.

"I understand, my king, but now is not the time for analyzing the nature of thinking beings," Manulir said. Then he picked up the map and began explaining the symbolism of the glyphs to the Mer-king. Although Librebe was high in the mountains the ocean floor existed tens of thousands of feet beneath them. It would have been easy to topple the landmass into the sea. The Mer-king knew this but he simply rolled the map up and looked out into the waters.

"We share life here with those who stood erect only a few years ago. We also share air with those who no longer need a form to exist. Those loving vibrations shine like the stars. But now we are dealing with Hu-men life forms that have not yet learned that they are a part of a grand equation. They want to take away something, thinking it will add another thing to their lives," said the Mer-king. He was debating himself. He knew that.

"How else will they learn to rise above it?" said Manulir. "They are amusing. You must give them that."

"I am not looking forward to their smell," said the Mer-king with a smile. The mermen laughed.

"And our queen, what does she feel about all this?" asked Manulir.

The Mer-king's fin fluttered in that anxious way it did when the sage spoke of his wife. "You are in love with my wife, sir," he sadly said. "I'm flattered."

The Mer-queen felt the current shift and she lost her connection. The wise woman of Earth's voice slipped away and her husband's voice replaced it. This was not the time for the king to corner the wise merman. Her husband knew they'd had many lifetimes together. He also knew they were committed to their lives at present. This fight, the war between the binary opposites was the only reason any of them had incarnated to begin with. They came to unify binary opposition so Hu-men could see the whole picture. So they could see as one. They came to help!

The Mer-queen thought of her life as a young dolphin. It was that life that had catapulted her from one dimension to the next. It didn't matter that she'd been trapped in a Hu-man circus entertaining children for her livelihood because she'd found the joy within it. It was there she met Manulir for the first time. He'd been a bottlenose dolphin that wouldn't give birth in captivity. She was the male in that incarnation, and she freed the female Manulir. She let her loose, and as a female, Manulir had their calf; her son and present husband in this life now. That was why Manulir addled him so. He always felt young in his presence.

The Mer-queen heard the woman of earth summon her again, and she listened.

"Yes," said the wise merman. "I love her."

"I'm sorry, my friend, it is not a judgment. It's only an observation. Forgive me for stating the obvious. You needn't explain or defend yourself, especially to me. I love her too," said the Mer-king.

Manulir was waiting for him to stop talking. His conversation made as much sense to him as saying there was water all around them.

"So, you are the wise merman. What do you suggest?" asked the Mer-king returning to the business at hand.

Manulir felt his heart beat erratically. It was true in this life, at this present moment he was a sage, not a mother or lover, just a sage.

"You are more than that. As you can see we are many things to each other," said the Mer-king. His friend's thought worried him in much the same way as his love for his wife did. He cared for the merman.

"The true question is, how do we become one with those that can't agree on anything?" Manulir asked.

"By employing those things they do believe in," said the Mer-queen upon entering. Both mermen rose up to greet her.

"Goodness to you both," she said. "A sage friend of mine on land had a wonderful idea. She believes we must become that which they believe in. We must become their ancestors."

"But isn't this war with their ancestors, their eldest ancestor to be exact? These people are plotting to kill their proverbial first cousins," said the Mer-king.

"Yes, they are committing Hu-men genocide, especially with the original twelve pods of their lineage. That is where most of the fighting above ground is centered, between those twelve great tribes," said Manulir.

"So, we must find the common thread of each warring side," replied the Mer-queen. "Preferably their highest side. They do love their hierarchies," she added.

"What or who is their highest creator?" asked the Mer-king.

"Remember, their instincts are to destroy their kings," said Manulir.

"What if we are looking at this from the wrong dimension? Who profits from the destruction of Hu-men? You mentioned something. The wars above ground are being waged primarily on their twelve original pods, or tribes whatever you call them," contemplated the Mer-king. "What if this is about their DNA?"

"Ahh, well thought, my king, of course it is! Someone wants to erase the Hu-men DNA. The Hu-man form is one of the most exploited of the blue planets. It is resilient and the neural anatomy makes it perfect for reasoning and storing information," said Manulir.

"And since it is direct matter from creation, it is made exactly in that image," exclaimed the Mer-queen. She was in terrified awe!

"So, these innocent naïve life forms have the ability to create willingly like no other creation in the entire solar system. These simple creatures either follow their instinctual oneness or some type of parasitic cleansing program, which is very destructive. Plus, they are programmed to seek their origin. However, if one of them were successfully able to create willingly and had centuries of superior technology, they could rule the music of the spheres," said the Mer-king before lapsing into silence.

"But if they eliminate the original God Seed as the Hu-men call it, they will have a reincarnating slave pool for eternity. That is why they are being programmed to self-destruct by creating division between the twelve family pods," Manulir sadly said.

"First things first, what if all life form above ground rebelled against this destructive tendency?" asked the Mer-queen.

"They have free will. They will willingly self-destruct. Look at what they've created above ground!" Manulir said. Now he was angry.

"We will lose many before they feel their connection to one another and the life forms that sustain them," the Mer-king sadly said.

They all became silent for a good—long—moment.

"Not if we connect them to each other," said the Mer-queen.

"Lovely intention," replied Manulir.

"Yes," said the Mer-king and once again they all fell into silence.

"It may work," the Mer-king finally said. "Let's call all of the inner realms. My love, you contact the fourth and sixth and eighth dimensions and get them to unite at once. Manulir you work with those spirits of matter existing in the third, fifth and seventh dimensional frequencies living here on Earth at present and I will hold consciousness with the beings of instinctual knowledge until we are all individually together again like rain from above."

"And me, father, what shall you have me do?" Sedina asked.

The three elder merfolk all turned in unison and a common thought went through their minds. How long has she been there? Again, there was silence. It was the Mer-king who broke from the tribunal and swam toward his daughter.

"You must make sure the channels remain open between you and our granddaughter. Because if this doesn't work we must bring her home immediately."

CHAPTER FIFTEEN

The mermaid was swimming in circles again. Equoo hated when his friend got upset. Especially when he was hitchhiking a ride in her hair. Now he was dizzy, so he used his nose to nudge her bun to one side and he freed himself. He'd had enough experience with Sedina to know trying to reason with her right now was futile. He had to let her swim laps until she came to some conclusion on her own. Thus, he slowly made his way to the brightest place in her cavern and munched on plankton until she calmed down.

Sedina could not stop thinking about her carelessness. Her actions had set this awful war in motion. She was the one responsible for the prophecy that all life as one knew it was going to change dramatically. Entire species were going to be erased. She now knew that one spark, that small glimmer in the distance, had changed everything.

"You are not responsible for this," said Equoo. "This event has been spoken of since I was a wee filly."

Sedina stopped. Why hadn't she thought about this before? She now remembered being forewarned. When she was a rebellious youth, she snuck into the sealed Akashic records of the Mer-ones. She read about the War of Binary Opposition, but she thought it was going to be an event in the future. She didn't think she would be present when it happened. And she certainly didn't think she would be the one to set it all in motion.

"What did the seahorses say?" she asked.

Equoo truly wished he'd kept his mouth shut. If he told her what they said about the times to come, she would feel even worse than she did already, but if he didn't tell her she'd think of something even more horrific. "They foretold of a time when the multi-elemental, *two-leggeds* on Earth would correct the imbalance in the world. They would be born with crystalline clarity and all their faculties would be wide open. They said the mean beings that wanted to siphon all life's goodness for their selves would try to kill them, but the children would prevail, however not before the majority of life was wiped out. Then they told us none of this mattered because life always exists anyway. And then they sang and whinnied and made as many babies as they could."

Equoo had no idea he would say so much. He really had to learn how to keep his mouth shut. No one wants to hear about the end when they were in the middle of a story. The seahorse managed to close his snout but his heart was wide open now and it was telegraphing all sorts of nonsense. "Seahorse stories always end happily," and he finally shut his mouth as well as his thoughts.

"I see," said Sedina. "What heralded the beginning of this story? How did all this start?" she asked.

"When we began going extinct. Hu-men started hunting us. They believed if they dried us in the sun and ground our bodies into a meal, we would make them well. They made medicine out of us until we dwindled down to next to nothing. Nevertheless, they began birthing the crystal-brained children with open hearts. The children healed them, so they stopped eating us because the children taught them to align with everything. And so on and whatever until everyone was happy in the end," he said, while looking at his belly the entire time.

"And do you believe it? Do you believe these multi-elemental children with crystalline awareness can save us? Did they mention a jackal?" she sadly asked the seahorse.

"I have never seen a Hu-man, nor has any other seahorse happily living in the sea. I imagine the only ones that have seen Hu-men never got to return to tell us what they looked like. No, I take that back, one-time Jod saw one. It had huge eyes and tubes coming out of it and it stared at him but that may not be true. Sounds a bit like a tall tale to me."

"It is very true, my friend. They are called scuba divers and they are learning how to dive deeper and deeper into the sea. One time they built a round cavern like bubble and they made it all the way to the ocean's floor. It was frightening," she said.

"If my kind had seen that they would have summoned every herd and friend in the sea to sink it. They would have never allowed it to sea-nap us. They have been so mean to seahorses and most of the other fish too. What I do know of their kind is they don't give up. They'd bomb the sea until nothing remained if it meant they couldn't have fish on Fridays," he said. He was trying to be humorous but the conversation kept going further and further downstream.

"And nowhere in your history did they mention a jackal?" she asked.

"I'm sorry, but no. They never mentioned a jackal or any other four-legged land animal, only the hairless two-legged Hu-men," he quietly said.

Equoo was frightened. He'd never had a conversation about those on land, especially Hu-men. Hu-men had been so cruel to seahorses. They'd kill them, or send them bad sounds, or try to pour oil over the water, anything they could so sea-beings would no longer be able to breathe. Hu-men had been trying to exterminate them since time began. He was sure some of the larger fish were so sick of it they kept their little sea legs into maturity so they could walk on land and exact their revenge. He'd heard many stories about them and they were never, ever, happy tales.

"I must contact the Mer-land seer. She was the one that told me this would happen. I hope I can summon her at will. Come," she said with determination.

"Where?" asked the baffled seahorse.

"To open waters where no one can hear us," she said. Then she picked up Equoo and shoved him into a large conch shell and swam across the stone path behind the royal hall, out into open waters.

❖ M ❖

Rose was ready. She had her passport and her shots were up to date. She'd bought a ton of crayons, pencils and some notebooks and protein bars for the children, and vitamins and dark chocolate for herself. She had an ample supply of toiletries. The rest of the space in her knapsack she filled with antibiotic wipes, a feminine hygiene sponge, and Himalayan salt and food grade hydrogen peroxide. Next, she placed a week's worth of underwear and a light silk sarong she'd made from her aunt's wedding gown plus an over-priced indigo wrap she bought ages ago at an African festival in Atlanta. When she bought the indigo cloth, she was sure she was going to make a lovely maxi dress out of it. She thought it would change the way women were perceived. She wanted to drape it from head to toe so it had an exotically sensual effect on the minds of the rabid orthodox, but that was when she thought like so many megalomaniacal others— that their way was best. She still didn't tolerate anyone thinking they were better than her. She simply stopped thinking she was better than any of them.

One final check and she was ready. She had everything. Then she went back into her bedroom and got the scarab ring she inherited from her great-great grandmother, and a link of the chain she'd broke before jumping the slave trader's boat and swimming to the island she now called home. It was her most powerful amulet. She needed to feel her power now and her family. Anything else she needed, she'd get there.

"*Rose, of light and breath so fair. Please be there,*" toned Sedina.

"Really, now," said Rose to herself and quite loudly. "Enough, I can't do this right now," she said throwing her knapsack into the back of her car.

"*Rose, speak to me of the prophecy that thee foretold. I am thee and you are we. Have we begun?*" toned the mermaid. She would not give up. She couldn't give up.

"Oh, my princess, you tried. You are not responsible. Maybe the Creator does not wish for you to know more than you do. Have you ever thought of that?" pleaded Equoo.

"I can't give up, Equoo. I have to learn all I can. Mianshe is my daughter.

I can't give up," she exclaimed. She was astonished at the thought that a divine plan wouldn't wish her to have awareness of it.

"Mianshe is the first of the multi-elemental children they spoke about, so I'm sure she will be okay," he said in the calmest voice possible. He wished his friend had more faith.

"No, Equoo! You said that it would take them a long time and most of the living would die. If she is the first, then she is most at risk. It's Hu-man nature to kill the messenger, Equoo. Look at Hu-man history!" The mermaid was crying now.

Equoo froze. There was no worse sound in the sea than the sound of a mermaid crying. It was so rare it took a moment to distinguish it but once you did, it remained in your cellular memory for eternity. Crying always paralyzed the seahorse. He couldn't manage the sound of a whinny from a spoiled baby sea-foal yet a sincere moment of tonal misery. He had no idea what to do.

"Listen, mermaid queen of mine. All, I promise, all will be fine. I am going to Africa by air over sea, and I promise to contact you as soon as I reach Librebe," toned Rose. And then all went silent for a good —long—moment.

"Did we hear right?" asked a shocked Sedina.

"Yes. How? Why is she going to your daughter's home?" asked a stunned Equoo.

"I don't know," she slowly replied. The mermaid had been shaken to her core. "What is going on?" she asked no one and everybody.

"It's begun. As was foretold," Equoo said without emotion. He was done feeling things for the day, so he shut down his bodily functions and gently floated in the sea.

Sedina grabbed the lithe seahorse before he went spiraling out with the current and she placed him deep inside the bodice of her breastplate. All her life she felt wrong for being so strong willed and adventurous. She felt too large because her laugh resounded and echoed or that she could swim a great distance in one breaststroke. She felt awkward for not tilting her head and because her tone was so deep, but today she called on all those things. She needed everything that made her who she was. She had to fill her own space and open her heart so wide the ocean would attach itself to her. She had to.

"No one will take my child, my life or any other life-form from me. No one can make that decision for me, but me!" she bellowed.

And the ocean roared and turned a blue so dark it made black jealous.

CHAPTER 16

Everyone was present for Mma Ellen's wake. The king sat beside his sister, the queen. The prince sat on the floor next to Adisa. The Fire-Tender sat outside by the fire, and the Man-of-Medicine moved around the house. Emadi was watching all of them. She wasn't spying on them per se; she was trying to avoid them. She'd had enough of people to last her a lifetime, so the Herb-Woman's daughter went into the pantry and hid. She needed some time to herself. The mourning wails of her mother's loved ones put her nerves on edge. Everyone's voice seemed so shrill and the drums were making her head throb. All the sound was intolerable and the colors were worse. Even midnight blue seemed loudly bright. She was grateful the queen had spread the message deterring the children of the village from joining them. The sounds of children laughing would have sent her scurrying into the bush for peace.

"Stop listening," a voice said and Emadi stopped and listened, but the voice said no more.

"Emadi, my dear, we are all leaving now. My dear, are you in there?" asked the Queen as light heartedly as she could. The queen slowly opened the pantry door, just a little and saw the Herb-Woman's daughter standing in the corner with her head resting on her arms, on the third shelf next to the rice canister.

"Emadi," whispered the Queen.

The queen motioned for the guests to go on home. She told them she would tell the young woman they had come. She asked them to be respectful when leaving. She told them again that everything was okay.

She told them she would see them all at the evening dama service. She even cried with them but she would not let them into the pantry. After the guests left, the queen gently opened the pantry door and walked inside and closed the door behind her. "They are all gone now," said the Queen.

Emadi never responded. She simply stayed exactly as she was; head resting on her hands on the third shelf of her mother's cupboard.

"Emadi, here drink this," the Queen said. She knew when your spirits were down it took a stronger spirit to raise them. She held the glass of whiskey and waved it back and forth under the young woman's nose.

"Please, my Queen, the smell is making me nauseous," said Emadi. She lifted her head and stared directly into her eyes. "I don't mean to be rude but the smell, and the sounds, Queen-Mother. They are so loud. And that man would not stop moving," she calmly and clearly said.

"My dear, listen to me," said the Queen. "I know you are tired. I understand. But you are going to have many guests this evening and they will stay until tomorrow's sunset. Now this was the shortest wake I have ever attended…" said the Queen before the young woman interrupted her.

"Auntie, what time is it?" Emadi asked.

"It is almost three in the afternoon, child. You've been in this closet since nine this morning. Drink this," she said.

This time Emadi listened. She downed the whiskey in one gulp.

"I had no idea I'd been in here so long. Last I remember I was trying to calm my mind so I stopped listening, until you called me," Emadi said.

"Listen, your mother's funeral is at sunset. That is in less than five hours. You have been in a brief daydream for equally that long. You won't have that luxury at the funeral. Everyone will be in a circle watching you and waiting for you to praise those memories they dearly hold of your mother. You will hear some silly and some truly sad stories that will make you want to tear your hair out," said the Queen.

"But I must never take off my head wrap," Emadi said with the faintest of smiles.

"This is not funny, my daughter," the Queen quietly said with authority.

"Please, forgive me. You are right. I'm sorry. I would never want you to think me disrespectful, my Queen, however I see more than anyone gives me credit for. I see you are worried, possibly frightened. I know the Fermemi Queen is to attend. Why? She never knew my mother. The Fire-Tender never took his eyes off the hearth, not once. I see he's worried too. And I see the Man-of-Medicine's yellow-eyed ambition. I saw so much I had to rest my head and eyes on this shelf," said Emadi with great control. "And I see we are out of rice."

The Herb-Woman's daughter was right. The queen was scared. She too had seen what the young woman saw but she had no idea what it meant. Now she was beginning to see it all very clearly. "The Man-of-Medicine wants the Hogan reinstated but as a governing force. He wants to rule," the Queen quietly said. "Is that what you believe?" she asked.

"Yes," said Emadi. "That is what I believe and I believe he's planning something for this evening."

"For this evening, Emadi!" said the shocked Queen. The queen composed herself and looked at the young woman. "The funeral is in five hours, so my wise young one, how can I be of help?"

"Well, I suppose we must first leave this closet. Then we must place a grid of protection around the communal fire. Then as long as we hold hands we should be fine. As for the shaman, he will expose himself soon enough and we must be ready for him, because he will take on the form of our first ancestor," she wearily said.

"The jackal!" said the Queen with alarm. "Who on earth would wish such a thing, especially on oneself?" asked the Queen, but she looked to the heavens for the answer.

"Because it will bring fear to those of pure heart. Nothing else would scare you, my Queen, and what could scare our King? Nothing. Not a thing but one thing, that very thing that scares everyone, the instrument of chaos itself—the jackal," stated Emadi. Afterward, she opened the cupboard door and walked out into the sunlight.

The queen closed the door and remained inside. She slowly made her way to her knees and layed down prone on the floor. With her face on the damp earth she prayed. "Dear Amma, it is I, your lowly, barren queen. I've never in all my years asked for anything for myself. I have been given a role to play and I am committed to playing it. Today everything you've created is at risk of coming undone by your son, the jackal. He is on a rampage and is defiling all that gets in his way. Dearest Mother Amma, please take over the upbringing of your son. Spank his behind and take him home with you. I am sure with your love this can be accomplished. And Mother, please take these murderous thoughts from my mind. With your grace, I exist. Thank you, I am your Queen."

The queen grabbed the first shelf and pulled herself to her knees. Next, she took hold of the second ledge and propped herself up onto her right foot. As she hoisted herself upward she saw a jar with no label. She opened it and smelled its contents before taking out enough castor seeds to put a large dog to sleep for the rest of its life.

"And so it is," said the Queen and she opened the door and walked freely into the sunlight.

✤ /\/\ ✤

"I am!" screamed the Man-of-Medicine. He was furious. His eyes were bulging and floating in the yellow space that had once been clearly white. His eyes darted back and forth in his head. He leapt up and in a zigzag direction made his way toward home. As he moved he cursed everyone and everything. "How dare she disrespect me? I brought her expensive tea and cakes. I came to her smelly house. I allowed her to work beside me and she ignores me!" he howled. The man pounced over to the sacred tree and punched it. "I will not be dismissed!" he screamed. "But I am not a pretty girl, or a showy fire keeper, or an ephemeral water-spirit, no, I am none of those things." Then the man fell to his knees and pounded the earth. "Now you will see me. You will see me now," he growled.

The medicine man opened his sack and pulled out the vial containing the strand of the mermaid-girl's hair. He got down on all fours and reared back on his haunches and began burrowing like a dog. The dirt went everywhere. Clods of dry earth smacked the trunk of the tree making the leaves shudder and fall to the ground. The shaman paid no attention to anything but the hole he was digging. He grabbed the falling leaves from mid-air and shoved them into the opening. Afterward he added some charcoal and dried roots and then he set it all on fire. Next, he took the strand of Mianshe's hair and tied eight tiny knots into it and he wrapped it around the stick Emadi had used to stir her tea. As he did this, he recited many words and guttural sounds in rapid fire. It sounded like nonsense.

"Amakremdanaiammaoneteneighteighteighteighteighteighteight eightommunommunommunooommunooomunooomun…" he said over and over again.

He continued chanting until the clouds blocked the sun from view. As the ebony shadow was being cast over everything, he swore an affirmation of complete annihilation.

> When the moon rises the fire will die
> Drowning the aliens from our eyes
> By force we'll eject the others from our land
> And water will cleanse water and the Jackal-man
> And he alone will rule the Nummos' inheritance
> For I am that I am, master from this moment hence!

Then he howled and sent his feet backward bounding off the tree to an upright position. "And so it is," he calmly said. And he spat eight times into the hole and the fire went out.

✦ /\\. ✦

CHAPTER 17

The prince needed to talk to someone, someone who wasn't his father. He needed an objective ear. The only person he knew who had never spoken ill of anyone was the Fire-Tender, but if he visited him Adisa might be there. He couldn't talk in front of her, not about his fears. He wanted clarity on the strange events surrounding the Herb-Woman's death. He had to know about duduju and if it was contagious. He wanted to know what role the Fermemi queen played. But mostly he needed to know if the Man-of-Medicine was still loyal to his village.

He wished he was in a city where he could simply phone the Fire-Tender or meet him at a café, but this was Librebe, the weird and wonderful little country that had isolated itself from the concerns of others. The prince remembered the Fire-Tender took his tea on the porch every night so he could smoke his pipe. Since the funeral service was in the evening, maybe he'd have his nightly ritual in the afternoon. He quickly washed and prepared his robe for the evening's ceremony. Then he slipped out the back, unnoticed. His instincts were right. The Fire-Tender was sitting on his porch smoking his pipe.

"Good evening, Uncle," said the Prince "Enjoying yourself, I see," he said with a smile.

"Well, what a surprise, my Prince, please come join me," the Fire-Tender said with a quizzical expression. "Adisa is in the square attending to matters, but I would love the company," he added.

"Thank you, Uncle, thank you," replied the Prince. "I'd hoped to find

318

you here alone. I wished to ask for your wisdom regarding some courtly matters."

"I see," said the Fire-Tender. He waited to see what direction the conversation would take.

"I don't know how to begin. Firstly, I'm ready and excited to ask for Adisa's hand in marriage but not during a funeral ceremony," he said before becoming quite still.

The Fire-Tender began silently praying for him.

"I'm worried about Librebe, Uncle. The Man-of-Medicine has changed since Auntie Ellen's death and it frightens me. Then there was Emadi's strange behavior at the wake. It makes me wonder if there is more to her mother's death than we are privy to," sighed the Prince. Then the prince looked at the Fire-Tender like a student looks up to a teacher. He was waiting for his answer or for enough clarification so he could solve the problem himself.

The Fire-Tender looked at the young man with a mixture of respect and compassion. It was a bold move to air one's fears. It was also a great sign of respect that he chose him to confide in. "Have you spoken to your father about these things?" he asked.

"Not so much spoken with as confirmed our sentiments. We are both confused by the events of late," replied the Prince. He never mentioned his father's concerns about his children or his own son's loyalty to his people.

"I see," the Fire-Tender politely said. "My son, I understand your worries. I too have seen symbols in the fire even I could not read."

"Like what, Uncle?" asked the Prince.

"Someone is visiting that is not from here, a woman. A cold storm is on the horizon, but it is the hot season, plus other signs I am not familiar with which may be from your daughter's world," he said.

"What do you think is happening?" asked the Prince. He felt oddly calm since having his doubts confirmed.

"I could never say for sure, my son. All I know is Ellen was scared the day before she died. She was frightened by something she'd seen or by someone she knew. Neither she nor the fire would tell me more. But tonight, at her wake the Man-of-Medicine would not stop moving. He did not want me to see him. He avoided everyone but at the same time he tried to spray his scent over the people too. He is not well in his body or soul," confided the Fire-Tender.

The prince listened with all of himself. He even listened to the nuances the Fire-Tender's answers brought up in him. "The storm, Uncle, is it sent by Amma or is it man made?" he finally asked. It was the question he most feared the answer to. He knew how to fight a man but he would not fight his Creator.

The Fire-Tender decided to be as open with the prince as he'd been with him. "My son, I'm sorry to say it is both. The storm will come from the heavens and from man," he said. Then he puffed his pipe and exhaled a large ring of smoke that never quite became a circle. It was broken in the west and it floated away like a continent did when it became an island during an earthquake.

⁂ /.\ ⁂

The Fermemi queen was verklempt. She loved the word verklempt. It got her all choked up inside when she said it. Another word she loved was wanderlust. That was how she was feeling today. Her wanderlust had left her verklempt. When the Fermemi caravan had crested the hill, the queen demanded they pull over for tea and mealie pies. They had been traveling for over an hour and she was parched.

"Come. Bring my umbrella here. This is the right spot," she said. And it was a good spot for viewing her village and the outskirts of Librebe as well. They were more than half way there, but it would take them a couple more hours to reach the center of town, thus leaving her only three hours to prepare for the festivities.

"Who are we going to see?" asked the Fermemi High-Prince.

"Oh, you, well, I'm just verklempt. How can you forget such things in such a short amount of time? If you were not who you are, I would have fed you to the pigs by now," replied the Fermemi Queen.

Truth be told, she didn't have a clue what the Herb-Woman's name was either. She pulled the young man's hand and drew him closer so his body shaded her face. Although he was her mate the young man often disgusted the queen. But he had a lovely body. It was firm and rippled in all the right places and was not scarred. His skin was as clear as a baby's. His body truly satisfied the queen in every way imaginable.

The Fermemi queen looked over the valley with pride. Her village was prospering and she was determined to keep it that way. When her spies told her of the birth of the twins in Librebe it upset her. She was envious. Twins heralded wealth, luck and wellness. It made things twice as good. She'd always wondered how the small village did so well in spite of its geographical disadvantage. She'd wondered if they'd found gold or better yet uranium. Maybe they were trading the expensive metals with foreigners, right under her nose. But given she had the only boat access to the waterway there was little possibility of that happening. Maybe they'd built a railway without her knowledge. She wished they had at least built a road wide enough for a motorcar. This walking up hill was downright barbaric.

She thought Librebeings were shy and old-fashioned. They worshipped the ancestral ways. They were good people, honest and fair to deal with but a bit too private and traditional. Granted they wore a combination of western and African clothes, and they were extremely well educated too; however, they simply chose not to get involved with any culture other than their own. They did not watch TV or listen to the radio. Why? They had electricity.

The tourists loved that sort of thing. They were so happy when the people were bare breasted and beating their drums. It made them feel enlightened and advanced. Tourism could bring in good money from the young European liberals. Even the entitled Black Americans were throwing cash around these days. Maybe she should create a homecoming ceremony for the children of the slave trade. People paid through the nose to call some place home and they paid even more to get rid of their guilt for not having to live there. Maybe tourism was why Librebe was thriving.

Needless to say, it was time to see what her neighbors were up to and what better way to hear the news than at a good funeral.

The Fermemi queen stood up and repositioned the young man so his shadow covered her from head to toe. "Stand here," she demanded.

The poor Fermemi prince was pouring sweat. He was so tired of being bossed around by the old woman. Since they had been married some twenty-eight moons ago she hadn't called him king once. She told him king made him sound old but he knew why she wanted everyone to call him High-Prince. A high prince had no rights to the throne. It was a useless title. It's only reward was he got to sleep in the main house and no one bothered him—well no one except the queen. So here he was a human umbrella for an old hag. If he hadn't seen a means of escape he would have feigned another hernia, but his body wasn't able to take any more medicines. He had faked being sick so often it was taking his toll on him. Now it was hard for him to get excited at all. Certain parts of his body would no longer obey him, but that might not only be due to the *dyodyonuno*'s medicines. Having to lay with his queen had that effect on him too. But the nightmare was almost over. He would help himself to the gold coin offering she'd brought for the Librebe king and go to Paris. He was sure he could get a job dancing there. First, he needed to get to Bamako.

"Watch what you are doing!" screamed the Fermemi Queen. "Well, I guess I won't get any rest now. Look at my face! It's melting, and my shoes are dusty," she nagged. "Ahh stupid boy, let's go. I'll rest there," she complained as she continued up the road toward Librebe.

"How will they know that, Nanny?" Adisa asked.

Leboya shrugged her shoulders and threw her hands up in the air. She had no idea how the people would know where they were to sit, especially the guests. Normally the community rushed in and sat where ever they ended up. Hierarchy among the people was not practiced in Librebe. Even the king and queen waited their turn when they were in the communal circle. The last time there was this much regalia over a death was when the queen died in childbirth, but then sadness ruled and the people simply sat down. Even though the people adored the Herb-Woman fear was guiding their behavior.

"I don't know," Leboya said. She was exasperated. "Why is the Fermemi Queen trying to take the glory from Ellen's funeral anyway? She can sit on a barrel in the back for all I care." Leboya wasn't having it, so she turned her back on the matter and continued sweeping the dirt.

Adisa agreed with everything Nanny Leboya had said, but she knew people. These people would stand and wail and compete to be the saddest one there if a foreigner was watching. Her father would be there in his place in the east. Everyone knew the king and the queen sat in the north and the prince sat to the right of them with his children on his left. If she could convince the prince and his children to get there early, then people would behave and act respectful upon entering the circle. She always sat to the right of her father, and the Man-of-Medicine would be in the west, so all she needed to do was place a cushion to the left of the king for the Fermemi queen. Adisa decided she would bring the pillow with arms that she'd gotten for her father on a trip in the city. It would support the visiting queen's back plus give her something to push off of when getting up. Hopefully she was able to manage getting up and down. The Fermemi queen was old.

Everything was ready. The wood was stacked and the square was swept. The blessing incense floated in the air. There was a nice breeze and a lovely cloud shaded the area. It was hard to tell what time of day it was because everything was steeped in the lovely gray-blue reflection of the sky. Adisa reached inside her wrap and retrieved two little vials of blessing oil. She wanted to protect the wood from being tampered with by any impure thoughts. She wanted Mma Ellen to have a peaceful ride home. She deserved it. She flicked the oil on the woodpile and surrounded it with good intentions and love. "Mma," she whispered. "You are loved." She quickly turned around to see if anyone was spying on her but nanny was the only one there sweeping down the steps one more time.

"For good measure," Leboya said as she swept. Then she smiled and went back to cleaning the dirt she imagined coming up that evening.

❖ ⋀ ❖

Rose was sticky with exhaustion. Her clothes were twisted around her like a ribbon on a maypole. She'd slept in three airports and numerous uncomfortable chairs for twenty hours, but she made it. She was in Pierreville with six hours to make the three-hour trip by car to Librebe. She had to find a driver and fast.

"*No one must know why you have come,*" toned the phantom Herb-Woman.

Rose jumped and dropped her knapsack. She hated drawing attention to herself like that. Normally she could manage being present when spirits talked to her from the other side, but this old woman was different. She was home. Rose imagined she was as much at home dead as she was when she'd been living.

"Don't talk to me when others are around," she whispered.

"*Someone is always around, Rose,*" she moaned with more control.

"Thank you," Rose said to the young boy helping her with her bag as well as to the old dead woman accompanying her.

Rose went out into the street and walked directly across it to the first market she could find. She haggled with the salesgirl in French and bought two pairs of underwear and some black soap. She made a point of asking the salesgirl for candles. When the girl asked her what kind, she told her white and then she paused for a long moment before asking her for some black candles too. It had just the effect she wished.

The owner came out from the back room and looked at the yellow foreigner with more interest. "Vous ne pas d'ici. You are not from around here," the owner asked her in a strange French accent she'd never heard before.

"Non, je visite ma tante," Rose responded. She made a point of being short with the woman when telling her she was visiting her aunt. It wasn't a lie. Just then Ellen knocked a small vial of oil off a shelf. She knew she had to buy it. "Cela aussi," she said to the salesgirl.

The owner ushered the girl into the back room and took over handling Rose's purchase. She was overly polite and extremely curious. When Rose asked her if she knew of someone who could drive her to the village near Librebe, she was baffled. She said there was no village outside of Fermemi. There was a town in the valley down the mountainside, but she had never heard of anyone living up that mountain but sheepherders. She told her it had once been a sacred spot built on crystals and rare metals that rang in the night and the people who lived there, spoke in tongues. They could communicate with the spirits. She said they had visitors from other planets and they flew in and out of there like witches on brooms. She said the place had bad spirits. She assured her that her story was no child's tale. Then she warned her that Librebe people were not to be messed with.

"*Hogwash*" toned the Herb-Woman's ghost and then she sucked the air through her teeth sending a chill up the shopkeeper's spine.

Rose assured the woman there was no need to worry. No one in her family was normal either, but they were still her relations so she had to go. She asked the woman again where she could find a driver that knew the way and could get her there fast. The owner offered her brother.

Her brother was a gentle looking man capable of killing a snake with his teeth. All he wanted was to end his journey with a full tank of gas and fifty American dollars. Rose smiled and gave the man what he asked for. He would earn it plus he'd never ask questions or let anyone know where he'd taken her. No one wanted their poor friends to know they had a pocket full of money and they got it by driving a yellow foreigner to a haunted town.

His name was Rambo. He always asked to carry her bag and he never demanded anything. He was always grateful for what he knew was rightfully his anyway. Rose liked him immediately. He had found a way to live in a corrupt world and maintain his dignity and that was not an easy thing to do.

All in all, his old Land Rover made it easily up the hill. Rose got used to the shocks and rode the car like a horse. She went with it and allowed her body to bounce in sync with the truck. After the customary greetings and small talk, they became good friends. She could tell because they allowed each other the grace of silence.

It was beautiful country. The pink limestone and copper enriched earth surrounded them like fairy dust and washed everything in a delicate flesh-toned hue. It was the perfect place to fall in love, but Rose wasn't here for that. It'd been years since she felt like being in love. The last time was at a festival in Colorado, when a kilted man came up to her while she was sitting on a rock in a mood just like now. He stood before her and would not leave. She didn't realize at the time that she'd fallen in love, but she did. She kissed him and sent him away on his path. She remained grounded in the rock, like Rodin's sculpture. Now after all these years she still wished she'd asked him to sit down with her.

Rambo reached over and touched Rose's leg and smiled. "I am well endowed," he informed her.

Rose laughed and wiped his hand from her thigh. Men had little knowledge of the art of timing. "Pull over," she said.

"But there is nothing here, miss," he said. "And the road ends soon so why walk now?" He was afraid his gesture of affection had insulted her. He hadn't seen the caravan of mourners walking on the ridge. It was an odd group. A woman in a bright purple caftan followed by a young man holding an umbrella and a mule pulling a cart laden with baskets.

"I'll walk the rest of the way," Rose said and she gave the man eighty dollars. "This should take care of your gas and some food for your journey. Merci beaucoup, Rambo," she said. And she grabbed her knapsack from the back seat and headed toward the ridge.

When Rose was sure the man was out of view she sat down and looked at the vial of oil the Herb-Woman had instructed her to buy. It was a thick sludge of sanguine goo that smelled like a gland from an animal.

"What is this, Auntie? What am I supposed to do with this?" she asked.

And the old woman's spirit came over her like a cool wind. *"Throw it in the fire. It will protect you and show you the way to the sacred cave and there, Amma will greet you, and take over your journey."*

After carrying the dead woman's message, the wind subsided and gently drifted away leaving Rose sitting in the setting sun of Librebe.

CHAPTER 8TEEN

THE START OF THE PROPHECY

The first person to attend Mma Ellen's funeral was the Herb-Woman herself. She appeared in the square beside the woodpile just as the sun hovered over the horizon. No one felt her presence. They were all too busy getting ready to say goodbye.

"Hello, my friend," moaned the Herb-Woman to the woodpile surrogate of the Fire-Tender. She lightly blew on the logs and smiled. She knew she'd miss him most of all. Why in all those years didn't she have an affair with the man? She was too busy worshipping her freedom plus she didn't want to cause him trouble. She must remind Emadi to pursue love above all else.

The community was beginning to gather. The Herb-Woman had until the full moon to make things right. She didn't want to experience her own funeral pyre. Fire was the tender's medium. She loved soil. She tried to dig her toes into the earth but her etheric body would not allow it. However, it was amazing how quickly a thought manifested, so she thought about making her mark in the dirt and it appeared exactly as she'd seen it.

Ellen sighed. She could see Adisa everywhere. The cushions were placed with such gentle care you could see her doing it. Déjà vu was nothing more than a different point on the time line. A strange expression since time had quite a curly figure. Her people counted it out in eight beats. Eight was the shapeliest of the numbers. You could write an eight from beginning to end and never finish it—8 stood for infinity.

Ellen thought Adisa would make a good queen and that would hurt her daughter. She remembered the time they'd all lived together under the same roof after the Fire-Tender's foul tango with the South African dancer. She never criticized him. She even included his daughter as her own and as a result, she lost Emadi. Her own daughter felt abandoned after that. She had to make it up to her before her voyage home erased her memories.

Ellen knew her daughter even if she failed, Emadi would be fine. She was strong, clear, and unpolluted. No one could get her to do something she didn't wish to do. She would've made an excellent Hogan. Nature loved her. But she would have made an intolerable queen. The village men would have killed her. Mankind has always had issues with strong women. That's why she was using the last of her strength to protect her warrior daughter. The roots woman was getting less rest in death than she did in life, when all she wanted was a good hot cup of tea.

The Fire-Tender entered the square and sat down. His daughter had already prepared everything, and she'd done an excellent job. There was nothing else for him to do so he sat down and took it easy. He felt as comfortable as he did sitting on his porch. He filled his pipe and added a nice dried pinch of mint in honor of his deceased friend.

Ellen deeply inhaled the smoke and smiled. Then she grabbed her heart center and disappeared into the ethers.

❦ M ❦

The prince was pacing. "Are you ready?" he asked. "I promised Adisa we would get there early!" he said in a slightly louder voice.

"Hold still," griped Verité. He was having a hard time getting his sister's hair wrapped. The short little ringlets were even harder to control than the long ones. "Please, stay still! I almost have it," he said with great concentration.

Mianshe had a hard time sitting still. Especially when someone had their hands on her head. It felt like she was being electrocuted by another person's mind. It was very uncomfortable. Still Verité did manage to get every single hair under her wrap. Now she looked like an apple muffin. Mianshe's cinnamon skin was crowned by a puff of orange-pink chiffon.

The color was very much her choice. She wanted to make the Herb-Woman smile. Her nanny tried to tell her that she would not only make Ellen smile; she would raise her from the dead with laughter, but she still insisted on wearing it. However, she did compromise with the color of her dress. Instead of the lime neon chintz she found in her nanny's sewing basket, she opted for the muted indigo cotton. This pleased her nanny to no end because the chintz made a crinkly sound when she moved and she was not fond of sitting still. Her nanny also told her in all her years of haggling getting her to wear indigo had been the hardest to accomplish.

"Children, please!" said the Prince. He wanted to say more but he wouldn't risk it. He'd been fighting the urge to scream all day.

When Verité came out in his T-shirt and khakis, followed by Mianshe in a dark purple convent uniform with a pink/orange chiffon wrap, the prince was shocked. He was pretty used to looking at his odd children but to have them dressed with time to spare was truly awe-inspiring. "Wonderful, let's go,' he excitedly said.

"One sec," said Verité as he ran into his room.

Mianshe gave her father a don't-look-at-me-I'm-ready look.

Verité lifted his mat and grabbed his learning box and retrieved his most powerful talisman—the triangle holding a four-pointed star. "I'm ready," he cried out as he rushed off to join the others.

❖ ⋀ ❖

Adisa couldn't believe she'd slept so long. She was just going to close her eyes for a second. She lifted her skirt and began running toward the square. When she entered she saw the prince already seated and she smiled. "Good evening, my Prince and Mianshe and handsome Verité," she said. She loved seeing the trio. There were nine others already there as well, and they were as quiet as lambs.

Mianshe pulled Adisa's skirt and drew her closer. "We are not allowed to talk or sing loudly or take the stick even if it is passed to us," she confided.

"I see," said Adisa. "I hope the others follow your wise ways, otherwise it will be a very long evening indeed," confided Adisa.

Mianshe hugged Adisa for a truly long time, much to the chagrin of the prince and Verité. When the mermaid finally released her, Adisa went and sat down next to her father. No one knew when Emadi and the queen arrived but they were there. Emadi chose to sit to the left of the Fire-Tender and the queen stood in the north waiting for the Fermemi queen and her high-prince.

The majority of the community had come early and they all held a sprig from some plant or a flower in their hands. The Fire-Tender was so moved by his people's expression of gratitude he spoke his thoughts aloud. "Look Ellen, look how much you were loved," he said. Then he felt the soft fur of a sweet grass stalk brush across his forehead. It was the Herb-Woman's favorite place to touch him. Only she saw the worry behind his calm face and she would always clear it from his mind with a gentle caress. He loved her for that.

You could smell the Fermemi queen before she got there. The smell of sweet musk and rose oil permeated the air around her. When the royal visitor approached, the queen instinctually lifted her hand in front of her nose, and when they embraced she held her face as far away as possible when hugging the perfumed Fermemi. The Fermemi high-prince understood the predicament of his Librebeing host, so he immediately grabbed his wife's arm and lowered her onto her cushion. It was the best he could do to repay the gold he'd taken and replaced with a small antique iron sculpture.

The dama dancers began their voyage. They circled the circle three times signaling the community to follow them so together they could all escort Mma Ellen home, but the king hadn't arrived yet nor had the Man-of-Medicine, so the drums continued to beat and the dancers continued to dance and the mourners began to wail as loudly as possible.

Emadi looked at the queen as she locked hands with the young man sitting to her left. The Fire-Tender took Emadi's right hand and his daughter's left in his and they waited. The prince was as fidgety as Mianshe. He didn't know if he should go look for his father or begin a word of praise for the Herb-Woman. Leboya kept her eye on the children from across the circle in case they decided to entertain the panicking crowd, and the Fermemi queen smiled and nodded at her imaginary audience. In her mind's eye all was well and she was very popular.

The queen knew something had to be done so she lifted one hand and signaled the crowd to be silent. Then she lowered her head and waited. The rest of the circle followed her actions and bowed their heads as well. The dancers stopped in mid-step. Not knowing what to do next, they repeated the step of the wind carrying the thoughts of their loved one away, over and over again. It was a perfect move given the strange thoughts surrounding her passing.

The queen said her silent prayer and listened to her heart. She tried to connect it with Emadi's and the Herb-Woman's because she was sure Ellen was there watching. When she felt her brother take his place beside her, she lifted her head. She'd never been so happy to see him in all her years of life, but he had changed. Not in physical appearance, he had changed in demeanor. There were no mushy contours. Her brother looked as sharp and keen as when he returned from his manhood ceremony. When the queen looked into her brother's eyes all her fear and worries left her. "As Amma says," she gently said. The crowd agreed and lifted their heads.

The king slowly looked around the circle and greeted everyone with his eyes even the Man-of-Medicine who sat in the north draped in black. He continued around the circle and barely stumbled when he saw a woman he didn't know staring respectfully at the earth. He stayed with her but she held her space so religiously no one recognized she didn't belong. The king continued journeying the circle until he gazed upon Emadi. He smiled at her then reached inside his boubou and produced a small wooden staff formed from a vine of the sacred tree. It was beautifully sculpted and inlayed with rubies and emeralds and a large aquamarine.

"My dear family, and relations," said the King acknowledging the Fermemi visitors. The strange woman lifted her head and reverently watched him. She had green eyes. It stunned the king for a quick second, but it didn't throw him off center so he continued. He turned and looked directly at Emadi.

"When I was young, I was in love with your mother. I thought about her all the time," he said. The king had everyone's attention now, even the Fire-Tender's. The Man-of-Medicine was held rapt by the king as well.

"So, when I had to make my journey into manhood, they sent me far away and left me alone for a very long time. I think they thought it would erase your mother's spell over me, but you cannot erase the magic of the heart. I had my vision and made my vows to my people and I became king. I was forced to let go of the little girl who wiggled and played in the field. All I had left of her was this," said the King. He held up the gem-encrusted staff. "I carved her figure into this piece of wood fallen from the sacred tree. I have finally finished my memorial to a most magnificent woman. That is why I was late. Please excuse me. Thus, my dear Emadi, in honor of your mother, Ellen and in service as your king, I ask you to accept my gift and my hopeful request that you will take over your mother's place in this village."

Before the words finished coming out of the king's mouth the community screamed and hollered and ululated and cried and laughed and sang in joy! The prince cried too. He loved his father so much in that moment. All he wanted to do was hug him and fall down at his feet. He would never be the man he came from, but he would happily carry his wisdom with him on his journey. The queen kissed her brother on his cheek over and over again. The Fermemi queen lifted herself up off the cushion and batted her eyes at the Librebe king, and then she punched her high-prince on the arm. She wanted him to feel what it was like to be a man.

The children giggled and watched carefully this way and that. They were trying to avoid being smacked by kente-clothed mammary glands or tangled up in the strands of beads everyone wore or being swatted with the fronds of plants everyone was holding in honor of the Herb-Woman. Even wrapped in cloth, or tucked in a shirt, or held in one's hand, a large breast or a strand of beads or a palm frond could do much damage. It could suffocate you or strangle you, or at the very least, leave a welt on your skin.

Thus, Mianshe and Verité and the other children rested their heads on the ground until the crowd regained their senses.

Emadi breathed deeply in and then out as she looked up at the sky and then she repeated the process all over again before holding her gaze down at her feet. She was so full of emotion she couldn't cry. She was lovingly stunned. Seeing how overwhelmed Emadi was, the king stood up and joined his sister's hand with the Fermemi queen's and closed the gap in the circle, and he walked his gift over to the Herb-Woman's daughter, and the crowd went wild all over again.

As he placed the staff in her hand the Man-of-Medicine stood up and screamed. "Will she be able to rid this village of those foul alien twins!" he screamed. That water nixie killed our Herb-Woman!" Then the medicine man looked up into the sky and began chanting the recipe for rain and it began to fall. But it was not raining hard enough for him, so he broke the circle and in one bounce he grabbed the Fire-Tender's water bucket and threw it on the girl.

The entire circle gasped! No one breathed or thought or cried or screamed because everyone, even the king was in shock. No one had ever in the history of life left a circle, or cursed a beloved's journey home, or stopped a ceremony. No one knew what to do because no one had any experience with that type of behavior.

Mianshe jumped up when the water hit her. Verité instinctually grabbed the wrap from her head so the people did not see her feet revert to webbed fins. However, he forgot about the short pixie cut he'd given his sister and the crowd gasped and shivered and cried to the heavens again.

"Look how he covers the webbed feet of the beast! Look at the shorn hair of the beast! They fed the Herb-Woman duduju and it killed her!" he screamed. The shaman was enraged and it felt good. He loved the look of fear on the people's faces, especially the Fermemi queen. She had broken the circle and had fallen onto her back, face-up to the sky; begging Amma not to curse her with the fatal duduju.

Verité couldn't stand the spectacle. His father was killed in just the same manner. People accused him of being a witch and they burned him and banned his mother so she had to go to the city to find work. The sorrow hurt her so badly she abandoned him altogether—her own son. That was wrong. This was worse. How could one person do this? She was a little girl, an innocent little girl!

"Duduju is not a virus or a sickness! He was my cousin Jean's lamb. We got sick because I loved him. I would never eat him. Duduju was my friend and Nanny cooked him in a stew is all," pleaded Verité. "Mianshe is my sister. She is kind and harmless," he said.

But it didn't matter. The little girl's hair was changing into a moonlit amber-gold-green hue plus the water made her little afro grow right in front of everyone's eyes. Her feet now had webbing between her toes and it mortified the people.

"Look!" screamed the Man-of-Medicine.

He kept manipulating the poor villagers' emotions. Two women passed out cold. One man ran home and the dancers kept walking around the circle like stick figures. It was chaos, complete and utter chaos, and the Man-of-Medicine loved it! Now he was ready to throw his final spear into the corpse of his rival the Herb-Woman.

The king regained his composure and watched the medicine man very carefully. "If you have a problem with my grandchildren, Ti-Temne, you should have mentioned it to me. To defame them at the dama of another puts only you in a bad light, my son." The king was furious. He'd used the shaman's childhood nickname instead of his title of honor and made comment of his age. The king was three years younger than the medicine man, but he had called him son. In any other culture the disrespect would have ended in a duel with one man dying in the end, but this was Africa, a very proud country that honored their ancestors. In this country an entire lineage was at risk of extinction when an insult was hurled.

The medicine man smiled a sharp-toothed grin and stood up and stared at the king. "If it is a ceremony you don't want defiled, Oumatadi, then you should sit down," he growled.

Emadi stood up and addressed the crowd. "My family, I accept your offer of wearing my mother's shoes," she said and she took off her head wrap and let her orange hair cascade down her back. "In the name of our eldest and wisest ancestor, Lebo, I accept. I know when we band together we can rid our land of this evil before us. Let us hold hands," she said.

But before she could finish her prayer and incantation, the jackal-man jumped up and spun three times counter-clockwise. He bounded across the circle jumping over the fire and grabbed Mianshe by her shirt and dunked her in a puddle. The mer-girl's feet grew completely together while her hair released itself and stretched down her small body.

"I will kill you with my own hands if you do not let go of my child, now!" screamed the Prince.

"People join hands! Do not let a bad spirit break this village," cried the Queen.

"Stop!" screamed Verité. The boy lunged forward and stabbed the medicine man in the shin with his triangle and star symbol.

The shaman tried to kick the child away, but he was as irritating as a mosquito. "Little nomad, slave trading boy, I will kill you," he sneered.

It was the strange woman with green eyes who finally stopped the pandemonium surrounding them. Throughout all the insults and accusations Rose waited for the Herb-Woman to guide her, but her guardian-phantom was mute. Rose could see the four directions splitting apart. She heard the man screaming his numbers and incanting the rain, and all became clear. She saw the agenda of the one creating chaos. He wanted everything to return to the black hole it was expelled from with a bang and a spark of brilliant light. The man was incanting all those who wanted to extinguish the heart and will of others. He called upon those who used technology to start passive aggressive wars, causing it to rain where it was not wanted or stopping it until the earth lay scorched underfoot. Where catastrophes were courted like harpies in a Greek tragedy. Where they genetically altered life and cloned meats and forced vaccinations on the people making genocide legal. He was calling upon those who had pitted cousin against nephew and relations against ancestors. Those that were trying to kill off the original DNA. Those that wanted to eradicate the twelve great tribes that willingly communicated with their Creator.

Rose had enough! No one had the right to take life away! Life was ever eternal and came and went as it seasonally pleased. She did the only thing a woman with the ability to create could do. She reached between her legs and dislodged the sponge holding her life's essence and she threw it in his face, the face of the vile jackal. "I have had enough of you!" she screamed. Then she poured the contents of the vial the Herb-Woman had instructed her to bring, into the fire.

Everyone heard the man scream. It was a howl that sent one's teeth cringing. "You!" howled the medicine man. But the Man-of-Medicine wasn't going to be beat, especially by a blood-bearing foreigner. He immediately fell to all fours and began shape shifting into his vile canine form. As the shaman was transmuting into the jackal, the prince grabbed a hot stick from the fire and thrust it against his exposed arm, then pushed his daughter safely out of the way of the fire.

Verité grabbed Mianshe by the hand and screamed at her to run, and she ran straight for the hills hopping from one stone to another, so no one could trace her steps, just like her brother had taught her.

The queen took Emadi and the strange woman's hands and guided them out of the square. The women went through the back behind the houses to the path that led up the mountain.

The Fermemi high-prince left the little iron statue on the cushion where the king sat and snuck down the opposite side of the mountain toward the closest city where he could get a lift to Bamako.

The Fermemi queen stood up and swore war on the village of evil beings and walked backward out of the square. She did not wish to carry any of the evening's events with her. She needed to close off their opening. She spat as she walked backwards vowing that if the jackal did not destroy them, she would.

The jackal-man grabbed some ashes from the fire and wiped the stranger's blood from his face. Afterward he ran into the forest. He had to think now. He'd never planned on being attacked by a strange woman who was on her moon. He knew Emadi's cycle was over and he had made sure the other women's cycles had ended too. Who was this menstruating woman with green eyes? He knew if he didn't panic, he could recapture what he'd lost. The people didn't respect him anymore of that he was sure. He could do nothing about that now, but they feared him and that was better. Where was the king? Where did the water-child go? He had to find her and kill her before she returned to the sea and summoned her mother. But two could play that game so the man finished his transformation, and when he had fully become the jackal, he bounded up the hill to find Mianshe.

The Fire-Tender stared down at the ground. Ellen had seen it all. The Herb-Woman had seen it coming before it began. He saw her symbol in the sand. He knew where he must go. He lifted himself to standing and felt his daughter come with him. She was still tightly gripping his arm.

"Listen to me, my daughter. Breathe," he instructed. When she came back into her body and began breathing, he placed a fig in her mouth. "Okay, we have work to do. You must grab as much wood as you can easily carry. I will take care of the rest. Okay? All you have to do is follow me and I promise you, all will be alright," he said. He brought his daughter's trembling hand to his lips and kissed her fingers.

While Adisa gathered wood the Fire-Tender sifted through the embers and selected a few. He put them in a tin can with holes poked in the lid and shoved it into his bag. When Adisa returned with her arms full, he grabbed some logs to lighten her load and led them up the hill toward the cave.

The prince ran back to his house but his children were not there. He grabbed his fishing knife, some cord, a flashlight and some water. He smeared his body with wax from a citronella candle to deter the bugs that bite. He had no idea how long he'd be in the forest. He only knew he would stay until he found his children and he wouldn't return until the medicine man had breathed his last breath.

Mianshe was scared. No matter where she went she could hear the dog howling. It was like he was everywhere around her. She remembered what Verité told her. She must go to the cave and wait for him there. But it was a teeny moon and its light wasn't bright enough to make it through the trees. She was so scared that she got lost. She sat down and toned a plea to her mother. "*Merma, I'm scared,*" she toned. But when she cried it vibrated into the forest past the jackal's ears, out into the ocean.

"Well there you are, little fish," snarled the jackal-man. He laughed as he ran up the hill toward his prey.

∗∗ ∧∧ ∗∗

The queen helped Emadi and Rose into the cave and then pulled the heavy panther's hide behind them.

"What happened, Queen-Mother," cried Emadi. Her hair was a tangled flaming-orange mass around her head. "And who are you?" she demanded as she stared deeply into Rose's eyes.

Rose was bleeding. Her dress was saturated in blood and it was dripping down her legs. Her stomach was in knots and it cramped horribly like a woman having a breach birth. The queen rushed around the cave preparing for what was sure to happen. Death was in the air and not only the scent of the unburied, there was the cruel smell of those that would make their transitions that night too.

"Quiet!" demanded the Queen. "You must clear your mind and think of your first moment of entry into this world. Your thoughts must be pure in here," she said.

But it was difficult to do. It was difficult to not be afraid. Rose was terrified. She could hear the jackal howling and she smelled the fresh blood running down her legs. As if their thoughts were immediately manifesting themselves, the women heard the heavily padded sounds of a huge animal pacing in front of the entrance to the cave.

"It can smell me. I know it!" Rose cried.

The queen ripped her head wrap off and began tearing it into little pieces. "Shove this inside you. It's all we have," she said.

Emadi looked at the queen with a fierce expression. "You know more than you are telling us, my Queen and we have a right to know," she said. Emadi's eyes demanded the truth, but it wasn't the queen who began talking. It was Rose. She fell into a trance and began speaking, but it wasn't her voice. It was the voice of the Herb-Woman.

The Mer-queen was frantic. She couldn't find Sedina. She'd looked in her cavern and in all the communal halls but she was nowhere to be found.

"My Queen, it has begun. You must come with us now," toned Manulir. *"The people are making their way down to the caverns in the sea's floor."*

"I will not go without my daughter!" she insisted.

Manulir lowered his voice to the most soothing octave available and began again. *"The dolphins have taken over the seas. I am sure they have taken her to safety, just as I am trying to do for you,"* he telepathically said.

"Where is my husband," commanded the Mer-queen.

"He is overseeing the dolphins and whales. He alone chose to go into the open seas. My queen, I promised him I would make sure you reached the crystal caverns. There you can see and feel all that is happening above. Please trust your king now. He is already out there rescuing your daughter," he ever so gently said and aloud.

The Mer-queen took a deep breath and coiled herself in repose. She toned a message to the open seas. *"Dearest daughter from all of me. I feel you in the open sea. I am with you always, call to me. Please, call on me,"* toned the Mer-queen. But there was no reply to her message. All she heard was the sound of a merchild crying.

"It is time, my friends! We shall sail into the beyond and incant the ancestors down from the sky into the sea to restore harmony. Are you with me!" roared the Mer-king.

And the dolphins and whales slowly circled him and in sync they all responded to his cry. *"We are you, my friend. From the beginning, it never ends,"* and the numerous herds swam off, one after the other; each following their syncopated clicks out into the ocean.

❖ ᴧ ❖

The jackal-man howled in joy and accelerated his chanting! He ruled the elements now. He could see the tide rising. He could smell her and her kind coming in with the mist. Now the entire planet was engaged in this one moment. Chaos ruled and nothing else mattered. He was returning the world back to its original form before they spoke and forced their will and shapes upon creation. He could smell the fear and smoke and hear the thunder and see the electricity. It was raw splendor! He was proud. He felt at home. Finally, he was who he was! But then he smelled something else. It was a strong smell and its gamey scent unsettled him. "Who would dare try me now," hissed the jackal-man. "I don't have time for you," he grumbled. "I have bigger fish to fry," he said. The Man-of-Medicine slowly fell to all fours and transmuted again into the jackal. There was no separating them now.

⁂ ᴧ ⁂

Verité ran until he couldn't. He stopped and tried to calm his mind, but it was difficult to do. She wasn't at their first rendezvous point. There was no sign of her, but he could hear her crying. "Please Mianshe, tell me where you are," he cried in return, and then he let his body tell him which direction to go next.

⁂ ᴧ ⁂

"I was young," said the Herb-Woman through Rose. "And no one understood me. I was like you, my daughter. Only one person saw through the mask I took to wearing. It was the man you call king. The man I knew as my daughter's father."

Emadi was stunned. She wanted to run, but the queen grabbed her. "Did you know this!" she asked.

"No, I did not," responded the Queen. "I had no idea. That's the truth. I thought he was forbidden to be with your mother because our parents wanted him to marry the Fermemi princess," she wearily said.

But the conversation was interrupted by the loud thumps of a large predator. It paced back and forth in front of the cave's entrance, but this time Rose was not afraid. Rose was not there. Only the Herb-Woman was present.

341

❧ M ❧

Verité ran up the hill toward the sound of Mianshe's whimpering. It was getting louder. He was getting closer to her. "Mianshe!" he yelled. But his voice was taken by the wind and returned to him. Verité tried running toward the last place he heard his sister's cries, but now the sky was turning black and the sea had started to rise. Although it was still at a distance it had curled up and stood as high as the mountain. If the wave hit the shore it would not only wipe out Librebe it would wash away the Fermemi village as well. He had to find Mianshe. She could stop it.

"Mianshe, please talk to me!" he cried, but the only sound that replied was the roar of the ocean.

Verité turned and ran as fast as he could. The young boy's chest burned. He was tired and he hadn't eaten since morning, but he couldn't think of such things. It left him hopeless. He kept seeing his dream over and over again. It was happening right now. He could hear his sister crying. He could see the jackal chase her, but he could not save her. "Don't give up! Think!" he yelled.

If he saw it all before in his dream, then he had to know where she was now. He sat down and remembered the nightmare he wanted to forget. She was in a little ball. He could see the sea curling up around her. The jackal entered in from the right and he grabbed her and ran to the cliff's edge. That is where he always woke up. He remembered she hid in a tree because the tree had opened its limbs so he could see her. The only tree that had that kind of awareness was Mr. Tree. That was what she called it, Mr. Tree. Only Mianshe would name the unnamable. But it was so dark out one could barely see the sacred tree. Everything looked the same in the forest at night.

Then, Verité had an epiphany. On the ridge you could see the stars. His sister loved looking at stars, and one star most of all. She would always smile and say, "Oh Sirius be…" Verité looked up at the sky and located her star and he followed its light down to earth until he saw a small form in the shadows.

⋙ ⋀ ⋘

"That's not why we couldn't be together," said Rose as she channeled the Herb-Woman. "We were too strong a force," she said. "Since my birth the elders knew I would be here in this moment. That is why there is a panther's hide over the doorway," she said.

"I don't understand," said the Queen.

"Neither did we," said the Herb-Woman via Rose. "We loved each other and then I got pregnant. No one knew this but us. They foresaw it, but they thought he'd been saved from me. But our love only got stronger, so we would see each other in our other forms at night when he was on his quest for his manhood."

"How did you do this, mother? He was locked away alone in silence for weeks. The only person to know where he was, was the old medicine man," Emadi inquired.

"Ahh love has its ways, especially with those it chooses," she replied.

Just then the creature roared and its shadow penetrated the panther's hide. The lion's silhouette was cast against the wall. It was huge. It was twice the size of the largest lion in Africa, and its roar was so loud you felt it. Rose covered her ears and slowly fainted.

⋙ ⋀ ⋘

"Mianshe! Verité!" screamed the Prince. He was filled with fear and adrenaline. He didn't care if the jackal heard him. He wanted it to hear him. He wanted to press his knife into its throat until its eyes rolled back in its head.

For a brief moment in time the prince had been happy. He had his children and a relationship with his father and he was to be married to a wonderful woman. He was to be king and he was excited to be mentored by his father. Only a year ago this same thought sent him running to another land. Why now when he understood the true beauty of having a family and community was it all unraveling? Why now!

The prince stopped. He had to catch his breath. He couldn't give up hope. They were his children and they were alone and afraid. He had to save them. It was this thought that gave him hope. The only other time he'd lost his children they were safe in the arms of… "The tree!" he screamed.

The prince ran with all his strength toward the ridge where the sacred tree resided.

❖ Ⲙ ❖

"Mianshe! Verité!" bellowed the Prince.

"Mianshe," screamed Verité.

"Be careful," the tree said.

The prince looked out to sea and saw a tidal wave that rose so high it blocked the stars from view. "Oh, dear Amma," gasped the Prince.

"Pére Prince," cried Verité. He saw the prince and he got scared. The prince wasn't in his vision. Why was he there?

"Popah," whimpered Mianshe. But they still couldn't see or hear her.

Verité ran to the right of the tree and began looking under all its roots. The prince started to climb the tree to get a better view. Neither of them saw the jackal digging in the dirt around the hollow log the girl had crawled into.

Mianshe had almost made it to the tree but the dark sea blocked her star from view, so she did what her brother told her to do. She stayed where she was until she knew where she was going. She found an old abandoned stump and burrowed in it like a rabbit and waited for him or her father or mother to come and take her home. But no one was coming.

The prince stood on limb, searching the area. There it was! The jackal, once a man, was sniffing a little mound of earth no larger than a sand dune, and he knew what the dog had found.

"Tree, grab my son, please," screamed the Prince as he descended its trunk.

The tree lowered its limbs and wrapped itself around Verité.

"No, I have to find her!" Verité screamed. This wasn't in his dream either so he knew the nightmare had begun.

The jackal howled and stood up on its hind legs and bayed at the night sky. The only constellation anyone could see now was Canis Major, the dog constellation. The wall of water had blocked all others from view. The jackal triumphantly yowled and thrust his snout into the hole, grabbing the little Mer-girl by her collar.

Mianshe screamed before going limp in the jackal's grip.

The Mer-queen shrieked and released her body into the dark sea.

The prince yelled and threw himself into the air toward the ground.

Verité cried and wrenched at the limbs of the tree.

Sedina moaned and furiously toned into the open waters. *"I am here. We are one. With love we are forever connected."*

But a lion came and flung itself onto the jackal, pushing all three of them over the cliff in front of the dark wall of water. The lion grabbed the jackal by its throat, but the jackal would not release its prey.

The prince rushed to the edge of the cliff and saw the lion and jackal battling on a ledge no larger than his porch. The immense lion had to press its body against the stone so it wouldn't fall into the ocean. The jackal knew its position would only allow the lion the use of its mouth and its front paw or he too would slide off the cliff and die with the water-girl.

Mianshe's body bobbed around the ledge. She was hanging by a hunk of cloth from her shirt. As the two animals fought, she could feel their spit and hear their bodies smashing against the rocks, but she never stopped looking up to where the stars had been before they were blocked from view.

Verité bit the tree and demanded it let him go. The tree did not agree, but it knew it had to honor the will of another living being. The tree had to release the boy. If the sorrow became too much for the prince's son, the tree would protect him with its leaves. It would shed itself until the boy saw nothing but his own tears, so the tree lowered its branches and gently released Verité.

The dolphins swam smoothly and efficiently in a circle around the entire planet. As they swam more of the life forms in the sea joined them until a delicate high-pitched hum was heard upon land. The sound vibrated within the earth, opening the ley-lines that ignited the earth's centers of power, canceling out the jackal's recipe for disaster. No paradigm or geometry or grid could oppress creation's love. Every artery on the planet lit up and hummed. Life was willingly singing!

The dolphins and whales continued dancing in the water. They would crown and breathe in the air and blow out a prayer to their creator. And as they called on their mother, the Sirius planet shined down on them, calming the waters. The tsunami subsided and the moon rose to its apex and the stars telegraphed their pure message of unconditional love for all life's forms equally, on land and in the sea.

The jackal was livid. He must win. He had to, even if it meant he might die. It did not matter to him. No form was the only form that mattered to him now, so he lunged off the ledge holding the little Mer-girl like a rag doll in his mouth. Nothing else mattered.

The lion knew what it had to do next. It had spent its entire life preparing for just this moment. When the jackal lunged the lion dug its claws into the rock and grabbed the dog with its right paw and pulled it close like a lover, and with its other paw, the lion ripped the jackal open from its throat straight through to its anus.

As the Mer-girl bounced in the jackal's mouth like a yo-yo, the disemboweled jackal fell backwards off the ledge, still holding his prey. However, their weight pulled the lion in with them.

And the Prince screamed!

And Verité cried.

And the lion flailed as it transformed back into the King of Librebe.

As the jackal's yellow eyes turned white, the Man-of-Medicine's disemboweled body hit the side of the cliff over and over again.

⁂ ⋏ ⁂

Rose woke up and sat cross-legged in the space. "It is done," she said. "Your father has surrendered to his love."

The Herb-Woman's faint apparition shrunk down and shape-shifted into a panther, and the large black cat stalked out of the cave in search of the lion—her king. She wanted them to share their journey home. Now they could finally be together. It was where they belonged.

⁂ ⋏ ⁂

The prince could not believe it! His father was a shape-shifter and in his lion form, he'd jumped from a cliff to slay the enemy of his family. But his daughter's limp body was still trapped in the jackal's mouth, and she floated in the air before falling into the dark abyss, right before his eyes. Now both of them were completely lost to him.

Verité tried to jump in after Mianshe. He was sure he could save her. He was sure. But the prince grabbed his only child and held him in his arms, and they stood together on the mountain and cried and cried and cried for a good—long—moment.

Mianshe hit the water with a splash. It became a *blooping* sound as the water engulfed her. It was the sound her boo-boos made when she popped them. It was a comforting sound. While she continued sinking in the sea, she listened to many sounds; the sounds of the dolphins singing, the sound of her father crying, the sound of her brother praying and the sound of her mother saying, "With love we are forever connected, you are forever connected to me."

Thus, the mermaid followed that sound until she gently fell into her mother's arms deep within the sea.

THE END

ABOUT THE AUTHOR

Michele Lamar Richards, most known as the actor that portrayed the sister in Warner Bros. blockbuster, *The Bodyguard* is an optioned screenwriter and successful blogger for michelelamar.com. Michele now lives in the Arizona desert writing books.